THE ICE MERCHANT

THE ICE MERCHANT

PAUL BOOR

Cover design by Asha Hossain

Print ISBN 978-0-7867-5493-9

ebook ISBN 978-0-7867-5494-6

Contents

PART 1

The Island City

1

Arrival

4 March 1889

Galveston, Texas

My dearest Ruth,

I have arrived in this peculiar island city safely, though greatly fatigued from our ten days with the cargo. The ice fared well & God willing, its rising price will shore up the profit, as was our good fortune in New Orleans.

I profess my loneliness for you, my dearest, & for the children, though I fear for your well-being & again entreat you to refrain from visiting that quack Valdis, or any of those other charlatans promising a cure. Surely your symptoms will eventually abate. It's best to remain snug at home, where our intrepid young Abigail (such a competent girl!) might seek your counsel during the final stages of the ice harvest.

I must be off to the docks now to find Adam & oversee the unloading. It promises to be an intriguing few days here. I am told that the local celebrations before the beginning of Lent are quite extravagant.

Yrs affectionately,

N

Nicolas Van Horne adjusted his tie and leaned across the writing table of the hotel's postal office. He sighed, then took a moment to listen to the Gulf of Mexico thrumming onto the beach just yards from where he sat. In a way, it felt quite good to be so far from New York. His mountain home was a magnificent place of clear lakes and dense, green woods, but it held sorrow, and worries, too. Others might think his North Country calm and peaceful, even idyllic, but this Northern man of commerce knew otherwise.

Yes, it felt quite good to be on this island.

Nicolas made a move to cap the ink bottle, then decided to dip the pen once more.

p.s. I hope you've had word on the whereabouts of our wayward son.

He gazed for a moment out the open window, admiring the bright morning and the blue-green expanse of water. The elegance of his beachfront hotel, the balmy breeze, and the gentle pounding of the gulf seemed so unnatural to a hardheaded Yankee who, just days before, had left his upstate village in the cruel clutch of an Adirondack winter.

Nicolas sealed the envelope, slid it across the marble counter to the postal clerk, and reached in his pants pocket for some pennies. With the coins' jingling, Van Horne's thoughts turned to his steamer lying calmly at harbor, and to the ship's cargo of ice, twenty thousand tons of it—dense, profitable, lucid three-foot blocks packed in sawdust and covered with canvas. And then there was the darker thought of the unusual goods concealed in the bottommost layer of his ice—the cargo he hoped to deliver quickly, quietly, and at a profit remarkable even for a Yankee trader.

Van Horne climbed into an open carriage at the southern entrance of Galveston's most elegant accommodation, the Majestic Beach Hotel. "Pier 22," he told the driver, a grizzled old man with a great chaw of tobacco stuffed in his cheek, and the carriage rolled off the sand and onto the bright brick streets of the city.

Warm salt air permeated the fine Irish wool of Nicolas's jacket, the smooth, long-staple cotton of his tailored shirt. "It's already summer here," he muttered to himself as the carriage whisked him past row after row of gaily painted houses. Pink. Blue. Purple. The avenues were broad and the houses were graced with intricate decorative work and wrapped by sprawling porches on both first and second stories. Undoubtedly the homes of the island's captains of commerce, Nicolas thought. Even finer than those he'd admired in the most elegant sections of New Orleans.

Nicolas removed his homburg and jacket, leaned back, and stretched his lanky, six-foot frame in the warm morning sunshine. As the carriage crossed Galveston Island from gulf to bay, the graceful homes changed to commercial brick, and the quiet of the neighborhoods became the bustle of the harbor.

"Could you tell me, kind sir," Nicolas called out over the clippity-clip of the mare's hooves. "Where would one find your new medical college?"

The driver slowed his carriage and pointed east, over the warehouses, to a four-story, red-domed building towering shiny and new in the distance. "That's it, right there," he said. He jerked the reins in the opposite direction, and the carriage drew alongside the wharfs.

"An impressive structure. Quite imposing."

"Huh. It's sure pretty," the driver grumbled. "But I'll tell ya, the folks in this town wisht it was on some other island. It ain't nothin' but a—" The driver was drowned out by the low-pitched blast of a steamer's horn as a great ship, low in the water from her load of cotton, eased from her berth.

Nicolas marveled at the many steamers and tall-masted sailing ships, flying flags from all points of the globe as they wove to and fro seeking berths for their cargoes of lumber; coffee; exotic, unnamable fruits; and tea and cloth from the Orient. In this booming port city, Nicolas's cargo seemed almost ordinary . . . almost, he thought, as his nerves gave a troublesome jolt.

He stepped down from the carriage at Pier 22 and held out a coin to the driver. "Would that medical college have a dock of its own?" he asked.

"Ask the stevedores, why don't ya?" the driver replied. Then, with a smirk, he said, "You won't be going there alone, I hope. No telling what might become of a person at that gawd-awful place." The driver spat forcefully onto the oily brick street, slapped the reins, and pulled away.

Nicolas spied his foreman, Adam Klock, waving from the bow of their ship at the far end of the pier. Adam was a sinewy rail of a man who stood a good six inches shorter than Nicolas.

"Ahoy there, Van Horne!" he shouted.

Nicolas wove his way down the dock, dodging around coils of rope, cotton bales, crates and barrels, and the dark, sweating stevedores who labored there—from men black as ebony to those who'd been roasted nut-brown by the sun.

"A good morning to you, Adam," Nicolas said when he drew near. "How goes it?" Nicolas scrambled up a rope ladder and stepped nimbly onto the deck of their steamer, a double paddle wheeler that had been their home down the mighty Mississippi and across the open water of the gulf. "Did you hire the men?" Van Horne asked.

"Six of 'em, sir. A good enough lot—experienced longshoremen, and strong enough, I reckon."

Nicolas lowered his voice. "How long will it take them, you figure? Unloading the top ice?"

"Don't worry, boss. I'll have 'em off the pier by nightfall, so's we can take care of that *bottom layer*. And I'm told the medical place has its own dock at the east end of the harbor, though it ain't much of a dock."

Nicolas gave Adam a clap on the back and took his foreman's hand, dark-stained and rough from the handling of horses and machines. "Good man, Adam."

As his employer in the business of ice, Nicolas had shared a berth with Adam Klock for many a night on the long and arduous voyages from their home near the Canadian border. Though friends from childhood, these two men knew their differences. Van Horne, the boss, was born to commerce and descended from wealth. Adam Klock, inveterate woodsman and jack-of-all-trades, was the grandson of a Seneca Indian and descendant of a long line of rough-and-ready mixed breeds who'd inherited their beloved North Country from the mighty Iroquois, then fought both the French and the English to hold it.

"But I'm afraid there's another problem," Adam said with a frown. "A harbor inspector was nosing around the pier early this morning, and he said he'd be back."

"I'll make for the medical college then, and arrange delivery. Keep an eye on those longshoremen of yours, Adam. They'll be asking questions . . . just make sure they don't touch that bottom layer."

Adam nodded. Then, looking down the pier, he whispered, "Oh-oh. Damned if it ain't him. Mr. Harbor Inspector himself."

A tub of a man with a full red beard walked up to the ship, clamored clumsily up its side, and stepped on deck. He wore a grimy blue coat with dull brass buttons. His breath stank of whiskey.

"Mornin', gents," he said. "I see the owner's up and about." He glanced at Nicolas without offering his hand. "I'm the tariff inspector, as ya can tell"—he tapped the tarnished badge on his coat—"and I'll need to have a look-see at your cargo here."

The inspector threw open a hatch and stared into the hold. "Ice, is it?"

"Yessir, yessir, that it is," Adam said.

"The finest Northern ice," Nicolas added coolly. "Pure and clear as crystal. We've recently unloaded her sister ship in New Orleans, sir, without event, I might add."

"You ain't got no apples, eggs, fresh produce . . . nothin' like that down there, eh?" the inspector asked as he brushed sawdust away, pulled up the corner of a canvas cover, and squinted into the ice. "There's a different tariff rate for such, and you ice traders been known to maximize yer profits thusly."

The inspector shaded his eyes from the sun and peered deep, where the morning light filtering into the bluish ice outlined row upon row of large, ill-defined shapes, like sides of beef wrapped in canvas.

"Somethin' big down there?"

Adam, his eyes like tea saucers, stared blankly at the inspector's broad back.

In a single motion Van Horne reached inside his jacket and smoothly extracted a well-worn leather billfold. "We're due to unload shortly," he said, flipping the purse open. "If there'd be an additional tariff of some sort, sir, I'd be happy to settle it."

The inspector turned. "Now that, sir, would be most expeditious." He dropped the hatch and stretched himself up; he was near six feet in height, almost as tall as Van Horne, though twice as big around. He reeled back on his heels, his hand extended.

"Would three be enough?" Nicolas asked.

"That'll do nicely."

Nicolas peeled off the bills; the inspector smiled and slipped them into his pocket. "I thank ya," he said, "and I'll make a note down at the office. You'll encounter no problem with yer commerce here, sir. I assure ya of that." He jumped from the ship with a thump and ambled down the pier. "And I bid ya both a good day."

Once the inspector was out of earshot, Adam asked, "Whatta ya think? He see something?"

"If he did," Van Horne said with a smile, "I'm sure a few drinks will help him forget . . . but I'd best get to that college straightaway."

"You figure to try their newfangled electric trolley, boss?" Adam asked, pointing to a bright orange trolley car that rumbled along the waterfront under a shower of sparks. "They tell me the college is only a few minutes away, if you dare ride that blasted thing."

"Come, come, my man." Nicolas guffawed, his ice-blue eyes twinkling. "Just because we're from the woods, we needn't act like bumpkins." He clapped his friend's bony shoulder. "I'm sure it's safe enough."

Just as Nicolas was set to swing over the ship's rail, another distraction—a young man of about eighteen years—bounded down the pier. The youth was red-faced and out of breath.

"Are you the ice merchant?" he shouted up.

"That I am," Nicolas replied. "Who are you?"

"A student from the college."

Nicolas scrambled down the rope ladder. Throwing glances furtively up and down the pier, he drew the young man near the ship's hull and asked, "What is it you want, son?"

"I'm to enquire, sir, if you have any fresh ones."

"Fresh ones?"

"Not embalmed."

Facing the young man so close, Nicolas perceived the odor of rot, a most foul stench, like that of a long-dead deer stumbled upon in the woods on a hot summer day. The youth appeared clean-shaven, eager, and bright enough, but he wore a tattered, badly patched coat and pants caked with a yellowish, greasy substance.

"My professor *needs to know*." The youth persisted. "*Any not embalmed?*"

"There's one, yes. One left." Nicolas felt his stomach tighten. Why had the last of his special cargo tried his nerves so? "It's a mere boy," he told the young man. "He was found buried in a snowdrift."

"How fresh?"

"Quite. Frozen solid. We loaded him in Buffalo."

"All right then, sir!" The youth's face brightened. "I'm also to ask when you might be delivering."

"We're hoping for tonight. Late."

"That's all I needed to know. Thank you greatly, kind sir."

As the youth turned to start down the pier, Nicolas took his arm. "Tell your professor I'll visit him shortly to make the final arrangements."

The student hurried off and Adam scrambled down from the steamer. "Whew." Adam sighed. "It's been a helluva morning. Will it be just me and you unloading that bottom layer tonight, boss?"

"I'll see about getting some help from this new professor."

"Good. Maybe he'll prove more obliging than them others . . . but you'd best get a bit of sustenance in ya before venturing that trolley." Adam pulled a warm, pungent package of butcher's paper from his threadbare corduroy jacket. "I picked this up for us at a little dockside spot," he said, uncovering a stack of fried oysters and glistening German sausages. From another pocket he produced two fresh-baked biscuits.

The travelers, still standing, bit at their breakfast, but while Adam commented on the fine taste of the oysters and the mild climate enjoyed by this new port city, Nicolas's mind flew ahead to their delivery. These jitters had kept his appetite at bay since Buffalo, and he wasn't sure why.

With a nod to his foreman, Van Horne walked off the pier and leapt onto a passing trolley car as it crackled and rattled along the waterfront. Adam, biscuit in hand, his knotty arms hanging like clubs at his sides, watched the car disappear into the frenzy of the harbor.

2

The Medical College

At the trolley's last stop near the easternmost tip of the island, simple frame houses lined streets that appeared to be nothing more than packed oyster-shell rubble and sand. The homes were two-storied, minimally decorated, and had only small, uncovered galleries. Nicolas was surprised by their bright new paint and the many colors, nearly as gay as the larger homes he'd admired earlier.

On the south side of the street stood an imposing three-story hospital built of brick—the Infirmary of the Ursuline Sisters of Charity—which was adjoined to a convent of the same name and similar construction. The hospital and convent were surrounded by a seven-foot-high black iron fence adorned with regally wrought inserts of a religious nature and topped by tall spikes.

Nicolas stepped back to make way for a young mare drawing an ambulance to the front gate of the hospital at a brisk canter. The only other movement on the street was a hearse, its black curtains drawn, being pulled from the rear of the hospital by a tired grey mule.

Taking up the entire north side of the block and rising high above its simpler surroundings was the Medical College of Galveston, a bright, four-story mass of pink sandstone with grey granite and buff-colored terra-cotta appointments. Three domes crowned the structure. A finely sculpted six-foot-wide star of Texas graced the archway of the entrance portico, now undergoing the final touches of construction. The waters of the bay lapped at a dock only yards from the back of the reddish building, while at the college's front, stonemasons, bricklayers, and hod carriers loitered on vine-covered piles of granite and sandstone debris.

Though it was only midmorning, Van Horne felt his shirt and hatband moisten in the glare of the tropical sun. He trotted up the dozen stone stairs to the main entrance, passed through the portico and under the five-pointed star of Texas, and pushed open the heavy cypress door. The interior was deserted and as cool as a tomb. He searched the directory in the spacious vestibule until he found the name he was after. His destination would be the uppermost floor.

A sharp, burning stench drifted down as he approached the circular stairway at the heart of the building. It was formaldehyde—an odor he'd grown all too familiar with since he'd added this twist to his livelihood. Making his way up the stairs, his nose stung. His normally sharp vision blurred. He felt his chest constrict with something like fear, but not quite fear. After all, what did he have to fear?

Nicolas Van Horne was a clear-thinking, proud man, proud of his Adirondack Mountains and the ice he harvested, as bright and pure as winter, as dense as stone. His ice brought joy to all who used it. Reputable medical men had proved it an excellent therapy for spotted fevers and the dread yellow fever. But this newer face of his enterprise had an acrid foulness to it. He'd come to dread the stink of his special cargo, and the medical men who seemed oblivious to it. And more than the stink, something about this particular cargo, details he couldn't put his finger on, had jangled his nerves to a frazzle . . . ever since Buffalo and those boys.

On the upper landing a blessed breeze from windows open to the gulf cleared the stench. There were only two doors; the opaque glass of the one Nicolas needed was clearly marked:

LABORATORY OF ANATOMY
Francis O. Keiller, F.R.C.P., M.P.H.
Professor of Medical Therapeutics and Morbid Anatomy
Dean of the Medical College

Nicolas had just stilled the fine trembling of his hand on the topmost balustrade when the door was thrown open and out filed two scrawny, red-eyed teenage boys, as foul smelling and outlandish as the youth on the dock had been. Both wore rubber aprons and scruffy beards. The first stopped in his tracks and cast an eye at the well-dressed Van Horne. "Visitor!" he shouted, and the two edged by and rushed down the stairway.

"Visitor!"

"Someone's here, Professor."

Nicolas watched the youths wind their way down the stairway, their boots tapping on the stone. When he turned, a tall, ascetic-looking gentleman was clicking the door shut behind himself. The man was dressed in a dark wool suit of European style, badly worn at the elbows. Slightly stooped, he looked at least twenty years Van Horne's senior, sixty years of age or more. The older man's smoke-colored beard was scraggly, and the pure white, wiry tufts of hair that remained on his gleaming head stood out as if charged with electricity.

"May I be of assistance to ye?" he asked with a lilt.

"I'm looking for a certain professor, name of Keiller. My name is Van Horne."

"Aye, yes, yes," he said softly. "Come along, if ye would, sir." The elder gent swiveled abruptly and motioned for Nicolas to follow. With a pronounced list to his gait, he crossed the landing to a door marked:

RESEARCH AREA
NO ADMITTANCE

"Please. We must pass through my laboratory," he said, holding the door.

On entering, Nicolas caught the strong chemical odors of sulfur and acetone, carried by the breeze that flowed through the south-facing windows of the lab, which was well lit by overhead skylights held open for ventilation. The laboratory benches—waist-high marble counters stretching the length of the room—were covered with a variety of scientific glassware. Beakers, odd-shaped flasks, calibrated cylinders. Glass columns reached nearly to the fourteen-foot ceiling. Retorts bubbled. Squatting along the far wall, an open incinerator smoldered.

At the nearest laboratory bench stood another scruffy student like he'd seen in the hall; next to the youth was a young woman. Both wore black rubber aprons. The woman leaned over the student's work on the lab bench, the bright windows behind her. Nicolas felt himself entranced by the striking line of the woman's profile, her lustrous dark hair pulled into a tight coil at the back of her head, and her willowy figure, a mere few inches shorter than his own. She was deep in concentration.

"I'm sorry, son. Sorry," she said, gently admonishing the youth with a lovely string of "s" sounds and a shake of the head. "This must be repeated. The solvent is wrong. Perhaps . . . acetone."

Alone at the next lab bench, some distance beyond the young woman, stood a short, heavily muscled man with swarthy skin, thick mats of neatly trimmed sideburns, and a powerful, square jaw. The man had a laboratory flask at a rolling boil over a Bunsen burner. Just as he reached for the flask, he flashed Van Horne a look of authority tinged, it seemed, with arrogance. Nicolas's initial good impression was dashed when the man knocked the bubbling flask to the floor, where it shattered. The clumsy fellow put his hands to his head and blurted a string of obscenities in squeaky, high-pitched Spanish.

At that, the young woman, who was glaring at the ham-fisted oaf, shook her head in dismay. When her gaze fell on Nicolas, however, the exasperated look on her face turned to a wry, endearing, slightly off-kilter smile, and her dark eyes flashed.

Nicolas knew this look. He'd seen it in the eyes of women as they discreetly took in the waviness of his chestnut-brown hair, or the elegant line he tried for in trimming his mustache. Perhaps it was the ruddy health of his windburnt cheeks, or the strength he believed a clean shave afforded a man's jawline. Whatever it was, Nicolas had seen this look before in the eyes of admiring ladies, though he seldom returned it in kind.

The attractive young woman gave a slight nod, to which Nicolas nodded back.

"Come along now, come along." Professor Keiller stood at a door labeled OFFICE at the far end of the laboratory. "This way, good sir."

Van Horne slipped past the woman and her student. A few steps beyond, he glanced back and again caught her dark eyes and silently admired her satiny hair—near ebony in color—and her graceful silhouette against the open window.

When Nicolas stepped into Keiller's office he was hit with a blast of heat and sultriness never before encountered by a lifelong Adirondacker such as he. The source of this discomfort was immediately evident along the north wall—an intense coal fire in a shallow fireplace lined by multicolored tiles Nicolas judged to be Italian. Steam rose from beakers of water set near the glowing heap of coal. The windows of the office were shut tight.

Nicolas took in the layout of Keiller's overheated inner office and found it quite elegantly appointed—for a place as steamy as a Turkish bath. The walls were of a lustrous cherry wood, intricately carved into seashells, pelicans, and Texas stars. The desk, two long, heavy tables, and the surrounding cabinetry were of dark walnut.

The professor turned to Van Horne and offered his hand. "I'm Keiller, as ye probably guessed," he said in his bouncy Scottish cadence. "Pleased to make your acquaintance, Mr. Van Horne, and I'm hopeful we may do business."

"As am I, Professor."

"Forgive the insufferable heat, but it's necessary for my insectary. I'm afraid those of the class Insecta prefer it tropical." Keiller chuckled and motioned to the further table, which was piled with oblong cages, each no bigger than a foot across, constructed of fragile slats of wood and screening. "My mosquitoes, you see. A certain temperature and humidity must be maintained. Please. Sit."

Keiller limped to his desk. Wincing, he lowered himself into his chair. "I was excited to receive your letter of enquiry, Mr. Van Horne. How did you hear of me, may I ask?"

"From the medical people in New Orleans. Your new college is well-known, sir."

"Aye, we're the largest west of the Mississippi, I'm proud to say. Twenty-three men, and serious students all."

"And such excellent new construction," Nicolas said, gesturing at the office walls.

Keiller leaned back and smiled. "Your first time in Galveston, is it?"

"Why, yes."

"Been trading ice long, have ye?"

"I began my enterprise shortly after college, nearly twenty years ago. In my early commercial endeavors I hauled ice to Albany and Chicago by train, but soon began shipping down the Mississippi to Saint Louis—where we now maintain our own icehouse—and then to New Orleans."

A moment of silence followed, and the two men locked eyes.

"How many have you brought me?" Keiller asked.

"Twelve."

"Only twelve?"

"And some parts."

"Twelve's a wee bit shy of our needs, but I suppose it'll do for the semester. They're mighty hard to come by, you know. We've a body-in-a-bag man, of course, but he's a clumsy dolt and his ill-planned grave robbing has raised the hackles of Galveston's populace, I'm afraid. The City Constable and the authorities as well. You see, I'd hoped for sixteen from you, Mr. Van Horne."

"Yes, well . . . twenty were required in New Orleans."

"Twenty? Damn New Orleans! We're as large as those rascals."

"Sorry I can't provide more. Perhaps next year."

"Tell me, how is their preservation? Have they decomposed badly?"

"Their condition is excellent, Professor. You may trust me on this. Remember, my business is ice—the hardest, coldest Northern ice."

Nicolas was sweltering and could no longer take it. He stood to remove his jacket.

"Do you also employ the services of an undertaker?" Keiller asked.

"My man's a true master of the mortician's art," Nicolas replied, hesitating as he envisioned Thomas Chubb, the undertaker, at his grisly work. Nicolas was reminded that it was indeed Chubb, that odd duck, that sly, secretive, but necessary accomplice in the body trade, who arranged the two dead boys in Buffalo. "This gent's concocted an embalming solution that's unmatched anywhere," Nicolas continued. "He uses extracts of hemlock bark, an excellent preservative."

"My student tells me you also have one aboard that's not embalmed—a child."

"That I have."

"Are ye familiar with how the child died?"

"Why, yes, I suppose. Somewhat familiar. A boy, no more than nine or ten years old. I learned of his availability in the city of Buffalo just as we departed with the ice. I managed a brief stopover there, where the boy was found frozen to death in a snowbank. Mercifully swift, really. No one claimed the poor wretch, is what I was told."

"Now there's a stroke o' good fortune."

Nicolas grew uneasy at the mention of this boy, and at the professor's zeal over the young body. He realized he'd grown callous toward the corpses over the years—he regretted that. Even so, a child in his hold always saddened him greatly. Indeed, this voyage had doubly saddened him since there'd been two such youngsters, two boys dead of unexplained causes loaded in Buffalo. Nicolas saw no reason to burden the new medical man with this minor detail, though, since the other boy had been unloaded in New Orleans. He needn't rouse this Keiller fellow any further.

It was puzzling to have two unidentified youths in his ice. Abandoned corpses, without family, most likely. Ruffians and misfits. This sort of thing was all too common these days, though there was something about those two young bodies . . . the look of them, different from the others in his hold.

"Yes, yes"—Keiller was grinning gleefully—"a young male, freshly frozen. He'll suit our purposes perfectly. We'll take that one direct to the research laboratory. Now, as indicated by your previous correspondence, Mr. Van Horne, your price stands at twenty dollars each?"

Nicolas nodded, though for an instant he considered the possibility of charging more for the child—this professor seemed so eager to have him. But then, this was his first transaction with Keiller; he didn't want to get off on the wrong foot with the old gent. And there was something else. In his years of travel along the Mississippi, Nicolas had met many of these medical professors, but this fellow was the first to invite him into his personal office. All the others had simply demanded delivery under cover of darkness and shoved the cash into his hand at the back door. Keiller seemed quite congenial. He was getting to like this rather odd professor.

Nicolas was about to return Keiller's satisfied smile when there was a knock at the door, it opened a crack, and the attractive young woman who'd been instructing the student in the laboratory peered in.

"Uncle . . . forgive me for interrupting, but Fernando and I are off to the barns to see about the experiment in the horses. While I'm gone," she chided gently, "you simply *must* look over my latest data. I'll leave it in the lab for you."

"Of course, dear, of course," Keiller said, waving her off.

The woman's dark eyes rolled toward the intricately tooled tin ceiling, and Nicolas grinned to himself. Seeing this, she blushed, flashed Nicolas a thin, slightly lopsided smile, and gently shut the door.

"So tell me, Van Horne," Keiller continued. "How'd you ever get yourself into this enterprise? You seem a relatively cultured chap to be supplying cadavers."

Nicolas settled back and smoothed his mustache before he spoke. "The idea first came to me some years ago, in Saint Louis. There was an incident of grave robbing while I was unloading a ship, and . . . well, I thought, how truly wasteful to bury a dead body if some medical gent might learn something from it. Why not put 'em to good use, eh, Professor?"

"Precisely my sentiments."

"I fostered certain connections with the medical men in Albany and supplied my first corpses . . . I suppose you'd prefer to call them 'cadavers,' eh?" He chuckled. "I admit I've turned a bit of a profit with it."

"Ye deserve every penny, good sir. Every penny. My students benefit immeasurably from the scientific study of anatomy."

Keiller struggled out of his chair and stood, as if lecturing at a podium. While he spoke he began waving his hands in small, questioning circles. "Anatomy and microanatomy—they're the basis of all medicine," he said, his voice rising. "My students study six days a week, in the evenings, as well. And morbid anatomy. Physiognomy! I ask you, Van Horne, how could one become a physician without knowing these things? Without knowing science? How? How?"

"I agree completely, Professor. Absolutely. By the way"—Nicolas cleared his throat—"is the payment available?"

"Oh, yes, of course." Keiller took three erratic steps from his imaginary podium to the nearer of the two tables, which overflowed with books and manuscripts. A safe squatted under the table. "I had the bursar prepare enough for sixteen."

Keiller twirled the dial and the door of the safe opened with a creak. He fumbled with an envelope thick with bills and began counting them onto his desk in front of Van Horne.

"As agreed. Twelve cadavers—two hundred and forty dollars."

"There's also the parts, Professor. One leg and six arms, a smattering of hands. Make that an additional twenty, if you please."

"Fair enough, good sir. And would ye be in need of assistance with the unloadin'?" Keiller asked as he dropped back into his chair and Van Horne tucked away his billfold.

"I was just about to enquire on that. Yes, I'd appreciate it greatly. I've only one man, though quite able. With assistance he'll make short work of it."

"I'll have my two people ready. You understand, sir, this needs to be done after nightfall. The folks in this town have not taken kindly to our new college, as ye might imagine." Keiller pressed his hands together in front of his face as if he were settling into his family pew at church. "There's such malicious talk these days."

"It's the same wherever there's a medical college, Professor."

"No, this island is not like other places. There are elements here, powerful elements that . . . well . . ."

"Rest assured, I shall exercise discretion."

"We'll set it for ten o'clock, then?"

When Nicolas stood and took up his jacket to leave, Keiller raised a hand to stop him. "Would ye have any interest in seeing my research laboratory, Mr. Van Horne?"

"Certainly. Exactly what sort of facility do you have there, Professor?"

"The most modern of medical research labs." Keiller hoisted himself out of his chair, lurched toward the fireplace, and bent over the insect cages. "You see, sir, here we're followers of the cellular theories of Rudolf Virchow . . ."

While he spoke, Keiller took a beaker of red, viscous liquid from the hearth and, with a delicate glass eyedropper, set a line of tiny drops onto the top screen of one of the insect cages.

"What's it you're doing, Professor?"

"Their blood meal. They prefer the human"—there was a buzz of insect activity—"but they'll feed on horse blood avidly enough."

Ever the inquisitive learner, Nicolas eased out of his chair and leaned over the professor as he worked.

"Best stay back, my good man," Keiller said. "I go to great lengths to make it hot as a Galveston summer in here—but they're lively at this temperature. If these critters should escape . . . well, I long ago became resistant, but a Northerner like yourself would not be so lucky."

At Keiller's warning, Nicolas straightened and stepped back.

"Ah, yes, Rudolf Virchow . . ." The professor, recalling his train of thought, went on as he fed his insects. "The greatest of observers, Virchow. What brilliance! What insight in his 'cellular' theory of disease. Rudolf's a good friend of Darwin's. Two of the greatest minds of our century. Yes, well . . . come along, sir. To my laboratory."

3

The Laboratory

The research laboratory was abandoned. Keiller and Nicolas strolled between the slate benches while Keiller rambled on about Rudolf Virchow and his theory of cells and their "morbid reactions."

"Top-notch scientists come to us from around the world, you know," Keiller said proudly.

"Like the Spanish fellow who was here earlier?" Nicolas asked.

"Well, no . . . that chap's still wet behind the ears. Fernando arrived only last week, recommended by Pasteur himself."

"And the young woman?"

"My dearest niece, Renée—the other Dr. Keiller in the lab. A brilliant physician and researcher in her own right." Keiller chuckled. "She's the real brains around here. Graduated summa cum laude. An accomplished scientist, and only five years out of doctoral training."

Nicolas lifted a heavy, oddly shaped piece of glassware from the lab bench to examine its finer details. "Exactly what disease do you study, Professor?"

"Yellow fever."

Nicolas's mouth dropped open and he set the heavy glassware down with a bang. "That's the miserable culprit that killed my mother."

"So sorry to hear that, sir. How unusual, though . . . you being a Northerner."

"Father had taken Mother south, to the Carolinas, while pursuing one of his financial schemes. I was but a child. It was early summer . . . an epidemic struck there. Father never forgave himself for leaving home."

Keiller pursed his lips and nodded sympathetically. "Where would your home be, Mr. Van Horne?"

"Northern New York, in the mountainous area drained by the Black River."

"And a right beautiful piece o' country it must be." Keiller took Nicolas's arm. "Let's get a breath of air, shall we?" He led Nicolas to the open window. "I imagine your home's something like my own dear Scotland."

"Yes, it is truly God's country, Professor."

"Ah, I've spent so many years in these hot zones of the world," Keiller said with sadness. "What's the name of your town?"

"Forestport."

"Forestport. That's where they're from then, the ones ye brought me."

Keiller, deep in thought, leaned on the windowsill and stared out. Rising on his toes, his gaze went past the convent and hospital, over the grey slate of the rooftops, to the green water of the gulf. The breeze blew the sulfuric odors behind the two men. The sun was high. Daylight streamed in.

Keiller turned and asked, "Do you know science, Mr. Van Horne?"

"Some aspects, yes, but I'm a practical sort. I enjoy tinkering. In point of fact I hold nine patents on devices I've invented for harvesting ice."

"Nine patents?" Keiller arched his bushy white eyebrows. "Indeed."

"You've spiked my curiosity, Professor. Tell me, exactly how do you intend to cure this horrid disease?"

"A few years back I discovered that yellow fever is caused by a living organism I'm callin' a 'particle.' We've succeeded in inoculating the guinea pigs we house deep in the bowels of the building with this particle . . ."

Nicolas enjoyed studying this professor, the peculiar way he had of rocking forward onto his toes and waving his hands about when he became excited.

". . . so you see, Mr. Van Horne, the key to yellow fever"—Keiller motioned toward his office door—"is the mosquito."

"In those cages?"

"Precisely. It's my theory that the particle of yellow fever is passed by the bite of *Aedes aegypti*, the common mosquito. I've said this since my days in Cuba, though not a soul in the scientific world believes me!" he laughed. "If Renée can only succeed in passing the particle to that boy's cells . . ."

"I see. A living particle."

". . . then we'll infect horses and they'll make buckets of anti-toxoid."

"The horse will make the cure?"

"Aye, the final step will be purifying the anti-toxoid from horse blood. That'll be our cure, my good man."

With his arms still in midair, Keiller glanced down at a leather-bound ledger lying on the bench top, open to a page freshly inked by a careful hand. "Ooh! My, my!" he cried with an old man's glee. "Renée's new data!"

Keiller bent over the ledger and fell silent. With a smooth, habitual movement, Nicolas slid his long-dead father's watch from a vest pocket and clicked open its gold lid. It was barely noon, but a sudden wave of mental fatigue made him wonder why he'd ever ventured to land a cargo in this strange new port.

"Forgive me, Professor, but I have business to attend to."

Keiller glanced up from the notebook. "Until this evening, then, Mr. Van Horne. I look forward to delivery."

4

Secret Cargo

Like wooden spacers the dead lay between the massive blocks of Van Horne ice. In the hold of Nicolas's ship, rich lay with poor, male with female, young with old; there was no order to their position in the ice, no preference to their loading. Potato farmers who'd tilled the weak Adirondack soil, sawyers from the mill at Forestport, Canadian lumberjacks killed in the woods, ironworkers from the village of Old Forge, whores from the poorest quarters . . . all lay together in the stillness of the ice.

These bodies had come to Van Horne's ship from locales flung far across northern New York State. Those from the village of Forestport and environs came through the trickery of Thomas Chubb, the village undertaker, who, without scruple, pocketed Van Horne's fee to bury coffins with lakeside rocks as ballast. Lumberjacks came from the camps listed as "missing in the woods." Victims of consumption arrived from the sanitarium at Saranac, where tombstones marked empty graves. Unclaimed bodies were sent from the lunatic asylum at Ticonderoga. And wherever a sawbones plied his trade in the North Country, he understood that the remnants of men—an arm off the sawmill floor, a hand lost to the leather chopper in Gloversville, or a leg severed by a lumberjack's false move in the great Adirondack woods—would bring a fair price at the Van Horne icehouse on the shores of Upper Spy Lake.

Just as an ice merchant must account for every cake of ice, Nicolas knew the source of each of these corpses and every odd part of man's anatomy that might bring a profit. He was a meticulous bookkeeper of the history of the dead. He had logged and cataloged this shipment with precision, each corpse, arm, leg, and hand—every human remnant.

The only exceptions were those two boys dragged from a Buffalo snowdrift, a fact that had eaten at Nicolas these past days . . .

It had been only moments before departing with the ice that his associate Thomas Chubb, the undertaker, alerted Nicolas of these two boys' availability. A quick and easy addition to their cargo, the two young bodies were handed over by a chap from Buffalo's medical college, a doctor Nicolas had never met before. Little was said at the transfer. As far as Nicolas knew, the "fresh one" so highly prized by Keiller, the new professor, was without human history.

Something odd he'd noticed about the boys as Adam stowed them in the ice in Buffalo had troubled Nicolas all the way to Galveston. There'd been an unnatural angle to their necks, a freakish, defensive pose of their limbs. And these youngsters had some sort of sinister tattoo—he could swear he saw it—a mark, a darkened, angry scar of some sort. Had he seen a thing like that before?

Nicolas checked his books while on the Mississippi and found a half dozen other unidentified bodies he'd transported in the past two years. Oddly, all were youngsters. Five were boys, ten or eleven years of age, and one a young girl—all arranged by Thomas Chubb. Two of the youngsters had been fished from the rivers or lakes, drowned. Three were found frozen in the snow. The girl was discovered one summer in the woods near Buffalo. His notes mentioned nothing about a mark on them.

Such deficits gave a careful bookkeeper pause. Worse still, these children's bodies reminded Nicolas all too vividly of his own, personal loss of a precious young son, gone now these many years, a boy of tender age and ill health, lost in the woods and never found . . . his sweet son Ethan . . .

With hoarfrost on their faces, Nicolas Van Horne's cargo of mortal remains had crossed America. Now longshoremen labored overhead. Canvas was thrown aside, sawdust swept away, and tons of ice were on the move in the tropical daylight. Only the hiding place of the dead, the dark, icy catacombs of the lowest layer, would remain untouched.

In the quiet of night the ship would be moved and the bottom layer of ice opened. And Van Horne's secret cargo would find its final resting place on the island of Galveston.

5

A New Business Partner

Nicolas studied the frenetic movement of the harbor out the open trolley window. He needn't stop at his ship; Adam oversaw these harborside operations with utmost competence. Nicolas was reassured by the sight of his great blocks of ice moving efficiently down Pier 22 and into Bonferri's Icehouse, a worn, wood-frame structure that squatted alongside the other aging warehouses on the wharf. The stevedores hired by Adam, a group of colored men, were hard at work with the hand-drawn carts they ordinarily used for bales of cotton.

Van Horne's present destination, then, would be the downtown office of Mr. Pierre Bonferri, midlevel merchant, procurer of dry goods, and go-between in the business of ice. Nicolas had corresponded with this Frenchman at length on matters of business; important final arrangements regarding Mr. Bonferri's icehouse and Nicolas's advance payment were pending.

From his years in the ice enterprise, Van Horne knew precisely what it took to become a successful ice man. Despite the myriad fine details of trading in ice, a man needed to pay attention to only three main principles. First and foremost, one should offer the finest product—pure, dense, Northern blocks, and at the right price. Next, the trader must ensure proper handling of his ice. Speed and strictest hygiene were paramount. Last—and most important—once the deal was struck, one must advertise. If these details were tended to, the demand of a local populace for ice would grow ten times greater with each year's shipment.

"Of course we'll handle your ice correctly, *mon ami*," Mr. Bonferri assured him, once Nicolas was comfortably seated in his downtown office. "I have dealt in ice for years now, as you know." Bonferri rocked gently in his commodious desk chair while twirling the tips of his handlebar mustache into pencil-fine points.

"I'm afraid it's an awfully small icehouse you have, Mr. Bonferri."

"Sir!"

"And poorly insulated."

"It is the finest on zee coast, *monsieur*."

"I'm sure. Nevertheless, I must insist, Mr. Bonferri—sharing profits as we are—that we charge a bit more than for that inferior Missouri ice you've been trafficking in. The public will gladly pay for a superior product such as mine."

"Yes, yes, *mon ami*, we'll up the price a few pennies. The public can bear it. Ice is practically a household item nowadays."

"And we'll need an exhibit."

"What on earth are you talking about, Van Horne?"

"An exhibit of my ice. I'll choose a perfect block and have it set out for all to see. It's the novelty of it. It's an advertisement, you understand."

"An advertisement. Clever, Van Horne."

"As many citizens as possible must see this block. Tell me, Bonferri, which is your finest, your busiest emporium?"

"That would be Slade's, a few blocks down the Strand."

"Then that's the place for it. My exhibit will be the talk of the town. Properly maintained, covered at night and so forth, it will last for months."

"Whatever you find necessary." Bonferri leaned back, gazed at the ceiling, and twirled with renewed intensity.

Nicolas continued. "At first we'll fetch a moderate price for our product. Then, when your summer arrives, the temperature will rise—"

"And so will zee price of ice. Excellent."

"You'll arrange for the exhibit?"

At Bonferri's nod, Nicolas stood and made ready to go. The Frenchman stood behind his desk, gave his mustache one last perfunctory turn, and offered a cool, greasy hand. "Of course you must collect your advance payment for my end of the bargain . . . when will you finish unloading, Van Horne?"

"The last of the shipment should be packed in your icehouse by the end of tomorrow."

As they passed through the outer office, Nicolas was startled by the sight of a pleasing, towheaded young woman standing at the upright desk along the wall. She was bent over a ledger book, keeping the tallies—a job usually done by a gent specially trained in affairs of business.

"How forward-thinking," Nicolas commented quietly. "I see you employ the fairer of our species, Bonferri."

"Ah, yes. *Très moderne.*" Bonferri chuckled. "I grew weary of the run-of-the-mill bookkeepers in this town. I've even ordered her a typewriting machine. The finest Remington."

The comely, curvaceous girl glanced up, flashed her peacock-blue eyes at the two men, and was back at her ledger.

"Tomorrow, when you've finished unloading," Bonferri said, "I'll arrange your payment. I'll send you a message, once my banker has it ready. I'm afraid you'll need to go to the financial offices on the upper floor of Hutch Sealy's Cotton Exchange Building for your funds."

"Is this Sealy the city's main banker?"

Bonferri took his eyes from his fair-haired bookkeeper and fixed them on Nicolas. "Sealy's our *only* banker. Hutchinson Sealy & Son Finance, Trust, and Title Company. You see, Mr. Van Horne, cotton controls this town, and the Sealys control cotton. The docks. The wharves. Every blessed dollar goes through them."

"Even for commodities such as ice?"

"Even ice. I'll make the arrangements. Remember, my financial officer's located on the top floor of the Cotton Exchange Building. I'll send a message to your hotel when the payment's available."

6

Delivery

At Pier 22 Nicolas found his ship riding high in the water, its topside secured. Adam had tacked a note to the ship's side explaining that he'd retired to his quarters at Molly's Rooms, "a stone's throw from the dock."

Molly's Rooms, typical of seafarer's quarters, was a flophouse located in the nearby neighborhood known as Sailortown, a rough-and-ready district of boardinghouses, dilapidated warehouses, rowdy drinking establishments, and bordellos. Nicolas entered the front door of Molly's and walked the musty first-floor hallway in near-darkness, calling for Adam, then he climbed a set of rickety stairs to the second floor, where the doors were left ajar onto the hall for ventilation. Seafaring men loitered in the hall, which was thick with cigar and pipe smoke. The guttural hum of foreign speech thickened the air further.

Nicolas called out again.

"In here, sir."

Adam sat on a narrow bed jammed against the wall, his legs crossed, a thin blanket thrown over his shoulders. His seaman's chest was set on end in the corner. Nicolas stepped in; there was barely enough room to stand. Large brown insects dashed under the bed to make way.

"It's settled, Adam. I fetched a good price for the bodies. Better than New Orleans. Did the unloading go as planned?"

"Smooth enough."

"The men saw nothing?"

"There was mumblin' but the bottom layer's untouched."

"Delivery's set for ten o'clock tonight at the medical college's dock. You'll have assistance."

Adam nodded. "I hired my two strongest longshoremen to come back tomorrow to unload the ice that's left in that bottom layer."

"We'll have those corpses out of there soon enough."

Outside of Molly's Rooms, Nicolas drew a breath redolent with the wharf smells of damp wood, salt, and tar. Gusts off the bay spun wisps of cotton around his feet. The sky was mottled and the feel of impending rain hung in the street as Nicolas walked clear of the harbor and hailed a carriage to carry him to his hotel to await nightfall.

With the evening's nerve-wracking delivery to the medical school drawing near, Nicolas decided he needed a stiff drink; lately, he'd found it difficult to relax without one. He strode up to the Majestic's finely appointed bar.

"What's your pleasure, sir?" the barkeep, a man the color of dark chocolate, asked.

Nicolas planted his boot on the brass rail and described a concoction of whiskey with a distinctive fragrance he'd experienced only in New Orleans.

"That'd be their style o' whiskey cocktail," the barkeep replied. "Nothin' to it." Flashing a smile, the barman doused a tumbler with yellowish liquor and spun the glass high overhead to coat its inner surface. "In the original, they used the absinthe of Sazerac de Forge et Fils," he said with authority in matters of tipular fixings. "Pity, years back the fever wiped out the family, sons and all."

"Yellow fever, was it?"

"Epidemic of '78, sir. Hit New Orleans a disastrous blow." The barman clicked the tumbler on the mahogany and poured.

Nicolas sipped. "Ah . . . Excellent. It's got a bite."

The barman smiled and stepped away to another patron. Here was a man Nicolas could admire, a fellow so different from himself and yet accomplished, well schooled, and in command of his profession. A mixologist of the highest caliber.

Nicolas studied his weary reflection in the bluish mirror behind the bar. A bath would be welcome. He badly needed a shave—hadn't been to a barber since Saint Louis. His mustache had grown wild, and his normally clean-shaven cheeks and chin were covered with a dusky thatch.

He tossed back the last of the cocktail and strode to the hotel's east parlour for a cigar. Leaning over the rail on the beachfront veranda, Nicolas smoked and admired the vast, restless water, so different from the lakes he'd left behind frozen hard as stone. But the panatela he'd chosen grew bitter. Suddenly weary, he retired to his room, stretched out on the bed, and dozed.

In recent years, when sleep finally found Nicolas, his repose was too often dashed by woebegone visions of his first son, Ethan—the one he'd lost to the woods as a young boy. On this evening, though, the cocktail he'd imbibed did its work, his recurring nightmare was held at bay, and he enjoyed some minutes of dreamless sleep.

Nicolas was wakened by the clatter of hail against the windowpanes. The room was dark as pine pitch. He lit a lamp at the bedside and opened his watch—still time for some supper to bolster him for the delivery.

In the hotel's main dining room he chose a plate of fried fish topped with browned almonds. A loaf of crusty French bread and a dish of greens, mightily spiced, were set on the table. Nicolas ate in haste, forgoing coffee and brandy. Delivery time was near. "Waiter!" he called. "Do me the kindness of calling a carriage."

Nicolas was pelted by a burst of rain and hail as he climbed into a covered cab at the hotel entrance and asked to be taken to the medical college. The driver had the attitude all these locals seemed to voice. "Mister," he said, raising an eyebrow, "might I ask what ya'd be doing out there at this time of night?"

"I'm a man of commerce. My business is ice."

"At the medical college?"

"Ice, my good man, has many uses in today's world."

When Nicolas climbed down from the carriage, the rain abated, but roiling black clouds obscured the moon. The palm trees were battered by gusts off the bay, creating an awful racket. A perfect night for the task at hand.

Professor Keiller waited on the narrow dock at the back of the red building. He wore a heavy rubber slicker buckled tight under his chin. Two brawny men flanked him: one a short, stout Chinaman whose deformed humpback had him perpetually looking to his left; the other a dark-skinned Goliath of South Seas origin, nearly seven feet tall, his bare arms and chest covered with sea serpents, anchors, and ships at full sail. Keiller linked arms with Nicolas, and this uncommon mix of men watched in silence as Van Horne's steamer came smoking in from Pier 22.

They made her fast and Adam climbed down. The harbor pilot who'd guided the steamer on its short passage was handed a dollar and, informed of the nearest tavern's whereabouts, set off on foot. Canvas coverings were unfurled. The frost on the faces of those wedged between the blocks of ice quickly turned to dew.

Keiller took charge, crying, "Straight to the vats with 'em! All but the child. Where is that boy?"

Though the corpses were icy cold, they weren't frozen solid, nor were there any remnants of rigor mortis; rather, the bodies were like grey, pliable lumps of clay dragged out from their resting places in the ice. A few were still dressed in burial clothes. Adam, aided by Keiller's sturdy, misshapen Chinaman, whom Keiller called Lee Ching, lowered the first bodies to the dock. The nautical giant then loaded the corpses, three at a time, into a wheelbarrow and rolled off to a low, steel door on the ground floor at the back of the college.

Keiller peered into the hold as Adam hauled up the boy, the fresh one, in his arms. "Yes!" Keiller grabbed Adam by the arm. "This way."

Sudden staccato bursts of lightning illuminated the look of sheer joy that shone on the old professor's face, and rain poured down.

"To the research laboratory with this one," Keiller shouted, his slicker awash, his hair pasted down by the torrent. "Give a hand here, Lee Ching."

Nicolas had turned up his jacket collar and pursued Keiller down the dock when a macabre thought struck him. "Professor," he called to Keiller. "You're not trying to bring the boy back to life, are you? With electricity or some such?"

"No, we're after his cells," Keiller called back with a maniacal cackle. "Only his cells. Like I told you."

"Oh, yes. Cells. But how do you get these cells?"

"Why, we extract 'em from his lymphoid glands, of course. Didn't I explain that?" The professor entered the heavy steel door at the back of the college and pulled off his slicker. "Renée's the expert there," he added. "She's prepared everything."

Nicolas dripped like a wharf rat. He fully realized, though, that the shiver rattling his spine wasn't entirely from the ghastly weather. All this excitement over the boy's fresh corpse had him riled. *Those boys, pulled from a snowdrift.*

"Come along, Van Horne." Keiller took Nicolas's elbow, stirring him from his dark thoughts. "Let me show you our storage facilities. Then we'll talk further in my office and drink to your successful delivery."

They stood in a large, windowless basement room that held the largest ceramic vats Nicolas had ever seen, each eight feet in diameter and shoulder high to a man, with barely space to walk between them. Keiller's assistants pulled the wooden covers off the vats, then began checking the corpses for signs of deterioration on a nearby marble slab. Any remaining burial clothes were cut away with a razor. A numbered label was tied on the big toe of each before it was slid into the murky fluid in the vats. Once the last corpse was on the slab, Keiller slammed the steel door shut and slid its bolt with a thud. The odor of formaldehyde became overpowering.

"The smell's a bit strong," Keiller explained, "because our vats are uncovered."

Chilled to the core, Nicolas watched bodies splash into the vats. The sight of a hand with dainty, bright red fingernails bobbing on the foul grey surface jangled his nerves. It was a whore, a woman who'd walked the streets of Forestport and died a miserable death during childbirth in her single room.

Once the county coroner had given her a once-over, Thomas Chubb had diverted her from a pauper's grave.

Nicolas couldn't catch his breath. "How . . . how long in the vats, Professor?"

"A wee bit more than a month, for complete fixation. I'm pleased with their condition, Mr. Van Horne." Keiller felt the coolness of a passing death mask with the back of his hand. "The preservation is excellent." Keiller smiled at the corpse. "A perfect temperature, and our vats will complete their perfection."

Nicolas's eyes welled over with tears. He fought to keep from choking. "Gad, man—it's vile in here!"

"This way, then." Keiller squeezed between the vats to a second steel door on the opposite wall. Nicolas followed into a long, narrow room, lit by electricity and bright with lime wash. "We store 'em here till we use 'em," Keiller said.

Heavy steel rails were secured around the walls of the room with bolts; sharpened hooks, like those used in an abattoir, were attached to each rail. Eight or nine corpses, hooked through the shoulder or back, dangled from the rails.

Nicolas did a double take. *Colored people,* he thought. The corpses were all colored people. Moreover, male or female, these corpses looked poverty stricken—malnourished, badly scarred by life, with hands thickened by the coarsest labor.

"This is all that's left from our previous acquisition," Keiller said. "And I doubt our unscrupulous pair of resurrectionists will be in business much longer." The professor tapped a leathery corpse and set it gently swinging on its hook. "Ye see, hanging 'em like this helps air out the formaldehyde before we dissect 'em. My students will be working on these fellows shortly."

Nicolas shuddered in his clammy woolens. His shoes squished as he followed Keiller to the door at the far end of the room.

"We'll get a breath o' air on the upper level," Keiller said, taking a narrow, darkened set of stairs to the entrance vestibule and central staircase of the college. "See, now, it's better here. My men will tend to matters down below."

Nicolas took deep breaths. He tried to still his shivering as he followed Keiller's slow progress up the circular central stairs of the college. The steady rumble of rain on the building's tile roof and the rattling of the skylights grew louder as they neared the upper landing, where Nicolas was surprised to see the smoky glass of the door to the anatomy laboratory brilliantly lit.

"Dissecting at night, are they?" he asked.

"Ha! That they are," Keiller laughed. "I'll wager there's no night dissectin' in Saint Louis or New Orleans, eh? It's sad, but most of these medical colleges springing up everywhere are more interested in bloodletting and water cures than they are in truth and learning." Keiller paused. "I'd be pleased to show you, Mr. Van Horne. A man of reason such as yourself should find a dissection in progress of great interest."

"I confess, I've never seen what it's all about."

"Come along, then. You'll understand better how my students profit from your specimens." Keiller swung his game leg toward the door. "There's normal anatomy, of course, but more important are the variations in structure, the growths, the morbid alterations of disease."

Keiller threw the door of the anatomy laboratory open. Nicolas was forced to squint, his eyes shocked by a line of powerful electric lightbulbs hung over three shiny, metal tables. The whitewashed walls, haphazardly strung with thick, black wires, added to the harsh brilliance.

"As ye see," Keiller said proudly, "we are totally illuminated by electricity."

Students draped with heavy black aprons surrounded two of the tables. At the nearest table, four students, their bare hands glistening, leaned over a freshly opened corpse, flaying the flesh from the belly and chest as if cleaning an enormous fish. At the next table two students encircled an advanced dissection of a severed arm with muscle, tendon, and bone exposed. The furthest table held a dismembered torso and single female breast awaiting another evening of study.

An explosion of laughter came from the two students dissecting the arm. Nicolas watched as one of them jerked on a central tendon, forcing the corpse's hand into an obscene gesture.

"This is"—Van Horne gasped—"the first I've seen what becomes of them."

"Think of it," Keiller said, gesturing at the youths. "It's nearly midnight and my students are still at their studies."

"They enjoy it more than I imagined."

"Perhaps they're a bit giddy with the late hour and the vapours. Gents!" Keiller said, raising a hand. "Take a break if ya like."

Knives and scissors clattered down on stainless steel. The young dissectors, their hands and apron fronts splattered with grey bits of tissue and glistening, yellow fat, abandoned their work and exited the dissecting room. Several carried a rattling bag of dried bones for later study.

Nicolas identified other human parts scattered on the stone floor—a complete pelvis, its bone scraped clean, and the severed head of an infant with the face dissected to expose the delicate muscles and nerves of its tiny eyeballs. In the corner, a mound of unrecognizable offal.

"We're still having a bit o' difficulty with disposal," Keiller said, shaking his head. "We've been dumping barrels of their earthly remains in the gulf, but it tends to wash up on the beach, which is a bit disturbin' to the local folks."

Van Horne's stomach churned. "I'm impressed with your operation, Professor," he said, his voice a near-whisper. "Very impressed, indeed."

A metallic, oily taste blossomed at the back of his mouth. Nicolas realized the plate of fried fish he'd eaten at supper was threatening to come up. "But, Professor . . . I believe . . . I'm beginning . . . to tire." There was a dull drumming in his ears, the pound of blood at his temples . . . and fatigue . . . such unspeakable fatigue . . .

Nicolas Van Horne's last thought, before his eyes rolled up toward the skylights, was how uncommonly good it felt to be sitting on the cool stone floor of the anatomy laboratory.

Then, nothing.

A Second Lesson in Science

It was hot, stifling hot and suffering damp. A hand gently cooled his cheek, his forehead, the back of his neck. When he opened his eyes he found himself wobbling in the oaken chair in Keiller's overheated office. A single bright light burnt overhead. A horrible ammonia smell…he snapped his head back and…was this an apparition? An angel leaning over him? He was looking into the dark eyes of a beautiful woman, like staring into a deep, still well. As his senses returned, Nicolas noted with unexpected pleasure the fine flecks of green light that radiated at the edges of her lovely, nearly black irises.

"Are you feeling better, Mr. Van Horne?" Renée Keiller, the professor's niece, asked.

"I . . . I fainted?"

Renée nodded, her eyes averted, then flashed a thin, understanding smile.

The elder Keiller was at Nicolas's side. "Come now, my good man," he said, settling a bony hand on Van Horne's shoulder. "Men faint, you know. It's strictly a matter of the vagus nerve. Nothing that a bit o' whiskey won't remedy."

Renée straightened. "Excuse me, gentlemen," she said, tightening the cap on the smelling salts. "We're at a critical step with the cells, and I'm sure your visitor will do fine, Uncle." She smiled warmly and opened the office door, allowing cooler air and the laboratory smells of sulfur and carbolic acid to drift in.

"You, sir, are in need of a drink," Keiller said, once the door had clicked shut behind his niece. He lit an oil lamp, then walked to the wall and twisted the electrical switch off. "I prefer the gentler light," he said as the single overhead lightbulb flicked out. "Perhaps I'm old-fashioned." He pulled the bottom drawer of his desk open. "Will Scotch whiskey do ye, Mr. Van Horne? I've a wee taste here from the highlands, a distiller near my childhood home above Dundee."

"Haven't had the Scotch stuff since my college days," Nicolas replied.

Keiller took two common laboratory beakers marked "150 milliliters" from a shelf and poured generous splashes. "And what college was it you attended?"

"Harvard, class of '68."

"Ah, Boston. I wisht I'd seen more of it. I was offered a position in Boston when I first came from Edinburgh, a fresh, young professor of morbid anatomy, you understand. But my research took me to Havana for a number of years, then here to Galveston, to the frontier."

"To build a successful school, I must say."

Keiller raised his beaker in the yellow lamplight. "Shall we, Mr. Van Horne? Here's to success—for your ice, our college, and future shipments."

"Yes, I'll drink to that, Professor . . . and to hell with these economic panics the past few years."

"Seems to me you've gained a reasonable degree of success."

"Production varies from winter to winter, which is worrisome, but my ice is of exceptional purity, and should my luck hold, I might expand . . . in fact, just today I've toyed with the idea of building my own icehouse on the island."

With another "wee taste" or two, the bottle of Scotch was emptied and Keiller again searched his desk. "I've another in here somewhere"—he produced a dark brown bottle—"aha!"

Van Horne removed his sodden jacket and hung it over a chair near the hearth. He pulled off his tie and starched white collar, limp from the deluge. They raised their glasses, their tongues loosened, and the formalities of "sir" and "professor" relaxed and were replaced by first names.

"Yes, Francis, you've a fine whiskey here."

Van Horne studied the screened cages of insects, puzzled by how the delicate structures were arranged into two groups, one marked by stripes of red paint. "Tell me about your mosquitoes, will you?" he asked.

"The particle of yellow fever resides in their salivary glands, you see. Here—the red cages are the ones that have it. Renée was able to pass the particle into our colony of guinea pigs. If she can grow it in the cells of this young boy you've brought her, we hope to eventually inject it into horses."

Seeing the puzzled look on Nicolas's face, Keiller struggled out of his chair and said, "Come—I'll explain better in the laboratory." He limped off, waving for Nicolas to follow.

The hour was late, the research laboratory empty. A single electric light burnt over the nearest lab bench, where the draped body of the small boy, the "fresh one," lay on a gurney, abandoned by the experimenters. Nicolas felt a strange thumping in his chest at the sight of the draped body. Keiller raced to the far wall and began fussing over a complicated apparatus; Nicolas followed. The professor turned a valve on his apparatus and struck a flint; an intense flame burst forth, scorching a stick of a chalky substance until it glowed white-hot.

"Calcium carbonate," Keiller explained. "It's limelight." He aimed the brilliant light at a mirror mounted under a microscope on the lab bench, then slowly passed a glass slide over the microscope's stage. When he appeared satisfied with what he saw under the lens, he motioned for Nicolas to look. "You'll be seeing at a power that few men have experienced," he said. "Only Wetzlar grinds optics to such incredible tolerances."

"What am I looking for?"

"The orange dots," Keiller said. "I've focused on the mosquito's salivary gland, stained with the acridine dyes I employ. That's the particles of yellow fever you're seeing, or the infernal Yellow Jack, as we call him."

"I see it, Francis. Yes, I do."

"Ah, Nicolas, so much has happened in the world of science since Jenner gave us an anti-toxoid for cowpox. So much has been learned."

Keiller displaced Nicolas at his scope. While peering into it, he began to lecture again, his hands sporadically shooting into the air. "Just as our greatest genius, Pasteur, has shown us the particle of rabies and given us a vaccine for anthrax . . . though Jean Toussaint still claims the credit, the silly old fool . . ."

Van Horne stepped to the open window. The rain had stopped. He took a breath of the storm's cool aftermath and shook his head clear of the sulfurous atmosphere. While Keiller lectured, Nicolas stared at the dull lights of the hospital across the street and thought how ghastly the place must be when the fever struck and filled its beds with dying men, women, and children.

"Ha!" Keiller chuckled behind him. "Wouldn't Toussaint like to know what we're up to with yellow fever, eh? The scoundrel's stolen Pasteur's ideas at every turn—he'd be quick to steal ours. Little does he know we're growing the particle on this very island."

While Keiller ran on, Nicolas walked to the other end of the lab bench, where the dead boy on the gurney was now brightly lit by the limelight. Nicolas lifted the shroud and stood back—it was his first thorough look at the body so hastily loaded in Buffalo. The marbled, bluish color of decomposition was just beginning on the boy's upper torso. A long incision ran the length of his chest and abdomen, where the experimenters no doubt took their samples. The incision had been neatly shut, baseball-stitched with coarse black suture. The body, washed clean, was still wet and shiny.

The dead boy appeared to be an ill-bred youth, and one who'd been poorly fed. His shaggy hair was in disarray, the jut of his jaw cantankerous and defiant even in death. With his head turned slightly away, his upper torso seemed strangely misshapen and mottled. His neck, desiccated to a brownish crust, appeared furrowed. On closer exam, was the windpipe severed?

As Keiller's science lesson droned on in the background, Nicolas bent over the corpse and stared close, wide-eyed. On the boy's right shoulder was a darkly pigmented scar about half the size of a silver dollar, a crisscross of thin black lines that resembled an X.

Ж

"It's that horrid *thing* . . . I recognize it from my dreams," Nicolas muttered as he flipped the shroud back over the body. "On the boys. The mark."

8

Morphine Dreams

A brisk north wind pushed Nicolas's carriage toward the beach at an easy trot. The rain had flushed the stench of horse droppings out of the street. Houses sparkled in the moonlight. This unusual freshness reinvigorated Nicolas, the tired traveler, but the sight of that boy on the gurney had his mind on a knife edge. Sleep would not come easily.

It was hours past midnight. The lobby of the Majestic Beach Hotel was deserted. Nicolas climbed the grand stairway to his room, turned the key in the lock, entered, and threw the windows open.

He tried to remind himself that, overall, it was a successful day. The delivery ended strangely, and there was the unsettling issue of the boy's corpse and its puzzling mark, but Nicolas had witnessed the inner workings of a medical college and met an excellent gentleman and scientist with some good whiskey. But, now, in his elegant hotel room, he had to force himself to forget the day's trials, and the nightmares. He needed to relax. Not any common means of relaxation would do, though. Nicolas aimed for a most modern, special form of relaxation he'd only recently learned to partake of.

From his steamer trunk he retrieved his "mix"—a small vial concocted for him by Forestport's apothecary, Mr. Boatmann, according to the specifications of the undertaker Thomas Chubb. Thomas's favored mix consisted of six parts morphine, one part cocaine hydrochloride, and a touch of chloral hydrate to prevent the morphine from "rattling one's nerves," as Boatmann had put it.

Nicolas took up the well-worn metal syringe Thomas Chubb had presented as a gift before Nicolas departed the North Country. He drew a single milliliter of Mr. Boatmann's handiwork into its cylinder—a dose he'd found reasonably relaxing. He slipped the coarse steel needle just beneath the skin of his forearm, the "subcutaneous method" Thomas had demonstrated for him.

A bright red weal rose up. Nothing more than a mild sting, really.

Yes, it had been a profitable day—now perfectly punctuated by something quite new, this warm chemical tingle. Joy crept through his body; his tired legs seemed to glide like a ghost's across the Oriental carpet. The bright light of

Keiller's dissecting room, corpses swinging on hooks, and the unsettling puzzle of two unidentified boys melted into a pleasant dreamlike state.

Ah, sweet morphia—a white cloud suffusing the room, cool air at the window, and the mesmerizing unrest of a vast, undulating expanse of salt water. He would undress in the pale light of the moon, and the last sound in his ears before his well-earned sleep would be the tranquil lull of the surf.

9

Uneasy Respite

On awakening, Nicolas discovered that he'd slept in his clothes. He hadn't done that in weeks, not since he'd first experimented with Chubb's steel needle.

Still in his damp shirt and pants, he stretched the stiffness out of his arms by the window and shook his head free of the cobwebs. Last evening's storm and strong north wind had been replaced by a mild sea breeze, warm by a Northerner's standards. The gulf was cobalt blue, the sky bright. In the hallway, Nicolas called out to a porter for a pitcher of hot water, then he undressed and piled his dirty clothing on the floor by the bed.

He checked his watch. Nearly midday, and he already felt exhausted. By now Adam would've made quick work of the remaining ice. That bottom layer, a mere three feet deep, would be packed in Bonferri's icehouse by Adam's trusty longshoremen. The hold would be cleaned, everything shipshape. As early as tomorrow they might board the train for home.

He was down to his last clean shirt and collar. He tied on a fresh cravat, knotting it roguishly long, and descended the grand hotel staircase to meander through the crowded lobby, his nerves rattling from the evening's morphine.

He sank deep into the plush purple of a lobby sofa and admired the high-vaulted ceiling and dark-stained woods of the bar, where a few diehards were downing their morning eye-openers. Porters and visiting businessmen passed by. He considered a visit to the hotel's barber for that shave and mustache trim, but the nerves, the jitters, lingered. The shave could wait.

On the Majestic's airy veranda he settled on a wicker chaise longue near the rail. The fine, grey sand of Galveston lay a few feet away, and the surf pounded a few yards further. A passing porter tossed a blanket over him to shield him from the drifting sand. He stretched his legs, pulled the thin cotton blanket tight about his neck, and watched with amusement as tiny yellow-and-blue-striped land crabs scuttled to and fro, then dove into holes in the sand no larger than a dime. Overhead, squadrons of raucous gulls hovered and swooped. The sea breeze whipped the blanket's edges about his middle and Nicolas sensed an undeniable energy there, a dark motive building in his groin. He hadn't paid heed to these urges for months, this stirring of his manhood, this carnal longing. Perhaps it had been all of a year.

Nicolas turned his mind to the possibilities the evening might offer. There'd be drinking and carousing in the bars along the wharf, though it would probably be wise to steer clear of that. He'd seen other, more elegant establishments where men of commerce like himself might imbibe and wait for the evening to unfold. A city this size surely had its share of distractions . . . brothels . . . slinky *femmes de pavé*, or "streetwalkers," as Adam had called them in New Orleans. Women of the night. Whores.

The roll of the surf and the laugh of the gulls soon lulled Nicolas from his lubricious reverie. His eyes grew heavy. He dozed.

He had the recurring dream about his son—the nightmare he'd had a thousand times. In it, he knew he was dreaming but was frozen in place, packed in cotton, unable to move. His son Ethan, his firstborn, the sickly fellow lost as a child, came toward him, staggering out of the pines after so many years, ragged, ghostly pale, forlorn, cloaked in white. Ethan called to him in a high-pitched child's voice, and he, his father, could do nothing.

But the past few days, ever since Buffalo, there was a nightmare within the nightmare. Other boys marched out of the woods behind his son, first two, then dozens, beckoning, silently mouthing, "Help us! Help us!" These new boys were covered with spiders, crawling from their mouths and staining their skin with strange black marks—symbols, or pictographs. The spiders went for Ethan, trying to mark him with the stain. Nicolas reached for his son; he pawed at the air, then watched the gossamer figures recede into the white and disappear, as if lost in a blizzard.

Nicolas found himself tossing and fighting with his blanket, wide awake and coated in sweat. His arms and legs were made of lead. He shook his head free of the nightmare and slowly rubbed warmth back into his tingling limbs. It was midafternoon.

Perhaps his nerves were jangled more than he'd thought.

10

An Unpleasant Business

Nicolas was enquiring in the hotel lobby about the location of the city's telegraph office when he again heard a lone boy's voice calling to him. This was no nightmare fellow who approached, but a gangly, smiling Oriental chap who appeared about fifteen years of age.

"Laundy, sir? Good sir have laundy for me?"

The boy was looking for work. Nicolas had the enterprising youth follow him to his room, where the nasty pile of last night's clothes and a bagful of soiled pants, shirts, and collars were whisked away, with a few extra coins promised for delivery that evening.

At the hotel entrance, Nicolas hailed a hackney coach to carry him to the wharves. As the coach approached Pier 22, however, he was shocked to see that his blocks of ice were *only now* being stacked into place at Pierre Bonferri's icehouse. This was work Nicolas thought completed hours ago. He shouted to stop the carriage, tossed a coin to the driver, and rushed to find Adam, who was on the ship, cursing and kicking at the deck.

"Damned longshoremen never showed up!" Adam said. "Neither of 'em. I found these other two, and even they were unwillin' till I upped the price. Ridiculous, for a measly two hours of work unloading that last layer."

"What's the problem?"

"From the looks these fellas gave me, boss, I'm afraid there's rumors about us. I heard 'em wondering out loud why we took our ship last night to the medical dock. You see, boss, it's nothing but cotton in this port, and the longshoremen are a superstitious lot. They're called cotton jammers 'cause of the way they jam a ship with cotton. They're the best in the world. Draw good pay for it, too. These cotton jammers are colored fellas, and they're all about voodoo, spells, and black magic. They even talk their own language, callin' it 'gumbo,' part Africa, part French."

"Let's hope these cotton jammers don't ruin this port for us. It looks like a good market for ice. Did you pick a block for the downtown exhibit, Adam?"

"Yep. Found a beauty. Wait'll you see."

Adam led the way to a corner of Bonferri's icehouse, where he pointed to a single three-foot square block covered with canvas and sawdust. His eyes gleamed as he pulled back the canvas and slid the nearby icehouse door along its rails for light. "Helluva hunk of ice, eh, boss? She'll last. And looky here," he said, pointing to the glassy blue surface where a plump fish the length of a man's arm shone through.

"Perfect," Van Horne said, nodding.

"A walleye. Good-sized one, ain't it? Foolish fish froze right there where it swam. That should keep 'em talking about our ice."

"Let's go to Slade's Emporium and speak with Mr. Slade personally. Once Bonferri's payment is ready, we'll be on our way. If railway passage is available, we may get off this island tomorrow."

"But for tonight, boss, I believe I'll find me a game of poque," the sturdy foreman said with a wry grin. "I done pretty good on the trip down, eh?"

Van Horne had seen firsthand Adam Klock's success at the New Orleans card game of poque, a Mississippi riverboat favorite. Adam, a shrewd North Country pitch player, had used the game to separate a fair number of boatmen from their hard-earned wages.

"Perhaps I'll find me a whorehouse, too," Adam added.

The two Northerners ambled elbow-to-elbow along the oily brick of the harborside, in the midst of all things nautical and the throbbing midday commerce of a busy port. They were about to cross into Sailortown when shouting erupted behind them and, turning back, they were met with a most bizarre sight.

Some distance down the thoroughfare, a buckboard rumbled toward them, pulled by two big-boned, well-lathered roan horses. The wagon was the same type as those crisscrossing the harborside stacked with bales of cotton, but its only load was four colored men seated in its bed. The men had burlap wrapped about their faces like hoods, with crudely cut eyeholes. The man on the driver's plank, also a colored fellow, was hoodless.

"Merciful Lord," Adam muttered. "Look at that."

The hooded men held heavy ship's ropes that led to two prisoners, their hands bound behind their backs with twine, pulled several yards behind the wagon. One captive shuffled along, his head downcast like a domestic beast's. As the wagon drew near, the second man stumbled, fell, and was dragged on the brick like a sailor keelhauled behind his ship for a crime committed on the high seas.

Wagons on the street halted. Cotton jammers and other laborers on the piers gawked. As the grim procession neared Adam, the fallen man twisted on the roadway, skidding along to shouts of "Faster!" and "Drag 'em!" as if the spectacle were the finest of sport.

"Poor devil," Adam whispered.

"No man deserves this," Nicolas said.

The man who was down regained his feet and staggered alongside his fellow prisoner—a light-skinned, freckled fellow with hair the reddish brown color Nicolas knew as "ginger," though now the man's shaggy mane was matted and soiled with road dirt and sand.

The taunts of the scruffy types on the wharf grew louder. The driver, whose face was a lighter brown, like coffee whitened with cream, gave his team a switch; the wagon jerked forward and the prisoner again stumbled and pitched forward onto the brick.

"Mercy!" Adam cried.

The miserable soul was dragged behind the buckboard like a sack of potatoes. His back and shoulders were scraped red and raw. The brick was bloodied. As he tumbled closer, the rope entangled his neck.

"Stop this! Stop it now!" Nicolas shouted at the driver. He stepped into the path of the approaching wagon and raised an arm. "What crime have these men committed, may I ask?"

The driver hauled up on the reins and scowled. He was a short, stout youth, with the blunted features of a colored man, but lighter skin. At close range, that coffee-colored skin gave off the distinctive yellowish sheen of a mixed breed, a mulatto.

"It's none of your business," the man shot back. His flinty eyes glistened. "Stand back, or y'all be next!"

The buckboard lurched, aiming dead at Nicolas. Jumping back, Nicolas saw this mulatto fellow close-up. He was clean shaven, no more than twenty years of age, and had the most unusual head of hair—jet-black, two feet long and straight, and tied in wild clumps into which were woven small bones like those of a chicken or the vertebrae of a small reptile . . . a snake or turtle. A necklace of similar making swung from his neck. This elaborate getup gave him the aura of an African chieftain.

"Let's git it done," he yelled to his men, and with another slap of the reins the wagon rushed down the street, its steel-rimmed wheels grinding loudly on the oily brick.

Meanwhile, unnoticed by their half-breed chieftain, Adam had pulled his fishing knife from his belt, slipped behind the wagon, and, with a single swipe at the rope, cut the dragged man loose. For a moment, the poor soul lay flat on his back, oozing blood, then he snapped to his feet and—with the look of an animal inexplicably freed from the jaws of a trap—he took off at a clip and disappeared between two warehouses.

The perpetrators pulled away with their sole victim, his eyes bright with terror. The chieftain stood in the buckboard, his headdress swaying to and fro as the wagon lumbered down the harborside. Pointing at Nicolas, he shouted:

"The Doctor will remember you two! Yes, he will. The Doctor remembers."

11

Gruesome Discovery

Unnerved, Nicolas and Adam hurried in silence toward the business district, shaking their heads in dismay as they mulled over their private thoughts.

Nicolas broke the silence. "What cruelty! These Southerners. I've heard of such things, but never—"

"What'd those men do, I wonder?" Adam asked. "Must've been some crime."

Nicolas and Adam rounded a street corner and came on a Sailortown drinking establishment known as Alciatore's Market Tavern. The sour stink of beer spilled in dark, moldy corners drifted out the swinging doors.

"I'm desperate for a drink," Nicolas said.

They bellied up in the midst of longshoremen, draymen, and drovers who were two deep at the bar swilling a yellowish brew.

"It's Isle Ale we serve, gents," said the barkeep, a burly, fully mustachioed gent. At Nicolas's nod, two murky pints of suds came sliding down the bar. "It'll cure what ails ya," the barman said, studying their long, grey faces. "And there's a first-class free lunch," he added.

Nicolas drained his glass in two quick draughts. Adam stared blankly at a platter of oysters the barman plunked down in their rough, grey shells. He reached for one but was stopped when a drunken laborer a few feet down the bar grumbled, "Dirty rotten Injun."

Adam Klock, grandson of a Seneca Indian and a born fighter, twirled to face the offender. Nicolas, however, saw the remark wasn't intended for Adam at all; further down the bar, a bronze-skinned galoot with long, black braids was the target.

"He didn't mean you," Nicolas said, grabbing Adam's elbow.

The two lurched together, punches were landed, and blood spewed from the drunken laborer's nose. The drunkard tottered. A bowie blade flashed. Adam broke free of Nicolas and made a move for the knife.

Nicolas knew his friend far too well. *This is a mistake*, he thought. "No, Adam!" he shouted, but Adam had already disarmed the drunkard; the big knife clanged against a spittoon and was lost in the sawdust that covered the floor. "Come on, man," Nicolas said, throwing coins on the bar. "Leave it to the barkeep."

"Gol–damn Southerners."

Nicolas tugged Adam through the swinging doors and into the street.

"You need to bottle up that Indian in you, Adam. You're too quick to act."

"Hey, boss, I acted quick back at the docks. Saved a man there, didn't I?"

"You surely did, I admit. But we've had too gruesome a day already."

Barely two steps out Alciatore's swinging doors, Nicolas saw that the most gruesome was yet to come. "Oh, no," he whispered.

The buckboard from hell rattled out of the alley, only now the men in its bed, crude hoods still in place, sat idle, their victim no longer in tow. The African chieftain hauled the wagon to a halt in front of Nicolas and Adam, and glared. A commotion in the alley drew the Northerners' eyes to a loose-knit crowd of citizens in suits and ties gaping at a man hung high from a telegraph pole in the shadow of a warehouse.

"Good God," Nicolas muttered. "They *lynched* 'im."

Nicolas and Adam dashed down the alley to the crowd of morbid gents.

"Leave him be, you two," the young chieftain on the plank hollered, shaking a fist.

The man spun slowly, hanged by a thick ship's rope. His unruly shock of reddish hair convinced Nicolas he was the man Adam failed to free at the harborside. A crudely drawn banner around the man's neck fluttered in the wind. As the body turned, it gave a faint shudder . . . the last throes of dying? Or just the gulf breeze?

"He's still alive," Adam whispered. "Boost me up."

Adam stepped into his boss's cupped hands and lunged onto the telegraph pole. He shimmied level with the lynched man and drew his knife, but it was too late. Flies swarmed on the man's eyes. His neck was stretched at an ugly angle.

"Let him swing," someone in the crowd shouted.

"It's a lesson to others like him," another said. "Don't matter, black or white. It's unnatural."

"Serves 'im right."

With his knife ready in hand, Adam stared into the dead man's bulging eyes, then down at his boss. "No sense in it," he said. "The man's a goner."

"Jump down, then. Quick." Two hooded men from the buckboard were approaching fast. "This way."

Nicolas grabbed Adam's arm and pushed through to the other side of the crowd, down the alley and away from the corpse. Glancing back, he caught a fleeting image, a still life on the back of the eye, of a redheaded man draped on his ligature, a crudely penned banner proclaiming the lynched man's crime:

. . . ROBBER

12

Details of Business

Nicolas had heard of lynchings but never been close to one. When the Civil War had ended, he was still a brash youth foundering at his university studies in Boston. Northern cities were rocked by unrest and riots after the war's end, when black men fled the South and Southern slaveholders came north to make trouble. Black men were ridden on rails, tarred and feathered, or whisked away in the dead of night. Marauders traveling on horseback hunted colored men like beasts and hanged them from the lampposts with no consequence for the perpetrators except a line in the next day's newspaper—usually little more than "Darkie lynched."

But Nicolas realized the thing they'd witnessed today was different. Very different. *A lynching party of colored men? Led by a mulatto? And the dead man white and fair haired?*

At Nicolas's side, Adam said, "Musta been a helluva job that robber pulled. A bank, maybe?"

The midday sun hammered down, but neither it nor the bustle of the commercial district did much to distract Nicolas. He and Adam walked the Strand up and down, up and down, until their hearts stopped pounding and gained a quieter rhythm. After what seemed like hours, they found themselves in front of Slade's Emporium, their original destination. Slade's was centrally sited in the bustling downtown, with a large display window perfect for an exhibit of ice. Nearby were clothiers' shops and an apothecary advertising itself as "Galveston's sole depot of leeches."

Inside the emporium, Nicolas and Adam found Mr. Slade behind the candy counter overseeing the operation of his new taffy-pulling machine.

"Ah, yes, the ice exhibit," Mr. Slade hollered over the rattle of his chain-driven contraption. "Pierre explained it all." He smiled broadly and stepped from behind the counter. "Such a novel idea. Bonferri's to be commended for his cleverness."

"We'll have your exhibit shortly," Nicolas said with a nod to Mr. Slade and a wink to Adam.

"Yessiree, sir," Adam added. "I'll get that block in here, lickety-split."

"Mr. Slade—tell me something," Nicolas said, lowering his voice and stepping closer. "Have you heard of the goings-on a few blocks over, near the harbor? A man's been killed, you know."

Slade's smile died. He averted his eyes to the rolls of sweet-smelling dough spinning off his taffy machine. "Why yes . . . I heard," he said, barely audible. "But here in the South, you see, when the cause is righteous, we look the other way in such matters. It would be bad for business to do otherwise."

Once the Northerners were back on the street, Adam asked, "When we leaving this town, boss?"

"All that's keeping us is the final payment from Bonferri," Nicolas replied. "He's yet to notify me when it will be ready. Blasted Southerners," he groaned. "They sure take their time with their commerce."

"Quick enough to a lynching, aren't they?"

"That they are."

In the fading light of day, Adam and Nicolas parted ways with Adam's promise to haul the ice exhibit to Slade's Emporium before dark. "Don't worry, boss," Adam told Nicolas. "I'll get the block set. Then I'm planning on staying safe and warm inside tonight."

Nicolas hailed a brightly polished barouche drawn by two spirited steeds. They were fine horses, dark spotted on a pure white background, of an unusual breed Nicolas heard called Opelousas in New Orleans.

"Majestic Hotel, if you please," he called to the driver. "But steer clear of the tavern they call Alciatore's," he added, shaking his head at the thought of the horrible thing drawing flies in the alley.

As the pretty horses eased the barouche smoothly in the direction of the beach, Nicolas recounted in his mind the litany of reasons to get off this island, and fast.

13

Surprise Invitation

Nicolas made a beeline for the bar to clear his mind of his and Adam's grisly experience, but before he could hoist his foot onto the rail, a clerk behind the main desk waved him over.

"A message, Mr. Van Horne!"

"Ah, yes, at last," he said, anticipating Bonferri's go-ahead for payment.

Puzzled at the look of this note, Nicolas broke its seal, a replica, in bright orange, of the Texas star he'd seen over the medical college's entrance.

> *Mr. Van Horne,*
>
> *Forgive my oversight in not mentioning it last evening, but I would be greatly honored by your attendance at the celebration of Mardi Gras to be held tonight at my residence, 708 Ursuline. Please arrive any time after 8:00.*
>
> *Although it is traditional to attend "en masque," I shall understand fully if your recent arrival in our city should preclude this frivolity.*
>
> *Looking forward to your presence, I remain*
>
> *Yours truly,*
>
> *Francis Keiller*

Now here was a turn of events for the better. A private party. He had no taste for one right now, but he'd be off the street and far from Sailortown.

"That laundry boy! The Chinaman! Where can he be found?" Van Horne asked of the desk clerk. "I'll need those shirts, and quick." Assured that the laundry boy would be summoned posthaste, Nicolas requested a hot bath be drawn in his room, then he set off to the hotel's barber.

Clean shaven and well trimmed, he returned to the room and threw open his trunk to study the neckties he'd packed for the journey.

"A mask?" he laughed to himself. "I don't even own such a thing." He chose the gayest of his ties, of black silk, hand painted with delicate Japanese pagodas. It always knotted perfectly and lay nicely at the neck. "Excellent for a party, I should think, but . . ." *Perhaps a long tie, with a stickpin . . . no . . . not with that ghastly burnished-steel thing for traveling . . . but then, one couldn't travel down the Mississippi with one's most valuable diamond stickpin.*

He was easing into the steamy water when a pounding erupted at the door. "Laundy! Laundy, sir!"

Nicolas pulled on his pants, opened the door, took the paper package from the boy, and tore it open on the bed.

"Ahh . . . excellent." He sighed, holding at arm's length a freshly boiled shirt, starched and pressed to rigid perfection. He was counting out three-penny pieces when the boy spoke up.

"Brothels, sir? Mister need brothels tonight?"

Nicolas smiled to himself. "No, boy, that won't be necessary."

"Brothels in Sailortown, sir!" The boy persisted. "I take you to Post Office Street. Nice ladies, sir. Very young girl, even, very young and you buy cheap."

"Well thank you anyway, lad," Nicolas said, a bit unnerved at the lad's insistence. He searched for another coin.

"And smoking, too, sir. Very good opium. Top-notch."

"No need for that old stuff." Nicolas chuckled, recalling his college years of opium puffing in the dens of Boston. Indeed, that was where he first met with the pleasures of poppy.

At Harvard, Nicolas was a star attacker on the football team, scoring goals whenever he got his hands on the ball. In the first half of the big Yale game his senior year, he took a hard tackle that left him an ache in his right knee that now—twenty years later—foretold the weather far better than any of the instruments he relied on during the ice harvest.

Nicolas had to be carried off the field that afternoon in Boston. His knee ballooned. An old quack near the college supplied him with a bottle of laudanum, but it was his brothers in the secret society Alpha Delta Phi who managed his "recuperation," as they put it, in Boston's opium parlours.

Nowadays, as Nicolas had discovered from Thomas Chubb, sweet morphia was so easily obtained from an apothecary's supply of the purest morphine sulfate, it was hardly necessary for a gentleman to spend hours in a smoky cellar.

Morphine, chloral hydrate, tincture of cannabis, cocaine hydrochloride—all plentiful and cheap, with thin, modern needles available, and the most accurate hypodermics, even some, he'd heard, fashioned of glass rather than steel.

"But, boy, one moment!" Nicolas called, stopping the laundry chap. "One more thing, son—would you run a message for me?" Van Horne uncapped the ink bottle at the corner desk and quickly scribbled a note on hotel stationery. "Take this to Molly's place."

"I know it. At Pier 22."

"On the second floor, call for a man named Adam." Nicolas pulled his watch from the vest that hung over the chair. "You must make haste."

Adam,

Have 200 lbs delivered to 708 Ursuline Street in my name.
Do this immediately.

Choose the finest, clearest blocks.

Nicolas

Nicolas sealed the note and handed it over.

"Right away, sir!" The boy beamed at the silver half eagle dropped into his hand. "Ten minutes on bicycle!"

Nicolas sank into his hot tub as the last of the day's sunlight stretched across the beach and streamed obliquely through the hotel window.

"I wonder," he said with a sigh, "just what is a Mardi Gras party?"

While downtown with Adam, he'd noticed banners of purple, green, and yellow hung about the commercial district that afternoon. In New Orleans, days before, raucous, raggedy bands of horns and fiddles had marched by. Hooligans wandered the streets late into the night. He'd been warned at his hotel to watch his purse.

These Catholic port towns were serious about the final days before Lent. A last chance for revelry. Rites of spring and all that. It was good for business, he supposed, as he leaned back in the hot soak and reached for the soap.

Yes. Mardi Gras. It would take his mind away from troubling occurrences. And it was good for business.

14

The Party

At nine thirty that evening Nicolas Van Horne, in stiff shirt and tie knotted to a perfect bow, felt sure his arrival would be fashionably late. His driver found Keiller's house easily, just one block from the hospital and new medical college. This end of town seemed quiet compared to the festive neighborhoods on the way, where the houses pulsed with revelry from the parties of the rich.

Keiller's house was a modest structure, in the French style, with intricate black ironwork on the wraparound galleries of both stories. The panel over the front door was graced by a stained glass in the image of a brown pelican. Nicolas banged the brass knocker twice and a maid appeared, a robust young woman of a milk-chocolate color, dressed in airy black cotton and wearing a dainty white mask over her eyes. She smiled and tilted her head in polite anticipation.

Nicolas nodded back. "I am Nicolas Van Horne of New York."

"Welcome, Mr. Van Horne. I am Sara," the maid replied in a seductively hushed baritone.

Sara beckoned Nicolas into a central hall warmly lit by the gaslight of alabaster wall sconces. Oil paintings of bucolic rural scenes were hung along the walls. Nicolas was particularly taken by one, the largest canvas—a dark, enigmatic woman in the style Nicolas recognized as pointillism, the latest rage on the Continent. At the far end of the hall, a staircase wound to the second floor past two lower landings, both lit by the globes of gas lamps protruding from the newels.

Sara took Nicolas's homburg and hung it on an oak hall tree finely detailed with carvings of sandpipers and soaring gulls. She motioned Nicolas through an open set of pocket doors to the dining room, where a half dozen guests, *en masque*, surrounded the dining-room table. The overhead gas chandelier was turned up full, illuminating a two-foot-high mound of chipped ice covered with boiled shrimp, hardly touched, in the center of the table.

"Mr. Nicolas Van Horne of New York," Sara announced to the group, her rich voice resonant. The guests turned masked faces to Nicolas; most held a crystal goblet and a shrimp dripping with a dark, pungent sauce.

"Aye, it's Van Horne"—Nicolas recognized Keiller's brogue coming from the craggy rubber face of a goat—"the ice merchant, and friend." The goat's ears flapped with excitement. "Come join us."

Keiller wore a faded black academic gown with a purple and yellow cape. His frizzy white hair protruded in tufts from under a top hat that had seen better days. When Keiller offered his hand, Van Horne caught a whiff of formaldehyde from the academic robes. Their handshake held firm as the professor turned and, with an elegant, sweeping motion of his free hand, declared, "Ladies and gentlemen, this is the generous fellow who sent the ice."

The few guests murmured approval and raised a glass or shrimp in a ragtag toast to the visitor from the North.

"As ye see, Van Horne"—Keiller pointed to the shrimp pile—"we're putting your ice to good use. And they're concocting slings with it in the kitchen." He lifted a sweating crystal pitcher in the air. "Care for one?"

"I believe I'd prefer whiskey, Francis."

Keiller smiled. "Sara, have 'em bring Mr. Van Horne a touch o' that one from Dundee, would ye?"

"With a chunk of ice, please," Nicolas added.

Leaning in close, the professor whispered, "Trust me, Nicolas. No one in this group cares what's been in your ice."

The door knocker resounded, and Sara stepped away to attend to a fresh flood of guests. While Keiller turned his attention to the new arrivals, Nicolas studied the costumes surrounding the table. The getups varied widely. Some guests were in ornate robes and gossamer finery; others had simply draped themselves with sashes of purple, gold, and green, or donned strings of gaudy beads. Nicolas felt a bit conspicuous in his best business attire, but no one seemed to care. Indeed, somber whispering among the guests suggested a different mood than Nicolas expected for the raucous festivities before the deprivations of Lent.

Sara introduced the new arrivals, labeling each with a dramatic moniker contrived as a clue to their true identity.

"Professor Sawbones and the lovely Madam Bodacious."

"The young Doctor Zeitgeist, lecturer extraordinaire."

These were easy to figure. *Medical types.*

The table was quickly surrounded. A glass of pale whiskey appeared at Nicolas's side. He sipped quietly and admired the lovely shrimp. A skilled observer of his fellow man, he was curious to hear what might be on the minds of the island's academics.

"Just heard about the setback," one gent said in a low voice, further muffled by his mask. "Pity we lost that one. A horrible way to go."

Hmm. Must be one of their unfortunate patients, Nicolas thought. *What ghastly diseases these men must deal with.*

"In broad daylight, too," another commented. "We're in a spot now."

"Yes, no telling where we'll get them, now that this fellow swung."

Swung?

"It was the rascal's own fault," another added with a shake of his dog-face mask. "They're all the same. Greedy and ignorant. They get one or two delivered fine, then start digging 'em up before they're cold in the ground."

"This fool's mistake was raiding the colored cemetery."

"Surely, though, when a body-in-a-bag man swings—"

The lynching!

"—another will come along!" the dog-face laughed.

While the men chortled, Nicolas's hand shook and a shiver ran down his spine. Blood surged to his face. He gripped his whiskey, tipped it back, and stared into the brilliance of the crystal chandelier to blot out the image that came to him.

Now he understood. *GRAVE ROBBER...the banner on the lynched man...*In their hurry to vamoose, he and Adam never had a good look.

He needed to calm himself. This was a private party, a time for gaiety, not the look of trepidation, of terror, he surely wore. He motioned to a servant with his empty glass.

"Ladies and gentlemen," Sara's voice boomed. "The members of the Mistik Krewe of Comus have arrived. First, I'm pleased to announce the Merry Ladybug, escorted this evening by Señor Cucaracha Cubano, the Cuban cockroach."

A comely, full-figured ladybug covered in red spots entered with her brown-shelled escort. There was a smattering of applause. Four other insects followed. Predictably, Keiller made the greatest fuss over "*Aedes aegypti,*" the common mosquito, pronounced perfectly by Sara.

The newly arrived academics crowded around the shrimp pile and drew Nicolas into conversation. He was asked to describe the impact of the recent economic panics on his business of ice. A second copious Scotch calmed the shock he'd suffered. More guests arrived.

"The Dark Prince of Dry Goods."

"Purveyor of the Finest Ladies' Accoutrements."

Now the businessmen.

Conversation swelled. French perfume was in the air. Despite their costumes and masks, guests recognized each other from a peculiarity of speech, a toss of the hair, or a distinctive smacking of the lips while downing a sling. Businessman mingled with medical man; the shrimp pile shrank. The room warmed by the time Sara announced the last, and the grandest, of the business guests:

"The Grand Duke of Finance, with his Grand Duchess."

A short, portly gent escorted a lady nearly a foot taller into the dining room. Both were dressed in hand-painted Japanese silks, with masks of rare feathers—though no feathers could beautify this lanky lady's face, which was as narrow and angular as an anvil, and looked as hard.

Nicolas sidled next to the Dark Prince of Dry Goods, who was fussing with his mustache under the hooked nose of his Satan's mask. "Keiller's invited some prominent merchants, I see," Nicolas said.

"*Mais oui*, a few attend a Keiller party," agreed the Dark Prince, readily recognized as Pierre Bonferri, Nicolas's go-between in the business of ice and notorious island bon vivant. "I'm shocked to see Major Walker here," Bonferri continued. "He's got no cause to celebrate. Word is, he's ruined. Tried to open an investment bank in this town, and Hutch Sealy destroyed him."

"Ah, bankers."

"No one loves a banker, eh, *mon ami?*"

"Is Sealy here, Pierre?"

"Right there—the Grand Duke of Finance, *naturellement*. Just arrived with his sourpuss duchess, the tall, gawky one."

"So that's the great man."

"A brilliant moneymaker, old man Sealy. He plucks the stuff out of thin air. Now there's one gent who belongs at a Keiller party. Sealy funded the college's construction, endowed its faculty . . . at least at its start."

Masked servants arrived with trays of steaming crabs, fried fish, and carved pineapples. In the crunch for food, Nicolas crossed to the other side of Bonferri and edged closer to Sealy. Snippets of conversation drifted his way; a fat white tomcat raised his voice over the crowd.

". . . fetch far too much for their labor, Hutch. Far too high a wage, I tell you. Now, your son Trey's got the idea . . . that cheap young Northern labor he's connected to. Why should the price of cotton be driven so high by a bunch of darkie . . . ?"

"So Sealy has a son?" Nicolas asked the prince at his side.

"Ah, yes, *mon ami*. Trey's the name. Biggest cotton trader in town. They've got it all in that family, eh? But there's more to that story," he added, drawing his face close and lifting his mask.

Nicolas leaned in.

"Listen, Van Horne—I'll share this only in the strictest confidence. It's a juicy bit, and it's to be kept between us. Agreed, *mon ami?*"

"I shall honor your confidence, Pierre."

"Sealy has a second son. A bastard."

"So, he keeps another woman. Frightfully common these days."

"But this liaison's a rich one, *mon ami*. Hutch Sealy keeps a *colored* woman. He has for decades. All the island knows, except his scrawny wife."

"How complicated."

"She's lovely, this ebony piece of Sealy's. Their mixed-breed son's near Trey's age, too. Old Sealy actually favors the half-breed, sent him off to school in the East, but the son prefers the low life. He stays in a Sailortown boardinghouse with the riffraff, mariners and such, and took to working the docks himself."

"Two brothers at odds, eh?"

"Precisely. Especially since Trey's one of those who wishes we'd won the Great War and slavery had never ended. Meanwhile, his half brother is a half-breed who leads the cotton jammers. Ha! Ha! . . . You know about our cotton jammers? All coloreds?"

"Yes, I've heard." Nicolas felt a chill despite the steam rising off the trays of crabs and fish in front of him.

"The bastard son's organized the cotton jammers into a force to be respected. Expert labor, well paid, but mostly of slave roots, the jammers. A superstitious lot, these coloreds and Creoles, and Sealy's bastard son has an unholy grip on 'em . . . Their 'Voodoo Doctor,' he's called."

The crowd began spilling into the front room.

"Voodoo Doctor," Nicolas muttered.

"That's him. It's his voodoo keeps those ships packed with cotton." Bonferri's attention was drawn to a far corner of the room, where the coquettish ladybug was throwing glances in his direction. "You see," Bonferri said, adjusting his mask, "what the Doctor says is voodoo law on this island."

"I believe I've seen the truth of that this very afternoon, Pierre," Nicolas said, rattling the ice in his whiskey as Bonferri worked his way across the room.

15

The Musicians

With this disquieting new information preying on his mind, Nicolas sought a quiet corner away from the crunch of the party. Whiskey in hand, he wandered into the hallway. *Damn! I've seen Sealy's second son—the Voodoo Doctor. I've seen the half-breed who lynches grave robbers, and I displeased him greatly.*

He was glad for the whiskey. Perhaps, once he was back in his hotel room, he'd settle his nerves with a dose or two of Chubb's mix. For now, he forced himself to study these paintings in the hall.

Pointillism, yes, that's what it was, and finely done . . . but what was that music he heard drifting from upstairs? An exercise, or étude, barely heard over the din of the party. He climbed to the first landing, listening. It was a fiddle, played well, and a second instrument, like nothing he'd ever heard.

At the top of the stairs the newel was lit by a casting of a lady in formal gown, with a hammer raised overhead and a gear tucked under her arm. He stopped to admire this tribute in bronze to modern American industry, which set Nicolas to thinking about a contraption he'd invented—a conveyor to lift the blocks of ice from the edge of the frozen lake to his icehouse. The thought made him wish he were standing on the ice of Upper Spy Lake. It was where he belonged, amid the clatter of the conveyor's chains and gears, its steam engine filling the air with wood smoke . . . but then, his daughter, Abigail, watched over the ice for him, and they'd be together at another ice harvest soon enough.

The fiddle's mournful line swelled. From the landing, Nicolas studied the players. The parlour at the front of the house served as their music room. Sheets of music were scattered on a table. A large harp leaned against the settee. An upright piano sat in the corner. In the center of the room a woman on a low stool faced away, toward the south window. She was wrapped in a scarlet kimono. A dark cascade of hair fell like black satin over her shoulders and back. She held a small harp on her lap; her hands flowed gracefully over the ringing strings. With a glimpse of her profile, Nicolas recognized the young woman he'd admired in the laboratory—Keiller's niece.

Seated on a stool in front of the lovely lady was a stout, somewhat elderly gent, unmasked, clean shaven, and with a bush of white hair that, in its total disarray, formed a spectacular aurora around his jowly red face. The fellow exuded health and vigor as he gave his blackened old fiddle a final flourish. When his eyes fixed on Nicolas, they flashed; he smiled and motioned with his bow. The harp crescendoed; the strings were damped, the piece finished.

"*Ja*, goot, very good," the old gent said in a thick Slavic accent. To Nicolas, he said, "Do come in, friend," and he waved the bow again.

Nicolas caught a faint floral scent in the air as he stepped into the parlour. Keiller's niece glanced over her shoulder. Her eyes were covered by a mask of peacock feathers. Her lips were painted a deep red, several shades darker than her kimono.

"Sir!" she said, her eyes widening. "I didn't see you there. But you . . . you've forgotten your mask. Don't you realize it's Mardi Gras?"

"I don't know about Mardi Gras, I'm afraid. I'm from New York, you see."

She chuckled. "That explains it." Her asymmetric smile had that youthful, roguish crookedness Nicolas remembered from the laboratory. "We'll forgive you this once," she went on, "but, oh my! New York? They say your Brooklyn Bridge is the seventh wonder of the world. You've seen it, I'm sure. Perhaps you cross it every day?"

The jowly fellow popped up from his stool. "Forgive us for not introducing ourselves." Holding fiddle and bow in his left hand, he offered Nicolas his right. "I am Rabbi Basil Prangoulis, spiritual guide for our town's industrious Jewish citizens and—as it turns out—also musician and instructor of the musical arts at the Ursuline Women's Academy, a Catholic institution, strangely enough. But it's a small island, you see . . . and this lovely lady—"

"Yes"—Nicolas hesitated—"we met earlier, though not formally."

"Well, then, may I introduce Dr. Renée Keiller, niece of the renowned Francis Keiller, professor of medical theory and . . . and whatnot. Renée is herself an accomplished scholar, scientist, and a student of music, sir, though a fair-to-middling one."

"Basil!"

"I make a joke, my friend. Truthfully, the Irish harp is the instrument on which she's most accomplished." Basil placed his fiddle in a dilapidated case on the floor. "And your name, sir?"

"Nicolas Van Horne, merchant of ice. But I fear a word of explanation is needed," he said, turning to Renée. "I'm not from the city of New York, miss. My home is in the mountains in the northern reaches of the state, far from the great metropolis."

"How delightful. You simply must tell me about it. But first let me find you a mask, Mr. Van Horne. I've had quite enough of this simple piece, I believe."

She shot Prangoulis a dark look, then stood, placed her harp in its case on the table, straightened her girlish kimono, and stepped into the next room. As her dark mane of hair sailed past, Nicolas caught that distinctive floral scent again. It recalled for him his uncle's orchards in the Hudson Valley, when the powerfully fragrant apple blossoms bloomed in spring.

"*Ja*, she's an excellent harpist, Renée," Prangoulis continued in the niece's absence, "a doctor of medicine and . . . what is it? Doctor of physiognomy or some such." He chuckled. "How shh-mart can one girl be, eh?" Turning serious, he lowered his voice and began shaking his head. "*Ja*, Renée's quite a young woman. Amazing, for one who's had such suffering thrown her way by the Almighty."

Renée swept back into the room holding a cumbersome theatrical mask fashioned of plaster. "I found *this*," she laughed, holding out the mask, which was in the likeness of a clown, its lips turned down in a grimace.

"Please, Renée," Prangoulis protested. "We might excuse Mr. Van Horne this one evening, don't you think?"

"No, no, I'll venture it," Nicolas said, pulling on the bulky mask.

"Bravo!" Renée stood. "Come, then. Let's join the party, shall we?" The two men followed Renée as she bounded down the staircase.

At the foot of the stairs, her uncle waved to her. "There's my lassie!"

Renée turned to Nicolas. "Forgive me, but Basil's music lesson was so trying, I'm afraid I've ignored Uncle Francis all evening. I do so want to hear about New York, though, and your lovely mountains. Will you tell me later?"

And she disappeared into the dining room crowd.

16

Uninvited Guests

"She's charming."

"*Ja*," Prangoulis agreed. "Sharp as a tack. Got a Scot's brain like her uncle. Lucky thing her feminine side comes from her mother, hah? It's the Creole French. Fair skin. Dark eyes. Hardy stock. Renée has taken the knocks, too, and poor girl, life and this island sent her plenty. But come, my friend, let's find where the brandy is hidden."

Prangoulis and Nicolas pressed through a crunch of masked revelers to the overheated kitchen, where Keiller's manservant was whacking away at the great block of Van Horne ice. The man proved to be an expert ice breaker, and Nicolas was grateful for the coolness wafting from the ice. He removed his cumbersome mask. His glass seemed to fill itself. Prangoulis's face flushed with brandy.

"Say, Rabbi Prangoulis . . . Basil . . . earlier, you mentioned certain hardships thrown Renée's way. What was your meaning there?"

"Well, Nicolas, as a physician of course her life is pure hell during these yellow fever epidemics. Then, two years ago the poor girl lost her husband and their only child, a baby boy, in less than a month, both to the fever."

"How tragic. She studies the disease that destroyed her family."

"They were in Havana for their research when . . ." Basil grew quiet. "Such things make even me, a man of God, question our God's good intentions. That little boy was everything to her. Now she has only her science."

Nicolas donned his mask and followed Prangoulis back to the dining room but lost him in the press of revelers. When he next saw Renée, she was sidling around the dining table, pursued by the mustache-twirling Dark Prince of Dry Goods, whose advances she rebuffed with a curt word.

"Enjoying our little ball?" she asked Nicolas, smiling sympathetically. "Please forgive me about the mask—you're such a sport about it."

Renée ran her hand into the pile of ice in the center of the table. She plucked out a chunk the size of a lemon and held it to the light. "Tell me about your ice, Mr. Van Horne."

"It's the purest ice available, I'm proud to say. Its clarity is unmatched by any in New England. Ice is changing the world, you know."

"It is quite pretty."

"The iron in the water gives it its density and healthful qualities."

"Where do you get it?"

"We harvest on a lake known as Upper Spy."

"There are mountains of course."

"Peculiar, rounded mountains. The high peaks of the Adirondacks are further north, well above Old Forge, near the town of Saranac."

"It must be lovely country. Perfect for raising a family, I suppose." Renée gave Nicolas a quizzical look. "But you are married, aren't you, Mr. Van Horne?" she asked. "You choose not to wear a ring, is that it?"

"Why, yes, I'm married," he replied, glancing down at his left hand . . . indeed, he'd not worn his wedding ring for a year, since that angry night he'd tossed it in the Black River and put it out of mind for good.

"I'm sure your wife loves New York as much as you."

Nicolas hesitated. "It's hard country, in many ways. The winters are long and bitter. Once the snow flies, there's little to do but dwell on one's problems. Many fall victim to melancholy, and what we call 'cabin fever.' For women, especially, the winters are difficult."

"I would love to see your North Country in winter."

Professor Keiller joined them at the table. He plucked a shrimp off the ice pile, dipped it in sauce, and peered at it. "The remoulade's superb!"

"You see," Renée explained, "we've finally found Uncle a cook who makes a proper Creole sauce."

"Yes," Keiller said. "I must get the formula."

"Oh, Uncle, you've never cooked a thing—outside the lab, that is." Renée took Nicolas by the arm. "Please come along. I'd like to show you something special about my uncle Francis. Just give me a moment."

"Now, Renée," Keiller protested. "Ye needn't bother our guest with none o' yer folderol, dear."

With a dismissive wave of her hand, Renée led Nicolas into the relative quiet of the front parlour.

"May I call you 'Nicolas,' good sir?" she asked.

"Please do."

"Truthfully though, yours is such a stuffy name. Too many syllables. Nic-o-las. You should change it. 'Nick' would be better. Much more modern."

"No one calls me Nick."

"Well, I do . . . now. And you'll call me Renée, if you please."

"I'm the lucky one, then," Nicolas said with a chuckle. "Your name's perfectly lovely as is." A faint flush rose to her cheeks. "You've an enchanting smile as well, I must say."

It was well past midnight. In the front parlour, guests settled heavily into wingback chairs, and couples lounged on the settees. The servants had cleared the dining table and were passing from room to room with trays of pineapple, oranges, and mango.

Renée led Nicolas to a gold plaque that hung above the mantel. "Uncle was awarded this when we left Cuba," she said. "It's from the University of Havana." The plaque was elaborately engraved and decorated with a tricolor caduceus and ornate garlands. Nicolas pulled up his mask to have a closer look as Renée translated the archaic Spanish script:

"'. . . awarded for scientific achievement . . . heroic and noble efforts to defeat the insatiable killer of men . . . yellow fever.'"

"His science is quite esteemed, then . . . and yours, Renée. Such a noble thing to fight this awful disease."

"Count yourself lucky, Nick, that yellow fever doesn't venture as far as your lovely mountains."

"In fact, the fever took my mother," he said, recalling the emptiness his dear mother's death left in the last years of his childhood.

"In ports like Galveston, no family escapes. My father and four of his brothers—the entire family except for Uncle Francis—were taken in the epidemic of '73. And then, my dear husband . . . I was married, you know."

His breath caught in his throat. "Oh?"

"A Cuban, from an aristocratic family. Two of the same mind, we were, both physicians and scientists, but my scientific work had already been published under the name 'Keiller' . . . so I kept my maiden name."

"Understandable. And your husband?"

"For six wonderful years we worked side by side in the clinics and Uncle's laboratory. But yellow fever came to Cuba and took him . . . along with our young son . . . in '87."

"So sad. How old was the boy?"

"Barely three. A perfect little darling named Benjamin." Behind her feathered mask Renée's dark eyes moistened.

"Long ago, I lost a young son, too," Nicolas said softly, his voice waivering. "His name was Ethan. Eight years old. A sickly boy; the doctors in Albany said he had a 'hole' in his heart."

"A common defect, I'm afraid. Was he blue at birth?"

"No, no." Nicolas cleared his throat and tried to shake the grievous memory from his head. "No, we learned of it in his first year. He didn't grow properly and, as you say, he would turn dusky and couldn't keep up with others."

Renée gave a knowing nod. "A serious condition."

"Despite his frailty, he was a game little fellow—too much so, in fact. He loved the woods and would wander, sometimes too far. That's why we lost him."

"How so?"

"He must've been tramping on a trail near town. It was late fall. He probably ventured too far for his fragile constitution. We searched and searched. Three days later, the snows came and . . . a body was never found."

"We never forget those we lose, especially the young ones." Renée turned toward the window that faced the street, a faraway look in her eyes. "That's precisely why Uncle and I must carry on."

"An unimpeachable goal, I must say."

"It's horrid in summer, as physicians. We spend countless hours tending to the dying, even as we must work for a cure. In Galveston, no hospital bed is empty. Every day before dawn the death wagons roll down our streets, the drivers crying, 'Bring out your dead! Bring out your dead!' The stench is horrible. The bodies are covered with quicklime and buried in common graves. As one graveyard fills, ground is broken for another."

Nicolas tried to imagine this island in the grip of an epidemic. The summer smothering hot. Whole families shut in, trembling at the telltale yellow in their loved one's eyes, the fever burning in their children's bodies.

"You must remember, Nick, never venture to the South in summer. Stick to your mountains. Wherever your business calls, you must never, ever—"

In midsentence, Renée was cut off by a thunderous clatter at the front of the house. "What's that?" she said. "What the . . . ?"

"It's a horseman," Nicolas said, stepping quickly to the window at the sound of a horse hard driven, snorting and whinnying, hooves clanging on the slate sidewalk. "And it's at your door!"

The hum of conversation was cut off by a crash in the entranceway, followed by the tinkle of broken glass. Utter silence gripped the house, everyone froze, then the hooves retreated down the street.

Nicolas and Renée stepped through the parlour door into the hallway, where shards of colored glass—the remains of the stained-glass pelican—were strewn across the floor. In the midst of the debris lay a large, red brick. A note was secured to the brick with several wraps of hemp twine.

Keiller limped into the hallway. "Not again," he grumbled. "Confound the rascals!"

Guests edged through the pocket doors as Keiller bent to pick up the brick and remove the note. Shuffling around the shards of the brown pelican, Nicolas and Renée crept up behind Keiller and all three leaned over a message scrawled in thick, black lines:

GRAVE ROBBERS
BEWARE

In his hand, Keiller cupped a sinister, scaly-looking object no larger than a silver dollar that had been folded into the note.

"What do you have there?" Nicolas asked.

"A charm, I'm afraid."

"A voodoo charm," Renée added.

Keiller went on. "I've learned a bit about them, lately. The wrapping is the hide of a black snake. What's inside is meant as a warning to those who go along with this sort of bunk."

Keiller unwrapped the charm. A coil of hair encrusted with dried blood protruded from the black casing of snake hide. Nicolas caught his breath. The lock of hair was the reddish-brown color he knew as "ginger." For the second time that evening, a coarse shiver rattled his spine.

17

Aftermath

Keiller turned to the guests standing behind him, their mouths agape. "It's nothing, ladies and gentlemen. Please . . ." Keiller's voice rose in pitch. He closed the charm tight in his fist. "We'll have this cleaned in a moment."

A murmur ran through the house while servants swept the fragments of colored glass into piles and guests meandered back to the dining room. The stocky Hutchinson Sealy stepped forward and removed his mask. His wife's face hovered unappealingly over her husband's shoulder.

"This should tell you something, Francis," he said with a shake of his head. "It's what many in town are thinking. Well then, we'll be leaving."

"Stay for coffee, Hutch."

"Thank you for the hospitality nonetheless," Sealy said, a hollow ring to his voice. He gave a slight bow and led his wife around the disarray. Other business types who'd lingered in the entrance hall unmasked and, following Sealy's lead, made for the door, excusing themselves as they circled the wreckage of the stained-glass pelican.

"There's brandy. More cakes?" Keiller pleaded to no avail.

The rude interruption, coming on the heels of an evening full of revelations, put Nicolas on a keen edge. He would take his leave as well. When he approached Keiller to deal with the formalities, the elder professor ignored him and called to the kitchen:

"Sara, would you see to coffee? And brandy?"

Renée, reading Nicolas's face, reached for his hand. "Come, Nick. Uncle's new cook makes wonderful coffee." She started toward the dining room. "Just a little longer," she whispered, "for Uncle's sake."

At that moment, Pierre Bonferri was headed for the door with the Merry Ladybug, whose cockroach escort was slung across a settee, blind drunk. As they crossed paths, Bonferri took Nicolas by the sleeve. "Your payment should be ready tomorrow, *mon ami,*" he said. "Remember—second floor, Cotton Exchange."

"Excellent," Nicolas said. "Good to do business with you, Pierre."

Bonferri gave a chuckle as he steadied the Merry Ladybug's erratic gait out the door. "But wait until well after noon, *mon ami*. You'll find business slow to start on the first day of Lent."

Throughout the house, the festivities were reduced to a low undertone punctuated by moments of deathly quiet. Guests unmasked. Chairs were dragged about. Coffee arrived on a silver serving set and Nicolas Van Horne, a Northerner raised on hot tea, settled onto a settee with Renée and drank murky Creole coffee.

As Sara poured a second cup, Nicolas asked, "Who's behind these attacks on the college? Surely you have an idea."

"It's our dissection, of course, Nick. Across the nation, resurrectionists pillage the paupers' fields while they leave the rich in their graves. The poor have rioted in Philadelphia and Baltimore. Here in Galveston, our supplier returns again and again to Galveston's colored cemetery, and I'm afraid he's opened one too many pine boxes. He may be leaving town soon."

Too many pine boxes. Nicolas's mind flashed to Sailortown. *She doesn't yet know about the lynching*, he thought.

"I can only hope," he said, "your attackers don't know about me. But won't the law help you?"

"We can hardly go to the constable, Nick. You, of all people, must realize that," she said with a dismissive wave of her hand. "And there's more to the problem. Elements I don't understand. Elements more pernicious, more powerful than the voodooists."

Crystal brandy snifters arrived on silver platters. While the last of the partygoers drank to the beginning of Lent, Nicolas's mind began to lag.

The sky had lightened with dawn by the time Nicolas settled into a carriage bound for his hotel, with the events of the evening spinning in his head . . . the masquerade . . . the revelation of the lynched grave robber . . . the rude interruption of their gaiety . . . and the lovely Renée.

There was something about a church, too, but at this late hour, details slipped his mind.

18

The Beginning of Lent

A German steamer had made port at daybreak, and long lines of immigrants seeking passage inland clogged the cavernous interior of Galveston's train station. Nicolas maneuvered his way to a window to arrange his and Adam's trip home by way of Chicago and Buffalo, connecting to the Adirondack Mail Express from the Buffalo–Albany line. He requested departure for late that day but was told by the clerk behind the bars that one of Pullman's private sleeper cars wouldn't become available until noon tomorrow.

As he stood outside the station and tucked the railway tickets into his jacket, Nicolas decided against stopping by Molly's Rooms to inform Adam of their plan. His foreman had been out late whoring and was better left to sleep, as were, most likely, the other occupants of Molly's establishment.

Nicolas thought how refined, how enchanting was his evening at Keiller's party. He'd felt friendliness and warmth last night, far more than at even the grandest balls at the lakeside cottages of the Adirondack railroad tycoons, especially near Francis Keiller's niece. Certainly an evening so fine could not be gotten at a house of ill repute.

Unlike most men of the day, Nicolas had only once in his life availed himself of a whorehouse. It was during last winter's trip with the ice when he'd succumbed to the needs of the flesh and accompanied Adam to a Canal Street haunt in New Orleans. He found the tawdry façade, the dark purple wallpaper of the sitting room, and the madam's false exuberance enormously disagreeable. Indeed, the boredom of the girls and abruptness of his failed encounter left him with a nervous melancholy that lasted for days.

Nicolas was not a man prone to dalliances, though men certainly did such things. Keeping mistresses was commonplace; even respectable ladies fell prey. He was well aware that his pale blue eyes, the clean line of his jaw, and his lean limbs were appreciated by women. He might easily have had his way with them, even those decades younger than his forty-one years. But for that one lapse in a New Orleans bordello, Nicolas chose to remain true to a rustic, rural New Yorker's ideal of marriage, and to a lifelong union with his childhood sweetheart Ruth Stuyvesant—no matter how drastically, how irrevocably, the years had changed her.

Settling in a hansom cab as it pulled away from the railway station, Nicolas was disturbed by the distinct floral scent that clung to his jacket. He'd noticed it first while dressing that morning. *Apple blossoms. Her perfume.* Had he been that close to Renée last evening? She had taken his arm, sat quite close, he remembered, but in the excitement that followed the attack, it hadn't seemed untoward. Perhaps he'd had too much of the professor's whiskey. There'd been brandy, too. And a vague discussion about a church, of all things, kept shifting about at the edges of his mind.

Moments after Nicolas had stepped down from his carriage and entered the Majestic's foyer, a clerk handed him an envelope with his name written in a refined, symmetrical hand. The envelope was sealed with the familiar star of Texas pressed into orange wax.

> *Dear Nick,*
>
> *Will we be meeting at the church, as discussed?*
>
> *I shall be there at noon. Saint Augustine's, in the 1700 block of Esplanade. Please do.*
>
> *Yours Sincerely,*
>
> *Renée Keiller*

A church? he mused. Of course, yesterday was Mardi Gras, making today Wednesday, the beginning of Lent. Well, one shouldn't be late to church, should one? It was still an hour before noon. The finalization of finances at the Cotton Exchange could wait till afternoon. Today was a day to attend church. Ash Wednesday.

Nicolas knew his mother to have been a churchgoer, but his own religious upbringing after her death had been spotty. As a young man in Boston, the atheistic college life and the rites of Alpha Delta Phi, his fraternal order, took precedence. He considered himself a sporting gentleman, an upstater whose Sundays were spent hunting or fishing. He found no time to worship a deity, except, perhaps, an ill-defined, personal God he felt near to when tramping alone in the Adirondack woods or standing on the frozen expanse of Upper Spy Lake before an ice harvest.

As he approached on foot, the brilliant white stone of Saint Augustine's Church shone from three blocks away in the noonday sun. A statue of Christ, with hands outstretched, capped the impressive structure. Citizens from all stations in life kept the massive front door swinging constantly to and fro. The crowd gathered on the sidewalk spilled into the street. For an instant, Nicolas nearly turned back. Had Renée arrived earlier? Was she already inside? He wasn't about to waltz into that place on his own.

A tall, dignified young lady in a chocolate-brown dress with a white lace collar backed away from the crowd. Her wry, tight-lipped smile and dark eyes were unmistakable. She hurried over, her two gloved hands extended.

"Nick. So glad you came." She wore a broad-brimmed hat with a shock of pink feathers gathered at the side. The feathers swayed in the breeze as she took his arm and steered him toward the church door. "Come along then, good sir."

"I'm not Catholic, you know," he said with a sheepish grin. "Actually, I'm not anything."

"No matter. Follow me and do as I do. It'll be fine."

The interior of the church was cool, dark, and laden with the sweet smell of incense. Renée gave a shallow bow toward the front, then walked down the aisle and pushed into a crowded pew, shuffling over to make room. Nicolas tried to mimic her bowed head but soon found himself craning his neck to admire the raised frescoes depicting Christ's life and the stained-glass windows throwing geometric patterns of muted color over the congregation. He'd seen colored church glass in Boston, but only from the outside. In the Adirondacks, church windows were clear; church interiors were bare of artwork and full of light.

What's this religion about? he wondered, scanning the stages of Christ's downfall portrayed in the colorful frescoes. The entrance to Jerusalem. The gruesome nails. The crown of thorns. Wasn't this the Protestant's story, too?

In Forestport, Nicolas knew plenty of Irish; they'd come in droves to build the canals, and most were Catholic, eating fish on Fridays, crossing themselves whenever they let loose an oath or mentioned the name of a relative who'd passed on. They believed in an afterlife, like most religions, he guessed, but it seemed to Nicolas that theirs was a particularly structured view—heaven, hell…and something in between.

The afterlife. Nicolas had never given it much thought. He was a practical sort, and though he'd seen too much of the dead, he'd never seen a soul.

Worshippers paced up and down the aisle, seemingly at random. Nicolas was enjoying sitting quietly so near Keiller's niece when she stood abruptly and motioned for him to follow to the front, where they knelt in a line of penitents with heads bowed. A priest in blue and gold satin vestments bobbed down the line, mumbling something that Nicolas recognized as Latin—not his best subject in school. In a flash, the priest smeared soot in the center of Nicolas's forehead with his blackened thumb. *The cross.* The next moment Nicolas was following Renée back down the aisle. She stopped to dip her hand into a stone basin near the entrance and cross herself. Nicolas blinked against the tropical sunlight as they stepped outside.

"See, Nick? That wasn't so bad."

"It was quick enough. Will your uncle attend today?"

Renée turned her face up at him, the cross of soot on the smooth ivory of her forehead. "Uncle?" She gave out a burst of laughter. "Huh! Uncle's only religion is science. Mine too, I suppose," she said, turning serious. "There's Easter and Christmas. In summer, there are so many funerals." She sighed and wagged her head. "I'm afraid church is hardly a priority. This afternoon I'll be tending to that boy's cells you so fortuitously supplied me."

"And I must locate this Cotton Exchange Building."

"Oh, that's simple. It's at the dead center of the commercial district. Say, why don't I accompany you? Indeed, on our way, why not stop by my house and take a cup of tea?" Renée hesitated. A frown rippled across her brow. "I live with my mother, hardly out of our way, and she'd be pleased to meet you."

Nicolas was getting to like this island. It had its fair share of violence and danger, but there was gaiety and growth, too. The place was moving ahead. One day, he thought, the name of this port city would be on the lips of the world. And here, strolling beside him, was an exceptional woman, one who remained lighthearted in the face of personal losses that would turn a lesser woman—or man—into a weeping, lifeless recluse. Renée Keiller. A physician. A scientist who, with her uncle, would one day find a cure for yellow fever.

As they strolled along the broad boulevards toward her house, Nicolas couldn't help but stare again and again at the smudge, the mark on Renée's forehead—the black cross found on citizens throughout the city today. A bolt of misgiving passed through him as—in his mind's eye—he saw that other mark, the thing that haunted his dreams and had marked the dead boy. A signature as black, as sinister as soot, but indelible, unchangeable . . . a scar.

19

The Medium on Ball Lane

The house was located on Ball Lane, a quiet, narrow street cut into the middle of the block, two streets down from Professor Keiller's. It was a modest, freshly painted pink-and-white two-story home with small, simply ornamented porches along the front and one side, where a towering, leafless camphor tree exuded its faint, medicinal odor. Renée opened the gate of the white picket fence and trotted up the stairs, leading Nicolas across the porch and into the entrance hall. She called for her mother, with no answer.

"Please take a seat here," she said, beckoning to a sun-filled, elegantly furnished sitting room to the right. She slipped off her gloves and set her hat on a hook. "It's here that we receive guests." Nicolas hesitated, his gaze drawn to the lightless room across the hall, its pocket doors half-closed.

"That other parlour is Mother's personal sitting room," Renée explained. "Here's more cheery." She motioned him into the sunlight. "I'll see to some tea . . . and Mother."

Renée walked toward the back of the house, but rather than sit, Nicolas shuffled across the hall for a quick look at the mother's "personal sitting room." A second parlour, it was nearly bare of furnishings. The outside shutters, closed tight against the tropical sun, allowed only thin slats of light to fall on a rug decorated with a large central zodiac sitting in a field of stars and a scattering of tiny numbers and obscure celestial signs. A stuffed screech owl, mounted high on the far wall, peered down with its large yellow eyes.

The only furniture in the room appeared to be a small, round, oaken table centered over the zodiac. The table was surrounded by four straight-backed chairs. It looked like a perfect setup for playing cards or board games, except that heavy curtains with a somber, floral pattern had been hung around the south-facing chair to create a freestanding "cabinet" that, if closed, would completely isolate the player seated there. More strangely, this chair sat on a large scale like those used to weigh bales of cotton or other produce. The legs of the chair had been sawed partially off to put its occupant at a proper level to the table.

Once his eyes had adjusted to the light, Nicolas noted a sideboard along the far wall that held a pair of writing slates, a box of chalk, and a "talking board," a sort of tablet covered with letters and numbers used for supernatural communication. Next to the sideboard stood a tall contraption composed of copper electrodes, a tangled nest of electrical wires, and a panel of gauges and dials.

Nicolas took two steps through the pocket door and gasped. To his astonishment, just inside the door stood a stuffed ape, upright and dressed in full formal attire. With wing collar, black cravat, tails, and silk top hat, the creature—a chimpanzee or perhaps a baboon—was about three feet in height and expertly preserved. The simian mouth of this masterpiece of the taxidermist's art was drawn taut in a wicked smirk; it held a copy of Darwin's *Origin of the Species* under one arm, and its other arm was fully extended with white-gloved hand signing a welcome.

A chill cut through Nicolas. He understood that a "medium" practiced her art here, but to what precise use this odd assortment of paraphernalia might be put was a puzzle. The smug-looking ape beckoning the visitor to the séance table was an obvious affront to modern science, specifically to Darwin's theories. So mesmerized was Nicolas by the ape and the whole uncanny business, he nearly jumped out of his skin when Renée spoke behind him.

"Nick—I'd like you to meet Madame La Porte, my mother."

"Enchanted," Nicolas said, spinning around with a quick recovery. "La Porte, was it?"

"My married name of course was Keiller," Renée's mother explained. "Celeste Keiller, but when my dear husband passed I reverted to La Porte. I thought it fitting since the dear boy, the love of my life, was a professor of linguistics, a Francophile who loved the sounds of words." She extended a pale, elegantly manicured hand. "So pleased to make your acquaintance."

Nicolas took the hand of the lady of the house, a handsome woman who had Renée's gentle face and Cajun dark hair, but with wide streaks of grey, like angel's wings, along her temples.

"I see you've discovered my special room," she said, her voice at once Southern and regal. "But please, this way."

She led them through the open pocket doors into the cozier sitting room, evidently a lady's parlour furnished with armchairs and a long settee. Sheer lace curtains were hung at the windows. The doilies gracing the side tables and antimacassars on the headrests and arms of the chairs were all of matching tricolor lace. A cluttered desk sat in the corner.

"I'll fetch the tea," Renée said, disappearing again to the back of the house.

Madame La Porte settled onto the wingback armchair and gracefully gestured for Nicolas to take the settee. "Renée tells me you're from New York."

"Yes, but from upstate," Nicolas explained for the second time in as many days. "My home is far from the city of New York."

"The countryside is so lovely, in its own way. But there's much to be said for large, established cities, too." Madame La Porte reached for a silver cigarette case on the low table between them. "Renée's father and I lived for many years in New Orleans."

She extracted a dark French cigarette and offered the case to Nicolas, who declined. He struck a match for her, a bit shocked to see a lady smoke. Renée swept into the room, set a tray down, and took the chair facing Nicolas. Exhaling a pungent, blue-grey stream of smoke, Madame La Porte poured tea.

"Sugar, Mr. Van Horne?"

"Milk, no sugar, if you please."

"Ah, yes. Canadian style." Madame La Porte passed a translucent bone-china cup. "I understand you know Renée through your business with the college."

"A transaction regarding . . . teaching, shall we say."

"Teaching?" She gave a deep, full-throated laugh. "With corpses in your ice? How novel, Mr. Van Horne. Please do tell me how you came on the idea."

"You see, madam, a Boston gentleman named Frederick Tudor was trading in ice several decades ago. He shipped as far as India. I heard that Tudor also packed apples and fresh-churned butter, which sold well in sunnier climes such as yours. I simply adapted the idea to a different sort of goods."

"And so you pack the freshly dead. It's utterly novel, I admit. But however did you come across your first bit of these 'goods'?"

"Several years ago I agreed to store two unclaimed bodies in my icehouse until they could be hauled to the medical college in Albany by horse and carriage. The medical men persuaded me to transport the bodies in my ice shipment instead, by barge, on the Erie Canal."

"And you saw the business potential."

"Yes, I supply similar needs in Saint Louis and New Orleans."

"And now here, to Texas. But tell me, my dear"—she drew on her cigarette, a clear, intelligent look in her eyes—"how do you come by them?"

"Many come from accidents in the woods. Arrangements are made by our town's undertaker."

"You steal them," she said, smiling again. "A body snatcher."

"It's . . . it's impossible to come by them legally, I'm afraid," Nicolas said, blood flooding his face.

"Do you open graves?"

"Never!" Nicolas, shaking his head, sat forward on the settee. He hated that this business was illegal, that he was thought a monster. "You see, madam," he continued, calming himself, "many are unclaimed bodies and are nothing but a burden to the state of New York. Lumberjacks. French Canadians who die far from their home, without family. There are accidents at the sawmill, in the ironworks, the garnet mines."

"It's true, my brother-in-law Francis has a great need. His school is growing so. Indeed, I admire your fortitude to enter a business that's usually taken on by such scoundrels. But my perspective is ever so different, you see. I have a certain . . . gift that makes it so."

"A gift?"

"The gift of sensitivity. I perceive what others do not. My worry, Mr. Van Horne, is that the lost souls you provide the medical college . . . these souls may not be ready to be dissected. At least some of them."

"I assure you, madam, they feel nothing. They are as dead as can be."

"You misunderstand. It's not their earthly remains I'm concerned over. I feel for their spirit, their essence. You cannot think all of life's energy, all that momentum, simply disappears."

"Certainly, I believe in the soul. But once the soul leaves the body, the body is nothing, is it not?"

"For most, yes. But a few linger, I fear, and they see what's being done to their bodies. Don't you think? You must realize this, being around the freshly dead . . . Well, perhaps you don't, but those disembodied souls make their presence known, at least to me. *I hear them.*"

Madame La Porte took a long draw of her cigarette, exhaled, and leveled her eyes at Nicolas.

"To speak the truth, Mr. Van Horne, I've heard voices these past few days. Strident voices. Then, yesterday, late in the afternoon, a horrible, prolonged scream, a woman in labor."

"Mother." Renée, who'd been quietly sipping her tea, shifted in her chair. "Mother. Please don't."

"And again, last evening," Madame La Porte went on, "a tiny voice came through. Two voices, in fact, young boys. They were weak, but perhaps if I tried to—"

"Mother."

Madame La Porte set her teacup down with a click. "I'm sorry, dear. I understand your material needs at the college. I do. And materialism rules the day . . . but it isn't everything. There's much to be said for the spirit."

Renée's eyes flashed. "I really don't think we need burden our visitor with the peculiarities of your personal pursuits, Mother."

Madame La Porte nodded and reached for her cigarette case. "You're right, Renée." Nicolas lit the cigarette. "Let's turn to more pleasant subjects, shall we? Tell me about these lovely mountains of yours, Mr. Van Horne."

Nicolas started speaking about his home, the lake, and the harvesting of ice, but he was badly shaken. *Dead boys? Two boys, at that? The way I'm talking I'm making no sense . . . I must stop myself before I'm babbling . . .*

Madame La Porte listened politely at first, but she grew still, something somber crept into her face, and her eyes emptied.

"You must excuse me, Mr. Van Horne. I'm feeling ill," she said, her cigarette at arm's length, its ash long and droopy. "Just being with you, I'm sensing a morose presence." She stood, her breathing shallow and erratic, and dropped her cigarette, still smoldering, into an ashtray. "It's showing me . . . I'd rather not . . . something ugly, those boys and a good man, and death . . . No! He doesn't understand the ugliness ahead—for him, for everyone."

"Is there anything I can do, madame?"

"*You?* No, least of all . . . nothing . . . I must find a distraction, something pleasant." Madame La Porte dashed into the hall. She looked around her, muttering as if she were arguing with thin air. "Yes, it is. It is! I'm afraid . . . no . . . No! I'd rather not . . . he seems a fine gentleman, I'll not spoil his stay. Damned voices!"

And she disappeared up the stairs.

Nicolas turned to Renée. "I'm so sorry. I hope I didn't offend."

"No . . . no, you see, she hears voices on occasion, but I've not seen her this upset since . . . well . . ."

"Such a fascinating person. Quite deep." Without thinking, he added, "And she's nearly as beautiful as you."

Color rose in Renée's cheeks. "Let's go, shall we? I'll accompany you downtown and explain more about Mother. I've plenty of time to tend my experiment, and I'll not be a bother."

In the hallway, Renée took up her hat with the pink feathers and stood at the mirror adjusting it. Faint strains of a fiddle tune drifted down from the second floor—it was a Gypsy melody as dark, as melancholic, as a funeral dirge.

"Is that jolly old Prangoulis?" Nicolas asked. "From upstairs. Playing such a sad tune?"

"Yes, Basil spends a great deal of time with us, you see . . . and he plays to Mother's moods." Renée turned and offered her hand. "Come, we'd best be on our way."

20

Downtown

"Clairvoyance," Renée explained. "Mother demonstrated the talent as a child. In New Orleans, she fully developed it."

"She's a crystal gazer, then."

"No, Nick. No crystal ball. Her sensitivity allows her to communicate with the afterworld."

"I confess, I'm a bit of a skeptic when it comes to the supernatural."

"Mother's no sorcerer, Nick. She's a medium. Her talents have been verified by the London Psychical Research Society."

"Verified?"

"The society's researchers measured electrical parameters in the room during several of Mother's sittings, when she communicates with the dead. By installing a scale under her chair, they determined how much weight she loses when she transmits her psychic energy—as an ectoplasm—into the room. The poor dear can lose three percent of her body weight when making a connection. The London folks authenticated Mother's clairvoyance, inspired writing, and ability to communicate with the afterworld."

As they strolled, Renée proved well versed in the architectural details of churches, city hall, the opera house, and the Ursuline Women's Academy. She pointed out Galveston's slave market, closed after the Great War. "Mother never passes this way," she said, hurrying by. "Her sense of past cruelties is too great."

As they drew along the harborside, fishmongers' carts lined the street. "I'd so love to see this ship that's traveled so far down the Mississippi," Renée said. "Would you show me?"

Nicolas led the way past longshoremen and coarse deckhands who stared at the lady. They found Adam pacing the deck of their steamer. Nicolas called to him, "Come meet this fine young lady, the medical man's niece."

Adam feigned a dramatic bow. "Adam Klock at your service, miss. Pleased to make your acquaintance."

"Renée's giving me a lovely tour," Nicolas said. "All's tidy now, I take it?"

"Yep," Adam replied. "Just waiting for the pilot to get his ship off our hands and back to New Orleans. I heard there's a crowd down to the emporium, gawkin' at our exhibit, sir."

"What sort of exhibit is that, Mr. Klock?" Renée asked.

"Why it's Mr. Van Horne's Northern ice, miss," Adam replied, raising his hand in the air like a politician. "An exhibition of the world's finest ice, right here, just a few blocks away, at Mr. Slade's illustrious establishment. I believe it'll soon be declared the eighth wonder of the world." Renée gave a chuckle. "Like Niagara Falls, it's sumthin' everyone must see before they die."

"Is it as good as the Brooklyn Bridge?"

"Better, ma'am."

"Well, then, Mr. Klock, I must see this wonder."

"And who better to show you than the ice merchant himself?"

"That settles it," Nicolas interjected, grinning. "We're off to Slade's Emporium. You'll settle with the pilot, Adam?"

"Yep. Before ya know it, I'll be off this tub and onto dry land," he proclaimed, giving the railing a slap and the lady a grin. "And not a minute too soon."

Nicolas and Renée strode off the pier and down the harborside. When they crossed through Sailortown, Nicolas glanced up the alley near Alciatore's tavern, a twinge in the pit of his stomach, then he pressed on, head down.

At the more civilized heart of the commercial district, they passed dry-goods stores and suppliers of sundries, until they reached Slade's Emporium. On the sidewalk stood a man with placards fastened front and back proclaiming, NORTHERN ICE HERE. He shouted through a bullhorn: "Ice! Ice! The finest ice on earth! All the way from Canada, folks! Git yer ice at Slade's! Yer modern icebox too!"

Slade's was at the peak of its business day. Citizens crowded in front of the display window, where a profusion of cheeses, plump game birds, and sausages was hung.

Nicolas forged a path through the crowd and pointed through the window to a three-foot block of ice, its edges smooth, its surface glistening, clear and blue. At its base was a label:

PURE NORTHERN ICE
DIRECT FROM BONFERRI'S ICEHOUSE
DELIVERY NOW AVAILABLE

"It's beautiful, Nick."

"Its hardness is unsurpassed. It'll last for months."

"And oh! There's a fish inside, with colors so vibrant! Look at that eye, like it's swimming by, casual as a fish can be."

Flushed with pride, Nicolas stared into the block of Van Horne ice. Here was the product of his labor, his livelihood, ice as hard as diamond, ice so pure it moved his heart to see it. "Well then . . . shall we get along to the Cotton Exchange?" he said with a sigh. "I've a payment to collect."

Located at the center of the financial district, on the corner of Market and Strand Streets, the Cotton Exchange served as the architectural heart and commercial nerve center of the city of Galveston. The building was three stories, though the trading floor took up the entire first two floors. Pink sandstone griffins clung to the finest Texas granite; tasteful rooftop gargoyles gazed down from high atop the building's spires.

Nicolas led Renée into the throng of cotton traders flowing through the high arched doors. Inside, the dealings of commerce raged on the trading floor.

Nicolas couldn't help but notice the look of wonder on Renée's face. "You've never seen this, have you?"

"I admit, it's my first time inside. Quite impressive, isn't it?"

The trading floor, a single, mammoth room with marble columns, crystal chandeliers, and an impossibly high frescoed ceiling, was as grand as any Roman temple. In the center of the floor was the bidding ring, mobbed by the traders, men in proper jacket and tie, their top hats undulating like the ocean's surface. Arms shot into the smoke-filled air as the traders, clutching their precious calculations in hand, shouted bids on the lot of cotton on the block. On a narrow runway two men frantically chalked bids onto slates.

At the edge of the ring dockworkers slit bales of cotton open like eviscerated animals for inspection by the bidders. As a plantation's lot of produce was bid on and sold, the carcass of cotton was hauled away and the bidders turned to the next lot.

Nicolas realized the unwritten rules of Galveston's grand Cotton Exchange required that Renée, as a woman, take a sideline seat on a long marble bench marked "VISITORS." "I'll be but a few minutes," he said, setting off across the expansive marble floor to the stairway on the far side of the trading floor.

Nicolas paused for a moment's thought at the perimeter of the bidding ring. The South had lost its slaves and economic panics had rocked its commerce since the late seventies, but cotton was still king. Nicolas glanced back at Renée, the only woman in the grand, airy hall, her eyes clear and intelligent, a satisfied smirk on her face. He felt his chest fill with pride at having forged his own Yankee way here in the land of cotton . . . and at being accompanied by such a fine lady to collect his just reward.

Nicolas took the long marble staircase at the other end of the trading floor two steps at a time. He quickly identified the proper bursar on the upper-level office of the Sealy & Son trust and title company, and received payment.

Grinning with pleasure at the bundle of large notes in his inner coat pocket, Nicolas skipped down the stairs and made his way across the crowded trading floor. He craned his head to see Renée over the crowd.

The visitor's bench was empty. He felt his pulse pound.

Renée stood some distance from the bench, her back to the wall. She was confronted by two men—a red-faced, corpulent cotton trader with a much taller, lean gent standing behind him. Renée stretched up on her toes, clutched her hat, and edged toward the fat man, peering down at his balding head. Nicolas struggled through the crowd, his heart going out to her as she stood her ground.

"We will not!" he heard her say. "That is absurd."

"Well then, we'll do it ourselves!" the fat man sputtered, his spittle spewing in Renée's face.

Nicolas broke out of the pack of bidders and rushed to Renée's side. The tall beanpole of a man was young, perhaps twenty years of age, and of obvious refinement and wealth. He wore a well-tailored suit and a dark, well-manicured Vandyke beard that failed to obscure a pinched face badly cratered by smallpox. As Nicolas approached, the tall gentleman bumped the fat one from behind, prodding him toward Renée; then he stepped back, looked away, and put on a disinterested look. The fat man pointed a finger at Renée's nose like a schoolmaster threatening to paddle the class ruffian.

"Sir!" Her hands trembled at her sides. "I'll not take such ignorant comments to heart. Our faculty will stand together, and my uncle certainly won't give up his life's work because of superstitious yokels like you."

Nicolas stepped in and faced off with the rotund, jowly gent, getting a sour whiff of the man's suit, like stale laundry. "Pardon me," he said, offering his hand. "I am Nicolas Van Horne of New York." The fat man glared. "Perhaps I can be of some assistance?"

"I was speaking with this lady here." The fat man sneered. "And it's none of your concern."

"I happen to be escorting the lady, which makes it my concern, sir."

The tall gent with the Vandyke edged forward again. He puckered his narrow, badly scarred cheeks and spoke over the fat man's shoulder. "The question my friend is putting to the lady, quite simply, is *why in God's name* they chose Galveston for their college."

"Please," Nicolas said, folding his hands behind him and addressing the tall gent. "Perhaps we might discuss this at some more convenient time. I'd gladly stand you gents a brandy after trading closes, or—"

"What? What?" the fat one blustered, rubbery jowls shaking. "The stench is awful from that place, and at all hours of the night." Again at Renée: "Bad enough your lackeys open graves, and the god-awful bits and pieces of human flesh turning up all over the island . . . now we've heard of your unholy experimentin' and . . . and this town won't stand for it!"

The tall gent nodded his head like a marionette and grinned at Nicolas.

The cotton trader again pointed a pudgy finger. "Why . . . the latest we hear, you're chopping young boys into bits and pieces for your blasphemous experiments . . . and don't deny it. Sorcerers! I say . . . a coven of witches drawin' down the moon, and you're the chief witch!"

"Sir!" Nicolas straightened to his full height. "I must call you out for such talk."

The man glared back, sputtering.

"I'll make you regret those words," Nicolas said, balling his fists.

The tall, ugly gent slid between them and, lowering his voice, spoke to Nicolas. "Really, sir, it's hardly your business, eh? Don't be a fool."

"I'll not hear a lady insulted."

"Of course." The taller man nudged the fat man away and backed him toward the trading ring. "Of course."

Nicolas took a step in pursuit, but Renée grabbed his arm and held tight. "Don't, Nick."

"The sooner it's gone, the better!" the fat one shot over his shoulder as his companion wedged him into the crowd. "Witch!"

With that final epithet they were lost in the crunch of traders.

"Come on, Nick," Renée said, clearly shaken. "We mustn't concern ourselves with such ignorance." Still holding firm on his arm, she steered their way out the door of the Cotton Exchange and gently tugged Nicolas down the Strand. "I'm so sorry."

"Who were those men?"

"I only know the tall one—Hutch Sealy's son. He goes by Trey. A highly respected family, the Sealys."

"Yes, I've heard. Well, the flabby one's as low as any on the waterfront, I'd say, and this Trey, egging him on, he's just as bad despite his fine duds."

Nicolas and Renée regained some calm as they passed out of the financial district, ambling along side by side with their heads down.

"Why are such men so set against the college?" Nicolas asked. "I can't figure."

Soon they passed a row of restaurants where the smell of grilled meats wafted into the street. Nicolas's stomach gave an unexpected turn; he remembered he hadn't eaten a thing since his brioche at breakfast.

"We call this 'Restaurant Row,'" Renée said. "It's famous throughout the South." She turned to him and touched the sleeve of his coat. "I'm sorry our little tour turned so ugly, Nick. It's been nice, otherwise, wouldn't you say?"

"Splendid, otherwise."

"I say we carry on from here. Shall we, then? How about supper later this evening?"

"Well . . ." Nicolas hesitated, unable to think. "I . . . I . . ."

"Perhaps it's forward of me to ask, but it's a modern day. People can say what they like."

"Of course they can. No offense taken, Renée."

"Then it's settled. I shall finish in the lab, make my evening rounds on the wards, and we'll dine tonight at Trudeau's. Their sweetbread omelet is simply divine. I don't care if it is Lent, we should enjoy ourselves, don't you think? Life must go on."

"It certainly must."

"Well, I'm off to the lab then."

"I wonder . . . might I observe?" Nicolas asked. "I saw that thing—your uncle's particle?—under the microscope, you know."

Now Renée was taken aback. ". . . Sure, Nick. You're welcome to accompany me." She took his hand briefly. "Let's ride the trolley. After I finish with the cells and rounds on my patients, I'll head home and you may call for me at eight."

Nicolas's mind raced. He checked his watch twice on the short walk to the trolley. Seated uncomfortably next to Renée on the trolley's hard wooden bench, he struggled to restart their conversation over the screech of steel on steel. "Those feathers in your hat—are those ostrich feathers?"

"Heavens, no." Renée tittered and leaned closer to be heard. "They're from the roseate spoonbill. It nests right here on the island. Touch them, if you like," she said, cocking her head toward him.

Nicolas brushed the back of his hand across the feathers, then blushed—a rarity for Nicolas Van Horne.

"They're not nearly as dear as ostrich," she added gaily, then settled back on the bench as the electrical carriage jerked and bucked its way to the Medical College of Galveston, where, in truth, Nicolas Van Horne—his cheeks suffused with color—had no further business.

21

In Her Laboratory

The laboratory was stifling. The floor-to-ceiling windows had been thrown open, but the breeze died and the midafternoon sunlight streaming in from the west turned the room blood-warm. Sulfur and carbolic hung thick in the air. Nicolas was relieved to see that the gurney with the dead boy from Buffalo had been removed. He imagined the partly dissected corpse floating in a vat below, locked with its secrets behind heavy steel doors.

The Spaniard, Renée's laboratory assistant, stared into a small microscope on the lab bench. Petri dishes—perhaps a hundred—were lined up in neat rows on the bench in front of him. Renée spoke a few words in Spanish. Fernando looked up from the microscope, shrugged his shoulders, and gave a long answer that, to Nicolas, seemed convoluted no matter the language.

This fellow Fernando was a handsome young man with brooding, dark eyes. His cheeks, nose, and jaw, framed by the jet-black bush of neat sideburns, appeared chiseled from dark granite. Nicolas guessed the young chap must've been close to Renée's age, in his late twenties, certainly not yet thirty.

"Fernando tells me the cells are alive," Renée said as she hung her feathered hat on a hook along the wall. "But I'd best check for myself . . . he's so slow to learn these techniques."

She pulled a heavy rubber apron from another hook and wrapped herself in it. With a well-practiced movement she bound her tresses behind her neck with a black ribbon, then displaced her understudy at the microscope, which was a simpler instrument than her uncle's ponderous contraption with the high-power lenses and brilliant limelight. She peered down the tube and adjusted the microscope's mirror to better reflect the light from the windows. Fernando, his arms crossed, stood by and fixed Nicolas in a stony stare.

"You see, Nick, if we're to develop the anti-toxoid my uncle Francis has dreamt of"—Renée sounded remarkably like her lecturing uncle—"the cells we extracted from the boy's lymphoid tissues must remain viable. Alive." Her face slowly lit with a smile. "And we're in luck. I believe the cells have divided."

"May I look?" Nicolas asked.

Nicolas leaned over Renée's shoulder and peered into the microscope. A petri dish containing a shallow layer of pink fluid lay under the lens. Shadowy blobs swam into view.

"We must count them to be sure," Renée said. "If they've doubled in number since yesterday, it's conclusive they're alive."

Renée took to her microscope again and began clicking a small handheld counter. Fernando fidgeted, his arms crossed, then cleared his throat. "He really should learn this," Renée said, steadily clicking. "I hardly trust the fellow to . . ."

Fernando paced two or three steps, up and back, mumbling, then blurted something in Spanish and abruptly walked out of the laboratory. Renée waved him off without looking up from her count, the laboratory door swung shut, and Renée and Nicolas were alone.

"I just don't understand that man," she said, still peering down the microscope. "For one thing, he's not the brightest star in the firmament."

"Perhaps it's his poor mastery of English."

"He supposedly worked with the finest minds in Europe—Cajal in Barcelona, then Pasteur's lab in Lille—yet he hasn't grasped our work. He has no scientific . . . what's the word? . . . objectivity. When we harvested the cells from the boy—you understand I had to autopsy the little fellow to harvest lymph nodes—Fernando became terribly upset." Renée looked up from the microscope and set down her counter. "Heaven knows we've enough superstition on this island," she said with a frown. "The way Fernando reacted, you'd think we were raising the boy from the dead."

Nicolas couldn't help but snigger. "I've had that exact thought, Renée. Just now, you *did* say the boy's cells are living, didn't you?"

"Yes, luckily."

"Then, in a way, you have raised the boy from the dead."

Her smile spread broader than he'd seen. "Touché," she said, sliding the petri dishes down the bench.

She took up a slender glass pipette, attached a small rubber hose, and, using her mouth for suction, drew pink liquid from a flask. Lifting the top off the first petri dish, she dripped a precise amount of the pink fluid onto the cells.

"What's that you're doing?"

"This is their nourishment," she replied. "I'm feeding the cells."

"May I try? I'm quite good with my hands."

"You'll need an apron."

Nicolas peeled his jacket off and plucked an apron from its hook.

"Like this, Nick . . . Yes, that's it . . . Very good . . . very good indeed."

At the end of the hour, Renée had entered her data in her notebook and the petri dishes were neatly stacked on the warm slate of the lab bench. They shed their rubber aprons. Renée slipped into a long white jacket. "I must be off to the wards now. The other physicians and students will be waiting."

"I don't believe I've ever met a woman doctor."

"Well, now you have."

"Until supper then?"

"Yes, my dear Nick. Supper at eight."

22

At Myer's Shop

Nicolas raced down the Strand, breathlessly scrambling from storefront to storefront in his frantic search. "What *did* she call it?" he asked himself. "Roseate . . . something . . . but no . . . Renée Keiller deserves something more precious than a local feather. A bird that nests on the island indeed! She's a lady doctor and a scientist searching for a cure. She needs an ostrich feather, the finest available, and dyed pinker than any silly bird rummaging about in a sand dune."

He settled on a shop owned by a Mr. Myer, whose goods were prominently advertised by a painted board on the sidewalk:

FOREMOST SUPPLIER
OF MEN'S AND WOMEN'S
ACCOUTREMENTS
PURVEYOR OF FINE SILKS

Nicolas noted how the window display caught the attention of Galveston's most elegant ladies in their light cottons and taffetas, modern puff sleeves, wasp waists, and full bustles, their silk parasols twirled overhead to shield delicate complexions from the sun. Clearly, Mr. Myer dealt in fine apparel. Ostrich feathers of the finest quality would be readily available, dyed to any color of the rainbow.

While Myer's shopkeeper wrapped the pink feathers with gaily colored paper and twine, Nicolas noticed a Japanese fan hanging on the wall. Of a diaphanous, ivory-colored paper, intricately hand painted, this was no common fan; it was an Oriental work of art. The scene on the fan depicted a Japanese maiden in a cherry-red kimono, surrounded by fire-breathing dragons. The maiden held a fan that itself was painted with a lovely maiden in a red kimono holding a fan, and so forth, to the tiniest fan—a fan within a fan within a fan.

"How unusual. How delicate," he said, admiring the fan's handwork.

"An object so exquisite," the shopkeeper replied, "would be suitable only for a particular type of lady. A truly unique person."

"I agree. I'll take the fan also."

His treasures wrapped and tucked under an arm, Nicolas hailed a carriage to carry him to the Majestic, where he requested a bath be drawn, his second in as many days. While buckets of hot water were hauled to his room, Nicolas laid out his evening clothes. A freshly laundered shirt, a stiff collar, his favorite vest—a Scrimgeour plaid. At the bottom of his steamer chest he uncovered his last fresh pair of pants. He chose his carmine-red tie.

With the details of his evening before him on the bed, Nicolas inhaled deeply of the balsam scent that clung to his woolens. Fleetingly, his thoughts turned to the Adirondack woods in spring, when the ferns first push through the snowpack and the afternoon sun warms the pines.

But springtime was not a pleasant thought for an ice merchant. *What if the ice goes out early?* The fear of an early thaw forever gnawed at Nicolas. Three years earlier his final harvest on Upper Spy Lake had been dashed by a premature spring; he'd had no ice to sell that summer, and his losses had been heavy. Worse, the bodies in the icehouse rotted and Thomas Chubb had to bury them in the woods.

Nicolas forced his thoughts back to the evening that lay ahead. He lowered himself into the tub, and the hot water worked its magic on the knotted muscle of his arms and neck. "After I clean up," he said with a sigh, "I'll be in need of a fresh shave. Must look my best this evening." He began to scrub.

23

Supper at Trudeau's

The air in the room changed as Nicolas dressed. The salty warmth of the gulf breeze was missing. When he looked out the open window, he saw the wind had shifted into the north, brisk and icy. It felt like autumn in the North Country. He hurriedly donned his woolens, choosing his heaviest jacket. Taking care to knot his tie to perfection, he trotted to the lobby for that shave.

Nicolas chose carefully among the hansom cabs waiting at the Majestic's entrance; he was after one with full side curtains. By the time the driver's fine roan gelding was pulling his cab off the sand, the wind whistled, the cab's coverings flapped, and a freezing mist was in the air.

Madame La Porte received Nicolas at the front door of the Ball Lane house. A coal fire in the sitting room's fireplace warmed the entryway.

"Yes, yes, I'm feeling much better," Madame La Porte said when Nicolas enquired. "Do you see what you've sent us from your mountains?" she asked, pushing the front door shut with her back while deftly extracting a cigarette from her silver case. "We call it a 'norther,' and this is quite a strong one. Renée will be down shortly. Cigarette?"

In a few moments Renée descended the stairs dressed in a white shirtwaist of light cotton, a black ribbon at her throat. Her skirt was dark and without a bustle, accentuating her trim figure. She'd fastened her hair back with tortoiseshell clips and fashioned it to fall in ringlets like fat sausages behind her.

"Hello there," she called from the bottom landing.

"My, but you're lovely this evening," Nicolas said, taking her hand. "I've held a covered carriage. It promises to be an icy night."

Blasts of wind rocked the carriage and puffed through its draperies. Shutters banged against the houses and sandy debris swirled over the street. On the short run to Restaurant Row, Nicolas removed his jacket for Renée to throw over her shoulders; she pulled it snug and inhaled its woodsy smell.

Trudeau's restaurant took up the entire ground floor of a large commercial building. The maître d'hôtel, a handsome colored man in formal evening wear, greeted them at the door and ushered them under brilliant gas chandeliers into the rich aroma of exotic French and Spanish spices. The dining room rang with quick-witted conversation and the clatter of silverware on china plates. Renée spoke French. The maître d' led them to the far end of the dining room, where the gaslights were lowered. A small corner table; an attentive waiter; champagne promptly poured; the clink of glasses.

"Shall I order?" Renée asked.

"I should say you must," Nicolas replied, smiling at the menu, which was entirely in French. "I trust your judgement."

Renée lifted her glass. "Yes, so here's to trust, and our friendship." Turning a bit more serious, she said, "I'm a strong believer in friendship, aren't you, Nick? An 'old world' sort of friendship. A man and a woman can be friends, can they not?"

"In many ways, yes. In other ways . . . certain things are assumed by society, Renée."

"Then society must change."

He considered this for a moment, then lifted his glass. "Here's to a changing society, then."

Supper arrived in six courses: First came golden fried fillets of pompano rolled in cornmeal accompanied by a spicy court bouillon. Spooning up the rich broth, Nicolas regaled the lady scientist with tales of the Adirondack skills of guides and North Country hermits he'd known. But when the subject turned to winter and how it left the landscape windswept and grey, Nicolas's mood turned somber.

"What's wrong, Nick," Renée asked. "Why so glum?"

"I was remembering a very sad winter." Nicolas retold the tale of the loss of his boy Ethan to the woods. He tried to remain stony-faced, but couldn't keep the emotion from his eyes.

"Back then, my wife, Ruth, was the schoolmistress. After Ethan disappeared, she was stricken with melancholy and never worked again. We tried cures from every charlatan in the state of New York."

"It's an awful blow to lose a loved one, Nick."

"You've lost, Renée, yet you continue your work."

"My patients and the lab are my comfort." She broke a loaf of crusty French bread. More quietly, she added, "I suppose you might say I'm married to the lab."

"Like Uncle Francis."

"Heavens no!" Her eyes, suddenly full of mirth, met his. "Not as bad as Uncle, I should hope."

Nicolas again cracked a smile. "As for me, I must count myself lucky to have my daughter, Abigail, such a bright girl, and my grown son, Schuyler…though there's one rascal who needs to settle down, I tell you. He's a talented musician, but I fear he'll never earn a living."

Renée gently set her glass on the tablecloth, where bread crumbs lay like freshly fallen snow. "You seem such an upstanding person, Nick," she said. "Have you any idea how dangerous your enterprise is?"

"I certainly do. I saw the man lynched in Sailortown, you know."

Renée's eyes opened with surprise. "You did? Why, I just heard. You understand, then, that since the end of the war, common citizens—in both North and South—have come to hate body snatchers. I know you're a fine gentleman, but they'd consider you the lowest of the low."

"There's one more way society must change."

"Why not leave it to the criminals, Nick? They have nothing to lose. You have so much."

Nicolas pushed back in his chair, and the ugliness of the two dead boys from Buffalo—the nightmare boys—flashed into his mind. Two twisted, frozen bodies from Buffalo, and he had no idea how they'd come to him or why they carried that strange mark he'd discovered.

"There are many, shall we say, 'side benefits' to my business, Renée. The students' learning, of course, but think also of your experiment with that dead boy's cells."

"Do you know where that boy came from, Nicolas?"

"From a snowbank."

"I mean, how he died?"

"I . . . truthfully, I don't know."

"I thought as much. Look—I'm as culpable as you now. I'll say no more, except . . . take care with this business of yours, Nick."

Their doting waiter brought stalks of cold asparagus and a stew he called étouffée. Renée had her sweetbread omelet; a truffle-stuffed duck came swimming in dark sauce. It was the finest meal Nicolas had had set before him in months, perhaps ever.

"And what about the danger *you* face, Renée?" Nicolas asked. "Those men at the Cotton Exchange?"

"I've thought long and hard about that. Believe me, there's more than meets the eye to those men."

"How so?"

"Cotton traders don't care about anatomy classes. In my opinion, they're after our docks."

"Docks? Why don't they simply add more docks? Galveston has an excellent deepwater harbor, one of the largest on the coast."

"No, they're after the east-end location of the medical college. We're separate, isolated really from the other piers."

"What advantage is that?"

"You know the story of our cotton jammers, don't you?"

"Sure. They're the best in the world at packing cotton, screwing it down tight into the ships, so they've monopolized the stevedore jobs."

"And they're well organized. Their wages are high. If new piers were built on our end of town, where the medical college is now, the cotton traders could hire their own, cheap labor."

"Bypass the cotton jammers. Seems plausible . . ."

The supper hour passed and the dining room emptied. Puddings soaked in whiskey sauce arrived and Renée called for "*café.*"

"Such a fine champagne you've chosen," Nick said, pouring more.

"It's French."

"Before coffee arrives, then, I propose one last toast—to Uncle and the cure!" he said, raising his glass. "And, of course, to our new friendship."

Renée sipped, then stared down into her glass. "Will you write me, Nicolas? When you're back in New York? As friends?"

"I'm not much with words, I'm afraid."

She looked up, her eyes gleaming. "I'm sure you write a fine letter."

"Then I shall try."

When they rose from the table, the restaurant was abandoned and the gaslights nearly all extinguished. Nicolas told the driver who'd held his carriage for them, "To Ball Lane," but Renée protested, her lips loosened by the French bubbly. "No! To the beach, sir!" she called to the driver. "We can't possibly end this lovely evening so soon. This gentleman from the North simply *must* see the gulf at night."

Nicolas shut the side curtains against the bitter wind and again covered her with his jacket. He felt a thrill beside her, free from eyes on the street. When their carriage rumbled onto the expanse of beach the tide was out and the north wind had blown the gulf flat as a pond. The scalloped, drifting sand glowed eerily in the moonlight. They stepped down. Their driver huddled under a horse blanket to wait. Renée took Nicolas's hand and led him to the water's edge and down the beach; in a few minutes they were out of sight of the carriage.

"Far enough?" she asked, slowing the pace, kicking at the sand. Then she looked up and came to a sudden halt. "Oh, look!" A line of brown pelicans glided over their heads; the huge, elegant birds, at least a dozen, low and silent, nearly motionless, flew in a perfect row into the north wind, their five-foot wingspans bright in the moonlit night.

When the pelicans disappeared over the sand dunes, Nicolas took her by the elbows and turned her toward him. "It's been such a remarkable day."

"Yes. Remarkable, indeed."

She stood with hands folded in front of her, head down. Her curls blew wildly in the wind; he caught wisps of them in his hands and held them to the sides of her face.

"I must kiss you, you know."

"Nick—"

He bent and kissed her, clasping her face in his hands. He'd not planned it, he intended only a harmless kiss, but her lips were smooth and warm . . . perhaps he persisted a moment too long.

She let out a tiny gasp, then took hold of his shoulders and kissed him back with surprising force. "Enough," she whispered, placing her hands on his chest and pushing him to arm's length.

"Forgive me."

"Oh, Nick," she said, studying his face. "I want to remember you just as you are. So serious."

Renée turned back, then broke into a run, calling, "Faster!" over her shoulder, taunting him. She veered landward into a line of sand dunes where the going was hard. Nicolas closed the gap. She stopped and faced him, out of breath.

"No." She paused, gasping. "No. It's time we go."

They roused their grumbling driver from the refuge he'd taken inside his cab, and he whipped his horse at a canter through the night. Renée pulled back the side curtain and the north wind rushed in. She thrust her face out the window, her hair flailing.

"I meant no affront, Renée."

She turned, her face in a nest of tangled ringlets. "Nick . . . It's been a glorious day. I haven't had a day like this since . . . well, I thank you for everything."

When the cab jerked to a stop at the house on Ball Lane, they sat in silence. Renée pushed the carriage door open and jumped down.

"Please! Shall we meet tomorrow?" Nicolas asked. "I must see you. I . . . I leave on the noon train."

". . . We'll see. I . . . Ta-ta."

She turned and loped through the gate and up the front steps without a further word. Nicolas sank into the seat, his heart pounding.

"The Majestic, sir."

Back in his room, Nicolas's eyes were struck wide open. He walked circles on the Oriental rug, retracing the odd events of a day that seemed like a dream. The feel of Renée at his side at the church, at supper . . . the scent of apple blossoms. The kiss.

It seemed a different world from the one he woke to, a world no longer muddied by two boys dead of unknown causes, nightmares, or those beastly cotton traders. He felt he could solve any puzzle, fix any problem.

Nicolas settled into a chair by the window and tried without success to force his eyes shut against the rising full moon. The gulf's gentle movement offered no soporific. Hours passed as he sat at the window. With amusement, he stared at the bed he knew would go unwrinkled, and then he saw them—the things he'd forgotten in his haste. The packages, the presents for Renée, still on the bed.

"The feathers! The fan!"

24

Departure

At sunrise, Nicolas packed his steamer trunk. His mind leapt about like a dervish. The hotel lobby was empty; he paced until guests appeared for breakfast, then he arranged for a carriage. Once his trunk was loaded he tucked the presents for Renée under his arm and instructed the driver to carry him to Ball Lane.

Madame La Porte answered the doorbell at the first twist.

"I'm afraid she's already in the laboratory, sir."

"I have something for her," he said, indicating the packages. "Perhaps I'll go directly to the college? I haven't much time before departing."

"I'm sorry, sir, but Renée instructed me . . . you see, her schedule's extremely demanding today. She chairs the faculty senate, and she's called an emergency meeting over that horrid occurrence in Sailortown."

"If I were to go to the college—"

"I think that impossible."

"Might I leave these for her, then? I'd like to pen a note as well."

"Certainly." Madame La Porte took the packages and beckoned Nicolas into the hallway.

"Could the message be taken to her? I'll hire a carrier, I'll—"

"Yes, yes, of course." There was an awkward silence; Madame La Porte smiled and gave a nod. "If you like, I'll see that your message is delivered to the laboratory with all due haste. Perhaps Basil . . ."

Standing in the hallway, Nicolas dashed off his thoughts:

> *Dearest Renée,*
>
> *My heartfelt thanks for the delightful evening. It seems a different world here, at least to this Northerner's eyes. If at all possible, please see me off—we depart the station at noon. Please come.*

Nick

Clouds of soot and steam belching from the locomotive's boiler hung like a pall over the departures platform of the Galveston station. Hired men loaded his trunk, but Nicolas refused to embark. Instead, he stood on the concrete alongside the train, searching the faces of the throng on the platform. The iron monster shuddered and smoked and the powerful pistons of its locomotive cranked once, twice, the great wheels turned, and then he saw her . . . or was it her? It was a hat like hers, pink feathers bobbing along the platform. Had she gotten the gifts?

From out of the cloud around him he heard Adam call out to him. "Van Horne! Climb up, man, she's movin'!"

Nicolas saw the train lumber forward; he loped alongside, then dashed to keep up, his thoughts accelerating with the locomotive, racing to the long days ahead, the loneliness of his sleeper berth.

He reached for the handrail and swung up. Renée had not come. In minutes he'd be off this sandbar and across the railroad bridge, the bay a blue-grey blur below, the roar of the engine louder, the click of the rails faster.

But no iron horse yet built raced as wildly as Nicolas Van Horne's thoughts, and the rumble of even the greatest train could not drown the fine trembling of his heart.

25

Alone in Her Laboratory

By now he'd be long gone, she knew—departed from the station and rolling across the Texas coastal plain. The ice merchant. His train was scheduled for noon, and the Galveston–Santa Fe Railroad was punctual, fair weather or foul. Earlier, while she'd imprisoned herself all morning, presiding over the circular discourse of her overwrought colleagues, Nick would have been tucked comfortably into his Pullman car, fast approaching the two-mile-long railroad trestle that crossed Galveston Bay.

He seemed such a fine gentleman, her ice merchant, so different from any other gentleman. This was a person with depth, ambition, an experience of life, and yet he was gentle and kind. She was fortunate to have made his acquaintance, to have shared such gay times and open talk. A true friendship had been forged.

Their moments together reminded her of the first time she'd spoken a foreign tongue—the excitement of making herself understood to another, though it was seldom a man. There was never a man like Nick, was there? Most men she'd befriended since her husband's death were from the university. Had there ever been a man with whom she could joke or speak so openly and naturally? Well, that would be quite a man.

Still, it worried her that this tall, stately man of the world didn't understand the extreme danger he was in. He treated it like business. She should've told him everything. She should have told him about the boy, the horror of it, the ghastly manner of the boy's death. Wasn't that what friends were for? Friends protected each other, even from their own weaknesses, their own mistakes.

Had she forged more than a friendship with this Van Horne fellow? She blushed at the thought of that moment on the beach. It was only last night, though it seemed like ages ago. Surely their tiny indiscretion had been a spur-of-the-moment fancy, nothing more. She would put it out of mind. Still, the tenderness of his touch, the sweet way he kissed her and stood there looking so—

"Renée! Your solution's bubblin' a wee bit briskly there."

"What? Forgive me, Uncle. How in the world did it get so—"

"This isn't like you, lass. Take care, or you'll burn us up!"

. . . Nick. Dear Nick. He'd promised to correspond, hadn't he? They'd agreed, practically taken a blood oath. Their enthusiasm was mutual. She wouldn't be the first to write, of course; that would be much too forward, as a woman . . . oh, damn! There it was again, that thinking she'd tried so hard to change, the silly idea that because she was born a female of the species she should act a certain way, or refrain from certain actions as improper. Complete balderdash! She must remind herself of that truth; women like her had been repeating it ever since the meeting of great minds—female minds—at Seneca Falls, decades ago. In the countryside of upstate New York, wasn't it? Nick's home.

Of course she would write the good Mr. Van Horne. She'd act as any decent human being acted toward another; whether man or woman made not a speck of difference in the modern world. She'd take up her pen, she would. "*Dearest Nick,*" she'd begin. Her letter was already taking shape in her mind.

Perhaps "*Dearest*" wasn't right. No . . . equality was equality. The shallow men of science and medicine could hardly accept her, a mere woman, as equal, but surely this forward-thinking gentleman from the North was different. Eventually, other men would learn to be like him. Like Nick. Yes, like Nick.

"Renée . . . Renée, dear . . . Will ye pay attention, lass? Your retort. Turn it doon, will you? What are ye about today?"

The smell of scorched rubber filled the lab.

"Oh, Uncle . . . sorry . . . I . . ."

Her solution was ruined, a whole afternoon's work. What was wrong with her thinking? There was nothing unseemly in forging a friendship with a man. With Nick, it was a natural meeting of two minds, two gentle souls, nothing more.

Yet . . . why had she rushed to the lab this morning? Her excuse to herself was that she must call an emergency meeting of the faculty senate to discuss the lynching. But she was sure nothing new would be said. Everyone already knew all the horrible details; the entire faculty was afraid to walk downtown, and now Uncle had no one to acquire cadavers. True, she had an experiment to tend to, the cells to count and feed, but she could've put the experiment off or instructed Fernando to carry on until her return. That way, she might've seen Nick off properly on the noon train, as a newfound friend would, with an embrace or perhaps a sisterly kiss on the platform. No harm in that. Instead, she'd rushed into the meeting room as if she were afraid to see the gentleman mount the blasted train.

She would wait before writing, not because it was the proper thing to do, but because this feeling in her was so alarming. Yes, she'd best wait for a letter from Nick, to judge its tone, its intent. She'd have plenty of time to ruminate over her response, the salutation, her deeper thoughts . . . Nick's Pullman car had just left the island; it was mere hours since he'd the crossed the bridge over Galveston Bay to begin his voyage.

It would be four long days before he'd arrive at his mountain home in the great state of New York, and that damned ice business of his.

PART 2

The North Country

26

Layover

"Layover! Ladies and gentlemen. Layover!" called the conductor who made his way between the cars as the train slowed, near to stopping. "Chicago it is, folks. Chicago. Boiler's in need of repair. With luck, we'll be departin' the station at daybreak."

Nicolas peered out at the black night and the ghostly shadows of telegraph poles creeping by. Chicago—gateway to the West, stockyard to the nation—the city of blood and meat, from porterhouse to headcheese, from chop to wurst.

In spite of his booking a private cabin with the most comfortable of Pullman's sleeping berths, Nicolas had climbed into his bunk only once in the last two nights. On the first day out, he tried his damnedest to put the island of Galveston out of mind. He'd forced himself to pull his ledger from his trunk and wrestle with the columns of figures, but waves of memory and trepidation washed over him. He shut the ledger. He stared out the window, never turned down the sheets. Instead, he took up paper and scribbled at the writing table till dawn, though he produced nothing more than a halting string of a hundred words. He was no good at it. Not words, not for this thing, this feeling he was fighting.

Besides, it was futile, was it not? Renée hadn't come to see him off at the station, though he'd asked, practically begged to be bid farewell. Her absence at the platform must hold some meaning, mustn't it? He should count himself blessed to be out of that strange, disturbing city and off that damp, salty island...But he didn't feel blessed...

With morning light on the second day after departing Galveston, Nicolas wasn't sure of anything. He had scribbled, scrawled, and searched for words until a sheaf of false starts stared back at him from the small table. No, he was no good at it. He'd hardly gotten past the salutation—*"Dearest Renée"* . . . *"To my dear friend . . ."* Then, in a fit that lasted till noon, he filled four pages with his finest hand and fell, dazed, into his bunk.

. . . dining with you . . . our walk on the beach . . . forgive me but . . . tossed on a sea of emotions . . . our friendship . . . what hope can I hold . . .?

As they chugged into the Chicago railroad yards, Nicolas reached for the mound of foolscap and chucked it out the window into the cold night air. Foolishness. He'd written foolishness. A letter to Renée could wait for eternity; it would never be finished.

The train wheezed to a halt, was rumbling and hissing when there was a knock at the door and Adam stood in the corridor. "Come on, boss. Let's get us a steak," he said, licking his chops. "I'm starved and the stockyards are walking distance."

Van Horne felt a hollowness at his center, an emptiness food could hardly fill. But the evening was young and his foreman needed sustenance.

A few blocks from the railway platform Nicolas and Adam crossed Thirty-Ninth Street and entered the stockyards and meatpacking district. The going became slick with a steady, icy drizzle that mixed the clay of the street and the blood from the abattoirs into a grisly muck. Stinking stockyard workers, their eyes bleary from twelve-hour shifts on the killing floor, pushed their way to and fro. The lowing cattle, the squeal of hogs, and the smell of raw animal fear filled the air. It was the sort of scene that kept ladies in their berths and gave pause to even the hungriest man contemplating a steak dinner.

Eight blocks into the district, they entered the neighborhood known as "back of the yards" and came on a row of public houses. Stockmen and slaughterhouse crews congregated on a particular street corner signaled the busiest and best establishment. The pair of New Yorkers pushed through the swinging doors into a poorly heated, drafty saloon consisting of a single cavernous room. The tables were packed with boisterous men. The doors to the kitchen—one in and one out—were so distant as to be a goodly hike for the dozen or so waiters hauling trays of grilled meats and sausages to the tables. Adam stepped to the bar and ordered beers from a tapman of great girth who spoke with a German accent. Two mugs skidded toward them from the taps and sloshed to a halt.

Nicolas set a foot on the brass rail; took a long, bitter swig; and studied the row of haggard faces at the bar for a sense of what this booming city was all about. Most appeared to be older, grey-haired workingmen in bloodstained blue shirts and woolens who sucked at their beer as if it were their last. A few younger men stared glassy eyed into nowhere. Nicolas found it impossible to tell which were about to start a shift on the killing floor or cutting tables and which had just gotten off work.

"We must count ourselves lucky," Nicolas said to his trusty foreman. "Harvesting ice is cold, hard labor, but at least it's clean. It's healthy."

"I'm beginning to think this business of yours might not prove so healthy." Adam leaned closer. "There's folks all over this nation who'd see us swing like that poor devil in the alley."

Nicolas gave a resigned nod, settled his elbows on the bar, and continued appraising the crowd.

He found that a surprising number of stockyard workers in this establishment appeared to be mere boys. One group near the bar looked eleven or twelve years old at most—dirty, ill kept, with musty hair and angry faces. Nicolas was reminded of the two dead bodies from Buffalo.

A couple of these ruffians leered at the older men as only youths intent on doing wrong might do. As Nicolas watched, a scuffle broke out between two of the boys, and the German tapman circled from behind the bar to eject the two combatants.

"They sure work 'em young in these stockyards," Nicolas said with disdain. "Are there no schools here? Have these boys no parents?"

"They're prob'ly orphans," Adam said. "The orphanages are filled to bursting these days. Poorhouses, too. Makes for plenty of able-bodied young ones, and a slaughterhouse don't care if they're only boys."

The shenanigans of these youngsters saddened Nicolas. His mind had been consumed by Galveston—the murderous events in Sailortown, the good professor and his lovely niece Renée, the scientists' work . . . the unsettling preoccupations of Renée's mother. Nicolas had given hardly a thought to his mountain home, the upcoming ice harvest on Upper Spy Lake, or his own son. Galveston occupied his mind so, Nicolas couldn't remember eating a thing since Trudeau's on Restaurant Row. Now, in the smoky barroom, the smell of frying meat piqued his appetite. He followed Adam's lead and called for the house's finest porterhouse with all the fixings.

Adam went on about the boys. "I've seen 'em in the North Country, too," he said. "Gangs of youngsters peddled as cheap labor. Some boss man takes their first month's pay and probably half their pay after that. In cities like Chicago I'll bet they cram a dozen of 'em into a flat with no water, no nothin'."

"These industrialists."

"And they call that progress."

Cuts of seared beef two inches thick arrived, piled high with sweet-smelling onions and fried potatoes. At arm's length from Nicolas a dull-eyed, balding worker, his face grey and drawn, sat hunched over his empty whiskey glass. The man glanced with something like disgust at the fine plate of food set before Nicolas, like he'd seen too much meat, had too many years on the killing floor. He had the look of a man whose whole purpose in life was a single, small, nightmarish task, performed countless times in the service of the company. Perhaps it was the fatal slash to the jugular, or hoisting the warm, twitching carcass into the air, or—most gruesome—the disembowelment.

On the bar in front of the man sat a single gold eagle, likely half his entire day's pay. He tapped the coin with a finger and called down the bar for another drink just as a second ruckus broke out among the ruffians. When the older man swung around to face the commotion, one of the boys broke from the pack, circled around, and slid between the old man and Nicolas. He shot the ice merchant a scowl, then whisked the old man's coin off the bar.

"No you don't!" Nicolas wrapped the youth's wrist in a steely grip. The boy's eyes swiveled around, snakelike. Nicolas twisted; Adam stepped up and cocked the boy's other arm behind him. Nicolas stared into the boy's hateful face. The boy sneered back.

"Hold on," Nicolas muttered. "I know you. I've seen you before."

"Leave me be!" the boy cried, wiggling, rising on his toes, and arching back toward Adam with the pain.

"You're the one they called Rainbow," Nicolas said. "I know from your eyes."

The hooligan's eyes were of two distinctly different colors, one dark brown, the other a translucent, fleshy grey.

"You were that boy on the lake at the first harvest."

The youth's freakish eyes darted about, searching for an accomplice. He could barely be a teenager. Frail with malnourishment, his growth into manhood stunted, the boy weakened quickly in the grip of the two Northerners.

"*Please don't, mister,*" he whined.

"You were on the ice," Nicolas said. "It was only a day or two, then you disappeared. Quit."

The barkeep appeared at their side, spouting a handful of German oaths. With startling dexterity for his girth, he grabbed the youth by the collar and tugged, ripping the boy's shirt as he pulled him away from the bar.

"Did you see that?" Nicolas said. "On his shoulder. Was that . . . ?"

The barkeep hustled Rainbow out the barroom door.

"I swear, Adam, I saw that strange—"

The barkeep was back, wiping his hands on his apron. "So sorry, gents," he said with a shake of his big round head. "No good, these young ones they bring here." He scanned the crowd for more trouble, but the pack of ill-kept boys had quickly dispersed into the large room. "*Mein Gott* . . . so many, and new ones all the time. They have no home, *ja*, so they come to steal and fight. Every minute my eyes open I must keep. Let me stand you two a drink."

Nicolas and Adam returned to their steaks. "You recognized that hooligan, too, didn't you, Adam?"

"I remember him well, though I hate to admit it. Rainbow. He was one of 'em in them crews, the young ones working the sawmill. He snuck away from the mill and come to me when I was recruiting for the first ice harvest in December. I'm afraid I hired him."

"Where'd he come from?"

"Never said, but a grown man said he was the boy's uncle come to me wanting the boy's pay. I gave him nothing. Told the fellow we weren't working the ice more than a day or two when the scalawag ran off."

"I thought I saw a mark on the boy's shoulder. Something like this . . ."

Nicolas dipped his finger in his suds, pushed his beer aside, and drew on the bar.

Ж

"I never seen nothing like that, boss."

"Well, I trust you won't hire the likes of him again."

On their return to the railroad station, Nicolas and Adam passed a row of brightly lit shops, among them an apothecary with a modern, finely outfitted display window. Seeing this, Nicolas suggested that Adam go ahead to the train. "I'll make a quick stop," he said, thinking of the depleted morphine mix given him by Thomas Chubb.

With a nod, Adam continued to the station. Nicolas entered the apothecary's shop, where he studied the exhibit of shining new hypodermic syringes at the counter. These were the latest thing, all the rage with their sparkling glass cylinders, ground-glass pistons, and finely tooled steel casements.

"Nowadays, they're drawing these needles as thin as wire," the apothecary commented as he laid out the various hypodermics on the counter. "They vanish beneath the skin with ease and leave the barest trace."

"The works I was given is certainly much coarser. Badly worn, too, I'm afraid."

"Now, this one, sir, is from the manufacture of Codman and Shurtleff of Beacon Street, a Boston maker. It's a most excellent instrument."

"The tooling seems quite precise."

"The ground glass and tempered metals guarantee perfect accuracy, sir." Nicolas worked the plunger slowly. "It'll last a lifetime."

"I dare say it will." Nicolas slid the works into its leather case. "I'll take it, and two vials of a mix, mostly morphine."

"Will Magendie's solution do?"

"I suppose that'd be fine."

"I'll prepare it with a dash of chloral hydrate, though I rather recommend the scopolamine," the apothecary said as he headed to his laboratorium at the back of the shop. "A mere tenth of a grain is most relaxing, yet without aftereffects."

When the apothecary returned, he bundled the kit and the bottle of mix, and pushed the brown paper package across the counter to Nicolas.

"Do beware that finer needle, sir," he said with a smile. "Just beneath the surface of the skin, small veins are remarkably plentiful. Should one wander into one, a certain unpleasantness may result. Some tingling, fatigue—nothing more, you understand."

Nicolas nodded, smiled a thank-you, and tucked the package under his arm.

"Take care, now," the apothecary said sternly. "As I say, they lie just beneath the surface. Steer clear of them."

The next day, swaying in his private cabin, Nicolas pulled the new works from its case, prepared an injection, and slipped into a state of blissful white dreams. Hours passed unheeded as the train beat the rails. Nicolas found the Magendie's solution quite successful at fogging the Galveston memories, both good and bad, the delights and the worries. It was so simple; one needed only choose one's dosage properly.

As they neared Buffalo, Nicolas decided to venture a second dose. He drew the apothecary's mix into his new works, gently inserted the needle into his forearm, and . . . blundered into a vein, precisely as the apothecary had warned.

"The gent was right," he muttered when the brilliant rush of intravenous morphine hit him squarely between the eyes. "They lie . . . just . . . beneath . . . the surface."

He settled into his cabin's leather bench and felt with exquisite sensitivity the rhythm of the rushing coach. "Ahh . . . how else can one forget the ghastliness this world brings?"

27

Buffalo

The train was deathly still, the only sound the faint thrum of rain on the Pullman coach's metal roof. Raw nerves pulsed at Nicolas's temples. Sudden, unexplained twitches shook his limbs. Something akin to sleep had passed over him since Chicago, but he'd still not climbed into his sleeping berth and now—it was already late morning—he found himself awkwardly draped over the private berth's bench, its hard oak arm his only pillow.

The Pullman's radiator gave a tired hiss. The train was shutting down. Snatches of conversation came from the passageway: they were talking about the city of Buffalo; it was unusually warm for this time of year. Also, it seemed the Buffalo-to-Albany train—their connector to the Adirondack Mail Express and home—was delayed to load coal. Nothing serious. They would connect the coaches and depart Buffalo today, but not until well after the supper hour.

Nicolas considered a small, settling dose of his mix of morphine to tide him over until the afternoon. Outside, grey lines of passengers filed down the platform for a stroll through Buffalo. With the coach cooling around him and the throb in his head, Nicolas formed a new resolve. He would pack his new works away and venture into town. That business of the two boys dug from a snowdrift sat uncomfortably at the back of his mind.

Nicolas had never extended the Van Horne & Co. ice trade to the boom city of Buffalo, New York. He had been content to supply local needs in the Mohawk Valley, before venturing far south with ice and corpses. For those Southern journeys Nicolas capitalized on the speed of the newest trains. He had cargo cars hitched to a fast locomotive at the rail spur at Upper Spy Lake and run through Buffalo's switchyard to Chicago. The load was then transferred to steamers for what the riverboat pilots called a "lightning run" down the Mississippi.

On this last run, to Galveston, there'd been less than an hour's stop in the Buffalo switchyard, barely enough time for Nicolas to retrieve those two boys found in a snowdrift from the medical college. *How odd,* Nicolas thought as he stepped from his Pullman coach, tightened down his homburg against the cold rain, and pulled his overcoat around his ears. *How odd to receive two corpses from a medical man, rather than the other way around.*

Thomas Chubb. That's who this all came back to. Thomas Chubb had informed Nicolas of two easy bodies in Buffalo just minutes before departing the lake with the ice. Thomas was always last-minute. And he'd been tight-lipped about the professor, Austin Flynt, who was "in a hurry to be rid of the boys." Few words had passed between Professor Austin Flynt and Nicolas at the transfer in Buffalo; Nicolas had Adam whisk the dead boys from the medical school and stow them in the bottom layer of Van Horne ice without even examining the bodies. Now, thanks to their locomotive's appetite for coal, Nicolas found himself with a small window of time to find this Professor Flynt again and discover what he knew.

New York State's medical college at Buffalo occupied a substantial brown stone building at the corner of Main and Virginia Streets. One of New York's first, the college was compact and plain compared to Galveston's new school. The building was topped by simple steeples and adorned only with churchy, peaked windows. A steepled entryway enclosed stone steps where one kicked the snow and ice from one's boots, though on this afternoon the steady drumbeat of rain had turned the scanty snowdrifts to slush, and there was no snow or ice to kick off one's boots.

The main door of the college creaked open with difficulty. The hallway floor was darkened and rutted with wear. Nicolas made his way down the empty hall to dry himself at the fireplace in the college's large central vestibule. He shook the rain from his homburg and overcoat, backed close to the fire, and examined the doors facing the vestibule, each marked with a professor's name. Austin Flynt, MD. He'd entered that door a little over a week before. His knock was quickly answered by a bright "Do come in!"

Professor Flynt was at his desk, writing in a ledger. He was a large, middle-aged man with a nearly bald crown, a well-trimmed goatee, and a broad, single eyebrow whose great weight beneath the glossy dome of his head gave the immediate impression of intelligence and wit. He appeared quite hale, with clear grey eyes and rosy, weathered cheeks. A look of recognition crossed his face when he glanced up from his oak desk and saw Nicolas; then his mouth set hard with obvious displeasure.

"Mr. Van Horne," he said without rising, his voice deep and full of gravel. "To what do I owe this unexpected visit?"

"I wish a word with you, Professor." Flynt's expansive brow arched, and his eyes widened. "It concerns our previous transaction."

"Why would you want to dredge up that distasteful business?"

"I've been perplexed, sir, as to why a medical professor would rid himself of these two unfortunate boys. I expect your own students could've used 'em."

Flynt sat back in his chair and, with a sigh, pushed away from his desk, pen still in hand. He was dressed as were all these academics—in a drab wool suit kept too long from cleaning or refurbishment. Holes at the elbow were left unpatched. A dingy cravat was knotted sloppily around a collar that had long since lost its stiffness. Boots as dry and wrinkled as any formaldehyde-soaked cadaver poked from under his desk.

"You're inquisitive, Mr. Van Horne—more so than the run-of-the-mill body snatchers we've dealt with. And you're correct; I would've gladly kept the bodies for our anatomy course, but for the special circumstances."

"What circumstances would those be?" Nicolas asked, stepping further into his office in his hope to push Flynt to the point.

"Well, Thomas Chubb gave specific instructions to transfer the bodies to you. In a rush, as usual. A big rush. Thomas had the boys dropped here only a matter of hours before your train's arrival."

"Where did the boys come from?"

"That I can't tell you."

"I thought they were found in a snowdrift."

"Most likely, yes. They were frozen solid."

"The boys' bodies just mysteriously arrived at your doorstep?"

"The snowdrift made a good story. Only Thomas could tell you the full details."

"I suppose I shall ask him then."

"Look, Mr. Van Horne," Flynt said, clearly agitated, "I'm an assistant professor, charged with anatomic acquisitions, and my superiors make it clear every day that I'll remain in this lowly rank forever. I've known Thomas Chubb for years, ever since he was first in Buffalo, and Chubb's always made it worth my while to handle an occasional problem like these boys."

"You've done this before, then?"

Flynt squirmed in his chair before answering. He tossed the pen he still held on his desk. Nicolas thought about Thomas Chubb for a moment and realized that if this professor felt well compensated, Thomas was likely better compensated. The village undertaker was a shrewd one when it came to calculating shares and profits.

Flynt continued, refusing to meet Nicolas's eyes. "I admit I've helped Thomas with disposal for years now. Mostly boys, an occasional girl."

"Girls as well?"

"Young whores, I've always assumed, got on the wrong side of someone. These disposals are not upper-crust, Mr. Van Horne. Quite the opposite."

"Whores or lost youths, Professor, they're still living, breathing beings."

Flynt scowled. "Don't lecture me, Van Horne. I was a field surgeon at Bull Run, fresh out of medical training. I saw the value of this human life you speak of, and it doesn't count for much."

Flynt settled his elbows on his desk with a sigh and continued more slowly.

"No, honestly, I don't know where Thomas comes by them," he said. "That's how Thomas wants it. One observation I've made, though, suggests some connection. Most of these ragamuffins have a burn mark. A cypher. Perhaps it's some secret Masonic thing or other."

"Can you draw one for me?"

Flynt reached across his desk for a scrap of paper and penciled a figure. As he sketched, he said, "Looks to me like an insect. Hardly noticeable, except under close observation."

Nicolas studied the scrap. He did not need to search his memory hard to know where he'd seen it.

Ж

His hands trembled. He folded the paper and thrust it into his inner jacket pocket.

"Tell me, Dr. Flynt—have there been others you know of in my ice excursions . . . before these two boys, I mean?"

"You didn't know? A half dozen, perhaps a few more these past two winters. Before then I was asked to sink the boys in the lake. Weighed down with rocks . . . or concrete boots, you know?"

"What?" Nicolas was aghast. "You threw bodies in the lake? But why?"

"Oh, back then Thomas gave specific instructions for what he called his 'special disposals.' I've no idea why he started taking them to store in an icehouse somewhere upstate—your icehouse, I presume—instead of my more permanent means of disposal. Thomas has his reasons, I'm sure."

Shaking his head in disbelief, Nicolas went on. "Professor, I'm still not clear on this. My original question remains unanswered. Why didn't you put these two special disposals, as you call them, into your vats?"

"That's obvious, isn't it? If someone here at the college should recognize one of these bodies, and the law should get involved . . . well, that would be it for me. As the low man here, I'd take the blame and end up jailed, or worse. Maybe hanged. They'll hang you in a minute in Erie County."

Flynt saw the baffled look on Nicolas's face and raised his broad brow in surprise.

"Come now, Van Horne. These children aren't like other poor souls who come our way."

"What . . . what can you possibly mean?"

"Those two boys were murdered, Van Horne."

Nicolas swallowed hard. "Murdered?"

"Garroted. Quite expertly, too. Strangled to death. The ligature marks were faint but definitive, as they've been on most of these young bodies." Flynt leveled his pale eyes at Nicolas. "Yes, Van Horne, you've had murdered children in your ice. I presumed you knew." Suddenly shaken, Flynt stood. "I think I've said enough."

"I . . . I can't fathom . . . but I appreciate your frankness, Professor."

Flynt leaned on his desk without offering his hand. "I must say, Van Horne, you seem a cultured gentleman. I trust that all this will remain between the two of us? That includes Thomas—I'd hate to cross the man."

"I'll try, but I'm not so sure," Nicolas replied, perplexed. "*Everything* is confidential in this miserable business I've forged, but someday, sooner or later, I'm afraid it will *all* see the light of day."

28

Icy Return

At half past three in the morning the Adirondack Mail Express, scheduled for a midnight arrival, wheezed to a stop at the Forestport station. Freezing rain had drizzled through the night onto the wooden platform; ice an inch thick shone like glass underfoot. Lightning scored the sky. Men went tumbling, baggage splayed across the platform; women refused to climb down from their cars. The stationmaster himself took a tumble at the mail car, cursing, "Ga-dang it!" when his elbow struck with a crack and the mailbag disgorged onto the icy planks.

Nicolas and Adam inched their trunks across the sheet of ice to the depot door. Inside the waiting room, with their backs to the potbelly stove, the fine scale of frozen rain on the men's overcoats quickly turned to steam.

"Not a pretty welcome for us, eh, boss?"

"The mercury can't be thirty degrees. The lake'll be soft."

"I hate to say it, boss, but the gents I've been associating with in the dining car say it's the most awful warm spell they've seen. This one fella claimed the ice is already out at Otter Lake. Big Tupper, too. Let's hope it ain't gone out at Upper Spy."

At the mention of bad ice, Nicolas's guts tightened like the coils of a python. Nausea rose in his craw. The tinkling of bells sounded in his ears. It had to be the morphine, at least in part, but more important, there was an ice harvest to finish, an icehouse to fill.

The depot's door was thrown open and a coltish, sandy-haired young woman in a red plaid hunting jacket strode out of the drizzle. "Father!" she cried, throwing herself at Van Horne.

"Abby, sweet Abby." Nicolas sighed. He opened his arms wide and spun her around. "Oh, my baby girl." He tugged her to him, all dripping woolens and sodden deerskin mittens. "I've missed you more than anything."

Abigail Van Horne was her father's favorite, the little North Country girl who'd chased after him from her first awkward steps across the kitchen floor. She'd trailed him into the woods, clung to his coattails while he stood at the bar over a whiskey, and skidded behind him onto the ice of Upper Spy Lake.

"Seeing you, my dear, it's good to be home."

Nicolas felt his chest flutter and his eyes fill with tears; the serpent in his belly loosened its grip ever so slightly as the girl's arms, strong as any man's, wrapped around his neck and Abigail pulled herself up to deliver an enthusiastic kiss.

"Well, Lordy, Lordy," Adam said, looking on. When Abigail released her father, and Nicolas stepped back to the platform to see to the trunks, Adam grasped the comely eighteen-year-old by the shoulders. "Abigail, girl—you get prettier and prettier every time I set eyes on you. It's only been three weeks, and look at you. All you need's a bit more meat on your bones."

"Oh, Adam, you rogue," she laughed, stretching to kiss his cheek. "Why don't you fetch the wagon round front, mister. I brought the buckboard."

"Not enough snow for the sleigh, eh, Abby girl?"

With a sidewise glance to see that her father was out of earshot, Abigail leaned close and whispered, "Haven't had snow in weeks, Adam. It barely freezes at night."

Van Horne's right-hand man pushed back with a nod and stepped out into the weather.

"So, Father," Abigail said, again approaching Nicolas. "Deliveries went well?"

"We were on time in Chicago. Lost very little ice in the transfer."

"And the riverboats?"

"Shipped out well, and we were blessed with extremely skilled river pilots. Made delivery in Saint Louis and New Orleans ahead of schedule, then on to the new port in Texas."

"A profitable voyage, then."

"But how's the ice at Upper Spy, Abby? We've heard talk."

"I've been dreading telling you, Father, but right after you left the weather turned, the lake softened . . . and we've harvested nothing."

Nicolas staggered back; it was the thing he most dreaded. "Not a single cake of ice?"

"At camp there was nothing but drinking and pitch playing. A couple of fights among the Lynch brothers, no injuries. I released the crew back to the village days ago."

"*Damn!* This is my worst nightmare."

"And Mr. Chubb the undertaker stopped by the house fretting about the lack of ice."

Nicolas was quiet for a moment. He'd kept his trafficking in bodies a secret from Abigail, though he suspected she knew more than he let on. Indeed, he guessed most of the town surmised there was more to the Van Horne business than simple ice.

"What did Thomas have to say?" Nicolas asked.

"I didn't speak with him. He came by and bothered Mother. She said he was concerned there wouldn't be enough ice for 'his end' of your enterprise, and you'd know what he meant."

Nicolas nodded. In the Van Horne icehouse, he'd long ago declared certain rooms off-limits for everyone but him and Adam. Even as a child, Abigail must've known that the transactions in these ice rooms were different; her father only entered them late at night or in early morning, often with Thomas Chubb, who, for a so-called "family friend," rarely set foot inside the Van Horne household.

Abigail knew these things growing up, and what little girl wouldn't sneak a peek into a forbidden room, even one filled with ice? Perhaps, too, Abigail realized that the folks in Forestport treated her differently. Since she was a teenager, her best friends had always been the newcomers to town—those who hadn't yet heard the rumors.

"How's your mother's health faring?" Nicolas asked.

"The same as ever," Abigail said with a scowl and a dismissive wave. "She never leaves the house except to visit that quack Valdis."

"I've begged her about this. I've begged. Damned charlatan . . ."

Nicolas's spirits sagged further. He linked arms with Abigail and leaned into her as they stepped out of the station and into the freezing drizzle.

Adam had loaded their trunks and drawn the wagon, a small, open buckboard that was the handiwork of local wainwright George Parsons, to the station's dock. In his hometown at last, Nicolas gave his daughter a squeeze before climbing into the wagon in the freezing rain.

The trip had worn on Nicolas's nerves; it had been four long days and nights on the train. The noxious by-products of his Chicago mix pulsed in his veins, his guts twisted, and his heart beat an irregular staccato as he settled into the open wagon between his daughter and his right-hand man. Abigail gave their chestnut mare a slap of the reins. Her watery blue eyes—exact copies of Nicolas's—flashed in the station's lamplight, and the wagon bumped and slithered into the darkness on its way along the Black River to the village of Forestport and the house that Nicolas Van Horne called home.

29

The Homes of Forestport

In the moonless night the inky surface of the Black River Road wound toward Forestport like a broad-backed serpent. The woods still held a heavy snowpack, but the road was bare, rutted, and slow going. The three travelers huddled together on the plank of the buckboard and pulled a canvas tarp around them. The wool woodsman's caps they'd donned were soon encrusted with a cake of frozen slush. The only sounds were the gentle hiss of sleet and the *clomp clomp* of the mare's hooves in the half-frozen mud.

"Father—don't fret."

"You say don't fret, but you know as well as I do an ice drought will kill our local business. The icehouse is nearly empty, and now a thaw? The last ice harvest sustains us through the summer, Abby. Without it, we'll have nothing to supply the towns in the valley."

"All we need is one more cold snap, Father. I'll check the prediction from Albany at the telegraph office tomorrow."

"I'll trust my own weather instruments, thank you, before the blasted wire from Albany."

Abigail knew well her father's fanatical obsession with his instruments, though she'd be the first to admit he was usually right about the weather. "You need rest, Father," she said. "You've had a long voyage."

Soon, the houses of the village began to appear on the roadside.

The village of Forestport sprang up where the Black River emerges from the great Adirondack woods; it had always been a town of lumberjacks and mill workers. Each spring, when the ice went out of the lakes, rafts of logs crashed down the Black River to be hewn at Forestport's sawmill. The finished lumber was then floated on barges down the Forestport feeder canal to the Erie Canal and the rising cities of New York State.

The Black River widened where it flowed through the village of Forestport, slowing to a broad, still expanse of water known by the locals as "Town Lake." Town Lake divided Forestport into two parts—the north side and the south side. Abigail turned their buckboard down Mill Street to the poorer, south side of town, where a row of small, off-kilter frame houses leaned precariously toward the slushy surface of Town Lake. She rolled the wagon to a stop at Adam's house. In another quarter mile, Mill Street ended at Forestport Falls, where an escarpment of granite choked Town Lake into the cascade that drove the flume for the sawmill's six-foot-diameter ripsaw—a blade notorious for its size and speed, and the reason Forestport was known as a town of one-armed men.

Father and daughter helped Adam drag his seaman's chest through the back door of his pride and joy on Mill Street, a two-story frame structure without porch or portico. Three steps and they were in the kitchen.

Born in an Adirondack "rough camp"—a shack with little more than a roof and four tarpaper walls—Adam Klock had been raised among the hermits, reprobates, and recluses who inhabited the far north shore of Big Indian Lake. Attendance at common school was mandated through age twelve by New York State law, and Adam's strong Seneca mother would have no criminal under her roof, no matter how humble the home she provided. So Adam snowshoed for an hour to Forestport Common School, where he proved to be among the brightest of his classmates. During summer vacations Adam forgot his books and became a leader of a pack of wild boys ages nine to twelve—Nicolas Van Horne among them—who roamed the woods, creeks, and encampments of the Indian Lakes.

After common school Adam ran traplines across the Adirondacks, from the summits of the High Peaks to the bogs of the Moose River plains, sleeping on the cold ground, in a hollowed-out log, or, at best, in a makeshift lean-to. He worked the woods as a lumberjack. He amused city slickers as a backcountry guide who guaranteed the biggest fish. When he joined in the ice trade of his classmate Nicolas Van Horne, though, he married a sturdy Dutch woman, bought a lot on the south side of Forestport and built this house, squaring every pine board and hammering every nail. To Adam Klock—trapper, lumberjack, Adirondack guide, and jack-of-all-trades—this modest house on Mill Street was a castle.

Flashes of lightning glared off the whitewashed clapboards of Adam's place as Nicolas ducked his six-foot frame under the doorjamb and into the warmth of the kitchen. The two rooms on the first floor, a kitchen and front parlour, were low ceilinged and simply finished; a steep, narrow set of stairs led from the kitchen to the second floor, where the couple shared a bedroom with their four sons.

Adam's wife, Gertrude, was pulling sheets of strudel dough paper-thin on the kitchen table. "Thank the Lord!" she cried, throwing up her hands. "Home at last, you two wanderers."

Gertrude Klock, the daughter of a failed lumber baron, was a stocky, deeply religious woman and the chief ledger-keeper at the sawmill. It was unclear how she ended up married to the crazy part-Seneca, or how she'd cured him of his wild Indian ways, but whatever her methods, it was strong medicine.

"Ah, sweet Gertie!" Adam said with a light in his eye.

Gertrude opened her arms and hugged her husband, leaving a perfect set of handprints in flour on the back of his damp jacket. "I'm grateful, Mr. Van Horne." She reached out to flour Nicolas's hand. "Bless you for bringing him back in one piece."

The excitement raised a rattle in Gertrude's chest. She turned away to stifle a ragged cough. "Pardon me, but this dampness, this thawing weather…I was ailing something fierce while you men were gone," she said, without mentioning the word "consumption."

The tiny kitchen smelled of baking pastry and the first vapours from a coffeepot set to boil at the back of the stove. Once her cough subsided, Gertrude brushed the flour from her hands, stoked the fire in the kitchen stove with a stout chunk of maple, and invited the three travelers to "circle round and dry out." She wrapped her hands in a towel and pulled a hot pan of strudel from the oven. She set the pastry, oozing butter and the smell of cinnamon, on the cooling rack next to the stove, then took a moment to catch her breath.

"Gracious me, you must be fretting about the thaw, Mr. Van Horne."

"How long has it been like this, Gert?"

"Weeks. We'll just cool this sweet strudel a few minutes, and it'll take your mind off this awful weather."

She fixed a kind, tired gaze on Nicolas's eyes. Her lips, dark and off-color, trembled when she spoke again:

"You're one who's most deserving of God's bounty, if anyone is. I'm sure He'll see fit to bring you another month of Canadian air, and more ice."

"I hope you're right," Nicolas said with a sigh.

"I'll be praying for it."

Though sunrise was still an hour away, a ruckus was raised in the bedroom overhead and four sturdy boys with dark, glossy hair and bright smiles tumbled into the kitchen to thump and hug their father. The oldest, nearly a man at fifteen, offered Nicolas a hearty handshake and prepared to set off for his job in the woods. The younger boys rushed back upstairs to finish homework before school. Gertie cut thick chunks of her apple strudel and poured coffee. Abigail and Adam ate like wolves, but Nicolas wouldn't touch a crumb; his stomach had been filled with lead ever since Chicago.

Freezing drizzle had been falling steadily. When the Van Hornes left Adam's place, sheets of ice fell from the wagon wheels and shattered on the street like fine crystal.

Town Lake narrowed back to a river at the end of Mill Street, just above the sawmill. Abigail turned the wagon onto the steel bridge that crossed the river to the north side of town. Abigail hauled back on the reins in the bridge's middle and father and daughter sat without a word, watching the water beneath the mesh deck of the bridge and listening to the rumble of Forestport Falls downstream. The river under them swirled through sheets of pale ice, cutting channels the color of tea. Town Lake was a boggy slush; pools black as obsidian gathered on its surface.

"It feels like blasted spring is here," Nicolas whispered. "I don't like it."

Abigail shrugged and snapped the reins. At the end of the bridge the mare wound her way uphill.

The north side of Forestport—the rich side—was built on a hill that rose to a sharp ridge. As the village grew, it crept upward toward the ridge. Climbing the winding streets, the turrets, spires, and cupolas that crowned the houses appeared progressively more intricate, reflecting the rising status of the homeowner. Midway up were the canal builders. Perched along the moneyed top of the ridge were the railroad barons' homes, like a row of finely decorated Christmas cookies with their expansive summer porches and brightly painted gingerbread.

The family home of Nicolas Van Horne sat halfway up this slope of prosperity, on a street named Walnut lined—strangely—by giant maples. The Van Horne house was three stories, straight and sturdy, its third floor a single room with dormers all around. The exterior was ornamented with fish-scale and Germanic-style gingerbread, but its green paint had faded badly and even peeled in spots. Bits of gingerbread had fallen away with last spring's windstorm, and the steeply pitched tin roof had rusted through at its valleys, causing reddish-brown stains to run down the clapboards. Nicolas often thought how disappointed his father, Friedrick Van Horne, would've been to see how the fine house he'd built had aged . . . but then, perhaps not. The senior Van Horne had been no perfectionist.

"At last we have you home," Abigail said with a sigh.

"Home . . . such as it is," Nicolas said, hearing the gruffness of his long-dead father's voice in his own.

Nicolas, an only child, had been willed his childhood home on Walnut Street; he'd settled back in after college, when he began to build his business of ice and court his childhood sweetheart, the local schoolmarm. As Forestport grew and new construction stretched up the hill, the young Nicolas Van Horne found himself coveting the homes of the railroad barons that rose like castles above him. Even now, as Abigail drew up to the front entrance in the darkness, Nicolas glanced up the hill and felt a vague pang of longing upon seeing the silhouettes of the mansions of those better positioned in life.

The business of ice had been good to Nicolas Van Horne. He was a frugal Yankee who—unlike his father—had guarded his money wisely and capitalized on opportunity. He wasn't rich, yet he opened his purse for a worthy cause as readily as any rich man. It was more in family matters that Nicolas felt impoverished. One son died as a boy. His living son was a rogue and a piano-pounding vagabond; there was no gentler way to describe the young Schuyler Van Horne, known to his friends and shady associates as "Sky." Nicolas hadn't seen Schuyler since New Year's Day; he had no idea of his whereabouts.

Nicolas's beloved daughter, Abigail, had always been the silent, steady one. But in the first week of the new year she had also abandoned the Van Horne household, moving all her things to the home of her friend Hildegard Blum, a solid German woman a few years Abigail's senior. Hildegard hailed from the valley, the town of Amsterdam. She'd taken the position of principal of Forestport Common School two years earlier. Abigail led a quiet, happy life with Hilda, and Nicolas was glad for that. What hurt him was that his daughter felt so little regret in leaving the Van Horne household, and her childhood, behind.

Abby jumped down to help Nicolas wrestle his steamer trunk over the sheet of ice on the front porch. A light glowed faintly at a second-floor window, but Nicolas felt sure his arrival wouldn't be noticed. He lit a lamp in the hall. He and Abby slid his trunk down the front hallway and into the dining room.

"It's so late, Abigail. Why don't you stay the night?"

"No, Father, I need to be home. Hilda will be waiting." She hesitated, refused to look him in the eye. "There's other news, too, Father. Sky's in town."

"Schuyler's back?"

"My long-lost brother," Abigail said with more than a tinge of sarcasm. "Sky, the wandering minstrel. He showed up two days ago, needing money."

"Already? What's he done with all I gave him at New Year's?"

"Please, Father—let's not have a scene like that again. Mother couldn't stand it."

"I should give him nothing. Not a single copper. Where's he staying?"

"He took a room at the inn. I suggested he at least visit Mother, and I believe he did, but then he was off in a flash to play at Thomas Chubb's Steinway. He said he had 'associates' to meet, whoever they are."

"He hasn't changed, then," Nicolas said with a shake of his head.

"Perhaps he's borrowed what he needs from his friends."

"More likely they'll be running up a tab at the inn. I must see the boy."

"He'll come around."

"Ah, my baby girl," Nicolas said with resignation. He encircled his daughter's lithe frame, rocked her gently, and felt the delicate, birdlike strength that had been her mother's so many years before. "This voyage I've been through, Abby . . . some truly ghastly things happened, but I'm back in one piece."

"And tomorrow is another day." Abigail broke away, then hesitated as she passed the stairs. "I'll not bother Mother," she said wistfully, with a shake of her head. "You'll see to her."

Nicolas stood on the porch to watch Abby go. Now it was rain—simple and steady—that beat on the porch's tin roof. The chestnut mare pulled away on its downhill run to the small house on Main Street that Abigail and Hilda shared. Nicolas watched the wagon disappear in the darkness. He turned, shut the door, carried the lamp down the hall, and entered the parlour. The time had come to face the other inhabitants of this darkened house—his wife, Ruth, and the ghost of his father, Friedrick Van Horne.

30

A Ghost in the House

Nicolas carried the lamp close, felt its scant warmth, and watched its arthritic fingers of light flicker across the blackened knotty pine of the parlour walls. He lit a second lamp on the side table. Around him loomed the heads of a dozen deer slaughtered by his father decades earlier. Bobcats. A grizzled old panther with yellow teeth bared. A spike-horned deer—Nicolas's first kill as a youth—draped with cobwebs. The fireplace was boarded shut, unused for decades.

An old country saying among the superstitious holds that those who die a sudden death may take years to leave the earth. So it was with Nicolas's father, Friedrick Van Horne, who, like these beasts he'd collected, had made a sudden and unexpected rendezvous with his Maker, then haunted the town for years.

Friedrick Van Horne was a born upstate New Yorker, a particularly shrewd one who'd made a fortune building the locks and canals that within the span of two decades traced along every decent-sized creek and river feeding the mighty Erie Canal. But when the railroad like a monstrous sea creature extending its tentacles reached out to every town between Forestport and the Saint Lawrence River, the elder Van Horne's fortune began to shrink. His assets dwindled with the crack of each spike driven, with the thud of each rail laid, until the Forestport feeder canal dried up, and the paint began to peel from the Van Horne house.

Friedrick, who'd grown accustomed to luxury and leisure, found it difficult to feed his wife and his only child, the young sprout, Nicolas. Without holdings in land, the senior Van Horne could hardly take up farming; besides, he knew nothing about growing hops or potatoes and didn't care to learn. He loved the woods but deemed lumbering operations far too strenuous and dangerous for a once-successful canal man.

By the time he'd lost his wife to yellow fever, Nicolas's father was penniless. He spent his days fishing and hunting to put food on the table, and his nights in the taverns grousing at the bar about the "blasted railroad" and how it had changed the Adirondacks. On one such dismal night, desperate for funds,

Friedrick forged an agreement with the local innkeeper, Mr. Hulbert, to run his newly built inn and tavern.

Hulbert's Inn proved easy enough to manage, but the long hours and hard liquor quickly robbed Friedrick of his health. He drank Canadian whiskey for breakfast; beer became his nightly antidote for the delirium.

When Nicolas chose to go off to college in Boston, his father, standing half-drunk by the fireplace in this very parlour, refused to pay a nickel for tuition.

"Find a scheme, boy!" his father had declared. "That's all a young man needs. An enterprise, any sort will do, anything to keep from laying rail for the blasted railroad."

It was a month into Nicolas's senior year when the sad news came from Forestport that his father had been found dead in the outhouse early on a frosty October morning, still in his flannel nightgown, his dead wife's favorite afghan wrapped around him, his nightcap fallen sadly to the rough-hewn planks.

"Heart stoppage," the town doctor proclaimed at the funeral. "The man never knew what hit him."

He hadn't been buried a week before the taverns were buzzing with talk of Friedrick Van Horne's ghost. Banging, thumping, and ghastly wails came from the top floor of Hulbert's Inn. An eerie blue light passed from window to window. The inn was abandoned by its regulars and shut tight by Mr. Hulbert.

Then, after Christmas, when old man Van Horne had been frozen in the ground for months, the strange happenings moved to the Van Horne house on Walnut Street. Erratic flashes of light were seen in the dormer windows of the third floor. Protracted moans were heard overhead. The place became impossible to heat, no matter how hard Nicolas stoked the stoves.

Nicolas boarded the family home shut. After graduation from college, he returned to Forestport, found his calling in the ice business, and wed the local schoolmarm, Ruth Stuyvesant, daughter of the town lawyer. The newlyweds aired out the family home, painted it, and refurnished it. Only Friedrick's parlour was left untouched. The hauntings became nothing more than a low moan that might be taken for the wind on a gusty night.

Nicolas stepped into the dining room from his father's parlour. He paused by the oak table, laid a heavy hand on it. An unlit oil lamp. Rusting candlesticks. A pall of indifference thick in the air. Nicolas and Ruth had raised their family here, taken a hearty upstate supper every evening in this simple room. Now there was disuse, disinterest, and dust; the dining room was as abandoned and forlorn as Friedrick's parlour.

Nicolas threw open his trunk and felt for his new morphine works. He slipped the leather case and the vial of Magendie's solution into his jacket pocket. He extinguished the lamps in the parlour and walked in semidarkness to the foot of the stairs, where, lost in the stillness of the house, he hesitated, as if listening for a sound. Then he took the first of the creaking stairs to the second floor, and Ruth's room.

31

The Lady of the House

Nicolas found his wife, Ruth Van Horne, seated at the window in her second-floor bedroom. He knew he would find her here in her sagging willow-caned chair, knew exactly how she'd be staring out the window; he'd pictured her this way all the while he'd traveled south with the ice. With its fine view of the village and Town Lake below, Ruth had always preferred this room, but after her change of life came so early in her life, once the melancholy set in and hardened, she had rarely left it.

Outside, the rain had changed to sporadic waves of sleet that beat against the glass. Weak light fell from an oil lamp onto his wife's expressionless face. Nicolas reached to raise the wick and bring up the light.

"Oh, Nicolas, no," she said, frowning. "My dearest. Please don't. It's too horrid a night."

He lowered the light back to dull yellow. A smile flicked across his wife's face as Nicolas brushed his lips across her dry, rough cheek.

"Your business down south was good, I take it?"

"Excellent. Have you managed?"

"What a blessing our dear Abigail is. And that lovely friend of hers, Hilda…every evening that good woman fed me a warm supper."

Nicolas straightened, waited for her to speak again, though he knew with certainty the only topic of interest to her.

"Valdis is recommending Saratoga again, dear. Another water cure."

Valdis! he thought. They'd argued about that quack just minutes before he left with the ice. Valdis haunted him throughout the South.

"Now, dearest, we'll have none of that old water cure business," he protested gently, the years of "cures" running through his mind . . . the hot soaks, the cold dunkings, the endless search for another spring. "Saratoga's waters surely must've lost any healthful qualities by now."

"Saratoga has facilities, dispensaries, manipulators. Valdis says—"

"Oh, Ruth, I don't know, I just don't know," he said, shaking his head at the more gruesome cures she'd tried—the fasting, the purges, the shocks of electricity. *Valdis.* "The man doesn't have a medical degree, for heaven's sakes, Ruth. I wish I knew what you need, what would help." He took her shoulder and looked into her slate-grey eyes. "Come daylight, I'll go to Boatmann and have the old boy mix up a fresh draught of laudanum."

Nicolas remembered the morphine in his pocket. He'd retrieved it with Ruth in mind but thought better of it. "For now," he said, stepping to the sideboard, "let's try a touch of the old laudanum, shall we?"

How had his dear wife come to this? The Ruth Stuyvesant he knew when he was a gangly schoolboy had been the gayest of girls, the cleverest and the brightest chalking the alphabet onto the board in Forestport's one-room schoolhouse. He singled her out at the lunchtime square dances. A schoolyard romance blossomed. At fourteen, Nicolas purposely crashed his toboggan at the foot of Carney's Hill, just so they'd be clutched together in the snow and he might steal his first kiss. He steered them to crash after crash after that, until Ruth stayed his hand as it wandered from his mitten to soft, forbidden places. She'd said, "We must wait for marriage, Nicolas."

Ruth Stuyvesant was destined to be a schoolmarm. From her first days in the classroom of Forestport Common School, with her face buried in a book, everyone knew. In the Stuyvesant household, she refused to cook, clean, or sew. Her three sisters groused. Her mother scolded. Only her father, Gustav Stuyvesant, the town lawyer and a dour, cheerless man given to deep fits of melancholy, encouraged Ruth's scholarly bent. He was devoted to Ruth. She read law in his library. He took her on mountain treks, instructing her in the fine points of fishing and hunting.

As expected, Ruth entered teacher's college. The couple made promises. Fidelity. Betrothal. Nicolas spent a year at Fairfield Academy, then Boston and college. Always there was gaiety and hope. That Ruth Stuyvesant of long ago was not the woman who sat before him now . . .

At the sideboard, Nicolas uncapped a small brown bottle, poured a splash of brandy into a medicine glass, and measured ten drops of laudanum from the bottle with an eyedropper. Thinking again, he added five more.

"I'll be off to the lake soon, Ruth. I must see how bad the ice has gotten."

"You're always away with the ice," she said. "Since...I can't remember...it's been—"

"Here. Take this."

Nicolas remembered the first blow that shook Ruth's foundation: It was her first year as the schoolmarm. She was freshly equipped with a "New York State Teacher's Certificate of Competency in the Modern Curriculum," teaching grades one through six. Her beloved father, Gustav—distraught over a pressing matter of law—was found hanging from the rafters of their horse barn, dead by his own hand.

When Nicolas returned to Forestport after college, he found his childhood sweetheart morose and distant. He remembered her for her woodsy ways, deep voice, misty hazel eyes, and shining auburn hair, and quickly pressed his youthful desire for the woman he once knew. Gradually, Ruth's melancholy melted away. She began wearing her lustrous auburn hair daringly bobbed.

Nicolas was madly in love, and Ruth could hardly defend against the charms of this tall, educated gentleman known in town as "that clever Van Horne boy." Nicolas was making a name for himself cutting ice. Indeed, Ruth was so smitten with Nicolas's advances that, despite her earlier intentions, a son to be named Ethan soon quickened in her womb.

When Nicolas learned of this twist of fate, the lovers took to long walks along the furthest bank of Town Lake, where secluded, grassy knolls and moss-covered outcroppings of rock offered the privacy they longed for. There they vowed to marry, lakeside, on a warm, moonlit August evening while clouds of bats swooped over the glassy water.

"Yes, we'll marry, sure," she said, her eyes alight.

"With your little secret, it's the proper thing to do."

"Oh, come now, Nicolas," she said, giving him a nudge. "What do we care about being proper?"

They were silent for a long moment, arm in arm, looking out over Town Lake.

"Aren't the bats marvelous?" she said dreamily. "Look at them . . . how they feed without a sound . . . thousands of them . . . perhaps it's a million."

Now, in her darkened room, Ruth's indifferent gaze was fixed on the dreary weather. A blast of slushy hail slapped against the glass, rattling the panes. "Heavens!" she cried, clawing at the air in front of her. "My nerves." She settled back; her hands trembled on the arms of the chair. Her dull hair, cracked and greying, sprawled across her eyes. "You see, Valdis believes it's a matter of a woman's spleen. 'Female syndrome,' he calls it."

"Melancholy, I call it. Now take your medicine."

"That laudanum—Valdis says there's a danger of morphine, a thing he called 'nervous waste.'"

"Enough of Valdis!" He groaned, immediately sorry. She was so fragile, like fine china. "Please don't fret over such nonsense, Ruth. Your doses are low. Now here, drink it all . . ."

Nicolas had heard plenty about nervous waste syndrome. It seemed that persons of a weak constitution or will had their brains addled by morphine. They lost all interest in life and wasted away as if starving to death. Nowadays such weak-minded souls were advised against the use of morphine, especially by hypodermic.

"Here now, I'll fix your coverlet," he said. "Soon you'll be fast asleep." He'd taken care to measure an adequate, relaxing dose. Fifteen drops would assure a full night's rest.

Ruth went quiet and slumped in her chair, fast asleep. Nicolas set the empty medicine glass down and organized the clutter on the table—a jumble of eyedroppers with worn rubber bulbs, powders, pills, and herbal potions. As he'd done so often in the past two years, Nicolas lifted his wife to her bed. She seemed lighter than he remembered, lighter even than on their wedding night, when he'd lifted her over the threshold of their room at the Butterfield House.

Once they'd decided to marry, Nicolas saw little reason to rush to the altar. After all, Ruth had no father to force a shotgun wedding. All of Forestport knew the simple truth. The memory of her gibbous wedding dress and grand reception at the Butterfield House was still fresh in the town's mind when Ruth went into labor with their firstborn child, Ethan.

But their infant son proved sickly. Slow to gain weight, he suffered bouts of pneumonia and colic. Nicolas hired a nanny. Ruth returned to her classroom. Nicolas, preoccupied with his blossoming ice enterprise, was absent for months at a time. Ruth filled her solitary days with teaching duties, her evenings with the frail Ethan, and her free time in the various social involvements of a quiet village rich in private intrigues.

Nicolas was surprised when a second son, Schuyler, came on the heels of Ruth's loneliness. With his rare times at home, he thanked lady luck. But while baby Schuyler grew hale and pudgy, Ethan took on a dusky hue. Boonville's doctor heard disconcerting sounds in the three-year-old's chest and advised a visit to the medical college in Albany for an opinion. There, a "condition of the heart" sealed the boy's doom; Ruth was despondent. Her first son would never grow to be a man.

During the ice season that followed the bad news, Nicolas lingered at home more than was his habit and a daughter, Abigail, was conceived. Ruth trudged through the snowdrifts to light the schoolhouse stove and chalk the three R's on her board. During summer break, Ruth retreated with her children to the Van Hornes' second home, a lake house on Upper Spy. The piney air seemed good for the sickly Ethan, and Ruth fished the shoals in her beloved Rushton skiff.

Then came the horror of Ethan's loss. At age eight, his growth stunted to the size of a five-year-old, the boy was lost to the Adirondack woods. He was off on a short jaunt on the Town Lake trail . . . alone . . . and was never found. After weeks of searching Nicolas came to accept this cruel trick of nature. The bereaved mother, however, was left with a deep, unrelenting melancholy.

Ruth was powerless against an endless assault of sweats, chills, and night terrors. She grew sulky. She drew into herself, irritated by Abigail's youthful antics, oblivious to Schuyler's uncanny talent at the piano lessons he took from Thomas Chubb on Thomas's fine Steinway piano. At the lake, Ruth's Rushton skiff sat in the boathouse unused, its fine cedar planking unvarnished. Her split cane fishing poles gathered dust, reels rusted, and fine silk line went to rot.

With autumn, the schoolmarm didn't appear at the front of her class. Nicolas made excuses. At first the town board listened and waited, but "youngsters need learning," as they said, and a new girl was hired. Ruth had already taken to her room.

Nicolas covered his sleeping wife with a feather duvet and swept the hair away from her face. He lit a candle, extinguished the lamp, and stepped into the hall to climb the steep, narrow stairs to the solitary attic room above. His room.

32

A Garret Room

Nicolas set the candle on the small bedside table. With Ruth's constant melancholy, a husband had become just one more irritation. Sensing this, Nicolas had moved his things up the narrow stairway to this third-floor garret, a room filled with the sharp, ugly angles of a steeply pitched roof and narrow dormer windows. He retreated here every day at sunset to watch the room fill with shadows. The pine planks of the floor became worn smooth under his step. Around him, the walls of horsehair plaster and lath, stained from years of sporadic roof leaks, began to crumble.

Sleep would not come easily this evening. The horrors he'd seen in Galveston and the powerful feelings he'd grappled with still haunted him. He couldn't shake the revelations of Professor Flynt about the dead boys in Buffalo. It seemed his life had been cursed with dead boys ever since the loss of Ethan. Now, more worries: a thaw, an early spring, bad ice. And Ruth.

At the north dormer, Nicolas cursed the hellacious weather. A winter's worth of melting ice and snow drooped from the roof and threatened to tear loose the tin gutters. The maple trees lining the street were encased in sheaths of ice, their branches bowed. To the north, lightning struck at the mountains, as if all of heaven's power were focused on the Old Forge ironworks in retribution for the open wound its mines had inflicted on the earth's fragile crust.

Nicolas's body craved morphine's dreamless sleep. He picked up the candle again and tiptoed down the stairs to Ruth's room. He slipped his works into his jacket from the sideboard. Turning to the door, he looked at Ruth, motionless under her feather bed, her skin pale and chalky. Ruth's weight was off; he'd felt it lifting her to bed, her limbs frail, her cheeks sunken . . .

Back at his dormer window Nicolas watched a cloud-choked sky refuse to give way to dawn. He set his works on the bedside table and curled into himself on top of his cold bed. Why was he constantly pursued, into his bedroom, into his sleep, by dead boys? Dead boys in his dreams, dead boys in his ice . . . though the two in his ice, murdered boys, were real enough. Too real. And the undertaker, Thomas Chubb, knew something about them.

He must talk to Thomas.

33

Sky Van Horne

He was snatched from sleep by the distant rumble of thunder. It was only moments past sunrise; pale morning light shone at the dormer window. Thin sheets of rain washed down the windowpanes.

Thunder sounded again . . . no, it wasn't thunder; the sound came from far below, downstairs, a low, distant slamming of a door breaking the silence of his garret room where even the wall clock, unwound, had not ticked in weeks. Then the scraping of a chair, barely audible.

Nicolas rolled from bed and pulled on pants and shirt. His head throbbed from too little sleep. The serpent coiled in his belly tensed. Groggily, he took to the stairs and staggered to their foot, two short flights. A lamp was lit in his study and there stood the wayward Van Horne, his son Schuyler, at Nicolas's secretary. He had its bottom drawers opened and papers pulled out.

"Sky?"

Schuyler looked up from the papers. "Oh! Father. You're home." He rocked back on his heels. "I was wondering when you'd get back from down south."

Schuyler's dark hazel eyes were shot through with a long evening's worth of carousing. The lids drooped unevenly. Despite his twenty years, Schuyler Van Horne had never reached his father's height, standing a good four or five inches shorter. A life of dissipation had softened his youthful middle and widened his girth to that of a man twice his age.

"What is it you're doing, Son?"

"Why, I'm borrowing some sheets of your stationery. I asked Mums, and she said it seemed perfectly all right. I'm planning a few small notes of promise in the village."

"Notes of promise? Promising what?"

"Ice. The businessmen are looking toward the summer, Father. The inns and such."

"You're writing notes for my ice?"

"It's that . . . I'm in need of funds for my ventures, Father. Mums said it was fine, a few small advances."

"But . . . but she shouldn't . . . you shouldn't," Nicolas said, perplexed, his voice rising, "and besides . . . how would you know what to charge?"

"Well, I'll ask them."

"Ask the purchaser to name his price? They'll tell you anything."

"Perhaps they'll have a bidding war."

"On my ice?" Nicolas circled the desk, leaned closer, and pointed out the window at the steady drizzle. "Look at this thaw, Son. We may have no ice this summer."

"But Mums said . . . Mums—"

"Schuyler—you disappear from the face of the earth when the first man steps onto Upper Spy, and now you sell my ice to put gold eagles in your pocket?"

"Father, you weren't here. I'm in need of funds for my musical enterprise in New York. The city is fabulous, I tell you. The cabarets, the dancing, the racket we make. They say it's like the beating of a thousand tin pans."

"Tin pans?"

"Until now, I admit, I've been nothing but a song plugger, hammering on the piano into the wee hours, but my chance has finally come. I mean it. The publishers love my work—they're playing my songs on the west side, on Twenty-Eighth Street, where all the gaiety is. You must see it to believe it. And my songs are published. They're published!"

Nicolas shook his head in disbelief. He knew little about New York City. The ice traders of Connecticut and Massachusetts supplied Manhattan; there was little reason for Nicolas to venture beyond Albany.

"But, Son . . ." Nicolas choked on the word. His face reddened. Rage ratcheted its grip on him.

Nicolas was not a violent man; he disliked fisticuffs, had no stomach for battles. During the Great War, he'd refused to muster with the Ninety-Seventh Regiment of Colonel Charles Wheelock to march south out of Boonville and fight on the fields at Manassas and Gettysburg. But now, this minute, he wanted nothing more than to grapple his only living son to the ground and throttle him.

Nicolas lunged toward Schuyler, then checked himself inches from his face. He struggled to keep his trembling hands at his sides.

"You fool! You're a disgrace!"

Schuyler's mouth dropped. He stepped back. "Father, I only meant—"

"How did I ever come to have a son who steals from me?"

"Steal?"

"Behind my back!"

"Just because you operate an icehouse? Because you're the trader? You should be happy to share with your kin."

"I give you everything!"

"I'm your son!"

Schuyler sidled away from the secretary with Van Horne & Co. stationery still clutched in his hand. He edged around his father and toward the study door.

"I'm your only son. Don't forget that."

The door swung shut and Nicolas, his head hanging, was left trembling in the middle of his study.

"My only son."

34

Thomas Chubb

Nicolas's mouth was dry with rage. "That miserable boy," he muttered, staggering to the kitchen to slake his thirst. "He'll rob me of my health, he will, along with all else that's gone so awry." Nicolas worked the kitchen pump with a fury. "I'll change that boy, somehow. I will." He took great gulps of cool, sweet well water, and the serpent released its grip on his innards.

"But first, I'd better cool down. Give it time. It's Thomas I must see today."

The house was silent. Nicolas was eager to check his weather instruments, but that took hours and could wait until after a talk with Thomas.

Nicolas climbed the stairs. Ruth lay motionless, fast asleep. Outside her windows the drizzle had turned to mist and fog. He collected their chamber pots and carried them out the kitchen door to the outhouse, which was tucked into the pines at the back of the house, nearly to the property line. There was neighing from the horse barn; the animals were in need of feed and water. He decided to stop by Abigail's on his way down the hill; she'd gladly do the morning chores—the horses, the henhouse, collecting the eggs, changing straw—all tasks that a loving daughter tended to in her father's absence.

Nicolas had eaten practically nothing since the steak dinner in Chicago, yet he didn't feel the least rumbling of hunger. He decided he'd fast today. He'd starve the damned serpent.

There were details of business to attend to, but foremost was a talk with his accomplice in the body business. And Nicolas knew just where Thomas Chubb was to be found; he need only trudge down the hill and slog through the mud of Mill Street . . .

Thomas Chubb, the third-generation village undertaker, had been groomed from childhood to take over the family business. As a young boy, he'd joined his father in the prep room in the cellar, where he quickly learned to assist with the pumps and fluids. In Forestport's schoolroom he was a loner among normal children but an inquisitive and bright pupil. After common school and a single, unhappy year at Fairfield Academy, Thomas was shipped off to learn the latest advances in the family's trade at the Buffalo Scientific Institute of Embalming, Undertaking, and Mortuary Sciences.

Thomas accomplished much in Buffalo. Embalming was a new art, and great scientific advances had been made since the Slaveholders' War provided so many bodies in need of burial. Thomas completed the institute's advanced course of study, excelled in the use of the trocar, and exhibited a singular talent in the reconstructive and cosmetic arts. He created a unique palette of rouges and paints, which he employed in unique and discriminating ways. Thomas was recognized as a strange bird, but clever, resourceful, and creative. His advanced independent studies during the wee hours of the morning in the institute's laboratories yielded novel embalming fluids with greatly enhanced preservative powers achieved by chemical innovations that were deserving of patents but that Thomas refused to disclose to his instructors.

Buffalo uncovered other, hidden talents in Thomas. He took up pianoforte and soon astounded the learned faculty at the Buffalo School of Artistic Expression with his exceptional musical talent, so much so that upon his return to Forestport his parents had the finest Steinway, the first and only grand piano in town, shipped from New York and installed in their downstairs parlour. At funerals, Thomas would tickle the ivory keys with gloomy renditions of the deceased's favorite melodies. Off hours, he bewitched the ladies of Forestport with his playing, giving private lessons to only a select few in the village. Indeed, it was Thomas Chubb's skilled tutorship that instilled a lifelong love of music in Schuyler Van Horne.

In his youth, Thomas Chubb cut a dashing figure in the village. Forestport had prospered; folks could afford coffins and funerals; and by the time his parents passed on, Thomas had become well-to-do. His company was eagerly sought by the town's young women. He indulged himself in food and drink, as had his father before him. He grew a bit broad in the beam.

As Thomas approached middle age, the eligible ladies of Forestport married off and the undertaker, whose light brown eyes and skill at the piano had once been so desirable, became reclusive. When no funeral was in progress, Thomas retreated to Stillman's barroom, his favorite haunt. He traveled often to larger cities, especially Buffalo, on business. It was well-known in the village that he indulged in daily doses of morphine, which—according to Boatmann, the apothecary—Thomas's great bulk seemed to absorb with little effect.

Nicolas steeled himself on the walk down Mill Street to Stillman's Inn, the small corner bar where the undertaker would be having his morning whiskey. The piles of dirty snow were melting fast. Trudging in the muddy street,

Nicolas felt the acute need of a whiskey; something dense and smoky like Professor Keiller's Scotch would suit him, but the thought of Keiller's whiskey brought a flood of disquieting Galveston memories, and he put it out of mind. Besides, Scotch as fine as Keiller's wouldn't be found at Stillman's.

Nicolas pulled open the barroom door and stepped in. It was hot and stank of stale beer and overflowing spittoons. Old man Stillman had hired a new bartender, a one-armed man who was a half-wit to boot. It was the mildest of late winter days; in spite of that, the simpleton bartender had stoked the potbelly stove in the corner to near its melting point. More than ever, Nicolas craved a cool whiskey.

Thomas Chubb was at the far end of a line of men hunched over their drinks at the bar. For Nicolas, the sight of his accomplice in the body trade, his belly rubbing against the mahogany, was a jolt. It was back to business now. Nicolas passed a greeting to the few men who looked up from their glasses.

Thomas shuffled his bulk further down the bar into the darkened corner. "Back in town, eh, Van Horne?" he said, motioning with a doughy hand. Thomas had a finely featured, round face that bordered on womanly, but for the three-day growth of stubble. Nicolas walked to the end of the bar, where he caught a sour odor from the undertaker. When he held a funeral, Thomas wore an expensive suit and was as fine-smelling as any citified dandy. Now, off duty, he apparently went unwashed.

Thomas made a hissing sound under his breath. "Christ, Van Horne," he said softly, "weren't you ever going to seek me out? How long have you been in Forestport?"

"Barely hours, Thomas."

The barman approached, wrapped in a moth-eaten winter coat and with a simple smile set on his face. "Rye," Nicolas said to him. "Canadian, with plenty of ice, and another for Thomas." The barman stepped away to the sink and began bashing away at a block of Van Horne ice.

Thomas said, "I stopped at your place the other day."

"You know how I feel about keeping my business out of the house, Thomas."

"I talked with Ruth. Did you get the message?"

"I did, from Abigail."

"We're in a mess. This thaw. Don't you realize?"

"Better than anyone." Nicolas turned and looked the undertaker in the eye. "But I've something else I want to know about, Thomas. You need to tell me about that delivery in Buffalo, the big rush." Nicolas saw Chubb's jaw clench. "How do you know this fellow Flynt, the professor with the bodies?"

"Oh, Flynt? Austin Flynt's been my associate for years."

"What kind of associate, Thomas?"

"He was of some small assistance in developing my embalming techniques. A bright boy, back then. Flynt's a chemist by training, but by no means was he destined for greatness in the medical world, despite his skills with alchemy."

"And those boys' bodies?"

"Austin Flynt's always been ready to negotiate for a specimen or two."

"He told me those two boys were murdered, Thomas. *Murdered.* That's why he got rid of them."

Thomas gave a halfhearted, shaky laugh. "Oh, nonsense. Old Flynt sees intrigue around every corner. Way back, he was sure I gypped him out of a patent, but that was nonsense, too. The man suffers from an overactive imagination."

The barkeep plunked their whiskeys down. Nicolas waited until the doltish barman drifted down the bar and was again feeding the white-hot stove.

"I'm telling you, Thomas, Flynt found physical signs. He was sure the boys were strangled."

"Well, what did *you* see, Nicolas? You had them in your possession."

"The one boy had dark grooves on his neck. I'm not . . . not exactly sure how to describe it."

"Then why get yourself lathered over nothing, eh?"

"There was a mark, too, a brand." Nicolas searched his jacket pocket for that scrap of paper Flynt had given him. He couldn't seem to locate it.

Thomas stared impatiently at his whiskey, turned it in his hand. "So what, anyway? What if some violence did befall them?" he said with a smirk. "We didn't do it. And profit is profit."

"Murder, Thomas, *murder.* Authorities must be informed, the culprit brought to justice."

"Oh, authorities, is it? Look, Nicolas—there are lost souls in this world. No one notices when one goes missing."

"Does it mean so much to you to make a dollar?"

"Look to yourself on that score, Van Horne. Whatever I've done, I've done for you—your business and your family. You know that. They're like my own. So, enough said."

Nicolas lifted his glass and drank. He should've expected as much from Thomas. The man was a talker, someone who could turn a thing around on you. Sure, his time in Buffalo had put a sensitive, artistic veneer on him, but under the silvery chatter he was a slick operator, a ruthless conniver. Thomas Chubb's funerals were heartfelt events with the overpowering aroma of fresh flowers and the plaintive tickling of the keys he did so well. But in reality, the undertaker was extraordinarily cunning with family members. He heartlessly overcharged the bereaved. He exuded compassion just moments after he'd lifted jewelry from a corpse and extracted its gold teeth. He buried empty coffins. For this—the empty coffins—Nicolas paid well. But now, watching Thomas stare into his whiskey, the ice trader wondered who else had paid the undertaker over the years, and for what services.

"I've put three new ones in your icehouse," Thomas said. "They came down from the sanitarium at Saranac. Got 'em into your ice, nicely embalmed, with the help of your daughter."

"Abigail?"

"Such a sweet girl. She knows the icehouse well. When we transferred the last one from my vault, the blocks in the icehouse were shrinking fast. The lake was mush, and that was over a week ago."

Nicolas pulled hard on his drink and waved the bartender over. He laid a coin on the bar and nodded at their two glasses.

"All we need's one last cold snap, Thomas."

"What if it doesn't come? Winter may be over; it's happened before. I've pickled them, sure, but they need ice. What will we do if they putrefy?"

"You'll bury them."

"Bury," Thomas said sourly.

"Don't worry. You'll be paid."

"And there's more coming, Nicolas. Two days ago I got word from the Moose River Lumber Company. That's what I went to your house to tell you. They've got bodies in an ice cave up there, waiting."

"I'll send Adam."

Thomas gave a perfunctory nod.

"How many are there?"

"I'm not sure. Two, maybe three. It's feast or famine, eh?"

Nicolas looked into the undertaker's watery brown eyes. "You've had them in my ice before, haven't you?" he said. "Haven't you? Those boys. Where do they come from . . . ones like Flynt had this time?"

"Oh, let it go."

"Where, Thomas?"

The undertaker waited a beat, then slurped more whiskey before speaking. "Mostly . . . mostly the cities," he said, reluctantly. "Buffalo. I've had them from Chicago."

"But why? *Why murdered children?*"

"*Oh Christ, Nicolas!* They're castoffs. Don't think twice about it. There's plenty of lost souls working the factories, the mines . . . there's profit for everyone. Let's leave it at that."

Nicolas drained his rough-edged rye in one chill slug and stared into the glass of ice clutched in his hand. This business was wearing on him. He crushed a sharp-edged piece of Van Horne ice between his back teeth, set down his glass, and gave Chubb a perfunctory wave. He'd get no more out of the undertaker. "See ya, Thomas."

Nicolas moved up the bar, passed a comment to the grinning barman. He bought a drink for an older gent who'd once worked the ice, clapped the fellow on the back.

Yes, business was wearing on him.

Once he'd stepped back onto Mill Street, the thawing earth smelled like the last of winter. He slowed his pace at the steel bridge, crossed halfway, and stopped to look over Town Lake where it narrowed into a flowing torrent of brown water. The lake's surface was grey with mist. Chunks of ice scoured the shore. Stillman's cheap whiskey hit his empty stomach hard. His head spun.

Just across the bridge on Main Street sat the U.S. Postal Office, where customers were filing in to make the noon mail train with their postings. He had much to accomplish before the last ice harvest, if it ever came. For one thing, there was a letter to compose, a letter promised to Galveston.

35

Instruments of the Weather

Nicolas turned back onto Mill Street and made his way to Adam's house. He knocked, waited, thought no one was home; clearly Adam wasn't about, and Gertrude Klock would be at her job at the mill. Then he heard a ghastly cough and Gert pulled open the kitchen door.

"Adam's off somewhere . . . ," she said, her voice a whisper. "I'm afraid I'm feeling poorly today."

"Sorry to hear that. Please have Adam stop at the house as soon possible, if you would."

"Surely."

"Gert, you must think seriously about a stay at Saranac."

"But, Mr. Van Horne, they're so costly, those places—"

"Now hush about that. We'll see to it come summer, so don't fret. Hope you're feeling better."

Nicolas crossed the bridge and set off down Main Street. Fog clung to the streets; it was a dead calm, so dreaded by seafaring men. Nicolas quickly settled accounts with the dry-goods merchant, Parson's carriage shop, the livery, and the railroad officer. Once the debts accrued from his trip south were cleared, he continued directly to Boatmann's Apothecary for Ruth's medicinals. Would there be something new for her? Something more potent? But Mr. Boatmann had little to offer.

"I'll alter her usual draught," the grizzly old apothecary suggested halfheartedly. "More of the alcoholic base might help, although you and I both know it's the laudanum that does the trick."

"She's also requested something Valdis recommended," Nicolas added.

"That'd be his latest." Boatmann reached for a bright blue bottle. "A clyster. Another fad from the good professor Valdis."

"Valdis is no professor, Mr. Boatmann."

"Of course he isn't," the apothecary said with a chuckle. "He just thinks he is, so why not humor the man? Now, with this latest preparation"—the apothecary held up the bottle—"have her add a pint of strong coffee before use."

"Snake oil, I say."

At the foot of Walnut Street, with Boatmann's brown paper package under his arm, Nicolas entered the Butterfield House, the largest of the town's three inns, to purchase a jug of hot chowder for Ruth's supper. Then, climbing the ridge, he caught a momentary breeze from the north. Was a chill in the air? His pace quickened.

Ruth sat in her chair and spooned up the fish chowder. "I suppose you'll be off to the lake soon," she said.

"I have yet to check the instruments."

"Would you bring me water for a wash-up?"

He heated water in the kitchen and filled her washbasin. When he carried the basin in to her, Ruth stood by the window. The pale grey afternoon light outlined a figure that was too full, too protuberant. He'd noticed that roundness last night as she slept. She looked like she was with child. It made him think of those treasured nights in bed when, pressed against Ruth's warm, healthy body, he'd felt the vigorous kick of a life that hadn't yet seen daylight. But this was something unnatural, a different sort of swelling.

Nicolas left her to her toilette and went to the shed at the back of the house, eager to check his weather instruments.

Early in his enterprise of ice Nicolas had dedicated a small, low shed at the fence line beyond the horse barn to serve dual purposes. For one, it was here he devised and perfected the machinery to harvest ice. Bolted onto the workbenches lining the walls of his shed were lathes, drills, and jigs for the cutting, turning, and fitting of metal parts. In the center of the floor sat the latest Van Horne innovation—a German engine that Nicolas had converted to run on a fuel called gasoline, rather than on naphtha, the highly volatile petroleum distillate that powered the motor launches of the great Saint Lawrence, and the broad expanse of Raquette Lake.

Besides machinist's tools, Nicolas had accumulated all the instruments of a professional meteorologist in his shed. On one bench top sat a barometric apparatus—silver filled—and a sling psychrometer. Mounted on the tin roof were a weather vane, anemometer for taking wind velocity, and rain gauge. Fixed to the outer walls of the shed were Nicolas's mercury thermometer and a glass cylinder filled with oil extracted from shark's liver—an ancient and accurate mariners' device for forecasting weather.

Nicolas made several entries in his log. He repeated all measurements three times. He found the wind velocity minimal from the south, the air temperature still well above the freezing mark, and the level of silver in his barometric apparatus steady. The shark oil appeared clear; the thin layer of white sediment on the bottom of the cylinder indicated the weather would hold. As he rechecked his entries, he noted that the barometer had fallen three marks, a slight change, over the past two hours. A chance for snow? The clarity of the shark oil suggested otherwise. It would be at least two or three days. Nothing indicated a movement of cold air from Canada.

Nicolas dutifully recorded his dismal observations. Back in the kitchen, he heard movement in Ruth's room and went to her. Ruth had changed into a long, somber dress with a tightly bound bodice. She'd tied her hair back and pulled her boots from under the bed.

Just past dusk, a large landau drawn by two bay horses pulled up at the front porch. Behind the driver sat five middle-aged ladies wearing fur hats and wrapped in shawls and afghans far too warm for such a mild evening.

Nicolas knew whose carriage this was . . . *Valdis! Valdis's landau, with Valdis's hired man at the reins and foot warmers stoked for ladies of a delicate constitution on their way to a snake oil show.*

"He's speaking at the Grange hall this evening," Ruth said.

"Ruth, please don't."

"I must be off. My friends are waiting." She climbed into the carriage in a lightly falling snow, and the carriage clattered down the hill.

In his study, Nicolas cleared his Chippendale secretary of the ledger books and tallies of his southern successes. Galveston, he knew, lay under a bright Texas sun, far from this village of tightly shut, simple frame structures. The medical college, its noble faculty and dedicated students, the scientists' troubles and their search for a cure for yellow fever—all of it came to mind with crystal clarity, unobscured by distance or time. He pulled a clean sheet of paper from a drawer.

He'd promised to take up a pen, had he not? Was he so false a person that he could not complete a simple letter to keep a promise?

36

The Willing Daughter

Nicolas's concentration was broken when Adam strode through the back door of the Van Horne household with Abigail Van Horne in tow. Both were breathless. It was well into the evening hours.

"We heard all about it, boss," Adam said. "They got something for us at the Moose River outfit. See, Chubb was coming out of Stillman's—"

"*Stumbling* out, I'd say," Abby added, pulling a face.

"Chubb said there's quite a number."

Chagrined, Nicolas said, "Watch how you talk, Adam." He threw a glance at Abigail.

"Come now, boss. Abby's no fool. While you were gone—"

Abigail nudged Adam out of the way and faced her father. "Let's drop the pretense, Father dear. I'm no longer a child. I know about your business. Everything."

"Well we needn't talk about it."

"Look at it this way, Father—Adam can use help fetching what's in the woods. Chubb wasn't sure how many there were in the cave, but it sounds like more than one man can handle."

Nicolas looked into the clear, knowing blue eyes of his daughter, so much like his own, and shook his head. "No, Abby, you shouldn't go."

"Adam says it's fine by him"—Adam gave a nod—"and it'll go much faster with two of us. We'll be off soon as we can ready a sledge to haul them out."

"This isn't for you, Abby. This is men's business."

"To hell with men's business," she replied with a scowl. "I know woodsmen as well as you, at Moose River, Big Tupper, Little Tupper, everywhere. And the damned woodsmen know me."

"I wish you wouldn't talk like that. They're lumberjacks. Anyway, you'd be more help with business in the village."

"To pay off Thomas Chubb? No thank you," she said. She crossed her arms and turned her back to him.

"Why not spend some time at the house with your mother, then? She'd like that."

"Father . . ."

With another nod, Adam tiptoed to the door. "I'll rig a sledge for us," he said softly. "The snowpack's still plenty heavy in the woods."

In the cold silence, Nicolas couldn't think what to say. She was strong headed, like him. She had always been that way. Now, a grown girl, she needed someone for herself, didn't she? There was once that young fellow who'd been sweet on her, a nice young man, a classmate of hers. If only she'd take to a boy like that, someone who'd work the Van Horne ice with them.

"Abigail, dear, whatever happened to—"

"Father. Don't. Just don't."

Late that evening Adam and Abigail pulled out of the Van Horne wagon barn under cover of darkness. Nicolas saw them off, watched them slip down the hill and turn into the woods. Then he went to his Chippendale secretary and raised the wick on the lamp.

"I'll make the midnight train with this. I will."

37

First Letter

15 March 1889

Forestport, New York

My dear Renée,

It is with the greatest trepidation that I pen this brief missive. I hope, my sweet new friend, that you shall not find my ramblings unwarranted or undesirable. I fear I have little talent at this writing business. Nevertheless, I will try my hand.

I must tell you that on my return trip I uncovered unsettling facts about the delivery I made to you. Other puzzling and troubling occurrences, and a warm spell that may kill my planned ice harvest, have made these first days on my return to the mountains trying indeed, & my nights are long and dark. (Perhaps a correspondence of some regularity will prove the remedy?)

I think of you often, Renée. Each morning upon awakening I worry that you have forgotten the humble gentleman who deals in ice. All through the long day I relive my first sight of you in your laboratory & especially at our lovely supper, where we held such brisk & illuminating personal discussions. Our brief friendship has come to mean much to me.

Please write! I must know if my new friend thinks of me as I think of her. Write, no matter how briefly. I assure you, your words will be worn out by my reading.

I trust that your work goes well & a cure for the fever will soon be at hand. Your uncle has a great mind in you, Renée. Serve him well & your work will be rewarded.

Entreating you to convey my warmest regards to your lovely mother, that rascally Basil & your kind uncle, I remain,

yrs most respectfully,

Nick

p.s. I have wondered, by the bye, if you received the feathers & the fan?

Bodies from the Woods

Where the Moose River joined the Black, the road narrowed to a footpath. Adam took the reins from Abigail and drew their sledge, a low-slung but sturdy affair, into the underbrush. They jumped down, unhitched the two horses, and hauled the sledge far enough from the trail to hide it from sight. The snow was still deep in the woods and the going had been slow in the darkness of early morning. Abigail hadn't said much, and Adam hadn't forced a conversation . . . not with the grisly job that lay ahead.

Once they'd stashed the sledge, they mounted the two dappled horses Adam had chosen for the trip, a perfect pair for the heavy woods and mountains, barely larger than ponies but powerful through the shoulders and haunches. Two hours later they'd crossed the Moose River Plains and were riding the trail along the upper reaches of the Moose River.

Logging had badly scarred the mountains. Devastated forest stretched along the river for miles. Giant stacks of logs called "skidways" lined the barren riverbanks. The logs, virgin white pine cut in twenty-foot lengths, awaited the spring melt, when they'd be rolled off the skidways and ridden downriver on a torrent to the mills at McKeever and Forestport. After passing dozens of skidways, Adam and Abby arrived at the advancing edge of the logging operation. A handful of lumberjacks were skidding fresh-cut pine on sledges downhill to the riverbank; they'd nearly completed a fifteen-foot-high stack. From atop the pile, an older man yelled, "Well, if it ain't Adam Klock."

"Sure as hell is," Adam replied. "Hiya, Fred."

As the fellow climbed down, a second lumberjack—the sledge driver—hauled up on his pair of played-out horses and jumped down wearing a broad grin. A clapping of strong hands on hard backs ensued. "Who ya got with ya there, Adam?"

Playing it up with a debonair wave of his hand, Adam said, "This here's Nicolas Van Horne's girl."

Fifteen feet above, a young man's face brightened. "Abigail, innit?" he said. "The daughter of the schoolmarm?"

"Hell if it isn't Jimmy Lamphear," Abigail replied. "Haven't seen you since sixth grade."

"You got it right, Miss Smarty Pants. My family moved this way, got a place in Old Forge. Your mom still teaching?"

"Hasn't in years, to tell the truth."

A flask of whiskey was brandished. The lumberjacks pulled their pipes from their pockets and leaned against their stack of fresh-cut timber, glad for the chance to chat with visitors and pass a bottle at the edge of the river.

"What's your guess on when you'll ride these logs outta here?" Adam asked.

"Shouldn't be long. Heard the ice is already out in the lakes south of Big Tupper."

"I heard the same," Adam said. "Damn early spring, huh?"

"Ice'll break up in a week, maybe two if the weather holds warm. Then the real fun begins."

"What they paying log drivers nowadays?" Adam asked.

"Moose company gives us four dollars a day. It's up to five on the Beaver River. Not looking for work, are ya, Adam?"

"Nah," Adam laughed. "Me and Abby are looking to find Big Mike." He hesitated and looked downriver. His voice went soft. "I drove logs once, ya know."

Every woodsman listened hard; even the youngest among them had heard the stories of Adam Klock's feats, his handiness with a crosscut saw and a pike pole . . . or how Adam had once paddled a canoe eighty miles through the Chain of Lakes, from sunup till sundown, to take a fellow lumberjack to his dying brother's side.

"Say, Adam, why don'tcha sign up again? Make yourself some real money."

"Nope," Adam replied. "You won't catch me wrestling no logjams no more. Had too many close calls."

Abigail and Adam mounted their ponies and left the woodsmen to their skidway of logs, the last of the Adirondack giants they'd soon ride downriver on a flood tide of melted snow and ice. Adam and Abigail made their way through a maze of stumps, mangled tree limbs, and wood chips known as "slash" to the upper border of cleared forest, where they found the man they were after, Big Mike Shaw.

The section foreman for the Moose River Lumber Company was a burly bear of a man twice Adam's size and three times Abigail's. Like the other lumberjacks, Big Mike was wrapped in woolens darkened by a winter's worth of wood smoke. The leather of his Croghan boots was molded to his feet by labor, and a rich-smelling pipe stuck from the side of his mouth like a permanent fixture.

"Whatcha got here, Adam?" Mike asked, smirking at Abigail from inside a pungent blue cloud.

"She's Van Horne's daughter."

"Name's Abigail," Abigail added.

"A Van Horne, huh?" The rough-hewn woodsman offered his hand with a flourish and a broad, brown-toothed grin. "And a charmin' young thing you are," he said, holding Abigail's hand as if it were bone china. "Keepin' rough company, aren't you, miss?"

Abigail chortled. "Sure am, but it's strictly business." She gestured across the ugliness of the slash to the standing forest. "That's some real pretty saw timber you're taking out there, Mike."

"Not much of it left, though. Up top of this sled road"—Mike pointed with his pipe to the mountain's peak—"ain't nothin' but pulpwood. Not a sawlog in it. Other side's all hemlock, and that's got no size to it."

"The tanneries paying much for hemlock these days?"

"Not much. They're boilin' more and more hides, but payin' us less for the bark." Mike paused to strike a match on his trousers and put it to his pipe. "Your dad's ice business doing good, Miss Abigail?"

Abigail shook her head. "I'm afraid not. We're in dire need of a cold spell to fill the icehouse."

"Huh. Never can tell. Been a rough winter up this way, what with the two blizzards. We survived it, though. Most of us, that is."

Abigail glanced at Adam, then looked Mike in the eye and broached the real subject at hand.

"As you probably surmised, Mike, we're here on my father's business." Mike nodded. "We heard you have something for us."

Adam chimed in. "How many ya got, Mike?"

"A gawd-awful collection," Mike replied with a shake of his head. "First off, 'bout a month ago two of my crazy Canucks got themselves killed skiddin' logs. A sledge full of timber run right over the middle of 'em both. They had no family, couldn't find nobody to notify. Crazy French Canucks, couldn't barely speak American. Then another—the craziest of 'em all—caught a widow maker off one of the big pines. Biggest damn limb I ever saw, come outta nowhere. And no widow to claim the body."

"That's three."

"Back in early February the crew on the Beaver River lost six men to a nasty grippe. Run through the whole camp. One body went unclaimed, so I stowed 'em with the others."

"In your cave?" Abigail asked.

"Yep. I guess Adam told ya about the ice cave, huh?" he said with a snicker.

"So that makes four," Adam said. "A damned bonanza. Same price as always be good?"

At Mike's nod, Adam pulled out a billfold and began counting bills. Big Mike tucked the bills into his pants pocket, then said, "You and the young lady best stay for supper."

"Naw," Adam said. "We need to get going, Mike. With this warm weather—"

"Sun's dropping fast," Mike said. "And them bodies are froze hard into that cave, ya know. Get some supper, stay overnight, and we'll getcha an early start."

At Abigail's nod, Adam agreed.

Mike said, "I'll give you two a hand tomorrow. We'll start at daybreak. Besides," he added, "I don't much care for that cave. I'd hate to be loadin' 'em in the dark, if you catch my meaning."

Canada blew a breath of winter that night, and the mercury dropped. The dining hall was toasty, the food hearty. In honor of the visitors, the rules of the camp—silence at mealtimes and early to bed—were suspended. Mike broke out six bottles of whiskey and the men entertained Abigail and Adam with tales of North Country hermits and larger-than-life lumberjacks. Adam tried to talk his way into a hand of pitch but got no takers. By midnight, the whiskey was gone.

At first daylight, the men climbed groggy from their bunks and pulled on their Croghans. Big Mike loaded a wagon with three kerosene lanterns along with pickaxes, sledgehammers, ropes, and chisels. He had their camp cook fix a package of bacon warm off the stove, then, without a word to his crew, he rode off with Adam and Abigail, leading the Van Hornes' two dappled horses behind the wagon. The three passed the package of breakfast between them as they rolled down the skid road.

The cave with the corpses was nestled in an outcropping of limestone only a few minutes' tramp above the river. They hauled their tools up an overgrown footpath to the mouth of the cave, which was covered by a thatch of wild blackberry and brambles. Big Mike put on heavy leather gloves and pushed aside the cave's thorny cover, revealing a slit in the limestone barely wide enough for him to slip through. Mike lit one of the lanterns, turned sideways, and edged his bulk into the entrance holding the lantern ahead of him. Adam and Abigail followed his lead, squeezing into the passageway with a lantern held ahead and tools and ropes dragged behind.

The narrow passage was a good ten yards long. At the halfway point, Abigail's breathing went fast and hard. The damp limestone closed in. "I don't like this," she called ahead to Adam, her voice pitched higher with each word. "I don't like this *one bit!*"

"Keep your eyes fixed ahead," Adam said. "On me."

"You know, Adam, we gotta pull 'em out this way."

"Well, hell . . . Mike got 'em in."

Big Mike already stood in the cave's main room. "Come along now, Miss Abigail," he called to her. "Gotta admit you got a point," he added with a chuckle. "With all the ice on them bodies, it'll be harder hauling them out than it was getting 'em in."

Abigail fought to quell her racing heart. "I . . . suppose," she gasped as she stumbled into the main room.

They stood in a large cavern, cold as a grave. From the ceiling twenty feet above, stalactites twisted down like ghostly fingers. The floor of the cavern was damp and slick, and covered by irregular, three-foot humps of stone that looked like Chinese pagodas.

"This way," Mike said, pointing between the rock formations. "They're a little further, against the wall."

"Damn, it's colder in here than outside," Adam said.

"It's the way this cave sits . . . the draft or something," Mike said. "It's froze all summer long." Mike lifted his lantern. "Here they are."

Four frozen corpses stood like boards propped against the grey-yellow limestone. Seepage from above had encased the bodies in translucent columns of ice stretching from the cave's ceiling to its floor. Mike raised the wick on his lantern. The ice columns were shot through with blue, green, and rust-colored streaks from the limestone water dripping from above. The dead men peered through their icy sheath—lumberjacks, still clad in their woodsmen's woolens and Croghans. The four faces were ghastly death masks contorted by shock and horror.

"Well, sir . . . and madam," Big Mike said with a nod to Abigail, "we have our work cut out for us." Mike hefted a pickaxe and took a tentative swing at the pillar of ice encasing the corpses. "Best get a start."

It took three hours with axes and sledgehammers before the column broke loose, the ice was chipped away, and the dead men were laid out frozen on the cave's floor. The room was still, the air laden with kerosene fumes from their lanterns.

"Now we . . . have to *drag 'em out*," Abigail said, her voice quavering at the thought of that long narrow passage, the only way to daylight.

Gasping for air, drenched from exertion despite the cold, they dragged the bodies to the passageway. Mike pulled the first into the narrow crevice. Adam pushed and prodded from behind. Abigail followed, her eyes wide. When the first body was out, Big Mike waved Abigail over to a rock by the entrance. He took her hand, felt her pulse pounding. "You stay put," he said kindly. "Me and Adam'll bring the rest."

It wasn't until all four bodies were lying on the ground in the late-morning sun that Adam and Abigail had a good look at them. Two were badly crushed through their middle by their deadly encounter with a sledge loaded with timber. The influenza victim's mouth hung wide open, as if gasping to fill his battered lungs. The last corpse—the one hit by the falling limb—was the grisliest of the lot. The man's head was split clean in two, skull and all, from dome to jaw.

"Which one's this?" Adam asked, pointing. The two halves of the man's face sagged apart like a gruesome carnival mask.

"That's the one caught the widow maker," Mike replied.

Adam crouched down for a closer look. "Don't look like no widow maker to me."

"It was a helluva big limb, Adam. Helluva big limb."

Adam circled and bent over the body to get a look at the top of the man's skull. It was split like a melon, except Adam was looking into shattered brain. He squinted at Big Mike.

"Yessiree!" Mike waved his hands and pointed high into the forest's canopy. "Biggest damn limb ya can imagine . . . fell from the tallest white pine I ever saw."

"No, Mike."

"You know them widow makers, Adam."

"No, Mike, this is somethin' else. A woodsman's axe done this."

Adam straightened and fixed his gaze on the camp foreman. Mike turned his back. "Nah," he said, looking off in the woods. "You got it all wrong."

"What happened here, Mike?"

"Nothin'."

"What happened?"

"Nothin', I said . . . well . . . okay. It was Jimmy Lamphear," Mike said softly. "He done it."

"Murdered him?"

"Not hardly, no. See . . . Jimmy's got a little sister lives over in Old Forge, and she's a real looker, this one. The boy keeps an Eastman print of her by his bunk. Well, this dumb Canuck persists in asking about her. Keeps at it, ya know? Then he's heading to Old Forge on Sundays, courtin' the girl. But he's crazy, this Canuck. He's one shoulda been in that asylum up to Lake Placid. See, he done the young girl wrong"—Mike glanced at Abigail—"real wrong. He had his way with her and when he finished, he beat her bad. Broke her arm, her nose, her jaw."

"So Jimmy gets even," Adam said.

"This Canuck's so crazy he comes back to camp jabbering French, picks up his gear, and skedaddles. But word was already back to Jimmy. He follows the Canuck into the woods . . . you can figure the rest. All my men are handy, but Jimmy, he's up from Paul Smith's and he's good as they come with a double-bit felling axe. And we keep 'em sharp in this outfit."

"Mike . . . Mike . . . ," Adam said, real low, wagging his head. " I don't think we can do this. We never had one like this before, never run into the situation."

"Only Jimmy and me know what happened. We decided the Canuck took a widow maker—that was the way it was going to be, no questions asked."

"I don't know. What if someone comes looking?"

Mike was quiet for a moment, then he turned to Abigail. "What's your thought, miss?"

"It was Jimmy's sister he wronged?"

"His kid sister. Sixteen years old and the prettiest, most pleasing girl, she is . . . or was."

Abigail, calm and steady, said, "You know what I think, Mike? This man had no respect for women. No respect whatsoever. I figure he deserved to catch a widow maker."

Big Mike turned to Adam. "Widow maker it is, then, Adam?"

"Biggest limb I ever heard of."

"I'll help you load 'em," Mike said. "You folks gotta get goin'."

To haul the bodies to their sledge, Adam took a hatchet into the woods and quickly fashioned two travois, cutting ash for the spars and pine boughs for the cross-hatching. He lashed the spars to their ponies' traces, and they loaded the bodies two to a travois.

"All set," Big Mike Shaw said as he secured canvas around the last of the corpses. It was nearly noon.

"We appreciate your help, Mike," Adam said.

Big Mike pulled a pint from his jacket. "Have one 'fore you go," he said. "We'll drink to these poor devils." In turn, the three of them tipped back the bottle, glanced at its label, and scrunched their faces.

With a wave, Adam and Abigail left Big Mike on the mountainside putting fire to his pipe. They led the horses with sagging travois stretched behind them down the skid road to the Black River trail. They pulled their sledge from the brush, loaded the corpses, unhooked the travois, hitched the two dappled ponies to the sledge, and moved out. From the cutoff on the little-traveled Brandywine Lake trail they made their way over a hard spring snowpack south of Saranac, then headed to Upper Spy Lake on a little-used corduroy road through a hushed stand of virgin white pine.

A breeze sighed through the pines; the only other sound was the scratch of the sledge's runners.

"About that crazy Canuck," Abigail said, "he can't be any older than me, you think? Maybe eighteen, nineteen? What makes a man turn so bad?"

"Well, Big Mike had something to say about that when him and me hauled those last bodies out."

"Yeah?"

"He told me this Canuck was an orphan from up Quebec way. The man never had no family, no home. Crazy Canuck just plain started out bad."

"I suppose that's reason enough."

It took the rest of the day's light to reach the Upper Spy trail by the route they'd chosen. It was a desolate, quiet walk in, leading their gruesome load down the narrow lake trail, sandwiched between the shoreline and the railroad spur to the icehouse. They reached Upper Spy at midnight, and the Van Hornes' dwindling ice gained four sad souls who'd met with unexpected ends in the Adirondack woods.

Midnight. That was when a certain young lady, the youngest Van Horne, locked the icehouse door behind her, and made a decision.

39

Cold Snap

It was the fourth time that morning he'd been to the shed to check his instruments, and with good reason. There'd been changes. The dampness and fog were missing. The wind had shifted at dawn and came from the Canadian side, its velocity rising. The shark oil hazed over; heavy sediment ran in thin rivulets to the bottom of the glass cylinder. And Nicolas's right knee ached. The old football injury—the surest sign.

Nicolas tore out of the shed after his fourth visit. The mercury was well below freezing, and dropping. On the stairs to Ruth's room, his knee throbbed. "We'll soon be off to Upper Spy," he said, breathless. "I'm sure of it."

Late that evening, Abigail—her eyes bleary from scant hours of sleep—rode to the house on the horse she most favored, a young stallion as black as night and full of spirit. Nicolas called to her from the porch before she'd even dismounted. "Ready the big wagon for tomorrow, Abby. Canadian air is on its way!"

"Adam's mustering the last of the workers at the inns, Father."

"And the men you already have?"

"Ten, and they're eager; their spirits are high."

"Supplies?"

"I took Mr. Finnegan away from his supper and made him open up the store. I've filled the cook's list."

"Bless you, dear. Come for me at dawn."

Abigail rode off without ever dismounting the rambunctious stallion. Nicolas climbed to Ruth's room. She had drawn the drapes against the bright moonlight and was already in bed.

"Ruth . . . Ruth." Nicolas shook her in the darkness. "Come now, please wake."

He lit the lamp by the bedside. Ruth stirred, fought her way out of a numbing sleep. A moment's blank stare, then she turned her face to the pillow. "I cannot," she said.

"Abigail and I are off to the lake in the morning. We must settle on your regimen."

All was readied—the laudanum, the pills, the compresses. Nicolas left Ruth and stepped outside the kitchen door. He didn't bother with a coat. The arctic night bit at his nose and cheeks. The black velvet of the sky filled with broad swaths of stars. Northern lights, the first he'd seen in weeks, danced on the horizon.

When Nicolas awoke the next morning, a blaze of first sunlight was at the frosted dormer window. The house creaked with the cold. Nicolas dressed and bounded down the stairs to warm himself by the kitchen stove, where Abigail was frying strips of venison in butter. She reached into a bag on the kitchen table and extracted three eggs with bits of straw stuck to them.

"From Hilda's goose," she said proudly.

Nicolas unwrapped a warm bundle on the table. "Biscuits, too?" he said, beaming. "Why are these Germans such fine bakers?"

Abigail spooned the venison onto a plate and set it on the table in front of her father, then tended the eggs that sizzled in bacon fat on the stove.

"Supplies loaded, Abby?"

Abigail nodded. She plated the eggs, then sat at the table and watched Nicolas down his breakfast. "So you see, Father, the wire from Albany was right."

"Bah!" He chortled. "Their instruments are no better than mine, girl." He dabbed at a bright orange yolk. "I only hope the cold snap lasts."

"We'll fill the icehouse, Father. I feel it in my bones."

Nicolas finished his breakfast, leaned back, and grinned. "Let's get going," he said, reaching for the satchel he'd prepared for the trip to Upper Spy.

40

Preparing to Harvest

A dusting of new snow covered the frozen mud and made the coach road to Old Forge treacherous. Abigail loosened the reins to allow the team to pick its way over hardened ruts as deep as a man's boot.

"Atta girl, Abby," Nicolas said with pride, his breath coming in clouds. "Let 'em set their own pace."

Steam rose from the glossy backs of the two steeds as they strained against the wagon's load. In the bed of the largest wagon that Mr. Parsons had built at his carriage shop, surrounded by potatoes, bacon, lamp oil, canned beans, and dry goods, lay Nicolas's new German engine, the power source for his most recent invention—a new ice plow.

By the time Abigail turned the team onto the Upper Spy Road, the late afternoon sun had tucked itself behind a mountain and the tops of the pines were ragged silhouettes against the steel-blue, darkening sky. She chose this time to say her mind.

"You were right, Father. I know now you were right."

"I've always said my instruments were as good as Albany's. When it comes to the weather—"

"I meant about this business. You said it wasn't for me, and you were right."

"The ice trade's hard, Abby, sure, but if you were to –"

"I'm not talking about the ice trade, Father. It's the bodies. I understand about the doctors and their studies, but too much can go wrong for us. Ice is fine, but I won't trade in the dead."

"I see."

"No, you don't. You'll see what's in the icehouse, then you'll understand."

The going was even rougher on the lake road. Jouncing along with pine boughs brushing by on both sides, Nicolas tried to wrap his mind around what Abigail had said about the body business. He knew better than anyone how things might go awry. Galveston taught him that. But Abigail couldn't possibly know about the murdered boys, could she? If only she'd stick to the ice business. Ice was all around them, every puddle, pond, and stream, solid with it. Ice.

Nicolas often pondered the scientific theories about ice and what it had once done to these Adirondacks. He was an avid reader of mail-order tracts on the subject from the university in Albany. According to the scientists, during the great Ice Age these mountains lay under glaciers—ice that was miles in thickness. The thousands of Adirondack lakes had been carved when the glaciers receded, gouging narrow, V-shaped grooves into solid bedrock, or so the theory went.

This made sense to Nicolas. The Spy Lakes—Upper, Middle, and Lower—ran parallel in straight north-south lines; all were four or five miles long, but none was more than a quarter mile across. It was as if they'd been scratched out by the sharpened talons of a gigantic claw, and scratched deep—so deep that folks in the North Country called them "bottomless," as if their dark waters penetrated to the center of earth.

Nicolas imagined, too, how the glaciers had molded the land alongside Upper Spy into these long, steep-sided mountains, like overturned canoes lying along the lake's length. At the northern end of Upper Spy, the mountains flattened into rounded hills called "drumlins." It was there—at Upper Spy's gentler north shore—that underground springs fed the lake its clear, iron-rich water, making Upper Spy a superb place to harvest ice.

When he started his ice trade, Nicolas had acquired a large, failed potato farm that once thrived on the drumlins at the north end of Upper Spy Lake. He purchased three hundred acres of land, and with the lakefront land came the rights to harvest ice. Nicolas shored up the potato farm's dilapidated barns and outbuildings to serve as stables, cook's shanty, and bunkhouse for an ice camp of thirty men. He dedicated one large shed to his ice-cutting equipment and—as in Forestport—his weather instruments and tinkering. To complete the ice operation he constructed an imposing, three-story icehouse, the largest in the Northeast. It was a unique design, with a capacity of over fifty thousand tons, natural ventilation, and double-walled construction to maximally preserve ice. Soon after its completion, Nicolas persuaded the Adirondack Railroad to run a spur to the icehouse, guaranteeing his commercial success at rapid delivery of large quantities of ice to the Mohawk Valley and points south.

Now, at the approach to the Van Horne ice camp, their wagon rolled along the length of the icehouse, and Nicolas's throat tightened. Only one of the icehouse's internal rooms held any ice at all; with an average harvest it might take three weeks to fill the massive structure. And there was no way to know if the cold snap would hold.

Night had fallen, the woods were still, the mercury was dropping fast. The only signs of life were the twin plumes of smoke rising from the chimneys of the cook's shanty and the bunkhouse. Despite their heavy wool caps, coats, and mittens, Nicolas and Abigail were chilled to the core. They stepped down at the cook's shanty, which also served as the men's dining and recreation hall. Nicolas threw open the shanty door and stood in the doorway, a cloud of ice crystals billowing around him. Adam, as the crew's foreman, was the first to jump up from his card game at the nearer of the two long dining tables. He grinned and reached a hand to each.

"A pleasant evening to the Van Hornes."

"A perfect evening," Nicolas agreed as he and Abby shucked off their caps and mittens. "Must be ten below zero."

The camp's cook, a white-haired woman in her eighties lovingly known as "Cookie," stooped by her stove, feeding oak to the fire. Fifteen hardy men sat around the rough pine tables, playing pitch. One by one, the men laid down their cards to greet the boss and the boss's daughter. At the far end of the table, two young boys were reading dime-store novels by lamplight; a third boy sat alone in the shadows.

"Little Jacky! Samuel!" Adam snapped at the two young readers. "You fellas get your faces outta them books for a minute and get that wagon unloaded." The youths marked their places in the stirring adventures of Deadwood Dick and Nick Carter; grabbed their coats, caps, and mittens; and tumbled out the door. "And you—Knox—go tend to Mr. Van Horne's horses like I showed ya. And I mean now. Lickety-switch!"

Cookie reached into a cabinet and pulled out a brown bottle.

"Here's a little warmer for you, Mr. Van Horne," she said, pouring for the Van Hornes and their foreman. "I sure hope you didn't freeze them potatoes on the way up."

"Nope," Van Horne replied, smiling. "Before we left I ran that German engine hot as she'd go, then packed your spuds and perishables near its crankcase."

After warming by the stove a minute or two, Nicolas thumped down his empty glass, reached for his coat, and declared, "I need to see the ice."

The night was dead still. A sugarcoating of new snow lay on the lake. The woods cracked with the cold. The Van Hornes, Adam, and a few of their crew stood at the lakeside, admiring the frozen expanse of white. Night air seeped through mittens and woolens. A sea of stars shone overhead and a curtain of phosphorescent blue-purple rippled over the treetops to the north.

"Excellent," Nicolas whispered.

Abigail pulled her plaid hunting jacket tighter about her. "See, Father. You got yourself a helluva cold snap."

"Let's hope it lasts."

"I measured fourteen inches before nightfall," Adam said.

"Still a might thin to work. Shall we chance marking it tonight?"

Adam kicked at the lake's crusty surface. "It was a good four hours ago I measured, boss, and it's colder'n a witch's . . ." He paused and took in a frigid breath. "I say we scrape and mark an ice field tonight."

"Have 'em do ten acres, then," Nicolas said, squinting out over the ice. "Take care near the middle. By morning it'll surely hold all the men, the horses, and the old ice plow, but we'll cut by hand until you measure over twenty inches. Then"—a gleam came into Nicolas's eye—"I'll break out my new plow."

That evening, after the Van Hornes ate their fill of Cookie's leftover venison stew, the crew hitched two light teams to the scrapers and hauled their marking tools onto the lake. Jack Casler, the oldest, most experienced member of the crew, put himself in charge of scraping the center of the lake, where the ice would be thinnest. Casler was a tough old bird with a great Santa Claus beard that hung clear to his belt. In his late seventies, father of eleven children and grandfather to many more, Old Jack hadn't missed a winter cutting ice since he was nine years old.

The youngest of the ice crew were the two hooligans Adam had sent to unload the Van Hornes' wagon. "Little Jacky" Casler—Old Jack's grandson—was a village boy, a barrel-chested, sickly child who took to periodic fits of wheezing that laid him up for days on end. Little Jacky's best friend, Samuel Smith, was his complete opposite—Samuel was a strapping boy who grew up on his father's hop farm south of Forestport and had the steely biceps and upper torso of a wrestler. This was the two boys' third winter of skipping school to work the ice. They were seasoned ice workers.

Old Jack led his grey-and-black roan horse, one of the prettiest matched pair in camp, out of the barn and hitched the scraper to it. Jack would scrape the crusty surface smooth. Little Jacky and Samuel's job was to clean horse droppings off the ice from their "shine sleigh," a light sleigh drawn by a quick pony, named for the shine left on the ice after its surface had been sanitized with a splash of formaldehyde.

Little Jacky and Samuel readied the shine sleigh and queued up behind Old Jack's scraper. The new boy scurried over the ice and hopped onto Old Jack's rig to add ballast to the scraper.

"Who's the new fella?" Nicolas asked Adam.

"Name's Knox."

"Where'd he come from?"

"Outta town somewhere. Abigail hired him, not me, boss. Damned if the boy hasn't already been a problem, too. Last night we caught him sneaking around the bunkhouse after lights-out, going through the men's pockets. He had a fistful of silver, and we found more under his mattress."

"Did you administer some justice?"

"I personally give him a Klock-style walloping. Today, he seems to have attached himself to Old Jack. Follows him everywhere, and I'll be damned if Old Jack hasn't taken a liking to the rascal."

Nicolas searched out Abigail, who was hitching their mule, a small but ornery beast, to the sleigh that would measure and mark the field. "Where'd you find that new boy, Abby?" he asked.

"Knox was volunteered by his uncle, a gent I never saw in the village before. They came all the way from north Franklin County."

"He's got family up that way?"

"I guess. His uncle insisted he get half the boy's pay, in advance. Said he'd be back in three weeks to collect him and the rest of his pay. I wanted him to learn the shine sleigh, but now Old Jack insists the scalawag go with him."

Old Jack's scraper sped toward the lake's center, trailing a cloud of crusty ice, with young Knox hanging on for dear life. Samuel and Little Jacky, their cheeks bright from exertion, their minds keen with dime-store-novel tales of daring, kept the shine sleigh in constant motion ten yards behind. The last harvest of the winter was in full swing.

Old Jack hadn't quite made it to the middle of Upper Spy when his horse suddenly stopped, and disaster struck. There was a low-pitched *frump*, and the pretty roan horse sank to its withers in the frozen lake.

"Air pocket!" Casler bellowed. "Horse through the ice!" His horse floundered. Knox was thrown against Casler's back, where he clung, terrified.

"Horse through the ice! Horse through the ice!" rang out across the lake as Casler's roan struggled in a roiling pool of frigid water and jagged chunks of ice.

Old Jack slipped off the scraper, crouched at the edge of the hole, and pulled with all his strength on the emergency lines, called "choke ropes." These lines, hung from his horse's hames, cut off a horse's air, thus calming the beast.

It seemed to be working until Casler slid toward the hole and went into the slushy mix himself, with Knox still clinging to his back.

"Chrissakes!" Old Jack gasped, before Knox sank the old man and a swallow of icy water shut him up. He let go the choke rope and the horse went wild-eyed. Knox flailed on the water's surface. Old Jack bobbed up, saw the boy couldn't swim a stroke, and with one mighty tug, heaved Knox onto solid ice.

Meanwhile, Little Jacky Casler edged the shine sleigh close to the hole. He slipped off the sleigh, scooted on his stomach, and grabbed his grandpa's coat collar. Little Jacky's friend Samuel hollered, "Hold on!" and, still on the sleigh, reached for Jacky's foot to become the last link of the three-man human chain. Moments later, Little Jacky broke through and Samuel, still clutching his pal, slipped off the sleigh and into the mayhem of thrashing bodies and roiling black water. The only one on solid ice was Knox, who lay, frozen with fear, where Old Jack had shoved him.

Abigail was the first close by with the light mule.

Nicolas fought to keep his voice calm. "Lead your mule around the hole, Abby. Rope the roan from that side."

Nicolas knew all too well that a horse might live for twenty minutes in the icy lake, but a man lasted only minutes, and boys even less. With a glance and a nod, Nicolas conveyed a plan to his best man, Adam Klock, who grabbed the free end of the rope Nicolas extended and trotted toward the hole, tying the rope around his waist as he ran. In one motion Adam slid to his knees, skittered across the ice, splashed into the hole, and latched on to the boys. Nicolas tossed a second rope to Old Jack, who managed to twist it around his arm. Nicolas dug his heels into a crusty spot on the lake and hauled. Two crew members came to help, and the half-frozen victims were on solid ice again. The fine roan, breathing like a racehorse after twenty furlongs, was drawn out from the opposite side by Abigail's mule.

"Hurrah!" A cheer went up as the crew rushed Old Jack and the three shivering boys, silent and numb, to the warmth of Cookie's stove.

Every man who worked the ice knew the importance of warming a chilled victim, especially a young one, before a deadly pneumonia set in. Nicolas shouted orders in Cookie's shanty. Adam handed a good-sized tumbler of whiskey to old man Casler. Abigail—to their chagrin—helped the boys strip so she could wrap their shivering, naked bodies in dry blankets. She made no pretense of hiding her eyes, warmth was so critical.

"Decided to go for a little dip, eh, boys?" Adam laughed. "Take this, now." He poured Little Jacky and Samuel a drop of the strong stuff and turned serious.

"You done good, boys. I mean it. You're real heroes—better'n old Deadwood Dick in them books of yours."

"Don't forget Knox," Old Jack grumbled. "The poor devil nearly drowned."

Adam poured a tad of whiskey for a silent Knox, who huddled near the stove, clutching his blanket around him.

To Nicolas's eye, Little Jacky looked the worst of the victims. When the boy had been carried off the lake, his lungs gave out a dull whooping sound and his lips were as blue-black as the night sky. Now, in Abigail's arms, his breathing turned to a high-pitched whistle, like a horse run too hard in subzero weather.

Nicolas set an old Union cot near the stove and fixed a bedroll for Little Jacky. Old Jack pulled up a chair and settled in, trying to calm his grandson's labored breath. Old Jack looked like he'd aged twenty years. Adam poured another for him, saying, "A bit more whiskey should help."

"Somebody stoke that stove," Nicolas said. "I want it hotter'n the damned equator in here tonight."

41

In the Icehouse

At midnight, Nicolas stood at the shore and surveyed the expanse of ice. The crew had measured and marked a ten-acre ice field and scraped its surface to mirrorlike smoothness, ready to harvest. Old Jack's roan horse, warmed and gently talked to in the horse barn, was bedded and made ready to join its teammate in the morning, none the worse for its chilling experience.

Back in Cookie's shanty, Nicolas shucked off his mittens and greatcoat. The crew began to retire to the bunkhouse. A big day lay ahead. Nicolas and Abigail talked quietly at the far end of a dining table.

When the last man left for the bunkhouse, Nicolas donned his garb again and walked alone to the equipment shed. He searched for the oil lantern he'd outfitted with the brightest available Argand wick. He didn't light it. Instead, he carried the lamp unlit to the east door of the icehouse, where Abigail, according to plan, waited in the dark.

Nicolas unlocked the main entrance. He pulled a match from his book of flexible phosphors, struck it, and lit the lamp—but only when he and Abigail were inside and had shut the steel door tight. Without a word, Abigail followed through the empty rooms. The only sound echoing through the icehouse was the creak and bang of doors opening and closing.

They went straight to the central room, the smallest in the icehouse, the special room kept double-padlocked. Nicolas pulled a small ring of two keys from his pocket. Here was the last of their dwindling ice; blocks were stacked no more than shoulder-high. Abigail led now, down the narrow ice alley to the far corner. On either side, corpses wrapped in canvas lay wedged in catacombs of ice. Nicolas held the lantern high.

"Here's the one, Father."

Nicolas turned the lamp up full. Abigail pulled the body partially out of the ice and crouched to unfasten the twine stays. She unfurled the canvas until the dead man's head was exposed.

"See?"

"A woodsman's axe," Nicolas said. "Who was he, Abby?"

"A Canadian lumberjack. From what Big Mike told us, the crazy Canuck deserved what he got. What he did to Jimmy Lamphear's sister was . . . even so, this man was murdered."

"I've seen enough, Abby."

"Now do you . . . you . . ." Abigail choked on her words. "Do you see what I mean? No matter how bad that man was, we're hiding it, Father, and that makes us just as bad."

"You're right, Abby, but what can we do? Wasn't there a family? Or relatives to tell?"

"No, he was nothing but a wanderer with a mean streak. Had a hard life, according to Mike. He grew up in some orphanage up Quebec way."

In the bright light of the lantern, Nicolas's jaw dropped. "An orphan? Here, hold the lamp for me."

Nicolas pulled the canvas lower, revealing the dead man's torso. The corpse was still clothed, except for holes in the arm of his shirt where Thomas Chubb had done his embalming. Nicolas yanked at the blood-soaked, frozen flannel shirt. He pulled a folding knife from his pocket and ripped away until he'd laid bare the skin of both shoulders.

"Closer with the lamp, Abby. Here." He saw it. The mark. "Oh, sweet Jesus."

The mark was fainter than those he'd seen, healed over years to a dull, flattened scar but still recognizable as a long-legged spidery thing stretching itself over the dead man's right shoulder.

"What is it, Father?"

"I wish I knew."

"Couldn't be an accident, could it? An old burn, where he touched something hot? Not sure if I've seen anything like it before."

"It was under different circumstances I first saw one. Bad circumstances." Nicolas rewrapped the body in its canvas and bound it with twine. Standing over the body, he paused in thought. "How old would you say the man was?"

"He'd be about the same as Jimmy Lamphear or me. No more'n twenty."

"That means they've been around for years, the others," Nicolas said, shaking his head. *Years. Those others were mere boys, eleven, maybe twelve.*

"What others?" Abby trailed her father back through the ice alleys. "What does that thing mean?"

Nicolas couldn't answer. He'd seen the mark on a dead boy, a murdered boy, and now on a grown man. *Thomas Chubb. It's the undertaker who knows something, who might illuminate the connection. But Thomas isn't talking.*

What could he tell his daughter? Abigail was right; there was no excuse for taking part in murder. Ignoring evil was evil itself. And no matter how much he reassured her, murdered boys would end up in Van Horne ice again.

At the beginning, things seemed so simple. The bodies came easily, and, once sold, they were gone forever into the vats and the dissecting rooms. Now it was murder he dealt in. There were boys murdered in Buffalo. Bad boys, according to Flynt. And bad boys grew into bad men. Whatever it was, it had been going on for years.

"We need to get some sleep," Nicolas said. He clicked the second padlock shut on the room of the dead. "In the morning, we harvest ice."

For their rest, Nicolas and Abigail trudged down the shoreline path to their lake house. When Nicolas converted the old potato farm into his ice operation, he had renovated the abandoned farmhouse into an Adirondack summer home, or lake house. Perched at the water's edge on a low stone bluff overlooking Upper Spy, the lake house afforded the Van Hornes the pleasures of clear, cool water and a piney breeze off the surrounding drumlins. The upstairs became sleeping quarters and Nicolas fashioned the first floor into an Adirondack great room fitted with comfortable sofas and adorned with trophy mounts, North Country paintings, and bearskin rugs. He constructed a spacious boathouse over the water, and enclosed and screened its upper deck against the voracious blackflies.

Now, in the grip of winter's last cold snap, the Van Horne lake house was as frigid and still as a mausoleum. Abigail built a fire in the kitchen stove to cut the chill. They gathered wool blankets and feather beds, and threw together two bedrolls on the kitchen floor. Once Abigail was wrapped in her bedroll, Nicolas reassured her with a soothing, fatherly tone. It would all work out. Ice had a future. He'd solve these problems. And no matter what, she was his daughter and he'd always love his little girl.

Abigail became still, her breathing steady and slow. Nicolas tossed for hours, his eyes open, mulling over the day. The evening's near-disaster on the lake. The riddle of the dead lumberjack.

In the years he'd worked the ice, Nicolas had never lost a worker to Upper Spy. Tonight, two fine Adirondack boys, the new boy Knox and an old, experienced ice cutter, had nearly died for the Van Horne ice business. Everyone on the ice had done right, and with lightning speed. The old coot Casler seemed none the worse for his dunking. But things might've ended differently. Things might've ended with corpses.

The thought made him shiver in his bedroll.

42

Season's Last Harvest

The lake came alive with ominous booming sounds, like a bass drum beaten in the distance. Nicolas knew the sound; he often woke to this *boom . . . boom . . .* on a clear, subzero night. It was the sound of the frozen lake's plates of ice shifting and buckling. Nicolas and Abigail scrambled from their beds well before dawn. Their hearts thrilled at the sound of the ice tightening its grip on Upper Spy.

Father and daughter dressed hurriedly and stepped outdoors. The cold penetrated their woolens. A freshening breeze shook shards of ice from the pines. The ice field shone like milk glass in the lingering moonlight. The hole near the center of the lake, the site of last night's mishap, had frozen into a roughened, bluish scar.

In Cookie's shanty the dining tables groaned under great piles of flapjacks, jugs of maple syrup, and bowls of mashed potatoes. Nicolas checked on Little Jacky, who lay listless on the cot. The boy wouldn't speak. His breathing was hard, and his color was off. Nicolas sent a man to fetch the town doctor in Old Forge, the closest village. He instructed Cookie to keep the fire stoked, report any changes in the boy's breathing, and pray with all her might that a fever didn't set in. It was all they could do.

The crew grew boisterous and cracked wise as they dragged their augers and breaker bars onto the ice. Nicolas had the men hitch Old Jack Casler's roan horses, freshly combed, their smooth haunches twitching with anticipation, to the old ice plow. But the team had no driver.

"Old Jack refused to get out of bed," Nicolas was told. "He never came to breakfast."

Adam ran to the bunkhouse to check on Jack. "It's not the whiskey," Adam reported back. "Hell, it's the man's first day off in fifty years, and he's drunk plenty of whiskey. No, it's something else. He ain't right."

Abigail took over for Old Jack on the ice plow. Nicolas assigned the new boy Knox to ride the plow's main beam for ballast, since Abigail was half the weight of Old Jack. Shivering with fear, Knox gritted his teeth and climbed up. Abby stepped onto the plow and sighted along its gauging planks. With a gentle "Gidyap," the plow shot like an arrow onto the ice field. Abby skillfully cut a grid of six-inch-deep grooves near shore, so the crew could start cracking out ice cakes. While they waited, the men stamped their feet, clapped their mittens, and puffed on their pipes. "Get a move on there, missy!" they yelled, chiding Abigail whenever the plow swung by.

Adam stepped onto the ice and chose the first square, or "header cake." He ceremoniously cracked the cake free with his breaker bar and sank it under the sheet of ice, thus starting the first channel to the icehouse. Raising his bar overhead, Van Horne's right-hand man gave the command.

"Okey-dokey, boys. Let's bring in some ice!"

Cakes were floated to shore; channels began to stretch across the lake. Shouts of "Get a move on!" rang out. In the icehouse, Nicolas adjusted his steam-driven conveyor and ice planer. Adam stoked the steam engine with oak, smoke billowed from the engine's stack, and belts began to whirl.

Nicolas dispatched Abigail to Forestport to raise fifteen more workers, bringing the crew to its full complement of thirty—all the bunkhouse would hold, and the most Cookie could feed.

Adam put in an order for a case of whiskey. "Don't worry, boss," he said. "I'll keep 'er under lock and key till the icehouse is full."

At the icehouse entrance, Nicolas watched over his ice planer as it ground the surface of each cake smooth and blue. Nicolas had every tenth cake diverted to another of his inventions, the stationary ice saw, which cut smaller blocks of irregular sizes and shapes.

Watching the saw work made Nicolas chuckle over how the patent officers at the U.S. Patent Office in Albany had marveled at its design. The Albany bureaucrats were totally baffled by his need for a mechanized, stationary saw in his icehouse. Traditionally, cakes of ice were cut by hand at the time of home delivery by the most skilled of ice men, the "ice breaker," who, with a single blow of his ice axe, divided the larger three-foot cakes into blocks of any size. Why, then, would this seemingly sane Van Horne fellow cut his cakes smaller in the icehouse, into a myriad of odd shapes, and with such uncanny accuracy? Was he filling an icehouse or building ice castles? Nicolas always smiled at the thought of Albany's patent men. They simply couldn't fathom true Yankee ingenuity, and, of course, they had no idea about the tunnels and catacombs Nicolas and Adam fashioned deep in the hold of his ships with these odd-sized, irregularly shaped blocks of ice.

The doc from Old Forge, a wheezy, portly old sawbones by the name of Shaughnessy, arrived at sunset. Cookie allowed that the doc's late arrival was designed so he'd be fed supper. After putting his instrument to Little Jacky's chest, Shaughnessy proclaimed, "Too early to know for sure," . . . and sat right down at the dining table. The only advice he gave for his fee of two gold eagles was to instruct Cookie to "keep the boy warm and feed him plenty of strong, hot tea."

"How much tea?" Cookie asked.

"As much as he can stand. And for heaven's sake, don't make the poor boy go out in the snow to pee."

"You might check Old Jack, too," Cookie suggested dryly. "He's not been out of bed."

After supper, Doc Shaughnessy spent a goodly amount of time examining the elder Casler. "His breathing's a bit labored," he told Nicolas, puzzling over Jack's condition. "He's grumbling about chest discomfort, too . . . but then, he's got an old man's heart. My guess is, he'll be fine. 'Course the man's pushing eighty, so no guarantees on that . . . Golly it's late. Don't mind if I stay over, do you?"

The doc checked Jacky the next morning, gravely assigning the youngster to "the will of our Lord" and to a fretful Cookie, who was brewing tea by the quart. Then he settled down to breakfast. The table was abuzz, waiting for the boss man to speak. Nicolas stood and raised his arms for quiet.

"Listen, gents. Adam measured twenty-two inches at the shoreline this morning, so I'm firing up the new plow. We've plenty of gasoline, and she's ready to go."

Three rounds of "Hip, hip, hurrah!" shook Cookie's shanty.

That afternoon, to more cheers from the crew, little Jacky Casler climbed onto the shine sleigh with his pal Samuel and their new understudy, Knox. Every man watched as the boys zigzagged crazily across Upper Spy. By nightfall the jubilant crew had cut thirty acres of ice with the new Van Horne ice plow, twice what they'd managed in the first two days.

On the next morning—the fourth day of the harvest—the breakfast table was unearthly quiet. Whispers drifted down the line; platters of flapjacks sat untouched. Nicolas stepped in and stood at the end of the table, a grim look on his face.

"I guess most of you've heard the bad news. Old Jack left us last evening. We found him next to his bunk at midnight, bless the old boy's soul. I guess Doc Shaughnessy didn't know how bad the old boy's heart really was and, well . . . that dunking set him back. So let's have a moment of silence here, get some food in you, and we'll get out on the ice. That's the way Old Jack would've wanted it."

A murmur of approval circled round the table. Chairs scraped as everyone stood. For a long moment, there was only the whisper of a wintry breeze at the frosted windows.

The crew wrapped the old man's body in quilts and set it next to the bunkhouse. By the time the men were cracking and floating the first blocks of ice, Old Jack was hard as marble.

For the next three days, Van Horne's gas-powered ice plow belched thick, black smoke. Its three-foot rotary blade whirred. The icehouse conveyer and planer devoured great quantities of oak and charcoal, and rumbled well past dusk. Giant floats of ice, dozens of cakes in breadth, were cut and solemnly pulled by two teams of horses to the icehouse to be divided.

With a single week's labor at the end of March, the crew had filled the Van Horne icehouse, every room stacked to the top, three stories high. Open water, black and still, stretched halfway across the lake. They fed and groomed the horses, oiled and put up the ice tools. Then the weather broke, the mercury rose, and spring rain poured down in sheets.

Nicolas and Adam stood on the shore without bothering to put on slickers. In dripping woolens, they tried to light cigars. Nicolas stared blankly at the undulating surface of Upper Spy, a soggy, unlit cigar in his hand.

"Nearly fifty-five thousand tons," he said with a resigned smile.

"Damned shame about Old Jack though."

"Did they pack plenty of ice around him in the wagon?"

"Yep. Betcha he's at Chubb's place already."

"Guess we'll have a funeral to attend."

"Look at it this way, boss. Come next winter, there's three boys be stepping out on the ice to take Old Jack's place."

"Including Knox."

"Yep. That's the way things work."

That evening the men polished off a stringer of lake trout, stuffed themselves on Cookie's cheese potatoes and blueberry pie, and cracked open the case of whiskey. Merriment rang out.

It was well past midnight before Nicolas and Abigail slogged down the path to the Van Horne camp. Before retiring, they warmed themselves in the kitchen and listened to the steady drumming of rain on the tin roof. Drunken shouts echoed across the lake.

Abigail asked, "Did you notice how antsy the men got when Old Jack went down to the village?"

"He was thawing out, Abby."

"But the men talk. The whole town talks, Father."

"You know I'd never allow Thomas to misplace Old Jack's body. Never."

"I know it and you know it, but in the village . . ."

43

A Correspondence Is Established

2 April 1889

Galveston Island

My dear Nick,

First, a confession, dear friend. Since your departure, it has been my greatest fear that your memories of the South would wane & I would never again hear from my new friend. But no! Your eagerly awaited letter arrived today.

I have read your lovely letter at least a hundred times & I see how your feelings go. I confess that I, too, think often of our brief time together. As you suggest, a correspondence of some regularity will allow us to explore these avenues of thought.

Please forgive me, Nick, for not bidding you farewell at the station. I am not one for sad departures & my work in the laboratory constantly beckons. Rest assured that I think of you, kind sir, perhaps more than you imagine.

I am pleased to report that our experiments go well. Uncle & I are confident that an anti-toxoid will be devised. As to whether we can perfect my methods to produce an effective treatment before summer, I have serious doubts. My trials with the human cells take time & we must be certain before we move on to develop the anti-toxoid in horses. It is work that cannot be hurried, no matter how great our dread of the next epidemic.

One disturbing bit of news. You undoubtedly recall how our local supplier of cadavers met an untimely death before your departure. No investigation of the horrid incident has been undertaken (I suspect Mr. Sealy intervened in that regard) but now Uncle Francis & our faculty are at wits' end to find a supplier. I know, Nick, that I advised you to steer clear of that perilous business, but now I ask you to do the opposite & consider delivering again to Uncle this resource our school so desperately needs. Exercise special care in doing so. Let me know the possibilities & your plan.

Experiments are calling & so I must end this now with the hope that you will respond with greatest speed. Until the joyous arrival of your next correspondence, with my warmest regards, I remain,

your admirer,

Renée Keiller

PS: Of course I received the lovely feathers & the fan, you silly boy. My warmest heartfelt thanks, sir. I keep both at my bedside so that I may see them when I first open my eyes each day. That is proof of something, is it not?

*****

14 April 1889

Forestport, New York

Dear Renée,

I've just returned from the final ice harvest with my hopes keen for word from you. How positively thrilling that I find among my correspondence a letter posted from Galveston. I make a brief response herewith; a more thoughtful missive shall follow closely.

I am taken with the simplicity & candor of your letter. It is with the same candor that I tell you of my thoughts. This vile body trade I have carved for myself continues full force & yes I shall have future supplies for your college. Of this I am certain. But this business wears on me. Complications have developed. I am greatly puzzled by how a few of these bodies have come to me. Facts I've discovered in Buffalo lead me to think something heinous is afoot & I wish you were here to afford me your valued opinion.

With regard to the business of ice, I am toying with the idea of constructing a Van Horne icehouse in Galveston. No better deal might be struck, I suspect, than to supply my pure & precious commodity to your tropical climate. What do you make of this proposal? Please take pen in hand and tell me your opinion. I ardently await the postal delivery that will bring me more of your admirable thoughts.

With my utmost good wishes,

yrs most sincerely,

Nick

44

A Funeral in the Village

The morning of Old Jack's funeral dawned sunny and crisp. The ground was frozen, the snow still piled high, but by late morning, when Nicolas and Abigail walked down Main Street to pay their respects, the snowbanks had begun to drip.

Nicolas chose a freshly starched shirt and collar, tied on a dark cravat, and donned a jacket of lighter wool. He planned the usual excuses about his wife's not being "up to snuff." It was the truth, after all. Ruth was at her window, morose and silent in spite of the beautiful spring day. Nicolas hadn't bothered to tell her about Old Jack. She'd hear of it, he was sure. Rumormongering and dwelling on the latest village passing were the favorite avocations of the Valdis coterie of melancholic ladies.

When Nicolas and Abigail entered the front parlour of Chubb's Funeral Home, the languid, gloomy strains of a popular tune drifted from the adjacent parlour, where the undertaker sat still as a statue at his Steinway. Adam fidgeted on a side bench with his wife, Gert, and his eldest son, who'd worked the woods with Old Jack last fall. Every soul in the village knew Old Jack. The settees, sofas, and benches of the place were filled.

Nicolas approached the coffin with Abby in tow. He paused to give a nod and a wave to the boys, Little Jacky, Samuel, and Knox, who sat in the corner, all well scrubbed and suited out in their Sunday best. The new boy Knox wore an ill-fitting borrowed suit. He stared glumly at the body of Old Jack in its open coffin and didn't acknowledge Nicolas's wave.

The music faded. Chubb put an end to the piece just as Nicolas and Abigail presented themselves to the line of Old Jack's relatives. Jack's brother—a geezer who was an exact image of Old Jack—stepped forward and offered his hand.

"Van Horne. Good to see you—" The brother's voice cracked. Visibly silenced by grief, he managed a faint smile. Nicolas and Abigail offered condolences.

"Sure are worse ways to go," Jack's brother said, shaking his head. "He'd a wanted it this way."

"There was no better man on a scraper or an ice plow."

The older gent stepped back, allowing others to take Nicolas's and Abigail's hands and smile at the Van Hornes' conciliatory remarks. When they arrived at the coffin, a younger woman with a narrow, pinched face and small, metallic eyes stepped forward and scowled.

"You're Van Horne, aren't you?" she asked, a flush of emotion rising up her neck. "The ice man?" She didn't offer her hand, leaving Nicolas's arm dangling in the air between them.

Nicolas nodded.

"You've got some nerve," she said, her voice rising shrilly in the sudden silence that overtook Thomas Chubb's establishment. "Come to view a body you're fixing to steal, are you?"

"I . . . I . . . ," Nicolas stammered.

"You'll not succeed in your grave robbin' with my grandpa, I'll tell you, sir. I've purchased Mr. Chubb's finest casket. He seals 'em with lead, makes 'em impervious to the likes of you."

Disconcerted, Nicolas stepped back and rose to his full height. "I should like to know," he asked of the other young lady standing by Old Jack's casket, "who it is that advises this misguided lady."

Thomas Chubb, master of funereal proceedings, wisely chose the moment to come down hard on his ivory keys with an "Ave Maria" that would've made Schubert weep. The other women pulled on the belligerent's arms, murmuring to her.

"No, I'll not hush!" the woman grumbled, trying to shake free. "I heard all about him and his dirty little business."

Nicolas hurried Abigail to the coffin to give the body a once-over. This was not the Old Jack he'd known on the ice of Upper Spy Lake. The body was laid out in a dark grey worsted suit like nothing the old boy had ever owned. Jack's once-rosy and hale countenance was crudely powdered and rouged over, his knobby hands were folded in an immovable pose, his hair was parted perfectly down the middle, and his bush of a beard had been brushed and curled like a dandy's.

Nicolas gave Jack's cold, hard hands a squeeze, then turned and led Abigail to the settee where Adam sat with his family.

Adam shuffled over. "Some secret, huh, boss?"

"Miserable woman." Nicolas prepared to settle on the settee, ignoring the eyes trained on him.

"Get a look at poor Knox," Adam said. "He's takin' Jack's death mighty hard."

"I wonder," Abigail asked, "where he got the good clothes."

"Jack's granddaughter took him in," Adam whispered. "The crazy one who was just screaming at your father. She dressed the boy up, Boonville style."

Nicolas gave a nod. "The kid looks well fed."

As soon as Nicolas settled, Abigail reached over Adam and tugged at his sleeve. "Father! Father!" Lost in thought, Nicolas at first ignored her, but she persisted like a little girl. "Father! Something just came to me," she said under her breath. "I saw that thing before, that weird thing."

"What thing, Abby?"

"The mark. That weird mark you showed me on the crazy dead Canuck."

"On his shoulder?"

"That spidery thing. I thought it looked familiar, but it was different when I saw it on a living person. I only had a quick glance."

"You saw it before? Where, Abby?"

"Remember when we stripped the boys in Cookie's shanty after they went through the ice? I saw that thing on Knox."

"Knox . . . the mark . . . ," Nicolas muttered, the truth of it sinking in, the truth that he'd found a boy who'd managed to stay alive, a boy with the mark he'd seen only on the dead.

"Yes, Father. On his shoulder. It's a sort of a brand, isn't it?"

45

Knox

The day after Old Jack's funeral, Nicolas sent Abby to the granddaughter's in Boonville to talk to Knox.

"He clammed up," Abigail reported, seated at her father's kitchen table. "Wouldn't tell me a thing."

"Did you get him alone, Abby?"

"Never. Old Jack's granddaughter is awfully protective of the boy."

"I'd best talk to him."

"I doubt you'll get in the house, Father. Once she recognized I was a Van Horne, that little witch was shutting the door on me. I smooth-talked her, explained how I'd worked the ice with Old Jack and just wanted a moment with the kid. She let me in for a few minutes but never let me out of her sight."

"We need to know more about Knox, Abby. Where he's been. Who his uncle is. I'll try talking to the boy myself, somehow."

"Only thing Knox gave away—he's sure not from Franklin County. He couldn't name me one town up that way."

"Did he admit he was an orphan?"

"No, but I'll bet dimes to silver dollars the man who brought him isn't any uncle. Knox couldn't tell me his name either."

"I suspected as much."

"'Mr. Wilson.' That's all he'd tell me about the man. Did you find what Thomas Chubb knows?"

"Damn him, no," Nicolas said, giving the table a thump with a balled fist. "Thomas disappeared after Old Jack's funeral. He seems to sense when I'm coming with questions. The word at Stillman's Inn is that he's back in Buffalo."

Nicolas asked himself, *Where do boys sneak off to in the spring?* The answer came easy. Once the snow begins to melt and the rivers run wild, packs of young boys wander the upper reaches of the Black River. Above Town Lake, the river becomes a racing torrent, a perfect place to launch cans, bottles, and wooden ships for a wild ride to Forestport, and to sift for treasure in the debris washed from the upriver lumber camps and cottages.

The trail that ran along the north bank of the Black River was rougher going than Nicolas remembered it as a child. Piles of debris left by the spring torrent blocked the way. Slushy snow made the going slow. Last summer's dead brambles tore at his trousers.

Boys were scattered along the riverbank, lounging on the melting snow, fighting, peering at the standing waves of rushing brown water. Nicolas recognized no one until he came on Samuel, Little Jacky Casler's friend, who was shot-putting heavy rocks from the bank into a deep pool. Samuel said he'd seen Knox. They'd been playing together on the trestle just minutes before.

The trestle loomed just upriver. Nicolas saw a lone figure sitting on the railroad ties where the track was still over land, where a boy could easily climb down if he heard a train whistle or felt a rumble. It was Knox, his legs dangling.

Nicolas walked closer and called, "Knox! Jump down!"

"It's you?"

"Yes, it's me, the boss on the lake. Jump down now. We need to talk."

"I ain't gotta do nothing just 'cause you say so, mister."

As if to prove his point, Knox stood and strode down the tracks toward the far bank.

"Come on, son. Come back and jump down. Train'll be coming along anytime." Knox swaggered further out; this boy had no fear. "Remember, Knox, I'm the one holding your pay. If your uncle comes for you and I refuse to pay . . . if I tell him you didn't work hard enough, or you—"

Knox stopped and turned. "I don't gotta," he shouted back.

Nicolas nodded and held up a hand. "No, you don't, that's true. But Old Jack would've wanted you to collect your rightful pay. It would only be fair, and Jack was a stickler on fairness."

Knox spun around and walked back a few steps.

"Come on down."

He slipped off the trestle, dropping ten feet to the packed pine-needle trail. He was a thin, gawky boy, but he'd had his growth spurt so his eyes were level to Nicolas's shoulders as they faced off. He jutted out his chin. Sinewy stretches of muscle ran through his neck.

"Whaddaya want, anyway?"

"I need to ask you a few things, that's all. I came out here so we'd be alone. Nobody around. You understand? We can talk."

"About what?"

"Where'd you come from, Knox?"

The boy's eyes darted to the woods. "Up north. Way up north, like I told that Abigail lady."

"Look, son, there's got to be something you want. Is it money?" Nicolas watched the boy fidget from foot to foot. "You worked hard on the ice, didn't you? When your uncle comes for you, maybe I can have a talk with him. You should get some of that money for yourself."

The boy's eyes shifted back to Nicolas. "He'd never do that. Besides, I don't need to tell you nothin', 'cause you can't boss me around. You're not the real boss man."

"So who is the real boss man?"

"I ain't tellin'."

Nicolas shifted from foot to foot, took a few steps closer and looked up. "Look, maybe Abigail and I . . . maybe we can figure how you could stay on here." Nicolas saw a light in the boy's eyes, a subtle twitch of his head. "Where were you born, Knox? Just tell me that much."

"In a hospital."

"A hospital?"

"Yeah."

"Where?"

"My mother needed an operation, see? They had to cut her open so's I could get born, but then she up and died. I don't remember any of it, anyhow. It's just what they told me."

"Who told you?"

"My stepmom, when I was little."

"Where was the hospital?"

"Poughkeepsie."

"You lived with your stepmom."

"Yeah, but she caught the grippe. By then my old man drunk himself to death. He was dead a year already when my stepmom got sick and they took her away to the hospital, seein' as she couldn't breathe."

"So they sent you to an orphanage."

"Nope. I was on my own. Then, on account of . . . on account of I got caught behind the counter at the soda shop, they put me in the Home for Wayward Boys."

"For stealing?"

"When the stupid old man wasn't looking I'd go quick to the cash register and pull a bill out from the high side."

"The big bills."

"Old fool. He left the drawer open for the taking." Knox reached in his pants pocket and came out with a corncob pipe. "Got tobacco?" he asked.

"All I have's a panatela."

Nicolas pulled the cigar from his jacket and handed it over. Knox smiled and pocketed his pipe. "Thanks." He struck a match on a rock and lit the cigar's tip. Leaning against the tarred beam of the trestle, he gave a few perfunctory puffs till the cigar tip glowed.

"How old were you when you went to the home?" Nicolas asked.

"Ten. Last year, when I was eleven, the men come to get me. They don't take boys too young. You gotta be big enough to work. When Mr. Wilson come, I jumped at the chance to get out. Like he told me, I just call him 'uncle,' and I was out."

"So your uncle's name is Wilson."

"They're all Mr. Wilson. A few call themselves Mr. Smith. They don't have no real names."

"Was he from Poughkeepsie?"

"Buffalo. A big city like that, there's lots of rich folks, see, and they'll make ya rich like them if you're one of the lucky ones, like me."

"But they stick you in a work crew. That won't make you rich."

Knox gave it a moment's thought. "Yeah, the crews are horseshit work, for sure. But not me. Uh-uh. They said I was special. After one more turn on a work crew, they're gonna make me a foreman. Then I'll have my own crew, I'll be in on it. No more factories and horseshit work for me."

"Work on Upper Spy is horseshit work."

"Yeah." Knox gave a nod and flashed a grin. "But I kinda liked it."

"You were good on the ice, Knox. Old Jack thought you were good, too. He told me so." Nicolas saw something flicker across the boy's face at the mention of Old Jack. "You could work it next winter for us, Knox. You'd replace Old Jack. We have summer work, too. If I talk with Abigail, you could start right away."

"Nah, they'll be coming for me. One more work crew and Mr. Wilson'll make me a foreman."

"Where do these work crews go?"

"All over. Big cities, mostly. Factories."

"Does anybody ever escape?"

"Uh-uh. They'll beat ya. They'll kill ya."

Nicolas shook his head, feigned disbelief. "Nah."

"I mean it, mister. If somebody tries to run away, they'll get 'im. We all know it. They make an example. You hear different things, but I heard they slit yer throat, or strangle ya. That's what I heard."

"How many like you?"

"I got no idea. The girls go off one by one, quick. Ones I knew all went to Chicago. But the boys go off in work crews. They sent one bunch of boys to Chicago, too, to the yards, musta been twenty. Lots go to the garnet mines here in New York. I was in a crew of six headed to the tanneries in Gloversville, but then the boss man had this idea to try the lumber mill in your town, so I says, 'I'll go,' 'cause I heard them tanning chemicals make you sick."

"That's when Abigail hired you on."

Knox chuckled. "Yeah, so's I could do your horseshit work." He stepped away from the trestle and studied the cigar in his hand, more like a middle-aged man than a twelve-year-old. "It wasn't so bad on the lake. At least it's upstate. I'd hate if they sent me out west or somewhere. I'd die working in that heat."

"It's not bad on the lake. Walk back toward the village with me, Knox. Just a little ways. I'll tell you about what needs to get done over the summer. It takes preparation to harvest ice. There's plenty of work."

"Horseshit work?"

"Some of it."

"Nah, I made a deal with them. See, I'm getting special treatment when I go back, when the boss man comes to get me."

"You want to be like Old Jack, don't you?" Knox gave a faint nod. "Old Jack never shied away from honest work, and he never needed any special treatment. I bet you don't either, not from people like them."

46

The Boss Man

Nicolas heard the pounding of the black stallion's hooves when Abigail was still a block down the hill. He'd already thrown open the screen door and stood on the porch, jacket in hand, when she drew the horse up. Horse and rider were both winded. Abigail's eyes were wide with excitement.

"He came for Knox," she called from the saddle. "The man who brought him."

"Where's he now?"

"I put him off, said I hadn't seen Knox and he'd have to wait. I told him I'd send word to him where he's staying, at the Butterfield House. His name's Wilson. Ernest Wilson."

"Best get word to Old Jack's granddaughter in Boonville, Abby. She needs to keep that boy out of sight." Nicolas pulled on the jacket. "I'm on my way to this Mr. Wilson."

The small, simply appointed lobby of the Butterfield House was deserted. An Oriental settee faced the fireplace, where a large moose head hung. It was a warm spring day; the snowbanks were melting fast and the fireplace had gone cold. Nicolas sent the desk clerk to Ernest Wilson's room with a message, then took a chair at the japanned writing table near the window. The dark velvet drapes covering the nearest lobby window had been parted, allowing a patch of morning sun to warm the writing table.

A pleasantly plump, well-dressed gentleman around Nicolas's age, with reddish side beards, came down the stairs into the hotel lobby. "I take it you're Van Horne," he said, extending his hand when Nicolas stood. "The name's Wilson. I'm here for Knox, to collect the boy's wages and so forth. Where's the boy?"

"Please, have a seat. I need a word with you."

Wilson frowned and cleared his throat. "If it won't take long," he said, sitting. "We need to be on our way."

"You see, Mr. Wilson, I'm afraid I've advised the boy to stay put until we straighten out this situation."

"Situation?" Wilson straightened and crossed his arms tight around him. His face hardened. "This boy's 'situation,' as you say, is that he's an unruly sort of fellow, a delinquent despite all my trying to keep him in line. That about sums it up."

Nicolas tried to sharpen his senses and concentrate. He needed to study this man. Wilson was so ordinary, so bland looking. A common brownish tweed jacket; no hat; a rounded, pale face with no distinctive features. He could've been a member of some agency, perhaps a bonds-and-futures man, or someone trading in assurances. On a closer look, though, well hidden beneath Wilson's thick side beards lay a raggedy, well-healed scar a good six inches in length. Also, there was a thin scar above the left eyebrow. Any one of a hundred common mishaps could've caused such lesions. A fall from a horse, a field accident, a tumble as a child in a haymow where a sharp tool lay submerged. Or something more sinister.

Wilson's face relaxed. He chuckled and gave a faint smile. "The boy's my nephew, you see. An orphan, so I feel a certain responsibility for his delinquency."

"You're from up north, I heard."

"Yes."

"Washington County, was it?"

"What does it matter? Did you get some work out of him?"

"Indeed we did. He turned out fine, working the ice."

"That's what counts, eh? And you know, Van Horne, I have several nephews willing to work, and work hard. Should you need to add to your crew, you might consider us. Now, if I can just collect the remainder of the boy's wages, and the boy, we'll be on our way."

Nicolas leveled his gaze. Wilson returned it across the table. "Sir, I saw fit to pay the boy those wages directly," Nicolas said, fighting to keep his tone steady. "He deserves the wages and, no offense, but I wondered if the boy would ever see their benefit."

"The rascal told you something?"

"I spoke with him, yes."

"Where's he at?"

"Safely tucked away."

"Listen, Van Horne, I've a right to the boy. He's family, so cough him up."

"Afraid not. The boy stays. I'm taking a personal interest in the lad."

Wilson's face reddened, the cheek scar suddenly more obvious. "You'll regret this, sir." He sighed and pushed back his chair. "In any case, there's plenty more fish for the kettle. I'm just as happy to quit your little burg." Wilson rose and made for the stairs as quickly as he'd appeared. As he grasped the first newel, he hesitated and turned. "You realize, Van Horne, the boy's legally mine. There may be repercussions to this."

"I assure you, we've totally competent lawyers hereabouts."

The edges of Wilson's mouth ticked up in a malevolent smile. "Oh, I was thinking of something far, far more serious, I assure you. There's a fellow in your town named Chubb. Ask him, why don't you. Ask him about repercussions."

His heart pounding, Nicolas kept to the shadows on Main Street until he saw a carriage carrying Wilson toward the bridge. He then took a horse from Abby's stable to the railway station, where a discreet enquiry revealed that the "gentleman" with whom Nicolas claimed he "had business" had purchased passage to Buffalo, as Nicolas suspected. Wilson was headed south and west, not north.

So he'd seen one of them—these men who took boys prisoner. Nicolas was nonplussed by what a gentlemanly appearance the fellow presented. Nothing special, a regular gent, reasonably dressed and so forth. The scars were the only things setting Wilson apart.

One other distinctive feature Nicolas observed, or perhaps imagined. When Wilson had climbed the stairs to leave, a ring flashed on the gent's left hand. It was something like a club or fraternity ring. A large sapphire glinted in the spring sunlight. Laid over the stone was a delicate gold filigree that looked awfully similar to the spidery cypher Nicolas had grown to abhor, the brand seared into the flesh of boys, both dead and alive.

47

The Undertaker

After slogging through the mud and slush to check nearly every barroom in Forestport—there were six—Nicolas found Thomas Chubb in the Antlers Inn. In Nicolas's mind the Antlers Inn, a dank, musty, poor man's drinking establishment, was not Thomas's type of haunt. It was a real hellhole. The local undertaker, one of the richest men in town, had stooped low. Thomas looked somehow smaller, too, sagging onto the top of a small table near the window, far from the noisy crowd at the bar, staring over his whiskey at the muddy street and the dirty, melting snowbank just outside the window.

"I saw you coming," he said.

Nicolas dragged a rickety chair to the table and pulled a grim face.

"I stashed another for you," the undertaker said, forcing a smile. "In my mausoleum. An old woman from the sanitarium. Send Adam, and we'll get her to the icehouse. Thank God you've got it filled, eh?"

"I'm not here to discuss business, Thomas. And don't try to look surprised. You've been dodging me, and you need to tell me what's going on. Something pernicious is afoot; tell me what you know."

"I can't, Nicolas."

"Yes, you can and you will. Who's this Mr. Wilson?"

The smile quickly disappeared from Thomas's face. "You of all people understand about a secret, Van Horne. Sometimes, they're very necessary in certain business arrangements."

"Who are these men?"

"They're businessmen like you or I, that's all."

Nicolas's thoughts went to Abby and her disgust with her father, with his business. He'd be better off without Thomas Chubb. He had depended on the man for too long.

Nicolas pushed his chair back and stood over the undertaker. "Business? Business?"

The place went quiet. He grabbed Thomas by his lapels, brought his face close, and whispered, "Those boys were murdered, Thomas. *Murdered*," he hissed. "Tell me who these men are."

"I . . . I can't say. They'll kill me if I tell, Nicolas. They'll kill me."

Van Horne saw the naked fear in the undertaker's eyes. He let go and stalked out.

48

Mud Season

Nicolas struggled to sit upright on the warm leather of the couch in his study. He cracked open an eye, shook his head, massaged the stubble on his chin.

Outside, mud season bore down on the village. The ice had gone out from the northernmost lakes, and the last raft of logs had crushed its way to the mill. In the village, rivulets of snowmelt ran through the streets, leaving only mud. Mud was everywhere—slick clods of it clung to every boot. Spring had come promising summer and sunshine, but for weeks all it offered was mud.

Nothing was going well. The morning after Thomas Chubb had refused to tell Nicolas anything of substance at the Antlers Inn, the undertaker left town "on business." That same morning, Abigail came to the house with more bad news. Knox had disappeared.

Nicolas thought he'd won the boy over, convinced him to hide from Wilson. He'd promised another season on the ice, more pay, the best bunk in the bunkhouse. Was the boy already dead? Strangled, and at the bottom of a lake? Nicolas's only hope was that he had fled before the murderous culprits came to collect the young scalawag from Old Jack's relatives.

Nicolas rode like a madman to Boonville to speak with Old Jack's granddaughter. The woman opened her front door no more than a crack, barely showing her weaselly face. "His uncle came for him and off they went—all good and proper," the shrew told him. "And good riddance. Now I'll thank you to get off my porch."

The skeletal hands of the clock on the mantel in his study pointed accusingly to noon; its ticking was like distant cannon fire echoing in his head.

"Oh, Nic-oh-las . . ." Ruth's voice drifted down the stairs like a siren's call. "I'm due a treatment, Nicolas. It's time. Are you in your study?"

His study: old leather couch, oak filing cabinet, Chippendale secretary that the years had darkened to a dense, grainless black. Nicolas stored his logbooks, contracts, and actuarial supplies here, but with the ice harvest finished there was little bookkeeping to do, and far too much time to experiment with the contents of the medicine chest that crouched like a mountain cat at the foot of the secretary.

"*Nic-oh-las?* It's time."

He climbed the stairs and measured Ruth's morning dose of laudanum. He'd had trouble lately bringing the yellow liquid to the proper line etched in the glass; the tremor in his right hand seemed worse each morning. He'd been adjusting his nightly morphine, trying for the pleasant white dreams it had once brought, but lately, they eluded him and the tremor lasted longer into the day.

"There you are. I've taken care."

He walked to the rocking chair in the corner, the chair Ruth had nursed their infant children in. The chair's creaking and its easy motion seemed to calm the tremor. Ruth took her eyes from the dirt-streaked window and blinked as if she'd wakened from a dream. A tense grin crossed her face and she began to reminisce. "How that Schuyler loved to eat," she said brightly. "More than anyone at the Van Horne table. Don't you remember?"

"Yes, I remember, Ruth."

"Abigail, meanwhile—frail as a stick." The smile faded from Ruth's lips. She turned back to her window.

Melancholy. Every cure, all the latest from New York and Europe, and still her body withers. Soon she'll be a skeleton. Where is the woman I once desired? The one who laughed at clouds of bats flitting over Town Lake?

"Schuyler was always the one who . . ."

Schuyler, her favorite. The second born, the healthy, sensitive son. Schuyler rebuffed her attempts to teach him to hunt, to fish . . . he spent his adolescence pounding on Thomas Chubb's ivory keys. All the boy ever cared about was his own entertainment. The good life, the gaming life.

"Why must you spend all day in your study, Nicolas?"

"I . . . I have details to attend to."

"All those letters? I've seen you at your writing station, you know. Letters are everywhere."

Nicolas's thoughts wandered to his study and his well-stocked medicine chest. Once, the careful use of morphine and a tincture of this or that gave his heart joy, his life color. Lately, no combination, no dosage, worked.

At night he tossed, dozing fitfully. He'd begun experimenting with a whiff of ether at bedtime as a remedy. A can of ether, uncapped; a bit of cotton dampened; the chill of the solvent. Ether's sweet volatility, so pleasant at the end of the day. With an extra whiff, it induced a lasting sleep.

"Here, now, Ruth. Your chowder." His hand trembled as she took the bowl. "You need to eat and build yourself up."

Nicolas left Ruth holding her bowl of chowder and returned to his study. In the mantel mirror, he examined his face. Nicolas had always taken pride in the fact that unlike many successful men, he had never allowed excesses of food or drink to cloud his mind or lard his body. He knew his carriage to be graceful, his midriff trim, his limbs firm. He'd always felt ten or fifteen years younger than his years. But now, at forty-one, he'd gone soft. Since the last ice harvest, he caught himself slouching. He needed a shave. His duds were long overdue to the tailor for refurbishment. The skin about his eyes had taken on the color of liver, and there was this infernal tremor of his hand.

Later, in the dead of night, Nicolas pulled on his boots, buttoned his musty jacket, blew out the lamp, and slogged down the muddy streets. It was time to check with the postal mistress on Main Street. In the months since the final ice harvest, the arrival of the Adirondack Mail Express had become the pivotal point of his day.

"Train seems late," he said to the postal mistress. "I thought I heard its whistle."

"Mr. Van Horne? You know the timetable, sir. Train's not due at the station for thirty minutes, and it takes another thirty to ride the mail bag over. Two trains a day, noon and midnight, Mr. Van Horne. Noon and midnight."

"I'll wait."

"We'll have the mail bag here by half past, weather permitting."

A letter was found. Nicolas rushed up the hill to the house, kicked off his boots, and retired to his study. The precious posting. He reached for his silver-plated letter opener, wielding it like a sword as he cautiously slit the envelope.

It was four in the morning when Nicolas applied his signature and sealed his reply. Time no longer counted for much; he sat at his secretary for hours, reading, rereading her letters, writing with the passion of a man who knows no timetable.

Dawn was at the window. His head seemed to have cleared. He'd managed an entire night without morphine. Now, with his pent-up thoughts on paper, he needed a deep, rejuvenating sleep.

With his ear tuned for the distant keening of the Adirondack Mail Express's noon arrival, he reached for the can of ether.

49

Letters: An Appeal

5 June 1889

Forestport

My dear Renée,

I cannot thank you enough for your letters. Their arrival brightens my mood & clears my clouded thinking.

I would tell you how our days grow longer & green things are blooming, but my mind has not been on the weather. As I've told you, recent discoveries have led me to suspect a dastardly abuse of children perpetrated here in the North Country. Of late, this has preyed on my mind and tortured my dreams, yet I get nowhere with my enquiries.

My first hope was that this is only a rare cruelty, however I now fear its scope may be larger. How to uncover the wrongdoers & expose them to the authorities remains the problem. I would so value your opinion in this matter, Renée. How I loathe the vast distance between us. I've always survived by my wits, but my wits fail me on this confounded issue, this puzzle that refuses to unfold.

Here is one bright idea that's hounded me. Might I not visit you before my scheduled ice shipment in the new year? The icehouse is full & we already have a reasonable supply of 'commodity' for your uncle (12 to be exact). Things are at a standstill, business-wise. Most important, I would benefit from your clear thinking on this odious scheme I've uncovered. A single passage by train to Galveston, in midsummer—is this not an excellent idea?

I admit, my thoughts are with you often, Renée. Morning 'til night I am ravaged by torrents of emotion & my mind wanders from matters at hand to my sweet new friend & her faraway life. Do I confess too much?

Write me soon with your judgment on this plan to travel posthaste to Galveston, & do not fault me for these confessions.

Yours with deepest feelings,

Nick

50

Letters: A Warning

Dear Nick,

I have your recent letter in hand & how my heart races at your mention of an early return to Galveston. I so want to hear more of this cruel plot you've uncovered against children. I will gladly offer whatever help possible to end such a detestable business, and I can only hope that I have not added to your confusion through some unthinking guile of my own during your earlier visit.

I confess, too, that the thought of my friend the ice merchant again setting foot on our sandbar is exhilarating. But alas, Nick, a journey south now would be ill advised. Consider it no further. The threat of yellow fever to the uninitiated, unexposed individual, a Northerner like yourself, is far too great. Your premature return would be a virtual death sentence. I worry too much for my good ice merchant's well-being to encourage a move of such rashness . . .

*****

. . . I shall heed the warning of one so expert in the area of epidemics, etc. Nevertheless, dear Renée, I am despondent. An early arrival was such an exciting possibility, and would so help me to understand and perhaps solve my present

predicament. The fact of the matter is, I wish to see you in the flesh, so to speak. But when?

Your letters bring me respite & warmth & yet, precious friend, I could use your advice, your intelligent assessment on this important matter that has me at wits' end. If only I could see your haunting smile & hear your soothing voice.

*****

51

In Her Lab Quietly

She was confused, and Dr. Renée Keiller had rarely known confusion. Throughout her years of university studies, her stay at the Sorbonne laboratories, and her travels along the South American coast in search of *Aedes aegypti* for Uncle Francis, Renée had always maintained a demeanor and confidence to match any man's. She thought and acted with crystal clarity. But now, ever since her gentleman friend from the North departed, she'd been distracted, and even confused.

In the quiet of her laboratory, especially late in the afternoon, she caught herself standing aimlessly at the laboratory window, thinking of Nick, the tall, strikingly handsome gentleman from New York. The trader in such lovely ice. She remembered how he entered a room, with every movement of his limbs purposeful and masculine, a man in command of his fate . . . though lately—in his letters—he seemed deeply concerned over this strange matter he'd uncovered. Hopefully, it had nothing to do with the wretched boy he'd delivered to her, for the cells. She yearned to help Nick, to see Nick.

Her feelings about Nick ran so deep, so visceral, she suspected they might be caused by a pathological fluctuation of the vagus nerve. When this emotional turmoil struck, it reminded her of the excitement of discovery in the laboratory. The same thready pulse, the same thump of the heart occurred when, entering her lab at the midnight hour, the electric lights flashed on the whitewashed walls and revealed the details of an experiment in progress. Those few instants when Nicolas had looked into her eyes caused a similar burst of energy, almost electrical in nature. Surprise, exhilaration, an acute release of excitatory chemicals into the bloodstream. Yes, this perfect gentleman had a powerful effect.

And Nicolas did indeed appear the perfect gentleman, though she'd been deceived by appearances before when it came to men. She judged these things poorly. There'd been the gentleman in Havana, a university professor, a researcher like herself, who'd spent the better part of the long rainy winter after her husband died trying to seduce her, unsuccessfully. She'd had European suitors, Spanish speakers with glib tongues. None amounted to much.

She needed to keep her head about her, to rethink this Mr. Nicolas Van Horne from New York. Perhaps she was wrong about him. Perhaps he was nothing more than a hardscrabble mountain man with a head for commerce. A well-traveled bon vivant, a connoisseur of younger women, an ice trader on the prowl for another meaningless dalliance.

No, that wasn't right. Somehow, she trusted herself about this man. Their moments together had been honest moments. She told herself that the passage of time would dull these emotions, but her heart knew otherwise. She worried about his entanglement in this dangerous business of cadavers. She so wanted to hear more about this thing, this "abuse" being perpetrated in the North. To be near him, to help sort out his theory about children being forced into labor.

It was a struggle to keep from revealing all these concerns to those around her. She couldn't help but blush at how loudly her heart pounded. Everyone must have heard its thrumming, especially when a new letter arrived.

Her mother certainly noticed. A woman of uncommon sensitivity, a medium, a clairvoyant scientifically proven to be capable of communicating with spirits, her mother was a lightning rod drawing unspoken energy from whoever came near. Just that morning her mother had told her, "I sense your feelings, Renée, and I understand. You're not wrong to harbor such emotions, darling. But we're living in the modern world, and above all, one must act like a lady."

"I realize that," she'd replied after a moment's thought. "He has a life of his own, but can we not have a fine friendship, nonetheless?"

"Just remember, dear . . ."

Basil Prangoulis, that clever old devil, sensed it, too. Basil could hear it in Renée's music, with each strum of her harp, the sadness, the longing. It wafted from the upstairs parlour after the supper hour; it was captured in the random little melodies she composed when she glanced away from her sheet music and her heart spoke through her fingers.

Her mother and Basil certainly must've noticed the letters. How could they miss them, stored carefully aligned in the slots of the secretary in the corner of her bedroom? Rows of letters worn nearly through with handling, read over and over by the light of the lamp at her bedside, a lamp Renée kept burning far longer than usual . . . The same lamp that lit the fan and the feathers, his parting presents to her.

"He writes you often," Madame La Porte had said at breakfast, some weeks before.

"We agreed to correspond, Mother."

"Is he forward?"

"Certainly not. He acts the complete gentleman."

"Well, then, you must answer him promptly. It's only polite."

Lately, the letters came in a flurry. She learned more about him than seemed humanly possible from mere writing. His fears, his dismay at the heinous things he'd uncovered. His concern for the unfortunate children he thought in danger. His tortured feelings over . . . their time together in Galveston. Was she reading too much into his words? She sensed words behind the words, parsed a deeper meaning, as if she were seated next to him at his inkwell.

Uncle Francis commented on her odd demeanor, despite the pain his tuberculous spine gave him. Dear Uncle was beginning to realize she spent more hours with paper and ink than with her laboratory notebook.

"I . . . I must finish this quickly." She whispered to herself, seated at her secretary, pen in hand. "A bit of rest and then . . . back to the laboratory."

The pen scratched.

"*I admit, Nick, that I share your desire.*' No, that won't do. Not at all. Perhaps this—'*I, too, am thinking of you in a different way.*'"

She thrust the pen back in the inkwell.

"*A different way.*' This must stop. It must go no further."

Another letter, half finished, torn and thrown to the floor. She paced by her bedside, kicking idly at the accumulated scraps of her smoothest vellum.

"I need to fight these feelings. Already patients are arriving at the hospital with fevers, and the anti-toxoid still eludes me. I must concentrate on my work, my calling."

52

Letters: Epidemic

. . . I confess, dear Nick, I grow despondent about our progress in the laboratory. We are well into the hot season & cases of yellow fever fill the wards. Uncle Francis & I remain convinced of our theories, we are working day and night, but with death bearing down, a suitable anti-toxoid from the horses seems unlikely. At best we will implement the cure for next summer's deadly assault.

And, yes, my dear Nick, I, too, think of you in a different way. But you must stay put. Our letters must do . . .

*****

. . . How I hate that you face such horrors, Renée. The death & suffering you describe is hard to fathom. I think of you & your colleagues often & I hope & pray for your successful experimentation to find the anti-toxoid & effect the cure. How lofty your purpose, how greathearted you are to care for these doomed souls.

If I could assist your noble work in some way, I would dedicate all my resources to it, but I fear your science is beyond my meager understanding . . .

53

Return of the Wayward Son

It was Abigail's voice in the distance, carrying over water from the far shore of the lake.

"Wake up . . . Father . . ."

Someone shook his arm. He stirred and found himself reclining in his study, as he'd been, he admitted, for most of the summer, the couch's dark, rutted leather fragrant and dank with sleep. It was late July, yet he'd dreamt of ice. He fought his way out of a ghastly dream of dead boys piled on the lake's frozen surface, a grisly heap of limbs forming unintelligible cyphers.

He squirmed and cracked an eye.

"Not again," Abigail said, her hands on her hips. "Another whole night on the couch, eh?" She stared at the disorder of Van Horne's study. The jumble of writing materials and stacks of letters. The drug paraphernalia. "You'll get no proper rest sleeping in your clothes."

Nicolas swung his legs onto the floor and rubbed his face awake.

"Sky's back in town."

"Sky's here? Sky? Ah, good. I need to speak with the boy."

"I heard he was at Stillman's, so I went last night and heard him banging away on their piano. I told him he'd better come by the house, or else."

"Oh, Schuyler, Schuyler, do I have plans for you, my boy."

Nicolas had been in the same room with his son only twice since New Year's, and both times they'd ended up in a row over money. But Nicolas had thought hard on Schuyler's waywardness since the night of his return from the South. He vowed to change his tack. At age twenty, it was time for Schuyler Van Horne to get serious about earning money the Van Horne way. But Nicolas would coerce and convince rather than rail at his son. He'd start with a reasonable but profitable proposition—one that involved Galveston.

"You see," Abby continued, "his money's run out. I confess, I lent him a bit after your last row, and even that's gone."

The morning July haze lifted, the sun shone, and deerflies swarmed in the warm pines. Nicolas threw open the kitchen windows and heated water. He prepared the steel tub for a bath in the spare room off the kitchen. He soaked a good hour, until the hot water had softened the dried, dark blotches that lined his arms. His attempts to decrease his morphine use hadn't gone well.

By noon Nicolas had eaten some crusts of bread with jam and donned lighter, summer pants and a fresh shirt. The afternoons had been exceptionally warm the past few weeks. Raucous finches flitted outside the window. Nicolas sat on the couch in his study, rehearsing his measured approach until Schuyler's resonant, deep profundo, perhaps a full tone lower than Nicolas's voice, penetrated the study from the kitchen.

"I tell you, Sis, I must! Gawd! The mess I'm in. I'll do whatever's necessary."

"You'd better, if you know what's good for you."

Nicolas sprang from the couch and rushed to the kitchen, where Abigail stood arm in arm with her older brother.

"Hello, hello, dear Father," Schuyler sputtered, embracing Nicolas. "I'm happy to be home." He backed away gingerly. "Truly, I am, Father."

"As am I, Schuyler. Might I ask, dear son, where you've been these past months?"

"In New York City, of course. Didn't I tell you? Ah, that greatest of metropolises," Schuyler said, looking skyward with an actorly gesture of the hand. "Entertainment, Father. That's what I'm all about. Playing my music in the public houses, the cabarets. Now they have me arranging shows. I hire only the finest of professional singers and dancers."

Nicolas scowled, despite his promise to himself to remain calm. *Singers and dancers, indeed. Trollops and streetwalkers, more likely.*

"The big publishers are finally onto me," Schuyler went on. "My songs jam the taverns, especially with the newcomers to the city."

"I heard him," Abigail interjected. "Last night at the inn—and I admit, he bangs 'em out. It drew quite a crowd."

"That was nothing," Schuyler said. "In New York, we run three, sometimes four shows a night. They arrive in droves, fresh off the boat. Irish, mostly."

"But, Son," Nicolas said, "it's been months since we've seen you."

"I'm sorry about that . . . you see, I have a little problem, Father."

"A money problem, I'm sure."

"No . . . well, yes, but this other . . . It's a bit personal," he mumbled, glancing at his sister. "It's a case of the clap."

Abigail groaned.

Nicolas put a hand to his forehead. "I should have guessed."

"But I have myself a fine doc now, a master with the dilator." Schuyler hesitated, then lowered his voice to a whisper. "I can pee again."

"And what about your drinking?" Nicolas said with a grunt. "Does the booze help you pee?"

"I'm afraid I owe the doc quite a bit."

"How much?"

"A little over fifty dollars, but I was hoping to get an even hundred to advance my ventures in the song-and-dance enterprise. Count it as an investment in my future, won't you?"

"What in God's name happened to all that I gave you at New Year's?" Nicolas asked, trying to control the slow boil in his voice. He knew too well his son's haunts and amusements, the fast horses, the games of chance. "And what became of the money Abigail advanced you?"

Abigail threw up her hands and turned away. "Oh, forget it. Just forget it." She pushed her way out the screen door and stalked onto the porch, out of earshot.

"How about the funds from those promissory notes you so glibly wrote, Schuyler?"

"The money . . . well, the damn horse wouldn't run."

"You lost it all on a horse?"

"It wasn't my fault! I was trying to capitalize on the funds . . . They were neck and neck!"

"And your horse lost."

"By a nose," Schuyler muttered, his head down.

Nicolas went silent, struggling again to compose himself. *All on one horse.* For Nicolas, who enjoyed playing the ponies as much as any man, a leisurely day at the races was a rare treat. For Schuyler, it was serious business.

He started again, slowly, in a firm, persuasive tone.

"Understand me, Son. You'll never win at gambling. That New Jersey crowd at Monmouth is too rich for your blood. You know that."

"You're right, Father. I've had it with horses. Song and dance and music—entertainment—that's where my talents lie, not the damned track. And now that the publishers are onto me . . . well . . . one needs to meet certain expenses, you see, to live in a certain style. It won't be spent frivolously, I promise. And of course, my doc needs payment."

The elder Van Horne wrapped an arm around his son's meaty shoulders, linking them together, these two men of dissimilar stature, Nicolas the taller, his features more finely carved and his mustache and chestnut-brown hair shades darker than Schuyler's sandy mop.

"Come sit a moment, Son." They sat and faced each other across the kitchen table. "Before I fork over any more money, I have a proposition for your future."

"I'll not harvest ice, if that's what you're after."

"It's not about the harvest, Schuyler."

"I told you, Father, it's too damn cold. I can't stand on that lake in winter. My feet freeze."

"How about a warm climate, then? How about building an icehouse?"

"Building?"

"I want you to supervise the building of an icehouse in Galveston." Schuyler gave a blank stare. "It's in the state of Texas."

Schuyler gasped. "Texas? With wild Indians and buffalo and—"

"Ha! None of that," Nicolas chortled. "It's quite civilized. First, you'll go to Saint Louis to study our icehouse there. Come October, you'll take the Saint Louis blueprints to Galveston and supervise construction of an icehouse on their harbor."

"I don't think so."

"I'm thinking of an even larger icehouse, perhaps big enough to hold forty thousand tons. We'll have to decide which is the best wharf to build on. We'll cut out the go-betweens, Schuyler! It'll boost our profits. The South's a perfect market for ice, nearly untouched. It's hot as Hades and ice is of great use for the fevers that plague them."

Schuyler, still unconvinced, shook his head.

"It's the family business, Son," Nicolas said. "Try this once, won't you? Wait until you see Saint Louis, boy. It's a boomtown. The cabarets are famous."

Schuyler's face brightened and Nicolas pressed on.

"Once you've built the icehouse, you'll be free to return to New York to this song-and-dance business of yours."

Schuyler seemed about to give in and agree when the stairs from the second floor creaked, and Ruth stood shakily on the bottom step.

"Schuyler, my darling," she said in a whisper. "I thought I heard your voice."

The wayward son rushed to embrace her. "Mother, it's wonderful to see you . . . but you're still ill."

"I'm never well, Son."

"You're so pale and . . ." Schuyler stepped back to study his mother. "You must come to the city," he chided gently. "Really, Mother. We've such wonderful medical men. I myself have recently made the rounds of the surgical institutes."

Abigail, meanwhile, stepped in from the porch with her arms full of potatoes and turnips. She skulked past Schuyler and their mother to the stove, where she stoked the embers remaining from the morning. She pulled a Dutch oven from the shelf and banged the pot onto the stove's hot spot. "We'll need something to eat," she grumbled, unnoticed by the others. She broke the seal on a Mason jar of preserved venison and dumped the meat into the Dutch oven, where it gave a faint sizzle. She opened a bottle of beer, tested a sip, then poured it in.

Steam rose from the heavy pot. Schuyler said, "It's getting too damned hot in here," and led his mother out the screen door to the porch, leaving Abigail at the stove and Nicolas at the kitchen table.

Abigail worked the kitchen pump, and scrubbed and peeled the potatoes and turnips she'd retrieved from the root cellar.

"Have you heard any word about Knox?" she asked, eyeing a turnip.

"Nothing. Adam's put the word out in town. Up north, too, as far as Saranac."

"I'm terribly afraid for Knox," Abby said. "That Mr. Wilson gave me the creeps."

Nicolas, too, was unsettled by the thought of another dead boy. "I've no idea what else to do about Knox," he said. "We may never know what became of the poor devil."

Abigail set the top on the pot, pushed it to the back of the stove, and turned to her father. "It's good to see Sky. He's fatter than ever but he looks well, despite his little medical problem. Do you think he'll take you seriously about Galveston?"

"I've been dreaming of this icehouse all summer. Think how good it'll be for business, Abby. I'll arrange funds for him, I'll do it all tomorrow, but he's got to get over his cantankerous ways. He's got to."

"He can hardly change what's in his blood, Father."

Nicolas gave her a stony look.

"I must give this another stir," she said, turning to her stew.

54

Letters of Intention

18 July 1889

Galveston

Dearest Nick,

I shall travel north! Uncle's colleagues at the university in Boston have devised new methodologies to obtain antitoxoid from horses. I must travel to Boston to learn from them. The timing is uncertain, but the sooner, the better. I will depart within the next few weeks. Final commitments are being wired as I write. How my heart pounds at the prospect!

I shall travel near you, Nick. May I impose for a brief visit? Let me know your thoughts. A day's rest in the coolness of the mountains would be welcome.

I fully understand the delicacy of your situation, but I so want to see your beloved North Country firsthand . . .

*****

. . . I can't wait to see you, dear Renée, & it's certainly no imposition. Indeed, it's a summer's long dream come true.

I would suggest, given the situation, as you say, that we settle on some mutually convenient venue for a meeting. Perhaps Saratoga. The racing in August is lovely fun, but you must make at least two days for it. I keenly await your response . . .

55

Upstate Arrival

For Nicolas, the noon departure of the Mohawk Valley Flyer was a quick ride to Albany. As the verdant hills rolled past his coach window, whole paragraphs of Renée's letters ran through his head. He'd memorized every word, especially the parts where she bared her feelings for him, even told him of her "racing heart" and her thinking "in a different way."

Nicolas was thinking differently, too. Schuyler had embarked for Saint Louis, set on the right path, and that progress emboldened him. Even the nagging problem of murdered children in his ice faded in his mind and seemed conquerable as the wood lots, fields, and valley towns whisked by, their chimneys busily belching the stuff of industry, their stations crowded with men of commerce. Perhaps, after all, Knox would be found alive. He had his best man, Adam Klock, searching the entire North Country.

As the train drew into the crowded outskirts of Albany, he imagined Renée in her coach, steaming east behind him, perhaps by only a few hours. His trip had been quick and comfortable, whereas Renée had endured four full days on the train in the August heat. She would be weary.

What a surprise, then, to see her step off the train at the central station, his dear friend the lady doctor, bright as morning. Glimpsed through the oncoming rush of debarking passengers, Renée's wry, intelligent smile lit the capital city's platform. Nicolas, not sure of what to expect, rushed to her, his heart ratcheting up in his chest. She came toward him, hands out.

"How well your youth serves you," he said with a nervous laugh. He took her two hands firmly in his. "You truly are a remarkable woman."

She leaned forward and delivered a peck to each cheek, very European. Nicolas caught a whiff of the soot and cinder-dust of long nights in a railroad coach—then, that lovely apple blossom scent, recalling in an instant his island visit months before.

"You cannot imagine," she said, stepping back with a sigh, "how I've dreamt of this moment." Nicolas felt heady, charmed by the familiar, sibilant ring of her voice. Here in Albany, though, had he caught a gentle, Southern cadence he'd not noticed on the island of Galveston?

"How is it possible you look so well rested?"

"To tell the truth, I'm in dire need of a powder room."

"I've just the thing," he said, leading her on his arm down the platform to the baggage car. "I've taken rooms for this evening at the Grand American—the best in Albany. As my honored guest you'll have whatever you wish, and after some supper and a good night's rest, we'll be off to Saratoga to play the horses."

A carriage waited. The lady's Pullman case was loaded and within a few city blocks they stood in the airy atrium of the Grand American Hotel, where arrangements had been made, rooms prepared, the staff alerted. Nicolas accompanied Renée to her room on the third floor and watched her nervously from the hall while she walked about the elegant, modern accommodation.

"It's lovely. You've done splendidly, Nick. Will you give me an hour?"

"I'll await your arrival on the mezzanine."

Nicolas stood over a whiskey, checking his watch and drumming his fingers on the marble of the mezzanine bar. The damned watch's mechanism, though Swiss-made, seemed agonizingly slow. When the gold hand had inched itself beyond the full hour, a waiter appeared at his side with a silver bucket.

"Something special, sir." The waiter swirled a dark bottle in chipped ice. "I've instructions from a certain lady, and a lovely one, I must say. You're to join her on the balcony."

Nicolas followed the waiter to a small second-floor balcony above a crowded veranda where guests were gathering to dine. Renée leaned over the iron rail, wrapped in a sleek, purple dress of Oriental silk, a matching velvet ribbon at her throat. She was watching the diners below and the activity in the town square. She turned and laid a hand on the bottle. "It's French."

"Champagne? All the way from Texas?"

"It's a bit of a celebration, don't you think?"

The waiter led them to a table for two set against the balcony's ornate balustrade. He poured. Below them throngs strolled across the square and a crush of carriages rolled by in the gathering dusk. The waiter backed away. They were alone. Nicolas leaned across the table, his heart racing.

"I can't seem to find words tonight. After your letters, seeing you seems so . . . exhilarating."

She reached absentmindedly for her glass. "I'm anxious to hear of everything that's befallen you, especially these troublesome developments you've uncovered, Nick. But first, there's something we must discuss." She sipped, set her glass down, and looked him in the eye. "Our arrangement. Our personal arrangement."

He was sure his heart skipped a beat. What did he expect? Surely she would put him off. He was a married man. Any demand of such an exceptional young woman would be absurd. "Whatever you wish, Renée."

"Others will see us differently, you know, being together like this."

"I understand."

"And I confess my thoughts sometimes run wild along lines I'm not accustomed to." A frown flitted across her brow. "Nonetheless, I propose that the friendship we forged in Galveston is of paramount importance. Let's keep it that way, shall we?" She reached across the table and grasped his arm in her two hands. "We must keep our heads about us, Mr. Nicolas Van Horne. Friendship above all. What do you say?" she said, giving a gentle tug. "Do you agree?"

"I . . . I should have said so myself." *So her letters meant nothing. Feelings put to paper are more fragile than the paper itself.*

"You're the perfect gentleman, Nick. That's precisely why I've come to visit." She settled back, glass again in hand. "Now, tell me what more you've learned about this strange plot you've uncovered."

Nicolas recounted everything, starting from the moment he left Galveston in an agitated state over the occurrences there. He told her of his stopover in Buffalo, where he confronted Professor Flynt over the dead boys. He described his confusion over how murdered boys arrived in his ice. As he spoke, Nicolas was surprised at how easily these unnerving facts—facts he'd never spoken of to a single human being—seemed to tumble out. Indeed, the telling of it all somehow assured him he was on the right track.

"All the facts I've uncovered," he said, "point to a coordinated gang of criminals who enslave orphaned, wayward youths."

Renée listened with a thin, attentive smile. Her champagne went untouched. When Nicolas told of Abby's discovery of the murdered woodsman dragged out of the ice cave and his later realization that the woodsman was one of the boys, grown to a criminal himself, Renée shook her head in dismay. "Your daughter's a brave one," she whispered. "The poor girl."

Nicolas felt his chest and shoulders tighten when he told the story of Knox, the new boy working the ice harvest, a lost boy whom Abigail had unknowingly hired. When Nicolas described his recent confrontation with the so-called Mr. Wilson, Renée's dark, green-speckled eyes widened in shock, telling him precisely how serious was the trouble he'd stumbled into.

When he finished, Nicolas settled his elbows on the table and reached for his champagne. Renée was pale and subdued.

"It's . . . it's terrifying, what you've uncovered. Your daughter understands this?"

"I've kept the murdered boys, and my worst fears, from her. She and Adam know only that the boy Knox is in danger. Indeed, this is the first I've spoken of it, all of a piece like this."

"You recall, Nick, my consternation over your body business. I confess something to you—I knew the boy you brought me had been murdered. The signs of strangulation were evident. Forgive me for not telling you."

"I recall your cautions. I remember everything about Galveston, especially our evening together. Our dinner. Trudeau's. The ride to the beach."

The faintest blush colored Renée's cheeks. "Yes. Cold, windy, and thoroughly delightful."

"But what's to be done about this mess? Knox has vanished—perhaps he's not even alive—and I have no idea how to hunt down this Mr. Wilson, or the Mr. Wilsons of this gang."

"I so wish I could help, because I'm as guilty as you. I should have reported the frozen boy to the authorities, but my experiments hinged on his fresh tissues. Such perfect specimens. Our best efforts at the medical college always seem to put us outside the law. Anatomy. Experimentation. It's a murky business, Nick, full of risk from all sides."

"But it's too late to turn back. I must do something."

"Well, you can't go to the authorities about these boys any more than I was able to." Renée's gaze wandered over the balcony's rail to the diners on the veranda beneath them. "My," she said with a gentle shake of her head. "We're in quite a pickle, aren't we?"

"I was so hoping for a lovely visit for you—"

"A lovely visit it will be."

"Yes, it will." He took up his champagne. "I feel I've known you for years, Renée, like an old school pal."

"And look where it's led us."

The waiter was at their side, pouring champagne. Nicolas felt the tension in his chest relent. A cool, dry breeze came from the street. Below, the evening promenade of passersby had begun, filling the walkways and streets, most in dark, formal evening clothes, the men's top hats bobbing, the women's full bustles aswirl as they took the cooling air with umbrellas clutched against the chance of a summer shower.

"Shall we dine on their veranda?" Renée asked, her wan profile betraying the fact that she'd not eaten much for days.

"The Grand American's not known for its kitchen. I propose a short walk to a German rathskeller I know, not much to look at but superb dining. Spiced meats and sausages. Potato pancakes. A delicate Moselle. Sound good?"

"Excellent. We'll talk more."

At the rathskeller, they stayed late at their table in a dark, underground corner lit only by candles, and Nicolas explained at length his plan to build an icehouse in Galveston. "It's an ideal market," he said. "I've already funded my son's efforts. Schuyler's in Saint Louis studying our facility even as we speak."

"I'm sure your son's a clever fellow," Renée said with a nod.

Nicolas settled back, warmed by the wine and the hope afforded by his son's newfound dedication to the Galveston venture. Perhaps that boy would make a business partner after all.

"But one thing, Nick. Be sure your son doesn't depart Saint Louis before October. Yellow fever took hold early in the South. The death toll in New Orleans is in the thousands, nearly that in Galveston. Every day at dawn carts full of the dead roll down our streets, rich and poor alike. We've run out of coffins, and the Magnolia Colored Cemetery has taken to burying in long, common graves. It's no place for a Northerner."

"How close are you and Uncle Francis to a cure?"

"We have a proper anti-toxoid that performs well in the test tube, but only small quantities. We must devise a method for large-scale manufacture. Only then can we understand the doses, the exact regimens necessary."

"So there's hope."

"Not for this summer, I'm afraid. In Boston, the professors at Harvard create anti-toxoids more potent than ever, in great quantities, and they're testing in patients at their General Hospital. I'm scheduled to begin my studies with them three days from now."

Three days. Three heavenly days. Nicolas leaned back and lit one of the rich-tasting French cigarettes he'd purchased while waiting at the bar. He rarely smoked a cigarette, this newfangled habit young men like Schuyler had acquired from the Europeans.

Three days entirely free of worries about dead bodies. So many hours, so many minutes, with Renée.

"Saratoga will be the perfect diversion for you," Nicolas said. "There's the racing, the gambling. Perhaps we'll take a paddle on the lake."

"And best of all, there's you, dear Nick." The corners of her mouth trembled, as if she were struggling to put on a smile. "Still . . . it's difficult to forget the suffering I left behind."

Nicolas raised a glass. "I propose a toast to the Medical College of Galveston, the good Professors Keiller—both of you—and to the cure you'll surely perfect upon your return."

They walked the city streets until past midnight. In the hallway outside her room, Renée took Nicolas's hand and pressed it warmly. "Thank you for a wonderful evening," she said as she pulled her door open. She hesitated. A simple peck to the cheek . . . "Good night, dear Nick" . . . and a second that lingered.

The next morning before catching the train to Saratoga, Nicolas and Renée walked arm in arm through the fashion district. The goods on display in the shop windows seemed more vibrant, more enticing than Nicolas had ever noticed in this city. Could it be the brilliance of the August sun? To others on the busy street, he was sure they appeared just another couple, more handsome than most, shopping for the lady's needs and laughing a great deal, and perhaps a bit flustered with each other.

Renée purchased a new straw hat at one of the finer shops.

At noon their bags were readied and they boarded a northbound car of the Mohawk & Malone Railroad for the short hop to Saratoga.

56

Saratoga

It was August in upstate New York: the sun shone bright, honeybees swarmed over meadows of clover, maple trees hummed with the sound of hives filling…and the horses were running at Saratoga.

Throngs of elegantly dressed men and women filed through the entrance gates of the world-famous Saratoga raceway. The flags of many nations fluttered atop the steeples of its grand pavilion. The track, the stables, the picnic grounds came alive with beaming spectators awaiting an afternoon of racing. From the furthest-flung points of the globe gamblers had come to stroll by the stables and size up the horseflesh. Laughter rang out. Wads of greenbacks were laid down at the betting booths.

Nicolas and Renée cut a striking figure as they strolled the grounds with race sheets under their arms and bets in their pockets, basking in the sweet, summery smell of freshly mown alfalfa and the neighing of well-bred horses. Nicolas had chosen his bow tie with the tiny brown diamonds, the Saratoga pattern, widely acknowledged to enhance one's luck at the track. Renée thrust a single pink ostrich feather into the band of her newly purchased straw hat; the hat's broad brim flapped in the summer breeze.

"Why, that's one of the pink feathers I left you."

"You see how perfectly I've kept it."

The trackside crowd was rambunctious; their hoots and hollers fairly drowned the bugler's call.

"Which is ours?" Renée asked as the hot-blooded steeds, strung tight as violin strings, filed toward the start line for the first race.

"Number nine, the chestnut."

"They're off!" resounded across the track and the horses flashed past the rail in a hail of flying turf. When number nine crossed the finish line, the handsome couple laughed aloud.

"Dead last." Renée chuckled. "We really must take a closer look for the next race."

They peered into the stables, inspected the horseflesh, and strained to overhear the high rollers whose pockets bulged with winnings.

"Now that's a horse I prefer," Renée said. "That dark one, the filly. What a beauty."

"She's running in the fourth race," Nicolas said, after he consulted his racing sheet.

"Let's bet her, Nick. Bet her big and she'll pay for our losses."

"That theory rarely works," he said with a smirk as he penciled a note alongside the filly's name. "Nice horse, though. Says here she's a two-year-old out of Morgan's stable in Vermont, and Vermonters breed fine horses, or so my son says. Schuyler thinks he knows fast horses."

Nicolas felt a burst of pride, mentioning his son's name. Schuyler's venturing to Saint Louis had buoyed his spirits ever since the boy left Forestport. Nicolas keenly awaited a report, though he well knew it might take weeks to get one's bearings in a strange city.

Nicolas and Renée bet losing horses in the next two races. In the fourth race Morgan's dark filly thundered off the start line, took an early lead, and easily held it to the finish. When he returned from collecting their winnings, a beaming Nicolas sensed that Renée's mind had wandered from the task of picking fast horseflesh. From under the shade of her straw hat, her gaze wandered to the distant pastures rather than the track. The summer sun beat down. Nicolas stopped under the maples along the stable path to remove his derby and mop his brow.

"What is it, Renée?"

"I was thinking about our discussion last night," she said. "And your problem."

Nicolas looked up, derby in hand, damp handkerchief in the other. "Yes?"

"I've read that in England, poor, desperate girls—mere children—are sold to older men as concubines. Apparently, it's a brisk underground business."

"Knox told me about girls sent off to Chicago. Forced into prostitution is my bet."

"In England it's called the 'white slave trade.' How horrid. Young girls, sold as toys to the rich."

"You're suggesting these lost boys I've discovered are like these white slaves?"

"Precisely. Slaves to work crews."

"Then they have slavemasters."

"Your Mr. Wilson and others like him."

Nicolas donned his derby and they wandered toward the track, discussing as they went. As the fifth race thundered past, he admired Renée from the corner of his eye. He longed for something, something he couldn't pinpoint. Surely he wanted badly to solve this problem of dead boys turning up in his ice, a problem that Renée saw to the heart of . . . yet there was this undefined longing. Perhaps he wanted nothing more than a touch of that pink feather rustling in the breeze. Better yet, a kiss in the warm sunshine. That thought sent a tingle rippling down his spine.

Renée stepped away from the rail and turned toward him. Her eyes met his. "What are you thinking?" she asked. "No . . . don't tell me. I see it in your eyes."

"Would you be shocked to know I'm tempted to steal a kiss?"

"That, good sir, would not surprise me in the least," she said with a smirk and a conciliatory laugh that hinted a small kiss, out of sight, might not be terribly untoward. "We're two people on a similar wavelength, I'm afraid. Like sympathetic strings ringing. But, as you know, given your situation—"

They wandered the grounds until they found themselves ambling through a stand of hemlock. Picnickers had spread colorful cloths on the pine-needle floor in the deep shade. Nicolas's mind flew to that impulsive moment when they'd shared a kiss on Galveston's beach. *This would be the time and place. Here, with the fresh piney scent of the forest floor under us.*

"The last races will be running," Renée said, a tinge of sadness in her voice.

"Let's catch them from the clubhouse, shall we?"

The clubhouse, where the elite of Saratoga dined at trackside, was a private area sheltered by the pavilion rooftop. Tables were set with fine linen and china. Men were required to check their top hats and derbies at the entrance to allow an unobstructed view of the track. To those fortunate enough to have gained a seat, summery iced drinks were served with flare from a long copper bar.

"Wretched packed, isn't it?" Nicolas said, surveying the tables, where couples gaily sipped cocktails and studied race sheets. A group of men of commerce stood along the outer rail, race sheets in their jacket pockets, enjoying an afternoon cigar. The waiter, who quickly gauged the elegance and position of each guest, seated Nicolas and Renée at an intimate trackside table with a prime view. Nicolas's heart swelled at the sight of Renée being helped to the seat beside him. He ordered a whiskey, fixed tall, with Saratoga springwater. Renée had lemonade.

They studied the steeds parading to the start line. Renée pointed out a particularly fine Arabian. "Some fine horseflesh," she said. "Your son would approve."

Oddly, Nicolas hadn't heard her comment. Instead, his attention was riveted on a man a few feet from their table, one of the businessmen. The gent, his hand on the rail, was leaning out to admire the dark Arabian stallion.

"What is it, Nick?"

Nicolas whispered, "One moment," and scrambled to his feet. In the next second he was gone from the table, facing the man, a robust, middle-aged fellow in a suit of quality wool with lapels encrusted with pins and ribbons. The gentleman seemed taken aback. He raised a finger in Nicolas's face. A rapid-fire exchange of words. Nicolas kept his arms stiff at his sides, his face reddening.

Nicolas took a step closer; the stout fellow turned abruptly and scuttled toward the entrance. Van Horne followed a few steps, his arm raised, then the man grabbed his hat from a hook at the clubhouse entrance and was lost in the crowd beyond.

Nicolas, shaking his head, returned to the table.

"What . . . ?"

"That man was one of them," he said.

"You recognized Wilson?"

"No. The man's ring."

Nicolas, breathless, waved their waiter over and made a brusque enquiry. The waiter looked off to the rail where the man had stood. "Why, yes, of course, sir," he said, smiling as he took the bill Nicolas slipped him. "I'll enquire immediately."

"His ring, Renée, his ring," Nicolas said. "It had the mark I've seen on them. A figure in gold on a stone, a sapphire."

Renée looked puzzled. "What figure, Nick?"

"Let me show you."

Nicolas reached in his pocket for his pencil and race sheet. He flattened the race sheet on the snow-white tablecloth and began to sketch in the margin. His hand shook. Scowling, he scratched out his first attempt and searched his memory, sketching slowly, carefully, as if he were drawing a design for the patent men in Albany.

Ж

Moments later the waiter returned and bent to Nicolas's ear. "The gentleman's name is Wilson," he said. "A regular at the clubhouse. His line of business isn't known, I'm afraid. Mining, perhaps?"

"And his city?"

"Buffalo, sir. Of that, I'm certain."

As a blood-red summer sun settled onto the mountains in the distance, and the last of the steeds filed by, Nicolas and Renée—such a handsome couple at a trackside table—were deep in conversation. They hardly noticed the sunset, or the horses.

57

The Fort Stanwix

When the ninth race ended Nicolas and Renée took to the busy streets of Saratoga.

"No, I've no idea of the mark's significance," Renée said, studying again the mark on the race sheet in her hand as they strolled side by side.

"But you've seen it before."

"Of that I'm certain. I've seen it on young women while on my rounds in the hospital."

"Have you ever seen it on boys?"

"No."

"That boy you used for your experiments—he had one."

"Really? I . . . I didn't notice."

"Clearly, you were preoccupied."

"Yes. Like I say, I've only seen it on young women, and only the type of woman destitute enough to come to our city clinic. I assumed it was some sort of ritualistic sign given them by their brothel-keeper or madam."

"In Galveston."

"Yes."

"That far from New York then."

Nicolas had chosen the grandest of the lakefront hotels for their Saratoga rendezvous, the Fort Stanwix, only a short carriage ride from the town center. Upon arrival, they retired to their separate rooms to prepare for the evening.

At the appointed hour Renée stepped down the Stanwix's staircase dressed in a light blue evening gown of feathery silk. The gown was high necked, with a tightly fitted, modern waistline, flowing skirts with no train, and puffed sleeves accented by lace at the wrist. Heads turned. Other lady guests, having played away the afternoon at croquet and lawn tennis, were strolling the lobby in jewels and black evening attire, heavily trussed and wasp-waisted, with cumbersome bustles that—even on the richest—seemed somber stuff to Nicolas. He caught a murmur among them: "That sea-blue dress, much too simple, isn't it?" . . . "a lady doctor" . . . "from the South, I believe."

Renée took his arm with grace in her step. Her wry smile lit the hotel lobby.

"You're the loveliest item here," Nicolas said.

"Oh, hardly. These others are simply dripping with diamonds, aren't they?"

Nicolas noticed Renée's effect on other men, who eyed the naturally slim waist and the blue swirl of her youthful step. Still others strained to hear the Southern ring in Renée's voice as she greeted her gentleman friend.

They walked a winding path and settled on a bench overlooking the lake, where they returned to their most serious topic of conversation.

"When you find these men, Nick, you must call for help from whatever connections you have, whoever might help."

"I have Harvard chums spread over New York and New England, I suppose."

"As far as Buffalo?"

"I've even a few associates in Chicago, though I never chose to open a market for ice there."

"Listen, Nick, while I'm in Boston I'll contact whomever you wish."

"An excellent idea."

"It sounds like the path leads to Buffalo. You'll be in danger, so go slowly. You mustn't do this alone. And we must think more on it."

In the smallest, most intimate of Saratoga's dining rooms, they continued over an upstate country supper: a bounty of frog's legs, speckled trout, and partridges, accompanied by the famous paper-thin Saratoga potatoes and sweet corn fresh from the cob.

"I've collected quite a number of bodies for my winter delivery to your uncle."

"He'll be pleased. Will you supply New Orleans?"

"I'm put out with New Orleans. They penned an invalid banknote last March. Once I've unloaded ice in Saint Louis, I'll make my merry way to your island. You know what recommends Galveston most, of course."

"The warm climate?"

"The pleasure of your company."

Nicolas thought he caught her smiling at that, but perhaps it was only the bright red of the strawberries arriving at the table in rich local cream that captured her fancy.

As dusk drew near, Nicolas hired a young boy to row them across the lake in his sleek Saranac guide boat. The strong-armed lad stood ankle-deep in the cool water, steadying the gunwales with a firm grip while Renée and Nicolas settled into low cane chairs facing each other. The evening was clear and calm. The lake was flat. A sliver of a moon lay low along the shoreline.

As his boat glided to the steady swish of his oars, the young boatman fixed his gaze on the shore. Nicolas saw that he'd chosen wisely. Here was a lad who'd learned discretion; he certainly wouldn't notice should a gentleman lean forward for a kiss in the falling darkness. But only once did Nicolas think to take the lady's hand. They never seemed to stop talking. There was hardly a quiet moment that might've led to something.

Later in the evening a five-piece band of violins, violas, and cello set up on the Fort Stanwix's rambling porch and worked through a repertoire of Strauss waltzes.

"Shall we?" Nicolas asked, offering his arm. He guided Renée onto the smooth planking. "The Blue Danube" played. His arms encircled her and Nicolas—who hadn't danced in years—quickly regained the solid frame and fluid step of his youth. In an extended interlude between pieces, he lingered and, in plain view on the empty dance floor, pulled her to him. Guests went quiet around them.

"Nicolas, not here."

He tightened his embrace and kissed her. The veranda came alive with whispers.

"You naughty boy," she said with a grin, pushing away gently. "Show off all you want, good sir." She turned and stepped along the veranda. "Still . . . I'm flattered."

When the band struck up another waltz, Renée held him at arm's length. "It's late and I'd best be off to my room," she said, waltzing gaily along the porch rail in time to the music.

Nicolas followed her to the staircase. "Till tomorrow, then?" he asked. She turned, nodded down at him, and was gone.

In the quiet of his room Nicolas found his heart bumping in his chest with a newfound velocity, a steady, warm thrashing. Perhaps his nerves needed settling. He'd packed his works and a bit of morphine mix in his portmanteau, but no, he'd not open it and resort to that false tranquility. Instead, he drew the curtains open to the night and paced the floor. The fiddles played on below, guests chattered on the veranda, but Nicolas could think only of Renée, that apple blossom scent, and the taste of tonight's stolen kiss.

He should have her, should he not? He wanted her—that was the truth of the matter. It would be wrong in the eyes of the world, but he wanted her. His life had changed. His children had grown. His melancholic wife was no longer the woman he'd known. This new life, these emotions, could no longer be denied. Renée had become everything to him, everything he wanted and needed. Now, deep in the night, he admitted this to himself, and decided to act.

"Tomorrow, I confess my feelings," he said to squares of moonlight by his bedside. "I must tell her she's the one. It will be our last evening. She'll not deny it's far more than friendship between us. She said as much herself, didn't she? How'd she put it? 'Sympathetic strings'?"

Nicolas settled into the hotel's fine-smelling sheets, content to relive the evening and mumble into his pillow.

"There's no other course," he told himself. "It's a matter of the heart."

Sleep took him quickly, as it will for a man with his mind set to action.

The next morning a fine warm mist hung in the air and towers of chalky clouds rose and fell in the dangerously dark sky. Nicolas arrived at the breakfast table where Renée waited, her dress a mysterious mixture of colors, Tyrian purple, sunset orange, and sea green, like some tropical orchid. She extended her hand and slipped back into her chair smooth as silk.

"Shall we spend the afternoon at the races, good sir?"

"We shall, weather permitting."

By the time they'd finished breakfast, it was raining.

58

At the Tables

Sheets of blood-warm rain poured relentlessly onto the track. Racing was canceled, the horses stabled. By noon, warm bodies in damp summer finery filled the casino, jostling and bumping around the green baize of the tables. Windows were thrown open, but any suggestion of breeze had long since died and the dark red walls dripped with dampness. Gaslights blazed hot and bright over the gambling tables; collars were loosened, jackets removed.

Nicolas Van Horne and Dr. Renée Keiller sat at the roulette wheel, spreading small bets on the black, playing the corners. Despite the oppressive heat, Renée appeared cool and at leisure in her brightly dyed dress with its formfitting bodice and light, elevated sleeves.

"Oh, my," Renée said with a sigh. "We're losing again, aren't we?"

Nicolas studied the table, wondering if that seven might be his lucky number. *Never had a lucky number. Lately, haven't had a stitch of luck, but that must be due for a change, mustn't it?*

Time was slipping away. Before long it would be evening, their last evening. On waking this morning, however, Nicolas had undergone yet another change of heart. With the dismal weather raining down, he realized that no matter how desperately he wished it, he couldn't press the issue of romance with Renée. He wanted Renée more than anything—he'd admitted that to himself last night—but to force his attentions on her was out of the question. She was too fine a lady for that. She was his friend, his confidant, his confessor, and now she had become his valuable accomplice in searching out and destroying the heinous child slave trade. He would confess his heart to Renée, his inner thoughts and hopes, nothing more. He would do it when evening fell, when the rain cleared and they would take another row across the lake.

"Blasted hot in here." Nicolas stood to remove his jacket and hang it over the back of his chair. "Hotter than Galveston, I suspect," he said, rolling his shirtsleeves nearly to the elbow.

"Few places are hotter than Galveston," Renée said with a chuckle, then the smile that pulled at the sides of her mouth went flat as her eyes became glued on Nicolas's disastrous forearm. "How long have you been injecting yourself?" she asked, taking his hand and giving his forearm a quick, clinical turn. "Morphine, is it?"

"I partake . . . occasionally. Hardly a problem."

"It most certainly is a problem, Nick. No doubt you've heard of a clinical syndrome—"

"A morphine habit such as mine could hardly—"

"You're wrong, Nick. Craving sets in at far lower doses than you might think. I'd hate for a fine gentleman such as you—"

"Don't give that business another thought. Please."

Renée saw something like desperation flicker across Nicolas's face, shiftiness in his eyes. She dropped his arm.

"As far as I'm concerned," Nicolas continued, buttoning his sleeves down with a snap, "it's folderol."

Renée looked him in the eye. "Just remember, Nick," she said, touching his hand. "I've seen what it can do, and it's extremely ugly."

Nicolas laid the last of their chips on the table. "All on the seven," he said. "Straight up."

"*En plein*," called the croupier.

Nicolas bolstered the bet with a handful of bills. "If this hits," he whispered, leaning close to Renée's ear, "it all goes to your lab."

The croupier spun the wheel. The tiny ball sang; all eyes were on it.

"Seven."

"Oh, Nick!" She wound her arms round his neck and gave a tug. A sisterly kiss on the cheek for their victory.

But what was this? Over Renée's shoulder, at the edge of his vision, Nicolas saw a hulking shape push away from a nearby table. A solid-looking, youngish figure, the fellow drew up to his full height and appeared to glare at their table. Was this local ruffian about to cause a scene?

The stout young gambler staggered toward their table, pushing others aside. Nicolas broke his loose embrace with Renée and turned to face the fellow and have a good look.

"Father? It's you!" Schuyler gasped—the wayward Van Horne son who, according to plan, should've been studying blueprints in Saint Louis.

"Sky?"

"You're here?" Schuyler's voice rose high above its bass note. "With a woman?"

Van Horne blanched, his face mere inches from his son's, which was blotched by alcohol and a morning at the tables. "What in the name of heaven…"

Schuyler's eyes shot to Renée. She blushed deep scarlet. "Who is this?" he asked.

"Why . . . this is Dr. Renée Keiller of Galveston. She's a scientist, a fine friend. We met during my stay in the South, you see, and—"

"Oh, I see all right," Schuyler said, backing away, his eyes wildly searching the room. "I've seen too much!"

"It's not what you're thinking, Schuyler. It's not."

But the younger Van Horne rushed away as abruptly as he'd appeared, leaving Nicolas and Renée speechless.

"Your son . . . ," Renée said slowly. "I'm sure he thought—"

"He must."

The blacks, the reds, and the spinning wheel forgotten, Nicolas settled both elbows onto the dark green velvet tabletop. His head sank into his hands.

"Don't hate me for this, Nick," Renée said, her voice trembly. "Don't hate me."

Nicolas lifted his head. "Never. I could never . . . *Damn Schuyler to hell! He's supposed to be in Saint Louis!*"

Renée stared out the window at the pale afternoon. "I should go, Nicolas. I'll arrive a day early in Boston, but . . ."

Dazed, Nicolas stood from the table, feeling for his jacket, looking about for his derby. He must . . . he must call a carriage to the Fort Stanwix. He would oversee the loading of her trunk.

The croupier called to the handsome couple as they wandered away from his table, but they didn't turn back. Their pile of winnings was left behind, abandoned on the number seven.

Contrary to all plans laid, all dreams dreamt, within an hour Nicolas and Renée found themselves entwined under the awning of the Saratoga station while rain poured down from an angry sky. They held firm until the last moment, stunned, unable to find words. Two blasts of the train's whistle, and still they clung to each other.

"We weren't in the wrong, Nick."

"It was right. It was always right. How . . . how could things turn so badly?"

"Don't forget me, Nick." She pulled back, fear wide in her eyes. "Tell me, Nick. Say you'll remember, say you'll write. Just tell me." The train began to move. She looked to gauge its speed, then plucked up the hem of her wet and bedraggled, multicolored skirts, and ran for it.

"Tell me!"

59

An End to Summer

Nicolas was a caged mountain cat—a wild animal, master of the forest, poised to pounce but with no prey in sight. The summer had cooled, and with it the local demand for ice. There was no business to be done. He had time on his hands, too many empty hours for reverie and regret. Soon he would turn to his needle and the numbing morphine that stopped time and cured all sorrow, at least for the moment.

On Nicolas's opened secretary sat three letters; the first, its edges frayed and worn, read:

> *My dearest Nick,*
>
> *Weeks have passed & still I have no letter from you. Torture me no longer with your silence, sweet friend. Why do you not write? I am desperate to hear from you on your progress in thwarting those evil men. What do you think of my further thoughts on the mark they wear? The brand? What have you discovered?*
>
> *As reported in my most recent correspondence, summer nears its end & yellow fever abates. Uncle is under a great strain & his health suffers. We are injecting the horses daily, but I find it difficult to concentrate & the Boston methods are not working as expected. I only hope that you are faring better with the perplexing conspiracy you've uncovered. I trust the list of names I sent was of use. Remember, stay safe.*
>
> *Oh, Nick, I would give anything to be in Saratoga again. If I could relive those days, I would show you the strength of*

my feelings. (And we would not be at that wretched roulette table.)

I await your safe return to Galveston with all my love & all my thoughts. Please tell me of your plans for arrival. Any word from you would be welcome. Know that I remain

Your loving friend,

Renée

Similarly worn, a letter posted from a wayward son to his father:

14 September 1889

Saint Louis

Dearest Father,

I write with grave reservations, given the nature of our last encounter. Nevertheless, I entreat you to hear my plight. Extraordinary circumstances have befallen me & only you can help.

I write this from Saint Louis, where I was forced to flee from my many creditors in New Jersey. Lord have mercy, dear Father, they will have my life if I do not pay up! I confess fully—my plan was to turn your loan into my deliverance at the tables at Saratoga, then return to New York to pay up. But Lady Luck was not with me. I couldn't return to the city I love. Saint Louis proved my last resort. The New Jersey thugs will never trace me here. I am unknown & there's the most unusual music.

Now, for my new plan—if you could see fit to advance me 300 dollars, it would be my salvation. I know this sum sounds egregious in view of my previous request for far less for my medical problems (which were total lies, by the bye).

Nevertheless, this amount is my only hope to appease my creditors, who are not pleasant people to deal with.

In return for your help, I pledge to fulfill your dream of building a Galveston icehouse. Yes, I am studying the fine art of icehouse fabrication. I now see your building on the quay of this booming river port is a true work of genius. The double-walled construction, so suitable to maintain temperature, the ingenious venting that solves the problem of condensation, & the clever layout of interior storage are all to be admired. Please advise as to your planned location for the new structure in Galveston & any further details of construction, whenever you send the money.

I cannot tell you, dear Father, how shocked & distressed I was by my discovery of you with that woman in Saratoga. In truth, I should not give a fig who you debauch. Nevertheless, as a part of our agreement, I promise to hold my tongue with Mother & Abigail, for your sake & theirs, provided you are willing to assist me, financially speaking.

Write as soon as possible with how you might provide the funds & when. Installments are not acceptable. I must settle quickly with those New Jersey villains, & I vow on my life's blood to follow through in Texas for you, where I plan to travel three weeks hence, after the yellow fever season, per your earlier instructions.

With hope for an amiable agreement,

Schuyler

Morphine, that's what was needed. He'd buy out Boatmann's apothecary, though he knew Boatmann's most powerful mix would fail to ease the pain of the third letter lying on the secretary—a letter in his own hand, freshly penned and awaiting signature for the midnight train.

My dearest Renée,

It is with the greatest torment that I break my silence. For too long I could not find it in me to lift a pen, though I ensure you the source of this paralysis was the extraordinary depth of my love for you. Above all, you must understand that. I think of you every minute of my day. Yet, as a matter of the heart, I must face the truth. It is wrong to torture you with an improper love.

I beg your forgiveness for this decision, Renée, but I must bid you well & farewell in this one letter & call it my last. I am no good for you. I will only bring you down. Trust, however, that you shall always remain in my heart of hearts, in my soul of souls, my darling pen pal, my greatest friend on God's green earth.

It's Ruth, my wife, who needs me most. I have been grievously wrong. Ruth is truly sick & deathly sick, at that. The doctors in Albany tell us her ovaries have gone cancerous & this thing, this horrible thing, has been eating at her all along. I must help her. I must concentrate on my life as it was before I met you, Renée. Before my landing on Galveston.

In spite of this decision, remember, always, I remain

Yours,

Nick

PART 3

Their Separate Ways

60

In the Laboratory

It was well into October before the hot breeze off the gulf died and for the first time in months an offshore flow crossed the island. The air felt fresh and cool, the death wagons were put up, the last corpses were covered with quicklime, and throughout the South city fathers declared the yellow fever ended.

Carbolic hung heavy in the laboratory of Francis Keiller. The elderly professor teetered on a lab stool, hunched over his student's laboratory notes, his eyes raw, his hair awry in the harsh electric light, his bones filling with pain.

"It makes no sense," he muttered to himself. "It's impossible."

The data seemed all wrong, yet this student was his best. He was a bright Texas farm boy, and Keiller trusted the lad's laboratory work as soundly as that of his own hand. The midnight hour had robbed Keiller of his edge; he shut his eyes and rested his head on his arms . . . for only a moment.

"Uncle. Uncle." Renée gently shook the old man's shoulder. "Please come home with me. It's late."

Keiller stirred. Wincing, he slipped off the stool, staggered, and nearly fell. "I need to understand this experiment, don't you see?"

"Tomorrow, Uncle."

"No, tonight. The experiment seemed so obvious . . ." Keiller steadied himself against the lab bench. "Have ye prepared the solutions, darling?"

A nod from his niece, her smoky eyes bleary with exhaustion.

"You're the one needin' rest, ye silly girl. Get yourself home and I'll begin the reactions."

Renée shut the laboratory door behind her, leaving her uncle muttering to himself. He lit Bunsen burners under a line of retorts. With the reactions under way, hours of observation lay ahead; there'd be time to reassess the boy's data while he watched his retorts bubble through the night.

Just days before, Keiller's student Patrick had failed to transmit yellow fever to a horse, despite using Renée's most potent sample of particle. The scientists put their heads together and decided Patrick had somehow killed the particle, though the young man swore he'd not altered established procedures, and Keiller's repeated searches of the student's notes found no flaw in technique. Patrick was admonished to begin the experiment anew.

"They're still only boys," Keiller told himself, laying down the student's notes. "Ah, youth. A simple error of transcription, no doubt." Keiller limped to his retorts and adjusted a burner.

What puzzled Professor Keiller most was that the particular horse they'd been injecting, a powerful draft animal, was now resistant to even the most deadly particle. This saddened him, since the horse, from a breed developed in the Clyde Valley of his beloved homeland, was a favorite. Now the horse would have to be destroyed. Keiller would miss the big fellow.

Lost in thought, with a keen eye on his reactions, Professor Keiller flipped the pages of Patrick's laboratory notebook. Then he saw it—a footnote at the bottom of the page, penned in the careful hand of his finest student.

"Acrylamide? Patrick added ten milligrams of acrylamide? That's it!" Keiller shouted to his empty laboratory. "The particle of yellow fever must've been weakened, denatured a wee bit . . . and that big horse is making a different anti-toxoid, a superior anti-toxoid that makes him resistant to the deadliest strain." Keiller struggled to his feet and made his way down the line of retorts. "Well, then, I'll test the idea with a simple precipitation. I'll begin immediately." He shut down the burners and went to his personal notes to enter objectives for a new experiment.

Within hours Keiller had an inkling of the answer—the method he hoped would yield the most powerful anti-toxoid they'd yet produced. He walked to the north window and threw it open to morning's first light and the pale, opalescent bay.

"What a fool I've been. Patrick's simple error has turned the trick. Now, with what Renée learned in Boston . . ."

Dawn broke and the morning bore down. Two hours later than was her usual habit, just as her uncle lifted his final test tube from its rack, Renée dragged through the lab door. Her eyes were red and puffy and a wan smile was pasted on her face.

"A new experiment, Uncle?"

"Yes, yes. Come. I need your help, dear." Keiller glanced at the clock on the wall. "Where've you been? Oh, look at ye, Renée. You've not slept a wink, and you've been crying again. Listen up, now—young Patrick added acrylamide by mistake, and that draft horse holds the answer. We must be off to the horse barn. We'll draw the big fella's blood, and if his serum's as potent as I suspect, well then . . . Renée, dear. You're so quiet."

Renée and her uncle rode the West End trolley to the desolate end of the island where the college maintained their barns. Along the way, Keiller jabbered constantly; Renée kept her face to the trolley's open window. Finally, Keiller took her by the chin and turned her toward him.

"Renée, I know ye so well. It's your Northern gent you're thinking of, innit?"

Renée shook her head free. "No, Uncle."

"Come now, I see those tears. He's a fine gent, our ice merchant, but it hurts to see you suffer so. Trust me, I may be a foolish old bachelor, but I know more than ye think. Everything will come out in the end. You'll find someone else someday. Aye, you deserve that much."

Renée dabbed at her eyes with the back of her hand. "I'm fine, Uncle." She turned to the window again, to the endless grey beach, the expanse of blue water, the waves of grasses shimmering over the narrow strip of island pastureland.

When her uncle lapsed back into his lecture, Renée felt for the letter tucked inside her smock, close to her bosom. She'd read it a thousand times; once she found a moment alone at the horse barn, she would read it again.

She must write Nicolas Van Horne, answer that horrid letter, and not take his words at face value. After all, she'd done nothing wrong, was guilty of nothing untoward. Why should she stand for such treatment at the hand of this gentleman? How many times had she told herself this? Yet . . . deep down she knew she wouldn't take up her pen. She'd keep her sullen silence, as she had for months now. It was what he'd asked for, wasn't it?

But he'd also asked for help, hadn't he? No matter what else happened in Saratoga, she sensed his eagerness for guidance in that ghastly business of the white slavers. She had plotted with him, told him in her letters every idea she'd had. Now Nick was forced to pursue those dangerous men alone. The risk, the danger, the prospect of facing those awful men—it was all on his shoulders. She didn't even know if Nick was still alive. Oh, heavens, how she hoped and prayed he was safe in his mountains, even if she couldn't have him for her own.

Her uncle was still at his lecture. "If our big barnyard fellow makes the anti-toxoid I'm hoping for, we'll begin trials of dose and treatment regimens soon. You must concentrate, lass. There's work to be done. Yellow Jack's held the upper hand all summer."

"Oh, Uncle, it's discouraging. We've no idea about doses. We'll need some volunteers. And why is it," Renée asked, "that each summer the epidemics grow worse?"

"A good question, lass. Damned Yellow Jack's made it as far north as Philadelphia again. Well, we've got the acrylamide step, thanks to Patrick. We'll find more Clyde Valley horses. They'll give us plenty of blood for you to purify anti-toxoid, and we'll be on our way."

The trolley screeched to a stop. Renée took her uncle's arm as he scurried painfully down the path to the college's horse barns.

"And about this Van Horne fellow"—Keiller, grimacing, stopped to make his point—"I admire the man, too, ye know. He's a fine, inventive sort. But there's your work, Renée. Your patients and your colleagues need you, too. And there's Fernando."

"With his constant chatter."

"Oh, come now. You know how it is with a new language. He needs practice."

"Fernando's been with us over a year, dear Uncle, and he's still full of silly questions." She gave this a moment's thought before continuing. "But you're right, he does try hard. Lately, I must say, he's been quite kind."

Long weeks crept by. At first, Renée's thoughts were only of Van Horne, but with her uncle, her colleagues and students, and the troubled, swarthy Spaniard Fernando at her side, Renée's anguish abated. She became less distracted. And her uncle had been right about the anti-toxoid and the big horses. They were on the final path to a cure, their laboratory's greatest achievement. She'd had success with the Boston purification method. Soon, they'd test the anti-toxoid in living patients, the final trials to decide the doses, to determine a regimen of treatment before spring, before the heat of summer arrived and yellow fever returned to kill again. That would be the final proof of their cure.

With her successes at the horse barn, Renée had assays to perform, horses to inject, and data to analyze with her uncle. Every day was filled with the familiar scents of carbolic and acetone . . . and the pensive young Fernando, talkative Fernando, to whom Renée turned in her excitement, in the heat of discovery.

"I think we have it. We do!"

"The reaction is good, yes?"

"Darling Fernando, would you hand me that large test tube, *por favor?*"

"*Sí*, my love. For you . . . anything."

61

Under the Skin

The syringe's metal casing was cool in his hand. He would take care to draw the tarry brown liquid to the mark . . . the second mark . . . no, the third.

"'A most excellent instrument,'" he said, quoting the slogan printed on his hypodermic's worn case. "'The superb workmanship of Messrs. Codman & Shurtleff of Boston.'" He'd taken to mumbling like this, reciting over and over under his breath. Advertisements in the newspaper. Placards posted along the roadside.

"Most excellent, indeed."

He injected. Precisely three marks' worth, a goodly dose, deep enough beneath the skin to touch, and pierce, a decent vein. He'd been using the veins, and a mix even stronger than Boatmann's usual. He'd upped the dose, too, and bought a shiny new needle for Codman & Shurtleff's syringe. A day never passed without morphine.

The leather couch creaked with Nicolas's meager weight as he leaned back, stunned, trying to clear the muddle of brooding thoughts that plagued his days and nights.

It was right, what he'd done to Renée, but it brought a high price. Visions of the woman scientist haunted him. Renée in her laboratory. Renée running ahead on the beach. Renée at the clubhouse at Saratoga. And her letters.

She'd sent many he'd never answered, was almost afraid to read again. In them, he remembered, Renée had analyzed his discovery of the slave trade, attacked it like a laboratory problem, listed her hypothetical courses of action, named those in Buffalo, Albany—even Chicago—who might help. Constables. City aldermen. University professors. "*Don't go it alone,*" she'd written. "*Use your connections, find good people, people in power who'll know how to put a stop to this atrocity.*" She'd even deciphered the damnable brand that was their trademark, though his thinking was so murky, he couldn't recall the details of what she'd said. Since Nicolas had stopped her with his last, desperate letter, nothing made sense any longer. His life seemed to stall like a seized, broken engine. He felt frozen in place. Defeated.

Nicolas Van Horne could no longer claim success at life. He'd once had a spirit, an integrity that so filled him, it seemed it would burst and pour out. His business of ice and his village position held such promise . . . until the Galveston delivery revealed an evil thing in his ice.

Young boys, orphans, were suffering and being murdered willy-nilly, their lives as grim as those of the African slaves who'd labored in the cotton fields, the cane fields, their masters' chambers. Boys like Knox suffered the horrors of the factories, the slaughterhouses, the mines. Young girls faced a life of subjugation. But Nicolas was impotent against the forces that buffeted him. He saw the sum total of his life before him, and a weak sum it made.

"Nicolas! Nicolas!" He was shaken from his dark musings. "It's time for the new medicines," came the call from overhead.

Van Horne climbed to Ruth's bedroom.

After his return from Saratoga, after his final letter to Renée, Nicolas saw for the first time the truth of his wife's deterioration. He took the ailing Ruth to Albany by train for an opinion from the same medical man to whom, years earlier, he'd supplied the first bodies for dissection. But this fellow, now a professor of anatomy at the medical college, directed Nicolas to yet another medical professor, Ashbel Smythe, an expert in "female matters." Smythe had recently joined the medical faculty from Europe. Nicolas saw immediately that here was a man like Galveston's Francis Keiller, a man trained in modern science.

In Smythe's office, Nicolas and Ruth found themselves surrounded by cabinets stacked with jars of exotic leaves, powders, and seeds. Twisted fragments of dried bark and tubers lay like misshapen bones on the shelves. Smythe, with his red rubber listening tubes slung over his shoulder, directed Ruth to disrobe and wrap herself in a sheet. He guided her behind a screen to an examining table, where Nicolas heard him prodding and probing. After what seemed like hours, Smythe dashed from behind the screen with a microscope slide in his hand, mumbling, "You may dress, madame."

At a side table, Smythe splashed a purple fluid on the slide and, still standing, observed it under his microscope. Nodding knowingly, he settled behind his desk and scratched in a notebook until Ruth took her chair, then he shut the notebook, leaned back in his chair, and addressed himself to the ceiling without meeting the two pairs of eyes fixed on him.

"This growth of Mrs. Van Horne's . . . ," Ashbel Smythe said slowly. "Yes, we'll call it that, shall we? A growth, an abnormal growth of cells—millions of them—well, they've gotten totally out of hand and traveled far from the female organs."

"It's bad?" Nicolas asked.

"They've taken her over. Filled her abdomen."

"Is it . . . fatal?"

There was a brief silence, an exchange of glances between the men. "I'm afraid so," Smythe said with a nod toward Ruth, who pulled from her bosom a small handkerchief with delicate lacework at its edges and dabbed at the corners of her eyes.

"But the battle isn't over, Mr. Van Horne. Not yet." Smythe leaned toward Ruth and addressed her in earnest. "I assure you, madame, we can gain time against it. You see, I studied for some years in the East, in Shanghai, where they've employed therapeutic herbs for centuries. Through the judicious use of certain combinations of exotic plants, the viability of tumorous growths such as Mrs. Van Horne's may be retarded, though never completely reversed."

Ruth brightened at Smythe's words. The doctor stood and wandered along his row of cabinets, sorting through items on the shelves until he held a gnarly, mahogany-colored root.

"This one works well on tumors of the ovary, the blight suffered by the missus," he said, slipping the root into his jacket pocket. "And this . . . this powder is for the swelling." Smythe extended the bottle to Nicolas to examine, then hesitated, bottle still in hand, staring at the line of unhealed sores at Van Horne's cuff line. "I see you are a user of morphine, sir," he said. "Yes. Morphine it is—that cunning fiend."

"A bit, yes, Doctor. For relaxation, you understand."

Smythe leaned over to take Nicolas's pulse. He lifted Nicolas's eyelid with his thumb and peered down. Nicolas thought of the tangled, bloody web he'd seen in the mirror that morning.

"Have you heard of nervous waste syndrome, Mr. Van Horne?"

"I'll not suffer from that, I trust."

"Your rapid heart tells me otherwise, sir. I strongly recommend you taper your use, slowly, very slowly, until you may comfortably put it aside altogether. For now, use only pure morphine. Do not adulterate it with cocaine or other stimulants. This tapering of dose may take a month or more, and will require a powerful will."

"I rather dislike that tapering idea. I'd rather just up and quit one day."

"Trust me, Mr. Van Horne. You must taper. If you were to stop abruptly, it would be utter hell. Indeed, it might well prove fatal."

"But—"

"You must do as I say, sir, or you'll be of little use to your wife. In my opinion, morphine's medicinal qualities have been extended far beyond the drug's purpose. Morphine should serve only for relief of the most excruciating pain." Smythe's eyes shifted from husband to wife and back to Nicolas. "And what pain have you, sir, compared to what your spouse may have in store? For now, I advise only small doses of laudanum for Mrs. Van Horne. There will come a time when she'll require the maximum, I'm afraid."

Smythe went to writing on a large pad on his desk. "I've made out my diagnosis, sir. If properly followed, the therapeutic regime I've prescribed should help. If a fever should occur, place her comfortably in bed and apply a warm mustard pediluvium . . ."

In the weeks that followed Nicolas was heartened to see Ruth regain a modicum of health on Ashbel Smythe's prescribed regimen of root extract. He followed Smythe's recommendation of only small draughts of laudanum, saving that for her pain to come. At noon each day Ruth took his arm and they stepped out of the house to walk along the Town Lake path. They sat on a lakeside rock—sometimes for hours—two skeletal specters against the pale river, reminiscing.

For his part, Nicolas found it impossible to follow Smythe's advice. He altered his mix to pure morphine, as suggested, but failed to reduce his use.

In fact, he injected more and more.

62

The Hunt for Knox

Word came to Adam from the garnet mines. He hurried to the Van Horne place, where he found Nicolas and Abigail in the kitchen. Nicolas was working the pump, gulping water from a tin cup.

"They say there's an awful number of new fellas, young ones, working them mines at North River," Adam told them. "A whole new crew."

"Must've struck a heavy load of gems," Nicolas said.

"Yep, a new vein," Adam agreed. "Our boy Knox just might be in the crew hauling it out."

"Then go check it."

When Abigail heard this, she volunteered to accompany Adam. "I know the route as well as anybody," she said.

Nicolas, in a black mood, grumbled. "Adam'll make better time alone." He leaned on the pump and gazed out the kitchen window at a steady, cold drizzle.

"Well then," Abigail retorted, "I'll go to Gloversville. The tannery's been hiring and Knox was supposed to go there—isn't that what you said, Father?"

"I seem to remember something . . ."

Nicolas considered a moment. Gloversville was a long distance, and it wasn't likely Knox would be there; the boy had hated the idea of the tanneries. Even in his muddled state Nicolas wanted to keep Abigail safe. And she was catching on to the danger these slave traders might pose, though he had shared none of the most gruesome details with her.

"A trip to Gloversville might be better, Abby."

"Suits me, too," Adam interjected. "This changeable weather's playing hell with Gert's consumption. I'll be back quick if Knox is in them mines."

"Good," Nicolas said. "Adam's off to North River. Abby, you ride to Gloversville."

Nicolas's stomach gave a turn at the thought of Gloversville. An acrid stench hung over that town, worse at night when the tanning vats were emptied into the Cayadutta Creek. With their latest expansion, the Gloversville tanneries ran their effluent through wide-bore sludge pipes, fouling the rippling crystal current into a brown slurry. The men who worked the tanneries had hands the color of the gloves they produced; their arms hung like leathery cudgels at their sides, their fingers twisted and stiffened with arthralgia. These were men eager to pickle their livers with whiskey the moment the bell rang to end their shift. Abigail wouldn't linger long in the stinking town of Gloversville.

The next day, the weather continued dismal. A chilly, late-summer shower misted down on Adam and Abigail's separate departures. Adam was off before dawn. Shortly after, Abigail made ready to saddle the spirited black stallion, her favorite horse in the Van Horne stable. The stallion was a yearling, barely more than a colt, but quick and agile, especially with a stick of a girl for a rider. Nicolas steadied the rambunctious steed while doling out last-minute cautions.

"Just watch for that Mr. Wilson. Gloversville's not much. They'll see you coming."

"They won't suspect a girl."

"Schuyler's the one who should be doing this." Nicolas reflected on that for a moment. "I always thought you'd find someone, Abby. You know, find yourself—"

"A man?"

"A husband."

"I thought you'd given up on that, Father."

Nicolas couldn't find words for what he'd always known, had sensed since the girl was herself a skittish colt.

"Dearest Father," she said, the saddle in her hands, "you know me better than anyone."

"Sure," he admitted, smiling a father's smile, a smile that held out hope.

"Then why must you be so bullheaded? I'm perfectly happy as I am. Hildegard and I keep our house quite fine, don't you think?"

"One never knows. You just might—"

"Don't."

She swung the saddle up.

"You're the perfect daughter, Abigail Van Horne."

"Almost," she said, cinching it tight, mounting.

Once Abigail and Adam were off hunting for Knox, Nicolas summoned the gumption to walk to the Antlers Inn for another talk with Thomas Chubb. He'd heard the undertaker was in town to hold a funeral for a town alderman. Despite the shakes that plagued Nicolas's mornings, he put off the day's first dose of morphine and instead poured himself a tumbler of whiskey before he walked out the door.

Nicolas found Thomas at the small table near the window. It was midafternoon and the barroom of the Antlers Inn was crowded. Nicolas called for a whiskey over a pack of drinkers at the bar. The barman, a humorless Irishman, gave a nod. Nicolas pulled an empty chair to Thomas's table.

"We need to talk," he said, leveling his eyes at the undertaker. "I've found out plenty about this secret business you're involved in, Thomas. I know about the boys and the work crews."

Concern passed across the undertaker's face, a chink in his confidence, though evanescent. "Just what is it you know?"

"I know it's a monstrous thing."

"Oh, Nicolas," Thomas said with a sigh. "You understand how a business operates. It's all in the numbers, my man, the profits to be made."

"Who's behind this, Thomas? Where are these criminals?"

Thomas settled back in his chair and stared out the window, watching Nicolas from the corner of his eye. "I thought you said you knew all about it."

Nicolas reached for his whiskey, the fine tremor in his hand obvious.

Thomas turned to him. "How goes the morphine?" he asked. "You still partake, I see."

"Perhaps too much."

"I guessed as much. The fact that you're here suggests to me that the morphine's damaged your perspective, Nicolas. Old man Wainwright keeps a fine supply, doesn't he?" The undertaker put a note of sincerity in his voice. "Honestly, Van Horne, you need only look the other way on this. That's what I do. It's what you would've done before the morphine addled your brain."

"Maybe, Thomas, maybe. But those dead boys in my ice, I've had too much of it." Nicolas pitched forward, elbows on the table, his head in his hands. "It's always a problem with boys in my life. It started with my own son."

Thomas blanched and again the undertaker's armor seemed to fall away. "Your son?"

"*My son, you damned fool.* Ethan, my first boy. The one I lost years ago. You remember."

"Yes, yes." Thomas gave a nod, his eyes averted. "I remember your son."

"That was the start of it. Then, thanks to you, I discovered two boys in my ice had been murdered . . . and this boy Knox told me all about the work crews."

Chubb arched a thin, delicate eyebrow. "Who's Knox?"

"He's one of the lost boys, an orphan. He worked the ice on the last harvest."

"I see. Look, Nicolas, you needn't take this so to heart. It's only a few that come our way. I tell you, if you persist in this I'll go back to sinking them in Lake Erie. It's plenty deep, and you'll be better off. Of course, you'll miss out on the profit."

Nicolas stood and leaned over his longtime accomplice, compulsively opening and closing his fists into balls. "You see how I'm at my wits' end over this, don't you? *Don't you, Thomas?*"

"I see the morphine in you, that's what I see."

Nicolas took Thomas by the arm, his voice rising. "Tell me about them, damn it! *You owe me this.*"

The bar went quieter.

"You owe me, Thomas. Who are these men? Where are they?"

Chubb snatched Nicolas's wrist. His grip was surprisingly strong. He rocked back in his chair and pushed Nicolas's hand away. "Ease off, Van Horne."

Nicolas felt his bowels tighten. Something deep in him hardened, like a fist closing. He reached down with both hands and grabbed bunches of Thomas's shirt and pulled him close. Chubb's chair scraped across the plank floor. "*I'm going to find Knox and, damn you, if harm comes to that boy . . .*"

The place was deathly quiet now. Eyes shifted. The deadpan barman shuffled from behind the bar and cleared his throat. "Um . . . gents."

Thomas, locked in a stalemate, hissed under his breath, "*You have no idea of the danger for us. These are not gentlemen, Van Horne.*"

"I don't give a damn. I'll get them one day."

"Don't you dare. Don't even try. If you anger them in the least, we'll be dead—both of us. Our throats'll be cut, or worse. Remember that. They'll do it in a blink."

The barman was at their side, a hand on each of their shoulders. "Come now, gents," he said. "Enough of this."

Nicolas released his grip and without a word went for the door. But his step faltered. "I'll do something," he shot back over his shoulder. "I'll straighten this out . . . I will."

Thomas shouted back, "Face it, Van Horne. You can't get yourself straight."

Chubb turned away and stared out the window, drumming his fingers on the table. Nicolas, his back hunched, pushed his way out the door. The barroom came alive with whispers and murmurs.

"What was that about?"
"Hmm . . . and those two, old classmates . . ."
"Something about a boy?"
"Somebody's son . . ."

63

At the Bottom of the Black River

It had once been so pleasant. Morphine—a distraction, a gentle, mellow addition to everyday life. But now it had dug in its claws, burrowed into his guts like a living thing demanding to be fed—and feed it he must. From early morning he thought of the needle. Such a talented thing, that finely drawn rapier. He was helpless in its path. It found its way to his heart's blood as if homing in on the heat.

Morphine had him in its grip, and what was the outcome? Wayward boys had undoubtedly died. He knew so little, and all the tools that might've helped had been stolen by the morphine. Renée had charged him with finding the men behind the work crews. In her last letters—those he'd ignored—she'd had ideas, names of people in Buffalo, elsewhere, even an academic-sounding lecture on the mark he kept finding on boys and thought he saw on Wilson's finger ring.

But Nicolas was no Pinkerton—a trained gunman able and eager to solve a crime, stop an uprising, or interdict a foul plot against his fellow men. Could he track villainous criminals into their haunts? Unlikely. Nicolas was a man of business—though he hardly did business anymore, thanks to morphine. Local demand for ice had dissipated with the cool, rainy days of September. Abigail kept the accounts. No, Nicolas couldn't bring himself to deal with villains or numbers, except to measure the drams of morphine by the lines etched into his syringe.

Morphine, pure and simple. Since Saratoga, Nicolas had thoroughly explored the anatomy of those hardening cords beneath the skin—his veins—their course traced by flaking scabs and open sores, like lines of scales on a fish. He'd learned to rotate sites, avoid the spots that became red or throbbed, and to direct his pleasure instead to unexplored blood channels, wherever they might lie.

When he dared draw the syringe past its third mark, he was guaranteed a jolt that surprised like an electric current. Every part of him, his skin, his muscles, even his innards, seized tight as a drum. Damn that miserable Professor Smythe . . . If he followed Smythe's advice and tapered his injections he'd be nothing but a cold, hollow shell. Morphine was brightness and the purest white light. Smythe, the charlatan, the quack, was dead wrong, though Nicolas had to admit Smythe was right about Ruth. She was doing better—she'd even gained a few pounds—and lately, she seemed to worry more about Nicolas than about herself.

Nicolas held the syringe to the late afternoon light at the windowpane. He checked the meniscus and slowly expelled the air. He'd take it to the fourth mark, perhaps the fifth. "A most excellent instrument," he muttered. So well conceived, the tempered metal of Codman & Shurtleff, the calibrations etched on the glass cylinder. And how finely they drew these needles nowadays. Hardly a bruise to be seen as the proboscis found its way.

"Ouch! Oh!" *This tingle in the face? This sinister weight on the chest?* "Gad! What?"

His limbs trembled. He couldn't move an arm, a leg . . . a finger. The morphine had wrecked his nerves. His power of speech, gone.

Nervous . . . exhaustion.

The afternoon turned to dusk, the dusk to night, while Nicolas lay immobile on his couch. Each breath was a labor. His eyes, half-shut, dried to a crust. Then, one by one, a nerve fired here . . . then there. He moved a finger, a hand, until raw, painful life flooded back into his limbs.

"Devil take these needles!" he cried, struggling to sit. There it was—the culprit had fallen from his hand to the floor beside him. "Much too thin."

He wasn't yet able to stand, but his head had cleared enough to know he could not go on, he could not live like this. The grim truth was that autumn would soon arrive, the ice harvest loomed, and morphine held him prisoner in his study. He was useless to Abigail, to Ruth, to himself. He could not go on living. Not like this.

Still trembling from the explosion of morphine inside his skull, he slipped off the couch, pulled on his jacket, and staggered against the doorjamb.

"I must not lose my nerve on this."

It would be quick. The cool evening air would give him strength to do the job that needed doing. Head down, eyes fixed on the street, he strode with conviction down the hill, to the bridge. He flung himself on the iron rail. The somber reflection of a tortured, powerless man lay on the water's black surface. Nicolas did not like what he saw. A murky life, obsession, untold secrets locked in a dark heart.

"I shall not lose my resolve . . . to go through with this."

He slung a leg over the cold steel rail, steadying himself, full of resolve. He reached in his pocket . . .

And the finest works of the Boston craftsmen Messrs. Codman & Shurtleff came to rest among the small round stones of the Black River's bottom.

64

The Arrival of Autumn

Nicolas was frantically working the kitchen pump when he saw Abigail ride up to the back door with Knox mounted behind her on her favorite black yearling. Knox peered into the kitchen with pale, forlorn eyes. He looked like a skeleton. His bony limbs added little to the stallion's load. Nicolas kept at his tin cup, sucking down the cool well water to quell the fever he felt rising.

"Got 'im!" Abigail said as the two walked through the kitchen door.

Nicolas, leaning on the pump, reached to clap the boy on the back. "Glad to have you back in Forestport, son. Wanted out of that hole, did you?"

"Yep. Thanks for sending her."

"You were right, Father," Abigail said. "The entire crew was boys. I waited till dark when they came filing out of the tannery. Knox saw me and bolted." Abigail fixed her father with a hard stare. "You look horrid," she said. "I better fetch you something to eat, too."

Nicolas, still draped over the pump, waved her off. "In a few days."

Nicolas had been twenty-four hours without morphine. He'd been shivering since he tossed his works at the bridge, mostly with fear at what was to come.

"We need to keep you close, son," Nicolas told Knox. "One of those Mr. Wilsons might come hunting for you."

"Damn 'em all anyway," the boy grumbled. "Liars. They were never gonna make me no foreman."

"I'll take him to Adam's," Abigail said. "Gertie won't mind. They've got an empty bed now that their oldest boy signed on with the Beaver River Company."

"Tell Adam that if Wilson shows, he should stash Knox at his cabin on Indian Lake." Nicolas turned to Knox. "Want to work the ice again this winter, boy?"

"Sure. At least you eat sumthin' good up there."

Abigail told Nicolas she'd take Knox to her place for Hilda to feed him. "Sure you don't want me to bring you something?" she asked.

"No, I've taken a bit of a grippe, that's all," Nicolas replied, struggling to calm the shaking. "Pay me no mind."

Once Abby's steed clip-clopped down the hill, Nicolas settled in his study, his arms wrapped around his middle holding tight to his guts, where the thing that had his teeth rattling seemed to originate.

October of the year 1889 came wandering into the mountains like a stinking hermit wrapped in rags. The landscape was dull and brown and smelled of rot; the red-and-orange blaze of the maples had long ago been washed to the ground by torrential rains. The last apples were gathered, the last of the cider squeezed. An early, killing frost shimmered on unpicked hop flowers. Desiccated cornstalks pointed to a grey sky like a million withered fingers.

"It's an ugly fall," Ruth told her husband. "And it means a long, hard winter."

But Nicolas heard nothing. He had retired with a "bad grippe" to his garret bedroom and was hardly seen. Wretched groans punctuated by the foul oaths of a wild beast drifted from the third floor.

Nicolas suffered through most of the dismal October. Abigail kept the stoves stoked below to warm the upper rooms. She cared for Ruth and was encouraged by her appearance.

"Look at you, Mums. It must be that new doctor's medicine."

When Abigail climbed the stairs to the third floor, however, she was shocked to see her father glistening with sweat and wracked by erratic, convulsive tremors. In a turnabout of family illness, she now feared for her father's life.

It was three weeks before Nicolas came to. He bathed, found fresh clothes, and began to carry chowder to Ruth. At night, he found himself joining Ruth in her bed, not as a husband might join with his wife, but solely for the warmth he might offer her in the hour before he retired to his room. He sensed that the grimmer proclamations of the good doctor Smythe still rang in Ruth's ears and sent a chill settling in her bones.

"Come closer, Nicolas. I'm dreadfully cold . . . and afraid."

In the last week of October a warm southerly breeze pushed up from the valley. The sheets of frozen rain that lay on the village fell away like scales, and Forestport was abuzz with talk of an "Indian summer." Ruth, the born Adirondacker, sensed that this was the sweetest of respites, a gift of the mountains granted specially for her. Indian summer brought with it a reprieve from her pain and time to think things over.

For Nicolas, it was a time to act.

65

Buffalo

His mind had cleared, and it was set. He would travel to Buffalo, as Renée had suggested in Saratoga. He'd take the noon train.

Nicolas wasn't familiar with the city of Buffalo. A booming port on Lake Erie, gateway via the lake to Chicago and the Wild West, Buffalo had sprouted big, violent neighborhoods, a patchwork of languages, a mishmash of immigrants. That was precisely what he was after, according to Renée Keiller.

Nicolas counted himself lucky he hadn't burnt Renée's letters. Once he'd dumped the morphine and the needle, and survived the consequences, he pulled the packets of letters from his secretary and studied those she'd sent after their return from Saratoga.

Renée had given careful thought to the child slave trade; her sound thinking was well detailed in her letters. She'd discovered that other European countries had developed white slave trades in young women and boys. In England, where laws were already enacted, a movement was afoot to outlaw children in a man's workplace. But the clincher was the scrap of paper she carried with her—the page of the racing sheet where Nicolas had sketched the mark he'd found, the mark of the slave trade.

Ж

Clearheaded now, Nicolas shuddered at the sight of it. Renée explained that according to a university colleague from Saint Petersburg, the mark was the Russian letter known as "*zhe*." It sounded like the "s" in "treasure" and was thought by children to represent an insect, or a frog on the surface of a pond. *Most likely a poisonous one*, was Nicolas's thought. *But what does that have to do with murdered boys, or a slave trade in child labor?*

The men they were after, according to Renée, had to be Russians. The city of Buffalo, Nicolas knew, had plenty of Russians, Poles, Serbs, and Slovaks, in addition to the more numerous Germans. Most of the Russians, he'd learned, were Jews, long-haired, fervent followers of their faith escaping starvation and persecution. But others were bad, the dregs of a giant country, criminals from the underbelly of Mother Russia. These men, Nicolas surmised, would live in tightly knit neighborhoods and form inner circles, or gangs, where they could speak their native language and draw others—perhaps even innocent orphans—into their web.

Nicolas judged that another discussion with Professor Flynt at the medical school would illuminate where such men could be found in Buffalo, if Austin Flynt could be coerced to give away any more than Thomas Chubb.

The brown stone that housed the medical college of Buffalo at the corner of Main and Virginia Streets was more accommodating in the warmth of an Indian summer than it had been when Nicolas last visited in the icy rain. He quickly found Flynt's office, but, on entering, was taken aback at the sight of an entirely different sort of gent behind the desk. This professor was a frail, elderly fellow, a mop of white hair atop a plethoric countenance.

"I was hoping to see Professor Flynt," Nicolas said, nonplussed.

"Flynt's gone, sir. I've been given his place here, good fortune for me. Just haven't changed the name on the door yet. Budgetary constraints and all." The elderly fellow rose on wobbly legs to offer his hand. "Name's Ainsworthy, sir."

"Mine's Van Horne. May I ask what's become of Flynt?"

"Disappeared, it seems. Are you a friend of his, or was it a professional association?"

"I had dealings with him last year."

"Then you know the sort he is. Well, most of us figure he simply tired of the routine. It makes sense. Old Flynt was under a great strain, what with the dastardly duties he'd been given. He moved on, perhaps no longer in medicine. No one's sure."

"No forwarding address? Nothing?"

"As I say, no one knows." Dr. Ainsworth leaned forward in his chair and pressed the tips of his bony fingers together as if preparing to say grace. "It was a bit disconcerting, his leaving. One Friday, late, he packed up his desk, mumbling about a 'vacation somewhere warm.' But the odd thing is, Flynt was a great fisherman. The next day his fishing boat was found washed up on the lakeshore, the Canadian side. I'd have thought he'd take it with 'im, don't you?"

"He's not been heard from?"

"No, but Flynt was an odd one. Always was. Kept strange bedfellows and all."

"Yes, I imagine he might've," Nicolas said, thinking of Thomas Chubb.

Nicolas had one last question for this Ainsworthy fellow. "Whereabouts in the city do your Russians live?" he asked.

"Why, they've practically taken over the lower east side. Quite an influx we've had. Along with the Polish, they're becoming quite prosperous, I must say. Why do you ask?"

Nicolas hailed a cab to carry him to the Russian neighborhood. "Yep," the driver told him, "that's where them Muscovites settled all right. Along William Street and Jefferson Avenue. Only a few blocks of 'em, but I'm sure there's more coming."

The driver's mare was old and slow. When their cab pulled near the neighborhood, dusk had fallen. Nicolas paid the driver and walked the blocks he judged to be the Russian area. The bright electric lights that lit the downtown hadn't made it here yet, and the shop windows threw scanty yellow light onto the sidewalks. Shadowy, ill-defined figures, many of them bearded, long-haired, and wrapped in brown cloaks, ducked in and out of the three-story brownstone buildings that seemed to be everywhere in this city.

In the monotonous darkness, everything seemed foreign, and when the evening chill blew off the lake, the desolation of the steppes fell with it over the streets. Nicolas realized he should've taken an earlier train to Buffalo. He had run out of light and couldn't have sorted out a Mr. Wilson if one were in front of him. He hailed a cab on Jefferson Avenue and asked to be taken to the finest hotel in the downtown area.

"It's the Hotel Fillmore, then," was the driver's response. "It's near the lake, too, sir."

The following morning, as he took tea and biscuits in the Fillmore's elegant dining room, Nicolas's thinking was at its clearest. He had a plan. He'd use the earliest daylight hours to search the city for lost boys and get to Wilson that way. The port of Buffalo was nearly as lively as Chicago. There'd be plenty of workers on the waterfront, where vast quantities of grains, flour, and Chicago meat passed from Lake Erie to the Erie Canal and the train routes.

On foot, Nicolas made his way to the waterfront in a tepid, Indian-summer predawn mist. Along the length of Commercial Street grain elevators constructed of wood towered at the edge of the lake. It was barely daylight, yet looking at the massive grey outlines, Nicolas realized what an ingenious idea this elevator was. It had been a clever New Yorker who'd linked an ancient invention—the bucket—to a modern steam-driven belt. Grain was scooped, bucket after bucket, out of the ships at harbor and carried high into a storage tower, where the buckets automatically dumped when the belt ran over a pulley. For as far as he could see, steam engines belched smoke and ash into the air.

Smaller ships, however, didn't benefit from this modern marvel; those vessels, mostly smaller side-wheelers, were unloaded on the backs of men, mostly grimy, impoverished Irishmen or—as Nicolas quickly noted—on the backs of young boys.

Taking a seat on a low, shoreside barrel, Nicolas studied the morning's labor. Sacks of produce were loaded directly onto barges here or, further along, directly into railroad cars. Many of the youngest workers fit the bill as Nicolas's lost boys—young and scrawny, mean tempered, and cursing like sailors. He needed only approach, pick out a sure one, and befriend him, or perhaps threaten him. He chose a particularly skinny lad.

"Say there," Nicolas called. "You." The boy plunked his sack of grain into the bottom of a barge. Nicolas fixed him with a stern look. "Hold it right there. I need to speak to you, and now!"

"Who in hell are you?" the boy said with a sneer, his eyes shifting this way and that.

"I'm a friend of Mr. Wilson. He sent me to check on you, boy."

The youth's eyes popped wide. "Me? I done nothin' wrong." He edged toward the gangway to his ship.

"Wilson sent me, boy. Now come here."

"I'm working hard, I tell ya. Leave me be."

"Wilson said he's coming to check himself, and soon."

The boy's forehead wrinkled. "He don't come this early."

"When's he come then?"

"Never until late, just before we quit after dark. Honest, mister, I been working hard. Daylight or not. You tell him that, will ya?"

"I'll do just that. Now back to work."

Nicolas walked the waterfront one more time. He had them now—these men who enslaved boys, the poor young devils suffering backbreaking work for their masters, and cheaply. Tonight, he'd have one of the Wilsons, maybe the Russian himself.

Nicolas had the rest of the day to find the two names that Renée had given him in her correspondence. The first name she'd urged him to act on turned out to be a university man who'd studied Buffalo's neighborhoods and the immigrants who filled the city. The man knew a dozen languages. The second name Renée had provided was the Erie County constable, who, her researches uncovered, was an old classmate of Van Horne's. Nicolas didn't remember too much about the gent, but they had a connection. Harvard, class of '68.

A congenial sort of fellow, and eager to help.

Late in the day, a different sort of Mr. Wilson walked the waterfront. Nicolas had taken a seat on a barrel near the barge-loading area he'd studied earlier. Darkness had fallen and most dockside workers were already in the taverns. The crew of boys, exhausted, were staggering under their sacks of grain when a fellow with stick-thin arms and legs, a potbelly, and dressed in an ill-fitting suit strutted alongside the barge. "Last one for today," he shouted. "Come on. Move it."

This Mr. Wilson was a redheaded Irishman. Hardly a Russian; Nicolas could see that clearly. And the slight stagger to the gent's gait made him a drunken Irishman. "Come on, come on, ya want some supper, don'tcha?" the irritable fellow snapped at the boys. Nicolas shadowed the Irishman down the harborside to the next barge.

"Sir! I need a word with you. Are you Mr. Wilson?"

The fellow turned and shot Nicolas a dirty look. The signs of alcohol poisoning were clear—the flush, the spidery vessels on the cheeks. The fellow stood, waiting, his pale blue eyes expressionless.

"I have a bone to pick with you, sir. You are Mr. Wilson, are you not?"

"I work for Wilson, and what's it to ya?"

"I'm a colleague of Thomas Chubb. You know of him?"

"I do not."

"Well, then, your top man does. Where's your top man, the big Mr. Wilson?"

"What would ya want with him?"

"We have a certain connection. I've done jobs for him."

"Where you from?"

"Upstate," Nicolas snapped back, deciding not to tell this underling too much.

"Yeah, yeah." The Irishman turned away.

Nicolas grabbed the Irishman's scrawny arm from behind and spun him around. "So where do I find him, huh?" He felt the man tense. "Listen, you, it's important business I have with the Russian."

"The boss'll be where he always is. Next door to Ted Sweeney's place. He's there every night, late, on Canal Street where we all report."

"Ted Sweeney's place."

"No, I told ya—the building *next* to Sweeney's. You'll find him there."

The brownstone next to Sweeney's Pub had a single, low entrance. It looked abandoned; the windows were unlit. Nicolas pushed the door open and stepped into a darkened hall. A sporadic murmur like some sort of machinery far below came and went. Nicolas took a set of stairs; the rumble grew louder. At the bottom of the stairs he stepped into a circle of bright electric light and realized the sound was the crash of candlepins. He was in a basement bowling alley, four lanes, all busy, and nearly midnight.

A player was standing idle at the first lane. When Nicolas asked for Mr. Wilson, the player gave a nod to another small door at the back. Nicolas walked the length of the hardwood lanes, past the pin boys frantically setting pins, returning balls, and jumping clear when pins went flying. Nicolas opened the door into a smoke-filled room with a dozen small tables where men in business attire were smoking cigars, and playing cards. A few women, dressed to the hilt, lounged near their men. A cluster of crap shooters stood along one wall, stooped over the dice.

Nicolas surveyed the card tables. Several of the men were large, well-built, beefy types, not unlike the Mr. Wilson who'd come for Knox and the one Nicolas had questioned at Saratoga's clubhouse. At one of the furthest, smallest tables sat the heaviest, most Herculean of the lot. This bigger gentleman wasn't playing cards; rather he had an alluring young brunette at his side, a bottle of clear liquor and shot glasses in front of him. Stout, broad across the shoulders, and dressed in an excellent business suit and fine silk shirt obviously tailored for his brawny physique, he presented the most powerful appearance in the room. The gent's thickened, boxed ears spoke of physical violence, as did the crook in his long, thin rudder of a nose.

Nicolas approached. He caught a few words, quite musical, in a low-pitched Slavic tongue. The couple's eyes shifted to Nicolas. They went quiet. He asked, point-blank, "You're Mr. Wilson, the Russian, aren't you?"

The man leaned back. Looking down the majestic angle of his nose, he nodded. "We're all Russian here. And who the hell are you?"

"I am Nicolas Van Horne, a colleague of Thomas Chubb."

"A useful man, Thomas. You come for him?"

"I come on my own."

"Well, then, sit and have drink with us." Wilson reached for the bottle, poured two shot glasses full, and pushed one toward Nicolas. The woman watched dumbly for a beat or two, then looked away, bored.

"What has Thomas Chubb to say these days?"

"I don't care what Chubb says. I've come to clear up this business he's gotten me into."

A frown passed across Wilson's broad face. "First, drink." The glass disappeared into his fist. He downed it in a blink.

Nicolas took down the liquor and continued unbidden. "I trade in ice, you see. I ship all over the country. Thomas is an old collaborator, but he drew me in, used my ice business for your purposes. It's a bad business, this cheap labor you deal in, sir. Do you hear what I'm saying?"

"I hear a man who's afraid, Mr. Ice Man. Here, another drink." Wilson filled their glasses. "For courage."

"I'm not afraid," Nicolas said, struggling to steady his hand as he reached for his glass. "I know about your business, and I want no part of it from now on. That's what I've come to say."

"How you know my business?"

"I've seen these boys with your mark, the burn mark, whatever it means."

A deep sound like a guffaw rumbled in Wilson's throat. "Haa! You say you know my business. What means my mark, then, huh?"

"It's meaning? I don't know."

"See, so now you learn something, Mr. Ice Man. That 'mark' you call it is the first letter of my name, Zhivakov. Russian is 'zh.'" Wilson sounded out the letter. "Look." He dipped his finger into Nicolas's drink and drew the letter in vodka on the table:

Ж

"See, now you know Russian language."

"I'm not Russian."

"Many men work for me not Russian, but they know good money. Young boys are good money. Young girls, too."

"But some are murdered. Why?"

"I tell you. See, business like a family, big family. I—Vladimir Petrovich Zhivakov—I look at work-boys and orphan girls like family. Sometimes necessary . . . how you say? . . . to 'discipline' in family. Sometimes my men too eager, the discipline is too much, too strong discipline, and what we got then, eh?"

"A dead body."

"Yes, but an example is what we got. An example to others, what we get rid of."

"And that's where Thomas Chubb comes in. And me. How long has Thomas worked for you?"

"Years. Thomas take care of many examples. Once you work for me, you cannot go back." Zhivakov thumped a fist on the table. "You see, Russian man is not like American man. Russian man knows how to discipline children, beat wife, how to keep control." Zhivakov glanced at his paramour and smiled. "And Russian man love to fight other man. We have war every ten years. In Russia, no man is without a war, no matter his age. We do not look at killing like American man."

"That doesn't make you better. It makes you worse."

Wilson's broad face cracked with a smile. "I like you, Ice Man. You come here to scold me, huh? You travel a lot, maybe you do special jobs better than Thomas Chubb. I can use smart man. I got people working everywhere, you know. America is great country."

Nicolas stood on shaky legs. "Thank you for the drink, Mr. . . . Mr. Zhivakov, but I won't be doing any more of your work. And I warn you, I'm not considering this matter closed. Not at all."

The big Russian's eyes narrowed to pinpoints. "You threaten me, Mr. Ice Man?"

Nicolas glanced around the room, which had gone eerily quiet. He thought of the long walk to the street. He sensed he'd entered a wasps' nest, and this Zhivakov, by a mere lift of a finger, could stir the nest to a stinging frenzy.

The Russian spoke again, softly now. "We Russians love sayings, you know. We have saying that 'you fight with me, or fight against me.' And men who fight me end up in lake. Or worse. Ask Thomas Chubb."

"We'll see about that," Nicolas said as he backed slowly toward the door. "We'll see."

He said the Russian's name perfectly. "Zhivakov," with the "zh" sound at the start. On his way downtown he whispered it to himself over and over, hammering it into his head. Nicolas was sure he'd get it exact when he reached the Erie County constable's office. He even knew the first letter, in Russian.

The constable had seemed like an intelligent man when Nicolas met with him earlier in the day. He'd be glad to have the information.

66

An Unpleasant End to Indian Summer

In long, white, perfectly starched coats, the learned doctors of Albany surrounded the bedside with equally long and pale puzzled faces. "A most interesting case," one of the more senior faculty commented.

Ruth Van Horne, the final patient on their ward rounds, lay flat in the bed in a fresh-smelling hospital gown, her belly laid bare. A circle of students in shorter white coats tightened around the medical scholars and craned their necks to see the patient and hear the pronouncements of their elders.

"The tests are conclusive," the long-faced academics agreed.

"The findings are unequivocal."

Students pulled notepads from their short white coats to record the startling effects of Professor Smythe's latest therapeutic regimen. Where before the tumorous abdominal masses had been expanding, now they were shrinking. The patient's outward health appeared greatly improved, despite an alarming loss of weight. Her pain had dissipated, but surely it would return.

Standing at the edge of the circle of physicians and students, Nicolas shook his head in disbelief. Ruth was better. Dared he hope?

Ruth, the medical miracle, began to fidget under the many male stares. One of the physicians snapped a sheet over her abdomen. Another set a larger tin of pills ground from Dr. Smythe's Oriental root on her bedside table. Extracts of thistle were added to her regimen "to improve the patient's mental state."

Dr. Smythe joined Nicolas at the outer edge of the circle. He spoke quietly. "To answer your question," Smythe said, "no, it is definitely not a cure. A brief period like this often precedes the worst." Smythe leaned in close. "My new pharmaceutics should help tremendously. Her vigor will return, though briefly. But I remind you," he continued gravely, "no nostrums or potions whatsoever, except what's been prescribed. No morphine. You must save the morphine for later, when her pain becomes too great."

"I understand."

"And what about you, sir? You seem to be looking in the pink."

"I'm over all that, thank you. It was hell, as you predicted."

"Commendable indeed, Mr. Van Horne. I've seen few men who could quit it."

Upon their return to Forestport, Ruth stepped down from the train without so much as reaching for her husband's arm. Soon, her appetite returned and she began taking breakfasts of cheddar and eggs, with only a rare twinge of nausea.

"That's some wondrous medicine," she said with a sigh after a week back in town. "But before the snow flies, I've set my mind on fishing one more time."

"This Indian summer won't last, Ruth."

"Surely there's a few days more. I've so neglected the skiff, and I'm quite strong enough to row."

Nicolas at first tried to persuade Ruth to stay snug in Forestport. His head was still spinning from his confrontation with Zhivakov. Knox had been dispatched to Adam's hideout on Indian Lake, and Nicolas planned another trip to Buffalo to consolidate alliances against Zhivakov and the slave traders. He'd steer clear of that woebegone neighborhood, for his own safety, of course. He trusted that the Russian would hardly expect him to prowl around Buffalo again.

In the end, Nicolas relented to Ruth. "Do take care on the water," he told her as he headed off to the station to board the train to Buffalo. "I'll be at the lake house in about three days, if business goes well."

Abigail hitched two good bay horses to a wagon and gently urged the team out of Forestport. Ruth, cushioned among their provisions in the wagon's bed, watched the afternoon roll by, and they made Upper Spy in time for her to settle into a big wooden chair on the lakefront and watch the sunset. The next morning, after two of Dr. Smythe's pills and one of the thistle, she felt a surge of strength. She and Abigail lifted the light, thin-hulled skiff from its rack in the boathouse and scrubbed off the grime left by years of neglect, and Ruth lovingly oiled its cedar planking. She tossed her cane pole in the bottom of the boat and rowed off to fish, the clean lines of the skiff's hull skimming low and quick over the misty surface of Upper Spy Lake.

Ruth fished for two days, spending most of the daylight hours drifting along the shoreline. The Indian summer held for her, but the nausea had begun to creep back. And the pain. No matter how skimpy her breakfast, the rock in her belly pushed up hard enough to take her breath away.

On Ruth's third morning at the lake house, Nicolas appeared, his business complete. Abigail cooked her mother's morning catch of brookies, their sides bright with fall color. Ruth stared at the fish untouched on her plate.

"The lake's been good for you," Nicolas said, forking the delicate pale flesh from his plate. "You're looking fit."

"Nicolas—I'm afraid I've had time to think, and it's still there. The growth. And it's getting bigger."

"No, you're over this thing. I can see it in your eyes. They're clear and bright now."

"The pills do that, but it won't last, and I'm taking more and more now."

Nicolas had cleaned his plate. He pushed his chair back from the table. "Listen, I'm heading to the village this morning; you and Abby can follow tomorrow. It'll be getting colder, so I'll put your skiff up before I leave."

"I'm telling you, dear, I'll not make it through another winter. You've a long, lonely winter in store."

"Oh, come now. It's always a long winter here."

Ruth followed Nicolas to the boathouse and watched in silence as he lifted the skiff onto its rack. His back was to her.

"Nicolas, you must tell me something." Nicolas turned, his hands still on the boat. "I need to know. Speak truthfully," she said, a sudden intensity in her eyes. "Have you ever strayed? Have you ever broken our wedding vows?"

"What?"

His mind flashed to that visit to a New Orleans bordello with Adam. Then, like lightning cracking the sky, he saw Renée Keiller as he'd last seen her, clinging to him at the Saratoga station, the rain pouring down around them. *Yes, my heart was untrue, but only my heart.*

"No," he said softly, and he gave the skiff a final shove.

"I wish to clear my mind of this," Ruth went on, her voice lowered to a whisper. "I did. I once strayed."

He turned. His mouth hung open. "You?"

"Once, yes, with only the one, but it went on for some little while, dear heart."

Nicolas stepped out of the boathouse onto the dock and fixed his eyes on the lake's cold, flat surface as if waiting for a returning boat. He couldn't bring himself to look at her. "I never dreamt . . . I never . . ."

"I've lived with this for our whole marriage, Nicolas. Back then—so long ago—you were always away with the ice, with business. All I had was little Ethan. The bouts of pneumonia. The worry. I was lonely."

"I cannot believe it of you," he said, his voice low and gravelly.

"It was so very long ago, Nicolas."

"You were the schoolmarm!" he said, throwing it over his shoulder at her, his eyes still on the lake.

"Schoolmarms can stray. And schoolmarms get lonely."

"Who was it, Ruth?"

"I won't say. No, never. I was so young and it would only do more harm."

"Someone I know?"

"It would be too cruel."

"Cruel, you say," his back still to her.

"Oh, you must forgive me, Nicolas. You must. Come embrace me one last time before you go off," she said. "Please."

"I can't bring myself . . . no."

Who was it? he asked himself. *Who?* He would ask her again. Later. In the village. He couldn't live with this mystery. He would keep asking until she told.

Ruth laid her hands on his back but he pulled away and strode to the end of the dock. Betrayed by his childhood love, his wife, the mother to his children. No, he'd not take her in his arms. Not now, not until she told. Perhaps never.

A chill was in the air. He lingered, already worrying about the danger he knew waited somewhere for him. He must make it to Forestport by noon, before the train arrived from Buffalo. Adam kept the lookout; he'd know if Wilson's murderous henchmen were about.

When Nicolas finally turned around, Ruth was climbing the path to the lake house.

The mercury dropped like a stone near the lake that night. In the blank sky, cascades of northern lights rose and fell. Abigail built a fire in the fireplace and set her mother's willow rocker on the warm fieldstone. Ruth settled in and rocked, a thin, stoic smile set hard on her face.

"We'll leave early tomorrow," Abigail told her. "Perhaps we'll catch Father still at the house. Lately, he doesn't stick around Forestport more than a day or two."

Ruth rocked silently, a distant look on her face.

"Don't pout, Mums. Summer's over, I'm afraid."

The next day dawned cold and dry. The ground froze hard and the bright, still Canadian air smelled of snow. Ruth insisted Abigail build up the fire before setting off to the barn to ready the horses and wagon for their return to Forestport. She filled a cup at the kitchen pump and took four of the tablets of thistle. Nicolas was right; the thistle brightened her eyes with nervous energy.

But its effect was short-lived. She'd not bother with Smythe's wondrous root. The pill no longer held sway with that rock inside her, she was sure of it.

She stood on the hearth to warm herself by the fire but she couldn't stay still. The pain in her stomach would not be ignored. It promised worse.

At the kitchen window, Ruth studied the lake. The water was flat. A skim of ice shone at its edges. A solitary wood-and-canvas canoe drifted along the nearby shore. Ruth recognized the boat, Canadian made, owned by two men who portaged from Brandywine Lake, braving this morning chill to fish. She watched the two gentlemen land a nice walleye. Surely they'd have a passel of plump fall perch in the bucket. But summer was over, Ruth admitted to herself. She'd not fish again. The rock inside her told her this. Abigail was busy in the stable with the wagon and the team; the time was right. She sat at the desk for some moments, then stepped into the muted wintry sunshine and took the boathouse path.

Summoning her meager strength, Ruth slid the skiff down from its rack. She hefted an anchor, laid it with its coil of rope in the bottom of the boat, and set off rowing, her breath coming in short quick puffs, her stick-thin arms sure at the oars.

The fishermen in the lone boat from Brandywine Lake watched her pull away from the boathouse dock. She saw them raise a hand as the sleek Rushton skiff passed near and traced along the reedy shoreline, but she kept her eyes averted. The cold soon cut to the bone. Her hands stiffened, the warmth of the hearth now far behind.

She rowed methodically, her will strong. She mustn't allow herself to slow until she reached her goal, the far northwestern shore of Upper Spy, where the steeper mountains met the lake. It was a place known as Pulpit Rock—she'd seen it from the kitchen window—a fifty-foot-high face of sheer granite dropping straight into the dark water. The rocky, unscalable cliff, capped by stilted, scraggly pines, shone bright pink in the oblique morning sun. It was the deepest part of the lake, and a spot as beautiful as any cathedral.

With each stroke of the oars memories welled up. Ruth was never one to think about good and evil, even with all the horrible things her cadre of village lady friends had said about the ice . . . The village always knew about those who thought their deeds were secret. People like her husband and Thomas Chubb. And her. The village knew the misdeeds of everyone.

Were the two fishermen watching? Not likely. Their view was clear across the lake, but they were busy catching fish along that far shoal. She stowed the oars and drifted to a stop within yards of Pulpit Rock.

She stood straight in the skiff, stretched, and steadied herself with one foot on the gunwale. The coil of rope lay neatly at her feet. She gauged the length she needed, bent to take up its free end, wrapped the rope tight about her waist . . . again . . . again . . . knotted it and turned toward the sheer face of Pulpit Rock. *Cold, so cold.* She trembled. *How fast will the light go?* With a smooth, well-practiced motion, she hoisted the anchor overboard and quickly now . . . quickly . . . stepped over the gunwale into the bottomless black water.

The fishermen from Brandywine Lake threw their rods in the bottom of the boat with a clatter and raced toward Pulpit Rock. The skiff they'd been watching, now empty, bobbed on the water's surface, cutting a slow arc. No sign of the woman. They paddled around the skiff, peering down, aghast, but there was nothing to see under a surface as smooth and dark as smoked glass. And nothing to be done. They dropped their anchor and let it out full, pulled it around the skiff, but the lake had no bottom here; everyone knew that. Their anchor never touched.

Eventually, they tied the freshly oiled Rushton skiff to their canoe and towed it to the Van Horne boathouse, eager to tell the tale of the extraordinary thing they'd seen at Pulpit Rock.

Late that night, after she'd ridden hard to retrieve her father, Abigail helped Nicolas search the boathouse. Ruth's cane rod lay in its rack. An anchor, the heaviest, was missing. The only sure indication of the meaning of what had occurred was the note on the kitchen table, a note scripted in the fine, looping hand of a schoolmarm, sealed, and addressed to her husband of many years.

My dearest Nicolas,

Forgive me for what I do, but I cannot go on. The pain has returned to my belly. A greater pain, albeit a much older one, is the secret I've kept from you for far too many years. You must believe that that secret is the only regret of my life. Foolishly, I toyed with fire, with evil, never dreaming of the repercussions. Only time taught me the truth, a truth I take with me into the darkness.

I love you & the children with all my heart & soul. Do not blame yourself & do not grieve for me. Get on with your lives, for I do this willingly & I swear on all that's holy, I go to my Maker without fear or trepidation.

Your loving wife,

Ruth

67

The Last Body in the Ice

It was not yet winter but the cold of winter had settled in and the earth seemed poised, as if waiting for the real winter to arrive. In the days after Ruth Van Horne's suicide, rotted leaves lay frozen hard as stone on the roadside. Each morning a dusting of snow swirled like ashes on the streets and drifted into the crevices of the village. The naked maples on Walnut Street scratched dryly against the clapboards of the Van Horne home. Inside, the fire in the kitchen stove was going cold. Nicolas and Abigail sat at the kitchen table. Adam paced the floor. Abigail began to sob, a telegram in her brief:

Cannot bear the news about Mother STOP

Will return Xmas STOP Love to Abi STOP

Schuyler

Adam went to her and gently took her by the shoulder. "Abby. Come now, girl."

Nicolas stood from the table and pounded a fist into his hand. "The grappling hooks," he said. "I tell you, we've got to try the grappling hooks again."

"They tried the damn hooks," Adam replied. "For two days. Come on, boss—you know Upper Spy better than anyone. At Pulpit Rock, the hooks ain't gonna do a damn—"

"Stop!" Abigail cried. "Stop about the grappling hooks!"

Nicolas sank back into his chair, his head in his hands, seesawing from anger to tears from minute to minute.

"Besides," Adam said, seeing the tears, his voice lowered, "it's too late. The lakes are freezing over. There's nothing to be done." Adam pulled a chunk of oak from the wood basket to stoke the kitchen stove.

Nicolas reached across the kitchen table with tears welling over and took his daughter's hand. "Abby, dearest Abby . . . I must live through the pain. I must. But I'm so sorry for *you*, sweetheart. To be so young, and no mother."

In November Nicolas took to long afternoon walks on the path along the north bank of Town Lake, far from Main Street and out of earshot of anyone. There, he sat on the same rocks where he and Ruth had watched the bats on that warm summer night long ago when he proposed marriage. It was comforting to sit in the open and speak aloud, his voice going out over the frail sheet of ice as it thickened in the winter stillness.

"Ruth . . . I forgive you, of course I do. I do . . ."

Nicolas came to this spot because here, he was alone. Here, with no wind on the river and no hope in his heart, his tears fell unseen onto the frozen ground.

By the time the snow flew and the woods began to fill, Nicolas was on the run. They were after him, Zhivakov's men, the Russians from Buffalo. Strange men—men named Wilson or Smith—were asking questions about him across the North Country. At first, Nicolas hid in the nearby towns, in and out of hotels, never at home for more than a day. He no longer found time to grieve. He was always moving. In Forestport, the Van Horne house was deserted. Adam and Abby hired men and prepared for the first harvest on Upper Spy.

Nicolas began hiding at the lake, alone. At Upper Spy, he spent the shortened daylight hours in the shed working on an invention he hadn't touched in months, an ice shaver he'd designed in his head before traveling with the ice to Galveston. Turning and fitting metal parts occupied his mind, but during the long, dark evenings, he was gripped by the thought that Zhivakov and his men might find him in his sleep.

In early December Nicolas made a quick overnight to Forestport, just long enough to retrieve a certain die needed to shape the ice shaver's blade. There'd been none of Zhivakov's men in Forestport for the past week. Nicolas sat at the kitchen table oiling and polishing the die. A light snow was falling when Adam came through the kitchen door, brushing big wet flakes from his shoulders.

"There's another body for us, boss," Adam said. "But you ain't gonna like it."

"Where is it?"

"In Boonville. He's at the undertaker's."

"Well then, get it into the icehouse."

"I'm not sure that's what you'll want."

Nicolas pushed away from the kitchen table and began to pace. "Damn that Thomas Chubb!" he grumbled. "He's been off in Buffalo how long? A month? And now when we need him to do some embalming, where is he?"

"He's in Boonville, boss. You see . . . the stiff is Thomas Chubb himself."

Nicolas stopped in midstride. "Thomas? Dead?"

"And somebody's already embalmed him."

"Damn that Thomas Chubb."

The buckboard had collected a good six inches of wet snow in its bed by the time Nicolas and Adam made Boonville. The funeral parlour Adam had been directed to was new in town, the second to open. The mortician who came to the door was a young man with a badly acne-scarred face. He seemed bewildered, wasn't sure why the body had been delivered to him or exactly who sent it. It had simply arrived on the train from Buffalo.

"The body came embalmed," he said. "Nice job, too. You know this guy? A sad case, this one. Lucky thing there was paperwork attached to him."

The unlovely young mortician opened a large envelope that was soiled by dark brown fluids. He reached in and produced a coroner's report. Nicolas held it at arm's length for all to read. The document described in gruesome detail the official viewing of the body: "*An obese male of the Caucasian race, fully dressed except for belt . . . blood under the fingernails . . . minor signs of trauma . . . a wide, darkly crusted ligature mark is consistent with the accompanying ligature, the decedent's belt . . .*" The report was signed and bore an official seal of Erie County.

"See, right there's the sad part"—the youth pointed to the bottom line—"*Final diagnosis, death by hanging. Manner of death, suicide.*"

Next, the young man handed Nicolas a page clipped from the *Buffalo Daily Courier*. "This came with the body, too," he said. It was a front page; near the bottom a headline read, UNDERTAKER FOUND HANGING. The article was brief:

A long-established undertaker hailing from a small community in Northern New York was found yesterday morning hanging from an inner door of his rooms at the Hotel Fillmore. The maid made the discovery. The ligature was the victim's own rather copious leather belt, which had been secured to the door's lintel with nails. Investigation by the County Coroner is pending, but all available information indicates the case to be an obvious, albeit somewhat strange, incidence of suicide.

"There's this note, too," the young undertaker said, handing a small envelope to Nicolas. The note was addressed in a delicate, feminine script to "the local ice trader Van Horne."

Nicolas's hand trembled as he opened the envelope. The content was also in a woman's handwriting, and well composed.

> *You forgot what I told you, sir, or perhaps you misunderstood. No matter, for it will come to the same end. As you no doubt surmise from this unusual gift, I no longer am in need of the services of your accomplice, nor of you for that matter. You fellows from up north are like fleas on my back, but sometimes the little fleas go too far.*
>
> *My men will settle with you next, ice man. I will send real Russians to do the job. Trust me on this.*

The signature was a scrawl. "Look how it's signed," Adam remarked, leaning in for a closer look. "It's not regular letters."

"That's Russian," Nicolas replied.

"Since when you know Russian?"

"His name is Zhivakov. I understand it perfectly. Must be he had one of his lady friends write the note."

Snow fell thick and wet on the Forestport Road, nothing that would stick for long, but enough to soak through their woolens and chill them to their core.

"Damnedest thing," Adam said with a nod to the load behind them in the buckboard. "He comes embalmed, complete with a coroner's report. Good old Thomas. He'd be happy, huh? Details to the end."

Nicolas wasn't listening. "Stop ahead, right there," he said, pointing.

Adam pulled the buckboard off the road at a flat place. Nicolas jumped down and walked around to the back. "Help me here," he said. Together they unwrapped the canvas encasing the body. Nicolas tilted Chubb's head back to expose the neck.

"Must be where the belt was."

"Yes, but look closer. See the thin marks?" Nicolas pointed at a purple line cutting deep into the soft tissues. "It's practically severed his windpipe."

"What did that?"

"Something like piano wire."

"So you mean—"

"The wire came first. He was dead, or near dead, when someone hanged him, nailed him up by his belt."

Adam shook his head. "Sure fooled me. Fooled the coroner, too."

They rewrapped the body, mounted the wagon, and continued in silence with their gruesome load. Nicolas had Adam turn onto the cemetery road and pull around to the Chubb Funeral Parlour's mausoleum.

"What're we going to do with him now?" Adam asked as Nicolas unlocked the door to the small stone building. "He's got no family in town."

"He had cousins out west, Missouri, I think, but they'll never come out for a funeral. Not for old Chubb."

"No funeral for the undertaker, huh?"

Nicolas smiled. "Nope," he said as they wrestled Chubb's bulk onto a cold shelf. "I suppose we might as well put him in the icehouse."

"Seems fitting," Adam agreed. "A small service in the village, just don't show the body."

"We'll set a nice marker in the cemetery for when the family from Missouri comes."

"Won't be many mourners at his funeral anyway, only those he taught piano and previous lady friends. Won't be many of them."

"Haul him to the lake after dark, would you, Adam?"

"He'll be in the ice before morning." The trusted foreman got quiet, his brow wrinkled. He didn't say a word until the buckboard had rattled down the hill from the cemetery, then he spoke out. "I gotta confess, boss—I'm gettin' tired of this business of yours. I mean, death's bad enough, but now it's murder."

"I'm afraid it's too much about murder, Adam. And it looks like I'm next."

68

The Time of Ice

Winter settled in hard during the first week of December. The first ice harvest was only a week or two away. Nicolas had taken a room in Boonville at the Continental Hotel after a report from the Forestport station that strange men disembarking the Buffalo train had been "asking after an ice merchant who lives in Forestport." But three nights holed up in a room at the Continental grew tiresome, so Nicolas decided to spend a day or two at the lake, and check the ice.

He rode the Old Forge line to the Upper Spy cutoff, shouldered his small pack basket, and tramped in on the shoreline trail. The vast whiteness of Upper Spy Lake stirred his heart. The broad, smooth outlines of the drumlins around him were like the comforting, protective shoulders of old friends as the light fell off into early evening and it began to snow in earnest. The lake's surface was a rough, opaque hide.

He walked out . . . two . . . four . . . six yards from shore. Alone, so early in winter and in the waning light of day, did he dare go further? The ice would be thin at the lake's center. He strode out, testing it. Snowy crust crunched underfoot. The shoreline faded, then the ice groaned; he felt it sink underfoot, a sudden *crack*, and he veered back toward shore.

When Nicolas spied the icehouse planted solidly on the lakeshore, his breast swelled with pride. The cook's shanty and bunkhouse looked abandoned and forlorn, barely visible behind the shifting curtain of falling snow. Nicolas unbolted the shanty's door and quickly searched for food. All he found was a small tin box hidden under a bunk, half-filled with tea from the Orient.

In the bunkhouse, Nicolas built a fire in the stove, boiled water in a cast-iron kettle, and brewed a pot of strong, black tea. He pounded the mustiness from a mattress and some blankets by beating them against the pine walls of the camp, then bolted the doors. He'd carried in a hunk of cheddar and a box of crackers, enough for a day or two. When he'd eaten and settled into a bunk, his sleep quickly filled with dreams of palm trees, purple orchids, and the salty smell of the sea.

He woke with a coarse shiver; he'd slept long and the fire needed feeding. Muted winter light seeped through the windows. He melted buckets of snow on the stovetop to bathe. He shook out his clothes, dressed by the stove, donned his greatcoat, and stepped out the door to survey a vast panorama of snow, powdery, clean, and as beautiful as the first day of creation.

A foot of snow had fallen overnight. The pines along the shore were flocculent with it. Nicolas wondered if such wild beauty, such stillness, could ever be penetrated by Zhivakov. Ordinarily, this landscape meant one thing to Nicolas—ice, pure and natural, of diamond hardness and clarity. Ice to be scored and cut, floated and stacked, stored, shipped, and sold. Now, Upper Spy meant solitude and safety.

Zhivakov knew he was an ice merchant, but how many lakes were there in the Adirondacks? The shoreline trail to the ice camp was unmarked; the camp was deserted. The Adirondack woods would be mystifying to a citified criminal, wouldn't they? Especially in winter? Only if Zhivakov or his henchman found a guide—a traitor from Forestport who knew the trail—could he find his way to Upper Spy.

Nicolas walked onto the lake, kicking up a fine powder. The sky was opalescent and a light snow again fell. Licking the flakes from his bushy, unkempt mustache, Nicolas saw Upper Spy Lake differently this morning. He had shaped his life from the ice of Upper Spy; he knew its worth and the price it fetched in many ports. But was there more to ice than gold eagles and silver dollars? Nicolas had heard how ice had quelled the fevers of the sick as far away as India. How big must a man's spirit be to turn his ice to that kind of good? What if all he saw before him on Upper Spy, all the profit of ice, were turned to the good of his fellow men—whether Chinaman, Northerner or Southerner, colored or white? Wouldn't he, the ice merchant, be richer for it?

Nicolas trudged northeast across the frozen lake. Pulpit Rock stood like a tombstone on the shore, pale and obscured in the falling snow. He slowed when he was sure he stood over the spot where Ruth's earthly remains were trapped under the ice. Tears came to his eyes at the thought of Ruth twisting on her anchor rope, her flesh preserved in the subzero currents until it turned to a soapy adipocere.

"Ruth"—a whisper in the steadily falling snow—"how I miss my dear Ruth."

Nicolas wouldn't call for another search. Come spring, there'd be no grappling hooks. He'd leave his beloved Ruth to the silence of the depths, to a watery grave, like a brave mariner.

The snow, falling faster, swirled in thick clots.

The ice would be ready in less than a week. In the village, machines were being oiled, ice plows sharpened, horses readied. Abigail and Adam had lined up the rehires from last year, men who wouldn't succumb to drunkenness and gambling once they got a pretty penny in their pockets. There'd be new men to test, to try their hands with the horses, the machines, the ice. And boys, good boys and at least one lost boy who, he hoped, would turn out good.

A busy winter lay ahead. Christmas was around the corner, a motherless Christmastide for Abigail and Schuyler. Nicolas would chance it at the house, he'd watch for the men Zhivakov would send, he'd listen for alerts from the railway station, from the barrooms. He would take down his rifle and load it. Should they surprise him, he'd be ready. With luck, there'd be time to clean out the old Van Horne home, sweep the chimney, warm the parlour with a fresh-laid fire, and cut a tree for the hallway. Perhaps Abigail and Hilda would decorate the tree in the way of the Germans of Forestport, with small candles and sugar-glazed cookies.

In the hush of falling snow, Nicolas's words were muted, softened. "There's much to be done before I'm back on the Mississippi with another cargo."

He turned and started toward the ice camp. An icy wind pummeled him from the north. The falling snow thickened, came at him sideways. If this kept up, it would be a blizzard. He couldn't see the icehouse, managed only to shuffle in its direction. The wind burnt his face and seeped into his clothes, his wool hat, his mittens. Finally, the icehouse loomed out of the storm, a ghostly silhouette in a wall of white.

He decided to see how much ice remained—the ice that held the poor souls he'd collected. He fumbled with the padlock, put a shoulder to the door. Inside, he lit a kerosene torch and set off to the middle room that held the last of the ice. The huge space of the icehouse was hollow and still, while overhead the wind roared so that the building's supporting timbers trembled.

Nicolas unlocked the center room and lifted the torch. Over two dozen bodies wrapped in canvas lay among the blocks, packages of cold flesh and bone preserved by the last Van Horne ice. Here was Nicolas's other harvest; the final canvas-wrapped lump, and the largest, was Thomas Chubb.

In the Van Horne business of death, Thomas had been a skilled and industrious ally. Only since Galveston had Nicolas understood Thomas's evil dealings with the slave trade, how Thomas had wedded himself to Buffalo for years. Nicolas admitted that his confronting Zhivakov was what caused Thomas's murder. For that, Nicolas felt remorse, though he had followed the right course—a course that made him a fugitive.

"Damn you, Thomas, I'm next," he said, retracing his steps. "I'm next, and damn you to hell for it." He hesitated, then muttered, "You're probably there already," and locked the double padlocks.

Outside, Nicolas struggled to shut the icehouse door against the howling wind. It was a blizzard, and judging by the gale-force wind, years from now the old-timers would call it the worst blizzard of the decade. Nicolas guessed he'd be snowed in, and would be for days.

Back in the bunkhouse, Nicolas checked the wood supply. He stoked the fire and went one last time into the cook's shanty to search for food. He didn't find much. A small can of beans; a few scraps of moldy, dried venison the chipmunks hadn't found. More black tea. Then, in the back of a cupboard he discovered a large tin of rice, a bonanza for a starving man, plenty for the days ahead.

That night the north wind moaned and the bunkhouse shook. Nicolas sat close to the stove and boiled a pot of rice. Plain and white as snow, it was the best rice he'd ever tasted.

PART 4

Return

69

The Ugly Mississippi

-PILOT'S LOG-
-15 March 1890-
River below Saint Louis near flood stage. Running under steam. Going rough and fast. Crew competent. No need to pump bilge. Cargo of New York ice shows little melt.

The *Jilted Lady* labored. Her thrashing side-wheels roiled the muddy river. A converted frigate, the *Lady* wouldn't unfurl her sails until the open water of the gulf, but her Scotch boiler supplied plenty of power. The twists and turns of the Mississippi demanded plenty of power from her paddle wheels, together with the keen attention of a seasoned river pilot, a "lightning pilot," as Captain Henry Rossbacher had called himself at the hiring. "I'm the fastest man on the river," was Captain Rossbacher's immodest comment to Nicolas. "We're an agile combination, the *Jilted Lady* and me."

Nicolas let go the rail and staggered to the rattan and bamboo lounge chair he'd bolted to the deck. Adam, tight-faced and off-color, leaned over the rail, his eyes fixed on the turbid river.

"Dang!" Adam exclaimed. "That's some dirty water."

"Stinks, too, doesn't it?"

"My guts can't take much more of this, boss."

"Should smooth out tomorrow," Nicolas said, easing into his deck chair. "Keep your eyes on the shoreline. It'll take your mind off it."

Nicolas had sensed Adam's glumness since they left the North Country. Their success in Saint Louis, where they'd unloaded their sister ship's cargo of ice and delivered four specimens of secret cargo to the medical men, had little effect on Adam's melancholy. Nicolas guessed it wasn't the wicked roll of the ship eating at his foreman. It was the thought of his wife back home, Gertrude, and her advancing consumption.

"Come this spring," Nicolas said, "I say you take Gert to Saranac. That high mountain air's just the thing."

"Easy to say, but—"

"And don't fret the cost, man. I'll cover it."

Nicolas's thoughts turned to his own home life and the sad, disrupted holidays he'd passed at the house on Maple Street. With Schuyler's return from Saint Louis, Christmastide was a bittersweet mix of holiday cheer and family mourning. A tree stood in the hall, but mirrors throughout the house were draped in black. Then, early on Christmas Eve, word came from Stillman's Inn that a certain Mr. Wilson, a hulking, brawny fellow, had checked in. Nicolas acted fast. Schuyler mounted a train bound for Saint Louis, Abigail scuttled down the hill to Hilda, and Nicolas was forced into the woods far from Forestport on a frosty Christmas morning.

Luckily, there'd been no January thaw. With Abigail at his side, Nicolas had quickly filled the icehouse with the winter's second harvest. His daughter was a great comfort, though her keen interest in his efforts to expose the slave trade gave him trepidation. Nicolas succeeded in keeping the fact of the murdered boys from her, but she'd deduced the rest. Naturally, he forbade Abigail to go near the Buffalo criminals, so she'd taken it on herself to visit orphanages across western New York to enquire how children might go missing or be taken from an orphanage by persons of questionable repute.

Nearly two months had passed since Schuyler left Saint Louis southbound for Galveston to construct an icehouse like the one he'd studied. When he departed Saint Louis, the once-wayward son had held a bankroll big enough to choke a horse, and he'd not been heard from since.

Nicolas settled in his chair and tried to put Schuyler out of mind. Since there'd be no delivery in New Orleans, he and Adam would make Galveston Island in two days. He'd see his son's progress for himself soon enough.

Adam refused to take his eyes off the muddy water. "I never saw my Gertie look so bad," he said. "And I been thinking." He straightened and faced Van Horne. "With the little lady's illness and all," he said, "I'm thinking I'll quit this business come summer."

Nicolas gave a start. Adam. His man.

"Sure, Adam. Sure."

"I figure I'll take Gertie to Indian Lake. Not as high as Saranac, but the cabin's snug and they ain't logged it out yet. Deer's thick as blackflies, too."

Nicolas went quiet and stared at the dark swirl of the Mississippi. Adam was right—the river was no Adirondack lake. It smelled of moldy laundry, or worse. A winter's worth of dross and flotsam bobbed on a skin of foamy scum.

Broad islands of brush and upended trees that the captain called "snags" floated by.

The *Jilted Lady* lurched sideways to the current; in his wheelhouse Captain Rossbacher swung the wheel to correct their course and keep their distance from the dangerous snags. Nicolas opened his ledger and spent the rest of the afternoon tallying the greenbacks and gold eagles they'd collected from Saint Louis and stashed in the ship's safe. When he looked up, the sharpest oxbows of the river had fallen behind. The river widened, slowed, and filled with ever-larger snags. Nicolas had a mental image of icebergs, with their vast bulk lurking beneath the surface.

When evening fell, the two deckhands climbed topside to light the ship's lanterns. In all his time on this river Nicolas had never seen a more motley pair than this couple of grimy, half-drunk river rats.

"You boys playin' ya some poque tonight?" the slighter deckhand asked.

Adam nodded. "Prob'ly."

"Count me in," the broad-shouldered, heftier deckhand said. This fellow, who went by Black Pete, was a mixed breed of some sort, his skin darkened to a chocolaty brown by years of ground-in soot. For three nights Nicolas had watched him lose big to Adam. Black Pete was good-natured enough, but as Adam put it, he was "one helluva glutton for punishment" when it came to cards. "A born loser."

"Where's that gamblin' man we took on board?" Black Pete asked. "I'd like to take me some winnings from that hombre tonight."

The "gamblin' man" Pete spoke of was an unscheduled passenger Captain Rossbacher had taken on somewhere early in their journey. A silent type in a seersucker suit and frilly shirt, he'd been sighted only rarely. According to Rossbacher, the gent claimed to be a river gambler, but he hadn't come topside to gamble and hadn't spoken a word to Nicolas or anyone else.

Shortly after nightfall Black Pete produced a deck of cards from the pocket of his dingy jacket. "Go below and see if that gamblin' man's comin' out tonight," he told his fellow deckhand. Pete pulled a stool across from Adam at a small table he'd set on deck next to the mast. Nicolas settled into his rattan chair near the rail and covered himself with a wool blanket.

Heavy cloud cover obscured the stars and moon. The engine of the *Jilted Lady* growled. Her paddles beat a tattoo. Flame and ash belched from the ship's stack into the pitch-blackness. The rock of the *Jilted Lady* and the monotony of the game of poque nearby—the cards dealt and redealt, coins tossed out and pulled in—all combined to lull Nicolas to sleep.

Sometime deep in the night the ship shuddered and Nicolas's coverlet fell away. His rattan chair creaked. He cracked an eye. Something was in the air.

In the lantern light, Nicolas saw Black Pete at the table, along with Adam and a broad-shouldered gent in a dandified suit—the gamblin' man. The pile of bills and gold eagles in front of Adam closely matched the winnings of the gambler. It had been a long night of cards, and the stakes were high.

Pete had his elbows on the table, a half-empty bottle of corn liquor nearby. His forehead wrinkled. "Reckon I'm all out," he said, throwing down his cards. "Ah, hell, it's my turn to stoke 'er boiler, anyway." He pushed away from the table and ducked below.

"My deal," Adam said.

Shaking off the fog of sleep, Nicolas lay in his chair and studied the gambler. The man must've had an appetite; he looked squeezed into that fancy, specially tailored suit. And Nicolas had seen that long thin nose before, hadn't he? That coarse, wide face? Or one like it?

"I got three of a kind here," Adam said. He laid his cards down. A smirk tugged at the corners of his mouth. "Aces."

The gambler gave a nod. "Got me beat. It's good hand."

The gambler's voice sent a bolt of misgiving through Nicolas. Something familiar in it, something foreign.

"You got good luck." The gambler collected the cards. "Maybe luck too good to be true, huh?"

Nicolas snapped awake. *A Russian accent.* He dared not move. A shiver shot down him and he couldn't help but let out a gasp. He felt the gambler's eyes trained on him.

"Uh-oh," the big man said. "I see it's time."

The gambler pushed back from the table and in one silky-smooth movement pulled a copper-colored Derringer pistol from his sleeve and leveled it at Adam.

"Do not move, you. You not my man, but your smart friend here spoil things."

The gambler held the pistol with remarkable delicacy in his big, powerful paw, and with equal delicacy he reached his left hand into his boot and came up with another pistol, this one a Remington Double Derringer, upstairs-downstairs barrels, with an opalescent mother-of-pearl grip. He pointed the second pistol straight between Nicolas's eyes.

For an instant Nicolas saw the future; he knew precisely the mistake Adam was about to make—that crazy half Seneca he knew like a brother, only a foot from a barrel loaded with sure destruction. *Don't do it, Adam*, he thought. *No!*

Before Nicolas could utter a sound Adam made his move for the pistol. Time stood still, the single barrel smoked a tiny puff . . . and yellow flame leapt square at Adam's chest.

Adam fell to the deck, heart-shot, without ever touching the filthy Russian cur. A spasm arched his back, then he went limp. Nicolas stared down two forty-one-caliber barrels—both still loaded, shiny clean, and steadily trained on his forehead.

"You see, I am sent for you, Mr. Ice Man," the gambler growled as he stood and moved away from the table. "Too bad I get this one, too. He was good at cards."

"You're courtesy of Mr. Zhivakov, I take it," Nicolas said, angling for time. "Perhaps we can discuss this. There may've been a misunderstanding of some sort and there may be a way of—"

"*Niet!* No talk."

The man smiled and nodded at Adam. "First, you clean here. Please to put your friend overboard."

"Surely. Anything to help." Nicolas edged toward his friend's body. Adam's eyes were glazing over like a fish at the market.

Behind the big gambler, Nicolas saw Captain Rossbacher lean over the bridge, then disappear back into the wheelhouse. Nicolas feigned getting a grip around Adam's dead body. He took his time with it. *Do something, Rossbacher . . . now, goddamn it!*

The *Lady*'s engine suddenly began to scream and her twin paddles flailed, spinning the ship in a circle. The gambler staggered, just what Nicolas needed—he grabbed a forearm that felt like a fence post and forced the pistol high. A shot rang into the black sky.

But the Russian's bulk was too much. Still holding the gun at bay, Nicolas twisted and bashed the man's hand on the table, upending it. The two fell to the deck in a chaos of cards and coins. Somehow, Nicolas loosened the big man's grip and the pistol skittered away. The two untangled and the big man sprang to his feet. Still on his haunches, Nicolas saw a flash as the Russian drew two metal bolts from his vest, a fine wire strung between them.

The gambler lunged, the bolts firm in his grip, the wire aimed at Nicolas's throat. Nicolas caught both the man's wrists, slowed the wire's progress, but he was pinned . . . pinned against the rail . . . slowly . . . bent backward, the wire closer and closer. He shifted his weight. *Use the big man's bulk against him . . .* He twisted, trying to pull the gambler over the rail with a death grip on the scoundrel's wrists. *The cur'll go with me . . .*

The gambler twisted a hand free, dropped the bolt, and shoved Nicolas further out over the Mississippi. Dirty water raced below. A blade flashed. *Thunk!* The assassin's knife sank into the wood right where Nicolas's hand had been . . . Nicolas pushed away and . . . dropped into the night.

The river raged around him. A shot rang out, then another. The ship careened downriver. Smack in the middle of the Mississippi, Nicolas chose a shore—didn't matter which—kicked off his shoes, wiggled free of his jacket and vest, and set a steady stroke.

Nicolas was a swimmer, but the river had a mighty grip. His strength flagged. Each bend in the river seemed to sweep him further from shore. The cold, silty water tasted of chalk. He rolled onto his back and floated motionless, watching clouds pass over the moon like smoke. Stiff with cold, his mind wandered to Adam's last moments, holding aces. *A lifelong friend, gone! First Ruth . . . now Adam. When will it stop?*

He'd taken a few stiff strokes when something solid jabbed his cheek. He wrapped an arm around an oak tree's limb, part of a giant snag racing downstream. He struggled to lift himself onto the tree's trunk, half out of the wintry water.

A few feet to his left something bobbed in the murk—a shapeless, pale lump the size of a man. Nicolas reached over and grabbed a shred of cloth and hauled. *Could it be? Adam, still a fellow traveler? Caught by the same snag?*

Fighting back tears, Nicolas pulled again, but it wasn't Adam Klock's dead body—it was nothing but a sack of flour fallen from some ship. When he pushed it away in disgust, a murky white paste oozed out.

Nicolas inched further up the oak's trunk, panting with exhaustion. He laid his head on the rough bark, until out of the gloom the riverbank emerged a few feet away. He gained his feet, balanced on the trunk, and leapt for shore. Landed in muck. Scrambled up the slippery clay bank into the underbrush.

A few steps and he was on a dirt road tracing along the riverbank. Shoeless, his hair fouled with red clay, he turned downstream, dripping fetid river water with every step. Strands of rank-smelling river weeds hung like ill-kept muttonchops from his face.

It seemed like hours before he stood in a village of low-slung buildings, swaying in the street in the grey dawn light. A gentle rain had begun to fall. Down a narrow path to the river, Nicolas's eyes fell on the *Jilted Lady*, tied to a dilapidated dock. He took off at a trot, then stopped himself.

"Is the murderous bastard still aboard?" he mumbled. He advanced cautiously, his feet raw, his filthy socks flapping on the road. Then he saw

Captain Henry Rossbacher sitting on the dock with his head buried in his hands. Rossbacher looked up and made a low, rumbling sound.

"Van Horne? I'll be damned . . . you're not dead."

"Thank God you're spared, too, Captain. How'd you manage it?"

"The goddamned privateer needed me to get him ashore. Once I docked the *Lady*, he forced me to open her safe, which he proceeded to empty. He even jettisoned your baggage, the rotten skunk."

"Left me nothing but the blasted ice, eh?"

"Devil take your precious ice, Van Horne."

Nicolas sank onto the dock and slumped against a piling. "Yes, damn my precious ice," he said softly. "My best friend. A man I've known since childhood, lost." Nicolas choked on a sob, tears falling freely now. He raised a fist, unleashed a woeful cry. *"Despicable scoundrel! Adam . . . oh, Adam . . . why'd you go for that gun?"*

"Git a grip on yerself, man," the pilot said, taking Nicolas by the shoulders to still his shaking. "We'll carry on. We'll get your damned ice to market."

Rossbacher plunked down next to Nicolas and wrapped an arm around him. He gazed stolidly at his ship in the weak river light. "Of course, my chickenhearted crew skedaddled," Rossbacher said with a chuckle. "So you, sir, will be feedin' her boiler."

70

Hasty Delivery

The north wind blew a gale over the open waters of the Gulf of Mexico, striking the side-wheel steamer *Jilted Lady* broadside with hail and ice that came like scattershot out of the night. High in the wheelhouse, Nicolas poured a touch of warmth for Captain Rossbacher from a bottle of rum purchased in New Orleans, where they'd taken on firewood for the *Lady's* boiler and managed to hire one additional deckhand.

Van Horne, the newly installed chief mate, had been stoking the boiler's furnace all evening. Soot was wedged into every crevice of his flesh. Besides that, he'd been forced to borrow clothes from Rossbacher, who was half a foot shorter. Nicolas Van Horne was a sorry sight. His bare arms protruded from a faded peacoat badly thinned at the elbows. He'd belted his pants with coarse twine. The borrowed shoes squeezed his toes like a vise. Rossbacher had offered a loan to buy clothes in New Orleans, but Nicolas felt in too black a mood to shop. Besides, his job as mate would've ruined any finer duds.

"I-is this tub seaworthy?" Nicolas asked through chattering teeth.

"She's been through a gale or two," Rossbacher said.

Nicolas passed the pilot a tumbler of rum and poured one for himself.

"Crossed the *Lady* to Mexico last summer," the pilot continued, turning serious. "Of course she's a might top-heavy with that boiler's big stack."

He took a slug of rum and swung the wheel a quarter turn to steady his vessel's progress against twelve-foot swells from the starboard. "This norther should blow itself out by morning," he said. "Then, with the easterly I'm expecting, we'll set some sail and make time." Casting a sideways glance, he added, "But for now, I believe she needs a bit more power, mate . . . if you please."

Nicolas tightened a weary grip on his tumbler before going below. The deckhand they'd taken on in New Orleans was a lazy no-good, and Nicolas had been doing most of the *Lady's* work.

The gale hardened through the night and pounded their starboard until daybreak. Once the storm relented, Nicolas, sleepless and covered in a salty crust, breathed easier.

By midday the swells subsided and the wind steadied from the east under an azure sky. Captain Rossbacher told Nicolas to let the *Lady*'s Scotch boiler go cold; they unfurled her cloth and sailed full and by on the easterly Rossbacher had predicted. Nicolas took advantage of the respite to duck belowdecks and scribble a note—a note he would post upon making port.

My dearest Abigail,

I am alive and well, but steel yourself for horrid news. Our dear friend Adam was MURDERED & lost on the Mississippi, may God rest his noble soul.

Surely I relate to you one of the darkest moments of my life. At Saint Louis our steamer shipped out well, all business having gone according to plan. Late that night Adam was SHOT DEAD defending me from a murderous slave trader, an assassin sent for me. I barely escaped into the river. Adam's killer is long gone, the ship's safe and our trunks emptied, the only good tiding being that we continue in the open gulf toward Galveston with cargo intact.

Regrettably, the task of telling poor Gertie Klock falls to you, dearest Abby, my courageous daughter. I am sure you will provide Gertie great comfort. Please extend my deepest, most heartfelt condolences. I look forward to finding Schuyler to see how his icehouse has progressed.

Until now, I've kept the worst of this from you, Abby. I've not let on how dangerous these slave traders are. Take caution, extreme caution. Stay close to home, and pray that my worst fears are unfounded, and Adam's killer will not pursue me to Galveston.

All love

Yr father

Near midnight Rossbacher sighted the light at Half Moon Shoal. When they slipped into the bay they lost the wind, and Nicolas fed the boiler's furnace one last time to steam around the tip of Galveston Island.

"I'd request that you dock at the first pier on the east end of the island," Nicolas told the captain. "And no need to blow her horn, Rossbacher. We'll pull in quietly, send your useless deckhand packing, and you'll be free tonight to find yourself a room."

"Gladly."

"Tomorrow I'll secure a permanent berth at Pier 28. We'll unload her ice there."

After making the Lady fast, Captain Rossbacher cast a questioning eye at the shoddy medical college pier, then strode off for a meal and a decent drink. "I'll be taking quarters at the Jolly Seaman's Inn," he said in parting.

Nicolas was heartened to see electrical lights from the upper floor of the college. They meant that even at this late hour he needn't roust old Keiller out of his bed.

The cool silence of the medical college's interior and the dark stench of formaldehyde on the long stairway were immediately familiar to Nicolas. Though it had been almost a full year, he felt like he'd never left the island. As he neared the upper landing, a door swung open and erratic footfalls came from the research laboratory. The professor limped out, his gait slower than Nicolas remembered.

"Professor Keiller!" Nicolas called up the stairs. "Hold on, sir."

The old man spun around slowly and squinted, a startled look on his face. He extracted a pair of wire-rim spectacles from his vest and fitted them clumsily around his ears. "Who? . . . Who's that?"

Since Nicolas last set eye on the elderly gent, Professor Francis Keiller had changed for the worse. He'd shrunk a half foot; his back was doubly crooked; his hair amounted to little more than a few wisps protruding like lonely wires from the sides of a wobbly head. The keen, professorial face was drawn and ashen, though his eyes still had a blaze to them—a blaze that flickered brighter at the sight of the ice merchant.

"Aye, it's Mr. Van Horne, returned to us in the middle of the night." Keiller offered a bony hand; Nicolas held it firmly.

"I've a delivery for you, sir. My ship's made fast at your dock."

"Ah, excellent. But you're lookin' a mite tatty, Van Horne. Difficult voyage, was it?"

"Unfathomably so."

"Come to the office, then, and we'll share a wee touch of whiskey."

With a wave of his hand, Keiller led the way back through his laboratory. Retorts were stilled, Bunsen burners extinguished. A solitary student, a slim figure against the glow of the open incinerator, was adding a powder to a cold Erlenmeyer flask that sat on the slate counter.

Keiller paused halfway across the lab and called to the student, "Patrick! I've an errand for you, son. Very important."

Keiller instructed the youth to run posthaste to the homes of his two anatomy assistants and shake them out of their beds. "Tell them our supplier's back," he said, "and there's work to be done tonight. Get cracking, boy."

In his blood-warm office Keiller poured two whiskeys and lowered himself behind his desk. Nicolas sank into the other chair.

"Professor, I'm afraid I carry terrible news . . ."

Nicolas's voice quavered as he imparted the grim tale of Adam's murder and his own near-assassination. For a long moment, silence hung like a pall over the two men. Keiller shook his head, then gave his desktop a resounding thump with his fist.

"Damnable cur! How ghastly. But, Nicolas—why would such a man be after you? This wasn't simply an argument over cards, you say?"

"It's a complicated tale, Professor. Since I left you last, I uncovered something I wasn't meant to, an enterprise run by ruthless criminals, and I'm dealing with the consequences. Earlier, your niece, Renée, helped me come to grips with the problem."

"I'm sure she advised you well. She isn't in any danger, is she?"

"I've been careful to go it alone on this."

"You best watch your back, Nicolas. But this is a great loss to your enterprise. Adam was an able assistant, as I remember. Is there family?"

"I'm afraid his wife's a consumptive in the advanced stages of the disease. I plan to see she gets proper treatment at Saranac."

"A world-class facility."

"There's four sons. The eldest works in the woods at the lumber trade."

"Fine boys, no doubt."

"I'll help however I can."

"I'm sure."

The two men went quiet again. Nicolas's gaze wandered over Keiller's office, reappraising the intricately carved wood of the walls, the books and manuscripts, the smoldering fire in the fireplace of Italian tiles he'd admired on his first visit. A faint buzz came from the carefully stacked mosquito cages of the professor's insectary.

This time Nicolas broke the silence. "Yes, it's been a troubling year for me, yet in many ways I count myself fortunate. Despite the loss of my wife—"

"*Egad, man!* You *have* had a rough time of it."

"Indeed, sir, I have, but my children—and Adam—carried me through. The ice business thrives, and we've collected a copious shipment for you, Professor."

Nicolas paused, having touched on the delicate subject of his visit.

"How many have ye brought me?" Keiller asked.

"A full complement. Two dozen."

"Ahh . . . Splendid."

"I did no business whatsoever in New Orleans, neither ice nor corpses. They're all yours, except the few I arranged for Saint Louis."

"Our students are greatly indebted."

"I believe there's a future for my business in your city. I've a new icehouse under construction, you know."

"Quite impressive, I understand. Everyone's been keenly watching your son, Nicolas. They're saying good things about him."

A faint smile—his first since making safe harbor—flickered across Nicolas's lips. "Schuyler's hit a few bumps in life," he said, "but I'm hoping he's turned a corner at last."

"An asset to the island, your boy. Very well-known. And now he's concocted this new horse-racing enterprise—"

"Horse racing?"

"A truly novel idea. A racetrack should turn a pretty profit in a busy port like this. And to locate in Sailortown in the . . . um . . . entertainment district. A brilliant move."

Nicolas hid a smirk. "Yes, I suppose." He hesitated before asking, "Is your niece well?"

"Yes, excellent," Keiller replied with a perfunctory nod. "Extremely busy. I don't suppose you know about her and Fernando?"

"Renée and Fernando?"

"Their betrothal."

Nicolas gaped for a moment, a sickening feeling in his gut. "You mean, Fernando and—?"

"It seems a tolerable match. The man's a good worker, steady and thoughtful, though hardly an inventive mind in the laboratory."

Nicolas fought to maintain his composure while Keiller rambled on. So much had happened since Saratoga. His confronting Zhivakov in Buffalo, the alliances he'd formed with the authorities—at Renée's urging—and now, Adam's murder...

"I tell you honestly, Van Horne," Keiller went on, "it was no surprise when I asked Pasteur about Fernando and the old boy didn't remember the chap ever working at the Université Lille. But then, Louis has gotten too damned big for his britches, I suspect. He probably overlooked the young man, and Fernando's the silent type—these Spaniards often are. He's worked so closely with Renée...the attraction...it's natural, I suppose..."

Renée. Keiller's lovely niece...When Nicolas was in hiding at Upper Spy Lake, alone, the empty feeling left by their brief summer interlude in Saratoga would well up, and his heart would ache. But Renée was pure infatuation, an impossible dream, a love never to be. For now, he had to put her out of mind. An assassin stalked him, and a hunted man had no time for idle thoughts...Still, the thought of Renée wedded to her lab assistant left a hollowness inside him.

Shakily, he set his drink down and stood. "We'd best get to my ship and get started, eh?"

"But you've not touched your drink," Keiller protested. "Ye likely need it, Nicolas. Ye look a bit woozy. Drink up, man."

Nicolas drew a breath, then another. Galaxies of sparkling white dots—an entire Milky Way—burst before his eyes.

"No . . . thank you, though, Professor. Let's get on with the unloading, shall we?"

71

On the Dock

Nicolas sensed from the start that it wouldn't go well on the dock that night. The sky was clear, the moon full and high. The evening was tepid, the bay flat as an Adirondack lake. Sound would carry for miles in such stillness. And he hardly had a taste for unloading bodies after the disastrous loss of Adam.

Keiller's grumbling assistants arrived on the dock half-asleep. Nicolas recalled the two men who acted as all-around porters and lackeys in the cadaver facility; one was the seven-foot giant covered with tattoos, the other a humpbacked Chinaman named Lee Ching. Both assistants immediately became unruly and bellicose. Keiller incessantly shushed them. But the biggest problem, Nicolas quickly realized, was that Adam Klock, his right-hand man, lay dead at the bottom of the Mississippi River instead of ably assisting in the ice.

Well before loading for the trip south, while still in the Upper Spy icehouse, Adam had devised an ingenious way to extract the bodies from the shipload of ice without first unloading the top layers. His new method, he'd rightly reasoned, would make for lightning-quick delivery in Saint Louis and Galveston. Adam had built a narrow chimney at one end of the cargo, and covered the chimney with a foot-thick trapdoor of ice. The chimney allowed Nicolas's slightly built foreman to descend into the catacombs at the bottom of the ship's hold and wrestle the corpses into position to be hauled up, one by one, with a rope.

The new method had worked perfectly at the unloading in Saint Louis, where within an hour of making port four bodies were unloaded. But now—as Nicolas recalled with a pang of remorse—Adam Klock had taken a deadly load of lead. The skinniest man on the *Jilted Lady* was gone. The ice chimney was far too narrow for Keiller's giant assistant. Likewise, Lee Ching's hunchback jammed at its entrance. Thus it fell to Nicolas to light a lantern, descend into Adam's chimney, crawl through the frigid catacombs, wrangle the bodies out of their resting places in the ice, and affix a rope so the strong arms topside could haul them up and out. Nicolas was rawboned from his winter of dodging slave traders and hard-muscled from the ice harvests, but he was still a much bigger man than Adam Klock had been.

The back door to the college was thrown open and the vats of formaldehyde uncovered, ready to receive the corpses. Nicolas dropped down the ice chimney and pushed the lantern down the narrow tunnels. But it went slowly, very slowly. Tons of ice seemed to press in around him. The rubbery bodies jammed. Nicolas fumbled with the icy ropes.

It took two hours before Nicolas saw the last—and the largest—of the two dozen corpses squeeze through Adam's chimney. By then, his breath came in harsh gasps; he was running out of air.

In the failing light of the lantern, he assembled a final bundle of his gruesome cargo—an assortment of arms, legs, and dismembered hands—and hastily lashed the bundle with twine. Topside, a hubbub broke out. "Hurry, Van Horne!" Keiller shouted. "Trouble's brewing."

With his lungs sucking at the vanishing air, body aching and stiff from the cold, Nicolas sent the final grisly parcel topside. When he scuttled up the ice chimney and peered out, he was greeted by a grotesque spectacle. The last of the bodies, a rotund and exceptionally buxom young woman, lay half on, half off the dock. Keiller's assistants stood over the corpse, dumbly passing a pint of whiskey between them. Nicolas remembered well the unnamed woman from a nearby town; she'd died of consumption at the County Home for Wayward Women and was destined for a pauper's grave until intercepted by Thomas Chubb.

Professor Keiller was distraught. "We were seen," he hissed. "When they were tugging on that last big one, I spied two young rascals in the bushes. I told 'em, 'Git!' but I suspect they were there all night, the damned hooligans." Keiller turned to his assistants. "Come on, you two," he said in a coarse whisper. "Let's finish, and fast! They're probably still watching."

The tattooed giant hoisted the naked female body onto his broad back; the corpse's pendulous breasts swung to a half-drunk rhythm as the giant made his way down the dock. Lee Ching dragged Nicolas's makeshift bundle of body parts off; Nicolas followed with Keiller hobbling alongside.

Once inside the back entrance to the medical college, Nicolas was done in and asked to take his leave of the professor.

"Yes, yes, get some rest, my good man," Keiller said as he prepared to swing the iron door shut behind Nicolas. "Our vats are at their capacity, thanks to you."

Nicolas, chilled to the bone, his hands blistered and lungs heavy with soot, staggered back onboard the *Jilted Lady* and collapsed into his bunk. His welcome sleep was broken only once, when, in the dead of the night, he heard a soft banging, or thumping, topside. Was it merely the creak of the mast? Also, he could've sworn he heard a rooster crow.

At dawn, Nicolas was wakened by stomping and shouting on deck.

"Father? Are you here?" It was Schuyler's distinctive bass voice. "Egad!" he exclaimed. "What is this mess?"

Nicolas pulled on his borrowed pants and shirt and ducked out from below. Schuyler was leaning on the ship's rail, looking prosperous and somewhat overfed in fine tweeds and a grey chesterfield jacket with a blue velvet collar. Nicolas raced to embrace his son, but at his first step he skidded on a slippery plank, his arms windmilled, and he hit the deck hard. Looking about, he found he was sitting in a puddle of blackened, congealed blood. "What in the world? *Blood?*"

"You've a mess all right," Schuyler said, casting an eye around the deck of the *Jilted Lady*. "It's chickens, Father. Look there. Chickens."

Schuyler pointed at the lifeless bodies of three bantam roosters lying on deck near the mast. The birds had been decapitated; their bright reddish-brown feathers fluttered in the breeze. Nicolas struggled to his feet.

Schuyler, still leaning on the rail, reached into an inner jacket pocket and extracted a cigarette. He lit it and took a long draw. "Looks like black magic to me," he said.

"Yes, and I notice the hatches have been opened."

"Hereabouts, this sorta thing's the speciality of the Voodoo Doctor."

Nicolas instantly recalled the ghastly lynching he and Adam had witnessed on their first voyage to Galveston. "You've heard of the Voodoo Doctor?"

"I've actually had dealings with the gent." Schuyler shed his chesterfield and rolled up his sleeves, the cigarette dangling from his mouth. "Can't feature what he'd hold against you."

"Obviously, he's heard of my arrival. Some town hooligans saw us unloading last night, and I guess news travels fast in this town."

"I doubt he cares about the medical college."

"No, Son, this fellow has it in for body snatchers. He lynches them."

"He hardly seems like the type."

"Believe me, Son. I've seen it."

Schuyler flipped his cigarette into the bay. "Well, let's get this mess overboard, shall we? I'm eager to show you the fruits of my labor."

They heaved the carcasses overboard and replaced the hatch covers. Schuyler donned his chesterfield and they were about to debark when he stepped to the mast and said, "Well looky here." The heads of the decapitated chickens were nailed on the low door that led below. The bloody heads were arranged in a triangle; in the center a small black object had been fixed with a brass tack.

"It's a charm," Nicolas said, recalling the bizarre trinket tied to the brick that had abruptly ruined Keiller's Mardi Gras party. "A voodoo charm." He pulled out the tack and turned the object in his hand.

"Cute little doodad," Schuyler said.

"I recall now, Son—the skin of a black snake wrapped around something…like a hank of hair." As Nicolas peered at the charm, a line of silvery droplets spilled onto the deck. He bent to examine the substance. "It's mercury, like in my weather instruments."

"Mercury was the Romans' messenger god, wasn't he?"

"Yes, but also the god of merchants."

"A message to a merchant, then, eh? An ice merchant, to be exact," Schuyler said with a smirk. "Come on, Father, toss that thing in the drink and don't give it a thought. Let's see your new icehouse. Adam, too. Is that lazy bum still sleeping below?"

Nicolas groaned. "Oh Lord, I've horrible news, Schuyler. I'll tell you as we go." He took his son's arm and led him to the *Jilted Lady*'s gangplank. "It's about poor Adam."

As they strode down the harborside, Nicolas relayed the tale of the Russian assassin and Adam's death. Though Nicolas had his finished letter to Abigail in hand, ready to post, Schuyler suggested his father telegraph Abby to advise her immediately of the bad news. Nicolas agreed, and they detoured to the Veracruz Cable Company office.

When Nicolas pushed his telegram under the metal bars, the harried cable officer looked up and raised his voice over the ticking of the machines. "Mr. Van Horne? Just so happens we've a telegram for you, sir." The officer searched in the chaos behind him, then reappeared. "It came over the wire two days ago."

He slid the cable across the guttered marble. Wired from the town of Forestport, it was from Abigail Van Horne:

Have news from Chicago STOP

Am learning much STOP

Slave ring bigger than thought STOP

Even in South STOP Take great care STOP

Abi

Last Nicolas knew, Abigail was in Chicago investigating a community house that sheltered runaways and misplaced orphans. The place, called Hull House, was newly opened by a certain Miss Addams, a renowned leader in the women's movement whom Abigail idolized. When Nicolas left with the ice, Abby was waiting for more correspondence from Addams. *Bigger than thought. Even in South.* A wave of shivers coursed down Nicolas's back.

Schuyler wrapped his arm around his father's shoulder. "Let's not dwell on this, eh? Knowing my sis, I'm sure she's got things under control. Come, let me show you your new icehouse."

"I'm in need of that, Schuyler. Indeed I am."

72

The New Van Horne Icehouse

When he stepped onto Pier 28, Nicolas's spirits were lifted from the abyss into which they'd fallen. The newest structure on the wharfs, Schuyler's icehouse was perfectly sited and appeared to have size and capacity far greater than Pierre Bonferri's, where Nicolas had previously stored his ice. Meticulously constructed of the hardiest swamp cypress, this was no jerry-built warehouse. What most caused Nicolas to take heart, however, was the "VAN HORNE & SON" freshly painted in bold red letters on the icehouse's white clapboards.

"I've never seen a finer structure, Schuyler."

"I specified your double-walled construction, Father, and the ventilation system, exactly reproduced, only larger. She'll hold over forty thousand tons, twice the Saint Louis capacity."

"If only Adam could have seen it."

"I might add that I accomplished it without spending the entirety of your funds. Pier 28's the perfect location, too. It's the busiest cotton wharf in town. You won't believe how much cotton they jam into ships on this wharf."

Father and son rousted the ship's pilot from the quarters he'd taken in Sailortown at the Jolly Seaman's Inn, a Galveston wayfarers' accommodation advertised as "cheap, lax in rules, and nearly free of bedbugs." Nicolas dispatched Captain Rossbacher to the medical college's pier to bring the ship around to the wharf at Pier 28. Father and son then proceeded downtown to make the bureaucratic arrangements necessary to unload thirty thousand tons of ice from the *Jilted Lady*.

On the ground floor of the Port Authority Building, they stood at window after window, dealing through steel grates with officials who, from their various cages, served as experts in matters of docking permits, port taxes, and harbor law. Nicolas was told that because all his assets had been stolen from the safe of the *Jilted Lady*, it proved necessary for him to "procure a financial advance"—in hard cash—from an established Galveston businessman to cover his unloading expenses. He immediately thought of Pierre Bonferri, his partner in ice.

Fortunately, Nicolas and Schuyler found Bonferri in the foyer of his nearby offices, keeping company with a stable of young women eager for a turn at his Remington typewriting machine. Schuyler dallied in the outer office with the young ladies while his father retreated to Bonferri's inner office.

Bonferri welcomed Nicolas warmly and quickly agreed to help with his problematic finances. As details were discussed, the Frenchman eyed the sad state of Nicolas's ill-fitting trousers and bursting shoes. His brow wrinkled.

"Say, Van Horne, while you're in town," Bonferri said, "you might consider a new suit. I recommend Myer's shop. He's my favorite clothier."

Nicolas agreed with a chuckle. "I'm afraid my garb's better suited to the high seas," he said. "Once we're unloaded, I must get myself to Myer's."

Back at the Port Authority Building to hire some stevedores, Nicolas discovered that virtually all Galveston's stevedores were tied to an organization controlled by the cotton jammers—the Island Society of Longshoremen, or ISL. The bureaucrat in his cage further informed Nicolas that the ISL prohibited its members from unloading "dangerous cargo" at the port of Galveston. "And Northerner ice is dangerous cargo," the man said. "At least according to the ISL."

"For God's sake!" Nicolas railed at the man behind the steel bars. "What's dangerous about ice?"

Nicolas and Schuyler were forced to walk the docks searching for laborers not tied to the ISL, though they found none.

It was noon when the *Jilted Lady* steamed in from the medical dock. Father and son, still without stevedores, sat on the pier, dejected, in the midst of stacks of baled cotton, hogsheads of molasses, and crates of bananas and pineapples. Captain Rossbacher scurried up to them.

"You and yer infernal ice," he said. "I've heard the damnedest things."

The river pilot explained that during his evening's stay at the Jolly Seaman's Inn, he'd heard dockworkers talking about an "ice trader" who'd crossed the wrong port authorities. Rossbacher further reported that while downing an eye-opener at a corner bar that morning, he'd happened to mention "New York ice" to one of the port authorities and was met with deathly quiet that fell like a curtain.

"Somebody in this port's got it out for you, Van Horne. Can't tell why," he laughed, "but I know one thing. Your ice is the most accursed cargo I've ever carried. I'll be right pleased to see her unloaded, so's I can get this tub back to New Orleans." Rossbacher looked up and down the pier. "I trust I won't have to wait till yer damned ice melts before I can fire the *Lady*'s boiler."

With that, Captain Rossbacher strode off the pier in search of further liquid refreshment.

"Looks like the cotton jammers have us stopped," Schuyler said. "Bet I can change your luck, though. As I said, I'm in tight with their leader. I struck a bargain with the fellow on a certain business arrangement."

"Would that 'certain arrangement' have to do with horse racing?"

Schuyler was taken aback. "Why . . . yes. It's guaranteed profits, you see."

"So I've heard," Nicolas said with a smirk.

"I figured Sailortown the best spot for a new track. This voodoo fellow has a lot to say about such things. He controls the port with his cotton jammers...cops 'em a fair wage, I hear. It turned out he was happy to have my track on a parcel of open land at the end of Post Office Street, just past the brothels. He saw my racing venture as good for his end of town, I figure."

"So you'll talk to him about men to unload the ice."

"Let me go see what the problem is." Schuyler paused. "Do you happen to know this voodoo fellow's connection to Hutch Sealy, the financier?"

"You do get about in this town, don't you, Schuyler."

"Quite an intriguing place. Sealy's two sons are the most powerful men in the city, from different angles. Naturally, they hate each other."

"I learned as much on my first visit."

"All very hush-hush. Doctor Voodoo's a prince of a fellow, once you meet him. Quite educated. He puts on a primitive act for his followers, but it's an act, believe me. They're a superstitious lot, these jammers. Curses . . . spells . . . Louisiana voodoo . . . they go for all that."

"He's got it in for us body-in-a-bag men."

"I'll go see him, Father. I don't want you to end up like those dead chickens."

Nicolas settled onto a cotton bale and heaved a weary sigh. "See what you can do, Son."

"With any luck, I'll fix things," Schuyler said. "Then we'll get you to my place for some rest. You can have the sofa, it's quite cushy. No nasty seafarer's quarters for you."

Schuyler wrapped an arm around his father and gave a tug. "I'll lend you some of my duds, too," he said with an extra squeeze. "You're looking so spare, you'll probably swim in them."

Schuyler hustled off to see the Voodoo Doctor while Nicolas sank onto a cotton bale, his head in his hands. The arduous voyage south would be a total loss if his ice sat at harborside, melting. But Schuyler seemed so changed, and for the positive. Perhaps the clever boy would finagle a deal somehow . . . but with this Voodoo Doctor fellow?

Nicolas looked up from his musings to find a blue-suited functionary planted in front of him, his hands on his hips, a stern look of officialdom on his face.

"Tariff inspector here, sir," the gent said. "I believe this here's your vessel."

A thin, athletic-looking young man, the tariff inspector stood eye to eye with Nicolas. His long, spidery fingers wrapped nearly around the blue notebook he held. The badge on his chest, freshly polished, shone in the noonday sun.

"I'll need to see your cargo."

Nicolas gave a shake of his head, and was slow to stand.

"Right now, sir, if you please."

Nicolas led the young inspector across the gangplank and aboard the *Jilted Lady*. The inspector walked to the line of hatches, threw the first open with a flair, and peered down for a moment before going on to the next. Nicolas followed, quickly shutting the hatches behind him.

"What's this?" the inspector muttered to himself. "Looks like a tunnel." The inspector made a brief entry in his notebook and set it on the deck. "I'll need a lantern. I'm going to have a look." Nicolas went below to retrieve an oil lamp—the smallest, dimmest he knew of—then watched as the inspector's lean frame disappeared down Adam's ice chimney.

Nicolas paced the deck. How long would this inspector be touring the icy catacombs? Finally, a cool draft wafted from the hatch and the inspector's head popped out of the ice.

"Damnedest layout down there," he said. "Tunnels everywhere. Nothing requiring tariffs that I can see, but heaven help me, at the bottom of the shaft I found *this* nasty item."

Delicately pinched in his fingers, the inspector lifted a human hand onto the deck.

Coarse and callused like a workman's, the hand had been severed well above the wrist, with half the forearm attached. The hand was missing the pinky finger from a long-healed mishap. A dingy brown crust covered the site of its crude amputation, immediately recognizable to Nicolas as the work of the Forestport sawmill's notorious circular saw.

"Any idea how this got down there, sir?"

"Perhaps an accident? During loading?" Thinking quickly, Nicolas added, "I don't recall such an accident, but I'd be glad to see to this thing's proper disposition, with the utmost respect and dignity, of course."

The inspector held him with a disdainful glare. "I suspect that where you come from, sir, folks know little about a proper burial." He pulled a paper sack from his pocket, slipped the severed hand into it, and set the bag on the deck. Then he was back at his notes.

"I'm takin' this to the city constable, Mr. Van Horne," he said as he wrote. "He'll be in charge of disposal and—naturally—the legal enquiry into the matter."

The inspector stepped down from the ship and called back at Nicolas, who appeared frozen in place. "You may proceed with your unloading . . . but do take care in our town," he added as he sauntered off with his grisly prize. "Take special care."

73

Voodoo Doctor

"Nothing doing," Schuyler said upon his empty-handed return. "No stevedores. The Voodoo Doctor wants to see you personally first. Seems to be some misunderstanding about your business at the medical college."

"I'm afraid this Voodoo Doctor understands too much."

"Don't worry. I made him promise he wouldn't harm you."

The headquarters of the Island Society of Longshoremen was a short walk from Pier 28, on the edge of Sailortown. It was located on Post Office Street, an avenue lined by brothels but quiet now, in broad daylight.

It was a plain one-story brick building, windowless, with the look of a warehouse. Inside was a large hall; Schuyler led the way to the front, past row upon row of wooden chairs. A few workingmen were taking seats. The men were of various colors and nationalities. The somber, muffled conversations suggested that a speech of some importance would soon be delivered, though the podium at the front of the hall, draped in red and white bunting, was empty now.

Schuyler stepped to a door behind the podium and gave a knock. "He told me he'd be available until the speech at three o'clock," Schuyler said. "Some foreign visitor or other."

"Come in," came from the other side of the unmarked door.

"His office isn't much," Schuyler whispered before reaching for the doorknob. "But very red."

They entered a small office that held a half dozen wooden chairs, a large round table, and a desk. The table was piled high with promotional pamphlets and tracts. Nicolas glanced over the material, which leaned toward trade unions, improving the lot of wage earners, and Marxism. Stretched across the walls were two banners, one portraying a hammer and a plow, the other a dagger's hilt grasped in a brawny fist.

Behind the desk sat the leader of the ISL, whom Nicolas had last seen at the lynching of the medical school's body-in-a-bag man. The mulatto who sat atop the nefarious buckboard a year ago was unmistakable. His hair, previously a tangled nest of darkness, was now plaited to a smoother mane, and the amulet around his neck that had called up some mysterious voodoo spirit earlier was missing. He wore a clean, blue work suit, common to the jammers. Seated at his desk, leaning over the litter of journals and handwritten papers, the young man's blunted features and bright skin gave him an entirely different air than Nicolas expected. The Voodoo Doctor appeared more business than voodoo. Still, his commanding, steely grey eyes cast a certain spell as he motioned, without offering his hand, for Schuyler and Nicolas to take the two chairs across from him.

"So you're the ice merchant," he said, his eyes burning holes into Nicolas.

"Recently arrived, yes."

The youthful mulatto began to gently rock in place. His desk chair squeaked. He picked up a hefty letter opener crafted of whalebone and began tapping it on his other hand to the rhythm of his chair's creaking. "I believe, sir, you are also a grave robber."

"No, sir, absolutely untrue. I never open graves, and I never shall."

"Body snatcher, then."

"No."

"How, precisely, does one obtain dead bodies without robbing graves or stealing them from loved ones?"

The Voodoo Doctor's tone, too, seemed surprisingly erudite, and calm. The man clearly had two different ways of speaking, two different personas.

Nicolas leaned forward in his chair. "You see, sir," he began in earnest, "the dead bodies I supply for the education of medical men come to me in various ways, mostly as unclaimed bodies, without family. They were never destined for a decent burial. They come from all parts of the Northeast."

"The North, you say?"

"The upper reaches of New York State."

"They weren't dug from potter's fields then?"

"No, sir. That would be outright thievery. I am not interested in burial clothes or jewelry or gold teeth, only their earthly bodies, and only so that medical men—scientists—can learn from them."

The surprise on the young man's face reawakened in Nicolas the sights he'd seen on his first visit to the Medical College of Galveston. He could never forget the lynching he and Adam had witnessed, with this odd ruffian leading the atrocity. But Nicolas also envisioned Professor Keiller's vats and anatomy facility at the medical college, the hanging bodies reeking of formaldehyde. Those corpses, he recalled, were solely of the impoverished, and nearly all colored folks. *From potter's fields.*

"How can I be expected to believe you?" the Voodoo Doctor asked. "For years, ever since the medical college opened, the graves of our people, the colored cemeteries and potter's fields throughout the South, have been defiled by criminals such as you."

"I've heard that, yes, but that hardly allows one to take the law into one's own hands, does it?"

The Voodoo Doctor looked away, stared at a banner on the wall. "I regret having to resort to violence, but that man was thoroughly warned, and he would not desist. The law does nothing to these grave robbers. In some cases, violence serves as a means to an end."

"I disagree," Nicolas said. "I've had too much of violence, and I find it accomplishes nothing."

The Voodoo Doctor refixed his stealthy stare on Nicolas. "I admit, sir, you surprise me." He motioned toward Schuyler. "I've come to know Sky here, and he seems a decent sort. Somehow, I expected something else of you, Mr. Van Horne."

"Perhaps your mind is open to the prospect of learning, then? Even at the medical college?"

"Oh, I don't fault them for their anatomy lessons. But the graves of my people, of the poor, those I will defend until . . . yet you say you don't defile our graves? I can't believe that."

"Perhaps you must trust me."

"No." The Voodoo Doctor leaned forward, set his letter opener on the desk with a thump, and swung back his mane of hair. "I must see these bodies you brought from the North," he said.

"I suppose . . . I suppose that could be arranged."

"If it's like you say, you and Sky can have your laborers."

"There's a professor at the college, a gent named Keiller. It's him you must see. I'll arrange what I can."

Once they were back on Post Office Street outside the ISL headquarters, Schuyler leaned in close and said, "I'm beginning to think this town's not safe for you, Father. In too many ways to count."

"Doomed to deal with murderers on all fronts, aren't I?"

"You'd best catch the first train and vamoose. Let me manage the ice."

"I'll not run," Nicolas said with a shake of his head. "I'd only be running again in the North Country, and I've had my fill of that. For now, I'm going to get word to Keiller about a visitor."

At dawn the following day six well-muscled stevedores of the ISL appeared on Pier 28. The crack team of dockworkers secured the ship's cargo of thirty thousand tons in the new Van Horne icehouse by the time the sun began to set over the bay.

"They demand a hefty wage," Schuyler said, "but they earn every penny." A broad smile lit his face. "I take it your professor convinced the Voodoo Doc."

In the long shadows at the end of day, Captain Henry Rossbacher waved farewell to the Van Hornes and the *Jilted Lady* steamed off. Father and son, weary from the unloading, walked to Schuyler's flat, an airy set of rooms above a local apothecary by the name of Tackleberry.

As they passed the apothecary's shop, Nicolas hesitated. The window display of hypodermics sparkled with a steely allure. The door swung open. A gentleman exited. Nicolas's heart lurched at the powerful medicinal fragrance drifting out. It was all too familiar. Tackleberry was preparing a mix in his laboratorium.

Nicolas shuffled his feet on the sidewalk. "My stomach's been sour," he said. "Perhaps I'll purchase some salts. You go ahead."

The heft of a hypodermic, the tingle at injection, the white dreams of morphia . . . all the thrilling sweetness of his past habit rushed back. Had he forgotten the misery the drug had wrought?

Tackleberry came from the back of the shop and handed a package to a young enough gent whose baggy black eyes and trembly hand gave him away. Tackleberry took payment, then stood at his counter and smiled at Nicolas. "How may I be of help, sir?"

"I've a sour stomach. Just arrived from a long journey, you see."

"I believe Colonel Hoestetter's Bitters to be most efficacious."

"I'll take them," Nicolas replied.

Tackleberry gave Nicolas a befuddled look. What sort of gentleman hid behind such scruffy beard, weary eyes, and cheeks made swarthy from exposure at sea? Not to mention the shabby secondhand outfit. "Should you be in need of leeches during your stay," the apothecary said as he wrapped the bottle of bitters, "our depot on the Strand keeps well supplied."

"The bitters will do."

Tackleberry hesitated. "Something more potent can be mixed, if desired."

Nicolas hefted the package of bitters. *Keep your wits about you,* he thought. *Adam's killer's out there.*

"That's all I'll be needing," he said. "Thank you, good sir."

Nicolas climbed the stairs and settled in the west parlour of the flat. Schuyler laid out one of his Scottish tweed suits, a fresh shirt, drawers, socks, and sundries for his father on the sideboard. He showed Nicolas the divan that was to serve as his bed, and Nicolas stretched out. The setting sun threw a purplish glow on the flowery wallpaper that covered the walls of the flat. Faint medicinal odors drifted up from below.

"I'll be joining friends for supper this evening," Schuyler told Nicolas. "Care to make their acquaintance?"

Nicolas thought for a moment, then said, "I think not, Son. I must be off to the college again to settle finances with the professor and perhaps discover more about this voodoo man."

"There's a Turkish bath in the next block. You'd best avail yourself of it."

"That can wait." Nicolas hesitated again. "I don't suppose you'd accompany me to the college before your supper engagement?"

Now it was Schuyler who paused; his eyes met his father's. "Tell me, Father—will *she* be there? The one I saw you with at Saratoga?"

"It . . . it doesn't matter, I haven't had a word from her since . . . since before your mother left us."

"Well, a medical college isn't exactly my cup of tea. Do join us afterward, though. We'll be at a Spanish spot in Sailortown called El Malhado. It's a simple tavern, but there's good eats, very rich, and a piano that's usually in tune."

74

Francis and Nicolas

In the first-floor vestibule of the medical college, Francis Keiller, professor of morbid anatomy and chancellor, was surrounded by a cluster of students. He was holding forth with an impromptu lecture on an obscure point of anatomy, but when he spied Nicolas entering the college, the good professor dismissed his students and greeted the ice merchant warmly.

"Shall we make our way to my office?" he said. "I bet you'll join me for a wee touch o' whiskey now that our business is finished, eh?"

Nicolas noted how slowly Keiller took the stairs, each step an obvious agony, though the old man's spirits seemed high, indeed ebullient after filling his vats.

"I've missed your company, Van Horne."

"But how's your health, man? You're looking poorly."

"Ah, it's my spine that's a bother lately," Keiller replied. "As is usually the case, I'm afraid it reflects something more serious. The tuberculosis has set up shop in plenty of places, including my bones." He chuckled. "One can know too much in this business, ye see."

In his office, Keiller searched for glasses and poured two whiskeys.

"I take it you were visited by a certain cotton jammer," Nicolas said.

"The king of the jammers, I'd say. Or maybe their prince. A fascinating fellow. You realize he's related to Hutch Sealy, don't you?"

Nicolas gave a nod. "I had qualms sending him your way, but there was no recourse."

"Turns out he's a sound chap, voodoo and all. We had a fine visit. Damned if he didn't brave the formaldehyde to inspect every cadaver in our vats and the few hanging in our storage vault. He found none from the potter's field among them, and no colored folks."

"As I told him, then."

"One has to respect a man of such conviction, even if it goes against our purpose at the college. In a way, he's the opposite of his brother, Trey, and the other cotton traders."

"How so?"

"Ah, the port's grown since you were last here, Nicolas. Once we had benefactors . . . hell, old man Sealy was our biggest benefactor, but no more. Now these cotton traders are all after us. With these economic panics of the past year, our real estate is more coveted than ever. The traders rile the whole town against us, but I suppose that's business for you."

Nicolas stared at the pale surface of his whiskey. "Yes, business and the almighty dollar," he said. "Not that long ago, I thought of the bodies I collect as a commodity, you know. It was easy profit."

"And now?"

Nicolas looked up. His eyes glistened. "You're doing noble work here, Professor, and I'm here to support you."

"I count us lucky for that."

"You see, I've come to a different period in my life."

"How so?"

"I've had losses—personal blows, financial losses. But when one's life is threatened, life takes on a different value."

Concern crossed Keiller's face. He pushed his spectacles up on his nose. "Yes, Adam's murder."

"You see, Professor, as I mentioned earlier, I discovered this dastardly business afoot in the North. My activities to expose it have put me in a degree of danger, I fear. It has to do with a bustling commerce in child labor—"

"Child labor, you say? The voodoo fellow mentioned something about that."

"The Voodoo Doctor knew of it?"

"Why, yes. Something about crews of young boys taking the cotton jammers' jobs."

"I must speak with our voodoo friend again."

"Yes, you must. Seems there are worse criminals than him on this island." With a grunt, Keiller pushed himself out of his desk chair. "I've nearly forgotten," he said, limping toward the safe that squatted under the nearby table. "Let's settle up, shall we?"

"We're square on that, Francis."

Keiller stopped and leaned wearily on the table. "What's that?"

"I'm doing it at no cost."

"No cost? Two dozen cadavers, and no cost?"

"It's the least I can do for your college."

"Van Horne, you are truly a savior."

"'Benefactor,' I believe you called it, Professor. Your college needs a benefactor to replace those who've abandoned you."

"Now there's a turn of events we must celebrate," Keiller said, reaching for the bottle.

75

In the Laboratory

At their third round of drinks Nicolas held up a hand to call it quits. "Don't bother to get up," he said, seeing the grimace on Keiller's face. "I'll show myself out."

"Before you leave, you must see our latest progress on yellow fever. I insist."

Keiller shuffled into the lab, sat at his microscope, and fired its brilliant limelight lamp. He updated Nicolas on their quest for a cure, explaining that the anti-toxoid they'd produced in horses completely prevented yellow fever in guinea pigs, their preferred experimental animal.

The scientists had a cure—for guinea pigs.

"But will it work in humans?" Nicolas asked.

"Now that's the question, and we're nearly at the stage of testing it. I'd be the guinea pig myself, if only I could," the professor said. "I'd inject myself with our anti-toxoid in the blink of an eye. Like Jennings did with his vaccine. Or like Koch."

"Why not do it?" Nicolas suppressed a laugh. "I've tested a few concoctions in my time," he said, thinking back on his year of reckless self-experimentation with the apothecary's myriad of mind-enhancing alchemy.

"You misunderstand, Van Horne," Keiller insisted. "Most of us at the medical college have lived too long in these tropics and, like it or not, we're constantly exposed by caring for our feverish patients, too. Oh, occasionally a new student volunteers to be a test subject. Valiant of them. Commendable, really, but we couldn't risk that."

Keiller motioned toward the eyepiece of his microscope. "Come. Look." Nicolas squinted into the instrument, adjusting his eye to the foreign landscape. "There's the culprits, Van Horne. See how thick they are! They're gaining. Each summer, each epidemic, they become more pernicious. And I fear the worst is yet to come."

As Nicolas peered into Keiller's high-powered optics, he was distracted by a familiar scent in the air. Did he detect a hint of apple blossom? Could Renée be near? More likely, he thought, it was exhaustion playing tricks, or simply some pleasant-smelling lab chemical. Renée was nowhere in sight, though Nicolas reflexively conjured her striking silhouette at the window—in his mind's eye.

"Yes, I see them." Nicolas felt his pulse quicken at the strange sight under the microscope . . . or was it that apple blossom scent that had him going? "The damned thing's packed with orange dots."

Fatigue and excitement had Nicolas eager for that Turkish bath and some supper. His stomach rumbled. He bid the professor good night and thumped away in his borrowed seaman's shoes.

"An assassin is waiting for me out there," he muttered to himself as he took the stone stairs to the street. Yet somehow, Nicolas felt excited to be back. He set off to Schuyler's flat with an unexpected lightness in his step. *There's much to accomplish before I leave Galveston*, he thought as the cool island night washed over him. *I only hope I leave it alive.*

76

Invitations

The evening was still and quiet, no one on the streets. Only a single man a block behind. Not a big, burly man. Nicolas drew a deep breath of the moist gulf air, picked up the pace, turned toward the bay. He was being followed. The man turned. A half block behind now. *Switch back toward the gulf.* When he swung around to look, the man was gone.

He slowed his pace, glancing over his shoulder at each corner. In the year since his first visit, newly built rows of houses had stretched further east, filling this end of the island. Now the dirt streets were bricked well past the hospital and convent.

No one behind him now. Two blocks further and he came on Keiller's house. Keiller's lamps had been lit for the evening. The window glass gave off a warm, yellow glow, but the stained glass of the pelican above the entranceway—the beautiful work smashed at the professor's party—had never been replaced. A plain board had been nailed over it. On closer look, a half dozen broken windows had gone without repair at the Keiller household.

Two men stood, smoking, on the corner of the next block. Nicolas crossed the street and set off. A slight detour one block to the left and he'd pass the little house of Madame La Porte. The men had tossed their smokes, crossed the street, and turned, too. Common workmen dressed in blue overalls, on the way to a job? Perhaps nothing more?

Best to get off the street. Renée would most likely be at the college. Nothing unusual in paying Madame La Porte a brief visit. He'd simply convey his regards and leave. He wasn't properly dressed, but since he was recently arrived in town and all, that might be forgiven.

Nicolas unlatched the gate of the white picket fence. A gas lamp flickered in the front yard. Nicolas stepped to the door and was about to turn the doorbell when from inside came the delicate strains of a fiddle—such skill could only be Basil Prangoulis's. Nicolas allowed a few bars of the soulful Gypsy tune to play out before he gave the doorbell a twist and the raucous ring stopped the fiddle in midnote, the door was thrown open, and the Hungarian music instructor of the Ursuline Women's Academy—and local rabbi—stood in the doorway. Prangoulis, dressed in a well-worn bathrobe, looked casually threadbare and avuncular.

"Ach! The ice man. Good to see you, Van Horne." Basil's grip was firm as he welcomed Nicolas into the hall. "Your winter has been good to you, *ja*? Got plenty of ice to sell?" Prangoulis motioned toward the sitting room, where his blackened fiddle sat on the low table. "Come join me," he said. "I am relaxing with music."

"Thank you kindly, but I think not," Nicolas said, taking two steps into the parlour. "I'll stay only a moment. I trust Madame La Porte is well?"

"*Ja*, but she's meditating right now, preparing for a session tomorrow night. She's seating a special circle. I must tell you, she's getting quite famous. Sure you won't have a seat? You look worn thin."

"An extremely strenuous voyage at sea."

"Will you be long in Galveston?"

"A few days, no more."

"But you must come visit with Madame La Porte before you depart. Perhaps tomorrow night for her session." Prangoulis stepped closer and lowered his voice. "I can't be part of her communications, of course. A modern rabbi can hardly condone the idea of a dead soul coming back from Sheol, eh? I think not. The abode of the dead . . . the underworld? Ha! I'm afraid the Torah strictly forbids that sort of thing. Still . . ." Prangoulis gave a nod toward the séance room across the hall. "I've seen firsthand Madame La Porte's extraordinary talents and . . . well, I'll tell you . . ."

While Prangoulis jabbered on, Nicolas stepped further into the parlour and glanced about as casually as he could manage. The armchairs and settee appeared as cozy as he remembered. Sheet music was spread next to Prangoulis's fiddle on the low table. There was a new desk in the corner, japanned dark red and highly glossed, where writing materials were out and a stack of notes penned on fine vellum paper appeared under way.

Edging closer to the desk, Nicolas recognized Renée's finely scripted handwriting; he'd seen so much of it. He couldn't help but stare. One note card was easily read:

Madame Jacqueline La Porte
of Ball Lane
Requests the Honor of Your Presence
for the Joining in Holy Matrimony
of Her Daughter

Renée Keiller
to
Señor Fernando del Diablo y Hoya
at
The Cathedral of Saint Augustine
1700 Esplanade
~~*June 15, 1890*~~

Nicolas felt the blood drain from his face.

Prangoulis took his arm. "What is it, Van Horne?"

"I see a wedding is planned."

"Planned, yes." Prangoulis chuckled. "They set a date, then they set another. Or better to say Renée sets a date, and then changes it. She's the one setting dates, *ja?*"

"I see. Do extend my sincere best wishes to her."

"Very thoughtful of you."

"I should like to speak with her sometime."

Prangoulis hesitated, then lowered his voice to a confidential whisper. "You know, Mr. Van Horne, we understand about you two, in the past I mean."

Nicolas's mouth went dry.

"Ah, well, with Renée's mother, you see"—he shrugged—"her sensitivity? Madame La Porte knew right away. Even Francis, the old bachelor uncle, huh?" Prangoulis chortled. "He understands his niece. Who could miss it, with all those letters?"

"That's all behind us now," Nicolas said, forcing a smile.

"*Ja,* water over the dam, eh?"

Nicolas edged toward the hallway. This talk had him flustered. "I must be off," he said. "I'll leave you to your fiddle."

"Do stop again. Certainly you might come for tomorrow night's sitting. I insist. I'll speak with Madame La Porte. I believe there's a place at the circle."

Nicolas took the hand Prangoulis offered.

"I'll tell Renée you stopped," the rabbi said.

"Yes . . . yes. Please do."

"Plan to arrive before midnight tomorrow—that's when she'll seat the circle."

It had been a bad idea to stop at Madame La Porte's. Too much had been stirred up. And the idea of talking to the dead, to those who'd passed beyond, was unsettling. *So many deaths. First, Ruth. Thomas Chubb. Adam.* Madame La Porte should let the dead lie.

As he passed Tackleberry's apothecary, Nicolas stopped, stepped back, and stared at the shop window. That enticing medicinal scent wafted out but Nicolas stepped to the stairwell; just as he did, Schuyler came trotting down in a dark suit with fresh shirt and tie.

"Perfect timing, Father," Schuyler said. "I'm off to Restaurant Row. Join us for a toddy or two before supper, why don't you?"

The sight of Schuyler calmed Nicolas's nerves. "I must tell you"—he clasped his son's shoulder—"I learned more about the Voodoo Doctor from the professor. It's possible our voodoo man knows about the child labor trade, maybe right here—on Galveston's docks."

Schuyler gave a start. "If anyone knows about the docks, it'd be him. Why don't we search out the fellow on our way to dine?"

"Excellent plan."

Father and son had taken only a few steps in the direction of Restaurant Row when a baby-faced young man approached. Nicolas recognized the lad as the student Patrick from the medical college.

"I've a missive for a Mr. Van Horne, the ice merchant," Patrick said self-importantly. "I believe that's you, sir." He produced a small rose-colored envelope from his jacket.

Nick—

So nice to hear of your arrival.

If you please, could you meet me at Trudeau's at half past eight for coffee?

We can talk, briefly.

Renée Keiller

Nicolas was so befuddled he began frantically searching his vest pocket for his watch, before remembering the timepiece lay buried in Mississippi silt.

"It seems I've something to attend to," he told Schuyler, tucking the note in the pocket of the weather-beaten peacoat he'd borrowed from the river pilot. "Perhaps I'll dine with you later."

"Do catch us at El Malhado," Schuyler said. He started down the street, then stopped and called over his shoulder. "I'll stop by the voodoo man's office on my way."

"Schuyler! That Turkish bathhouse? You say it's in the next block?"

77

Coffee at Trudeau's

Antoine Trudeau, the French restaurateur, had expanded his accommodations since Nicolas last dined at his establishment. All told, six dining rooms—elegant, spacious, and spread over three floors—were new. Counting the kitchens and smaller, private dining rooms Trudeau had tucked away beyond the general public's line of sight, the expansion engulfed the entire commercial building.

Nicolas entered Trudeau's original, street-level dining hall, precisely as he had when he'd dined with Renée the year before. Faint streaks of shaving cream still clung to Nicolas's chin. He wore Schuyler's grey tweed, hardly a suitable fit as it was much too big in the midsection and a tad short in sleeve and pant leg.

Trudeau's ornate pressed-tin ceiling seemed familiar, as did the dining hall's tropical-patterned wall coverings. Starched tablecloths glowed warmly in the yellowish gaslight of the chandeliers. With the supper hour barely under way, only a few tables were occupied; there was a quiet undercurrent of conversation, the occasional click of silverware. Nicolas's heart began to pound as memories of that night with Renée flooded back: the elegant supper they'd shared, the walk on the moonlit beach, the stolen kiss.

Nicolas spied Renée seated at a nearby small table set against the wall. She had pulled her hair back straight and sleek, much simpler than the curls she had worn on that wondrous night. A waiter at her side poured from a silver urn. The aroma of coffee roasted with chicory wafted up. Renée's dark eyes lit briefly with recognition. She stood and offered a cool, firm handshake, nearly masculine in its strength.

"So glad you've arrived safely," she said with a hint of her tight-lipped smile. "You look well. Quite ruddy. Is it the southern sun?"

"I've been at sea."

There was an awkward scraping of chairs on the floorboards as Nicolas helped her regain her seat. The waiter poured Nicolas's cup; with a nod from Renée, he vanished.

"I thought it would be best to talk here," she said.

Renée sat straight as a poker. Nicolas caught her eye for a second but read nothing there. The faint scent of her apple blossom perfume drifted across the small table. *Those feelings . . . so far in the past. So much has happened . . . water over the dam, as Prangoulis put it.*

"I can't stay long, Nick. I'm analyzing a new batch of anti-toxoid. They vary so in strength, though we have little idea why," she said with a bright burst of nervous laughter, followed by a lingering silence. "Uncle Francis told me of Adam's murder," she said.

"The bullet was meant for me."

"Thank God you're all right."

"You see, I've been quite successful at pursuing these slave traders. Perhaps too successful."

Renée's eyes met his. "You found them, then?"

"In Buffalo. Russians, as you guessed, at least their ringleader. I relayed details of his operations and headquarters to the county constable there. I also contacted my old college mates in Boston, as you suggested in your letters . . . before . . . you know . . . my final letter. Anyway, the plan in Boston was to go to the press with details. They managed to make one arrest in a shoe factory in New England, though the Buffalo culprits are still on the loose, as far as I know. I must thank you for all your help, Renée . . . though it's made me a hunted man."

"I had no idea, you know . . . being out of touch. Perhaps you should never have taken my advice."

"No, it was the right thing to do. These men are savages. And their dealings are broader than I imagined. My daughter, Abigail, discovered they've established their hideous human trade as far as Chicago. Abby's in touch with a woman there who's tracking orphans and runaways. She liberates lost girls from the brothels and provides a safe haven."

"I've heard of this place. It's called Hull House."

"Abby also suspects this ghastly slave business may stretch to the South."

"Have they followed you here, do you think?"

"I'm sure of it. If not Adam's killer, some other they've sent."

Renée leaned forward, studying the cup in her hands. "I remember Adam quite well. So full of spunk, that man. I met him only the once, but . . . how tragic."

"Everything goes wrong at once, eh? My wife died—"

"I didn't know . . ."

"Last fall. Her illness finally . . . and then my associate, the undertaker, was murdered by the slave-trade scoundrels with whom he consorted."

"How ghastly."

"Once I'd stirred the Russian's nest in Buffalo, they took their revenge on Thomas . . . bad luck for him." Nicolas leaned closer. "It's been bad times in the past year, but good in other ways."

"Good?"

"I've also known great happiness."

"You deserve that," she said with a nod.

"I was thinking of Saratoga, Renée. Before my son arrived on the scene, that is."

She fell silent. When she looked up her eyes were misty.

"You were right," she said with a tremble in her voice. "You were right to do what you did, Nick. Your last letter—I understand now. The way we are...it's for the best."

"I—I've heard of your intentions to marry," Nicolas said, the words catching in his throat. "And I wish you every happiness."

"Thanks so much," she said with a hint of her old, sly smile.

Now it was Nicolas's turn to stare at his cooling coffee and take a moment for thought.

"Another thing, Renée. When I'm alone, especially at the lake, I think often about you in your laboratory, your work, about science, and I'm convinced that someday—someday soon—I shall hear of your fame."

She laughed, but Nicolas went on. The lump in his throat seemed to vanish. "I mean it. You'll perfect your cure, you and Uncle Francis. Your medical college will be known over the world for defeating yellow fever."

"I think not, Nick. This city, this island, they're forcing us out. It's difficult to work, to concentrate."

"My son's made connections here, you know. If need be, I'll speak with these cotton traders, the Sealys—whoever needs to be set straight."

"Oh, come, Nick. You're in enough danger, and you have your ice to tend to."

"Ice isn't everything."

"It's lovely ice, Nick. I've always thought so. Besides," she said coolly, "I rather doubt there's much you can do."

She pushed her chair from the table and stood. When she did, she accidentally overturned her cup. "Oh, dear. How stupid." A dark brown stain spread on the tablecloth.

Nicolas rose in his chair. "Renée, couldn't we—"

"Nick, Nick—" She cut herself short, shook her head, then took a breath and went on. "I want you to know something, Nick. I remember Saratoga, too.

I shall always remember Saratoga." She stepped away from the table and turned her face toward the door. "It's best, really, that you don't linger on the island. But it's been good, very good, to see you."

She brushed past and was gone.

Nicolas sat back and stared blankly at the overturned cup she'd held in her hands just moments before.

He handed a half-dollar to the waiter on his way out and set off in no particular direction. It surprised him how unchanged Renée seemed. Her eyes, hair, voice—all of her—so familiar. And her scent.

As he walked his heartbeat slowed and he felt that a weight had lifted from his shoulders. Renée spoke of Nicolas's ice without knowing that now ice and its profits served a higher purpose in his mind. Saving wayward boys, the medical college, the cures of tomorrow—so many noble callings. As if fate had drawn him to this island for a reason, in spite of its dangers.

His mind raced. He wasn't sure of the first step to be taken, but the way of his future was clear. As clear as Van Horne ice.

78

El Malhado

The crowded streets of Sailortown made it impossible for Nicolas to know if he was being followed. He honed in on El Malhado quickly, drawn by the jaunty piano refrains issuing forth. Looking over the swinging doors, he found a barroom packed with Spaniards, foreign laborers, and generally scruffy types. A swarthy hulk of a waiter launched a good-natured fusillade of Spanish at him as he pushed open the swinging doors and looked about, adjusting to the semidarkness, tobacco smoke, and pungent aroma of grilled meats.

Seeing Nicolas's blank stare, the waiter smiled and grumbled, "In or out, *señor.*"

Schuyler was at the upright piano at the far corner of the bar, surrounded by a half dozen admiring young compatriots; a few others were seated at the table next to the piano. Sky was banging out a tune one part minstrel show, two parts raggedy improvisation. He glanced up and beamed.

One of Schuyler's companions called over the din. "Sir!" He motioned to Nicolas. "You must be Sky's father. Come over."

Schuyler beat an ending on the ivory keys and lumbered off the piano stool. "So glad you came." He took his father's arm and led him to the head of the group's table. "Believe me, the food here is fantastic." Lowering his voice, he added, "And we need to talk."

The men at the table shuffled over to make room. Once Schuyler's friends were again noisily chatting, Nicolas leaned close and asked, "Did you find out anything from the Voodoo Doctor?"

"I found him in his office, but when I asked what he knew about crews of young Northern boys on his docks, he clammed up. The only thing he'd say was that he was 'dealing with the scoundrels.'"

"Hmm."

"And he wanted to talk to you."

"He knows something, then."

"I told him we were meeting here for supper."

Plates of shrimp and whole crabs cooked in savory rice arrived. It was the first good meal Nicolas had had in front of him in weeks, and he ate voraciously, then settled back to enjoy the jovial banter among Schuyler's young friends.

As coffees and confections arrived, the doors of El Malhado swung open and the Voodoo Doctor stalked in. Nicolas and Schuyler watched the voodoo man's shock of hair sway to and fro as he sauntered the length of the bar, tight-lipped and stolid.

"Mr. Van Horne, sir," he said, standing over them. He yanked a chair close, then turned and straddled it, his arms crossed over the chair's back. His cold stare was within inches of the Van Hornes' faces. "You must tell me what you Northerners are up to."

"I presume," Nicolas said, "you're speaking of the slave trade."

"You know what I mean. The young boys on my docks this past year. Crews of them for sale. Sky seems to know. How about you, sir? Are you part of this business?"

"God, no, man! I've been trying to stop it."

"Your business is supposed to be ice, yet you sell dead bodies. What else do you sell?"

"You've got me wrong. Last year I delivered the body of a boy—a murdered boy—to your medical school. That's how I discovered this slave trade."

"Come now, Van Horne. You're a man who's out for profit. You arrive in town broke, looking like a vagabond. Everyone's seen you. Evidently you've fallen on hard times, made bad deals. You have no financial resources and you need more—"

"I was forced to obtain a loan, sir. No fault of my own."

"You expect me to believe you have no part in this evil scheme? These boys are treated like slaves. It's only me—and the ISL—that's kept them off the docks. And Northerners like you try again and again."

Schuyler, standing it no longer, spoke up. "You've misjudged him. He'd never do such a thing. He's my father, and I know . . ."

The Voodoo Doctor focused his steely glare on Schuyler. "You businessmen are all alike. Whether it's cotton, ice, or your racehorses—everything's for your gain and the workingman suffers. Now it's children your father trades in."

"Look"—Nicolas's voice rose—"we could help you. We could, but you've got to believe me. I told the truth about the bodies I brought, didn't I?"

A crease flitted across the Voodoo Doctor's brow, then he gave a nod. "Yes, you did, and I helped with your ice. But now I've heard this about you and these crews. There's something afoot, some plan to undermine all the ISL has done for the workingman." The voodoo man's eyes went cold. "And you, a trader from the North in dire financial straits, you're not connected to this Northern plot?"

"I give you my word as a gentleman."

"Well, then . . . we'll see. I'll get to the bottom of it, believe me. My men are on it, and I'd better not find you're lying."

"But . . . you've got to give us something to go on. Who's involved here?"

The Voodoo Doctor thought for a moment, then shook his head and pushed off from his chair. "Just remember what I said. If I discover that you're part of this, in any way . . ."

Without a further word he stood and stalked down the bar, jostling rough types out of his way. Once he'd stepped out the door of El Malhado, a buzz rose among Schuyler's friends, who'd been straining to eavesdrop.

"You'd best not mess with the likes of that fellow," one of Sky's comrades offered. "He's clever, and he can ruffle the feathers of the workin' stiffs."

A second friend at their end of the table, one who'd not said much, called out, "Hey, Sky—play us something, will ya? I've had enough of this dark palaver."

Schuyler sat at the piano and ran his fingers down the keys. "I believe I'll try an original," he said, then launched into a tune of lost love and heartbreak. His full, bass voice resonated over the raucous tumult in the tavern. The men finished their coffees and egg custards and began to light cigars.

Schuyler played a raggedy finale and came to the table. "Gents," he said, "we'll take our leave of your fine company. My pops looks like he needs some sleep."

Under the light of the gas lamps on the street, Nicolas shook his head in frustration. "We're getting nowhere, Son," he said. "This Voodoo Doctor knows plenty, but for God's sakes . . . he suspects me? I may have a word with the father of that man."

"Good thought. He certainly knows the cotton business. In the South, cotton is at the bottom of everything."

"And Hutch Sealy begot the two sons who control cotton."

79

A Visit to Hutchinson Sealy

Nicolas slipped from bed and dressed quietly. He found another of Schuyler's oversized jackets, one of Scottish tweed, and departed for the upper floor of the Cotton Exchange, dead set on having a word with the city's most powerful financier.

Nicolas easily recalled the impressive Cotton Exchange Building. Elaborate stone façades, elegant high-arched entrances, the turrets, the intricate gargoyles overhead . . . Hutch Sealy had succeeded in building, and controlling, the finest architectural achievement of the city. *How does a man amass a fortune such as this?* Nicolas wondered. *With profits . . . profits stained by corruption, perhaps? The forced labor of children? Even murder?*

Nicolas climbed the marble stairs to the top floor of the Cotton Exchange and found the offices of Sealy & Son Finance, Trust, and Title Company. He was eager to meet the man, but the man was not eager to meet him. Nicolas was informed by all three of Sealy's gentlemen secretaries of the financier's "extremely busy schedule" and kept waiting for the entire morning. He paced in the vestibule. Midday approached. He cursed under his breath. It was past noon when Nicolas recognized Sealy as he slipped out of a side door, and was able to intercept the handsomely dressed financier.

"Mr. Sealy, I believe?" He matched several strides with the portly gent. Sealy ignored him, scurried across the vestibule, and took to the stairs.

"Mr. Sealy!" Nicolas called, pursuing.

Hutch Sealy had changed only slightly since Nicolas last saw the banker abruptly depart Keiller's Mardi Gras party with his sour-faced beanpole wife. The elder gent was stouter now and wore his beard in an immaculately trimmed French fork style, with sharp, greying tufts sprouting obliquely to either side. At the sight of the renowned financier, the story of Sealy's two sons—one a successful cotton trader, the other the mulatto leader of the ISL—echoed through Nicolas's mind.

"Mr. Sealy!"

The points of Sealy's beard shook with displeasure when he finally turned back to Nicolas, barely slowing his progress down the stairway. "Please, sir," he said. "I'm on my way to dine for heaven's sake!"

"I wish only a moment of your time," Nicolas said in a confidential tone. "It concerns a matter of some importance."

Sealy paused at the building's entrance to eye the ill-fitting jacket and the freshly boiled shirt Nicolas had borrowed that morning from Schuyler. "A matter of importance? Men come to me all day long with matters of importance," Sealy said with a smirk. "I'm sure one of our financial officers could've assisted you with whatever you're in need of."

Nicolas offered a hand; Sealy made no move to take it.

"I am Nicolas Van Horne of New York," Nicolas said. "You may remember me from your Mardi Gras celebrations last year . . . with Professor Keiller and the medical people?"

"You're the ice man. With a new warehouse, correct?"

"Recently constructed, yes."

"You and your son seem to be doing quite well with your ice, though you hardly look it yourself." Sealy glanced at Nicolas's outstretched hand, then pushed open the door, stepped onto the sidewalk, and began to walk away. "Can't imagine what you want of me. Hope it's not a loan."

"It's not a matter of business," Nicolas said, following.

"Not business?" Sealy hesitated. "I suppose, then, it's to do with the damned medical college you're so enamored of."

"It began with the medical college."

"I hardly need concern myself with that, thank you." Sealy stopped and turned to face Nicolas on the sidewalk. He motioned toward the finely ornamented Cotton Exchange, its magnificent granite façade, the pink, the grey, the gargoyles leering down. "You must understand, Mr. Van Horne," he said. "You, sir, are in the South. Since the Great War, hereabouts we've not taken kindly to Yankee traders. Oh, in the name of business we'll smile and put on a show, but we all know a Northerner when we see one. And everyone in this town's heard of your part in that business out at that college, ice man, so I'd tread lightly if I were you."

"It's a cure for yellow fever they're after, Mr. Sealy."

"Ha! I've heard that for years. A cure? From the hellacious fumes and stench issuing from their laboratory? From caged vermin in the basement? That will get us a cure? So where is it? Most businessmen in this town would see the college gone from our island."

"And these same Southern businessmen, do they also deal in slaves, sir?" A shadow passed over Sealy's face. "Child slaves to work their cotton?"

"Gad, man!" Sealy groaned. "What are you talking about?" He turned and strutted down the street, with Nicolas alongside.

"It's my suspicion, Mr. Sealy, that young boys are for sale in the South, to work the docks, perhaps even on your island."

"You're insane, Van Horne. I'll not hear it."

"Sir."

The two men glared at each other. Restaurant Row's eating establishments were filling with a mayhem of lunchtime patrons. Nicolas wasn't sure how far he could go with what he knew, but he decided to venture it.

"There are those on the docks who agree with me on this," he said. "Certain persons—"

"Certain persons?"

"One special gent who knows plenty when it comes to the docks. And for some reason that gent—*your son!*—suspects that because I'm from the North, I'm involved."

Blood suffused Sealy's face. "You . . . you," he blustered. "My son is an honest cotton trader."

"Your *other* son, sir."

"*What?* You . . . you'll excuse me, but I'll leave you to your bizarre suppositions. I must dine."

Sealy dashed across the street, sidestepping carriages and buckboards as he went. Nicolas was left on the curb. Then the financier seemed to have another thought; he turned and shouted over the clatter of the traffic passing between them.

"You'd best quit sticking your nose in others' affairs, Van Horne. Get back up north, man. If you don't, I'll ruin you. Hear me? I'll ruin you."

80

An Evening Circle at Madame La Porte's

Nicolas walked the street as if it were covered in eggshells. Sealy had meant it when he said, "Tread lightly in this town." But could Hutch Sealy know about the Russian assassin? Was he *part* of the slave trade?

At the flat, Nicolas found a note:

Join us again at El Malhado —Sky.

Sailortown was too frenetic, too crowded; it was bound to be dangerous after dark. Instead of venturing to El Malhado, Nicolas decided to stretch out on the divan in the flat's west room while dusk fell and the lamplighters made their way down the street below. He planned to attend Madame La Porte's séance at midnight. He'd best stay off the streets until then.

As midnight drew near, a stimulant and some quick sustenance seemed in order. He donned the tweed jacket he'd borrowed, found a bowler of Schuyler's that was a bit too large but a passable fit, and hustled down the stairwell and onto the street. He took care to stay in the light of the gas lamps and steer clear of the seedy chaos of Sailortown, where an assassin's work would be easy. The elegance of Restaurant Row should prove safe, shouldn't it? He regretted thinking like a hunted animal, but if he wanted to stay alive to see the North Country again, he had to.

On Restaurant Row, hungry patrons rushed to and fro; those already satiated strolled and chatted under the streetlamps, patting their bellies. Nicolas chose a respectable-looking corner tavern. He stood at the end of the bar with his back to the wall and ordered a toddy to combat the damp chill of the evening. The sweetness of the liquor blunted his appetite; he called for a second toddy. The clock behind the bar showed an hour before the toll of midnight. Time enough for a third before an on-time arrival at Ball Lane for Madame La Porte's purported activities with the unknown.

Nicolas was certainly no spiritualist, but the supernatural craze that had swept the country for more than two decades was impossible to ignore. Circles, or séances, with their supposed visitations, were commonplace, and after all, Nicolas considered himself a forward-thinker. He kept an open mind about the likelihood of life after death. After all, there were so many different ways to spend a life, surely there'd be differing paths in the world of the dead.

He wondered what he might expect at Madame La Porte's little circle. For one, he'd heard a soul could linger for months on earth if death were sudden, unexpected, or premature. The folks in Forestport claimed that was true of the ghost of Friedrick Van Horne, his father. Ruth's suicide was certainly unexpected.

It was also his understanding that the recently dead were most apt to communicate with the living. Come to think of it, Adam was the only one who fit the bill on both scores—unexpectedly murdered, and only days ago. He'd probably have the best chance of talking to Adam, though he really wanted most to speak with Ruth . . . to explain, to apologize for those last minutes together at the lake. To make his husbandly love known.

The stimulant effects of Nicolas's third toddy sent a tingle down his arms and warmed his face. It also afforded him courage for the walk to the house on Ball Lane, where the streetlamps grew sparse. He glanced over his shoulder at every corner. An occasional laboring man was all he saw, a cotton jammer or two; they were so very common.

Prangoulis answered his ring at the bell and stood aside to welcome Nicolas into an empty hall. "Madame La Porte hoped you might attend." He took Schuyler's outsized bowler and hung it on the hat tree. "They're just about to be seated," he said, then scurried away.

The séance room to the left was dimly lit. Madame La Porte was speaking with two guests who stood in the elegant lady's sitting room, where the gaslights burned brightly.

"Do come in, Mr. Van Horne," Madame La Porte said, motioning to him. "Basil mentioned your interest in tonight's activities, and I'm so glad you came."

"Will there be a place at the circle?"

"As it happens, just one, for you. After all, you've traveled a great distance to be with us."

The guests were introduced by Madame La Porte as Mr. Simon McCandlish and his wife, Beatrice, local citizens who had recently "suffered a great misfortune."

The McCandlishes were somber-looking folks of modest means. The husband was bald as a billiard ball, red faced, droopy jowled, and in a disheveled suit. His wife, Beatrice, wore a dowdy brownish dress. Her face was grey and drawn; lines of dried tears tracked down her cheeks.

"These dear folks lost their lovely child just days ago," Madame La Porte explained.

Mrs. McCandlish spoke, her voice wavering and weak. "It was 'the strangling angel,' they called it."

"Diphtheria," Madame La Porte added. "Jonathon was the boy's name, a child of eleven years, poor dear; he was taken swiftly."

"There was nothin' they coulda done," Mrs. McCandlish said, "though they tried valiant enough, the doctors did."

Nicolas took the wife's hand and patted it warmly. Beatrice turned to Madame La Porte. "Your daughter, Renée, the lovely girl, she was the greatest comfort to us at the hospital."

"Well now—let's step across the hall and begin our circle," Madame La Porte said. "Please remember that we must all maintain strict silence, unless, of course, you are the one designated to communicate, or you're asked a direct question by a presence that's joined us."

The three nodded agreement.

"Remain seated, maintain physical contact with the others at all times, and do not allow your mind to wander." She stopped in the hallway and turned to Nicolas. "You do believe in the afterlife, don't you, Mr. Van Horne?"

"I have an open mind about such matters."

"Is there someone you wish to contact in particular?"

"Yes, two. For one, my dearest friend, recently murdered."

"How dreadful. His name?"

"Adam Klock. It's been scarcely a few days since his death on the Mississippi. I doubt his body will ever be recovered."

"And there's someone else?"

"My wife, deceased last fall."

"So sorry. That's quite some time ago. Were there unresolved issues?"

"There were indeed."

"Shall we begin our sitting, then?"

Madame La Porte led them past the stuffed ape that beckoned at her séance room's entryway, to the table. The room was exactly as Nicolas remembered: a small oaken table in the center; three straight chairs at the table and a fourth enclosed by curtains to form the "medium's cabinet." The chair of the medium, as before, sat on a large scale like those used to weigh cotton bales.

The outside shutters to the room had been closed, allowing only thin slats of moonlight through the window glass. A single gas lamp burnt dully along the wall. While the participants took seats, Madame La Porte lit a candle in the center of the table, extinguished the gas lamp, and stepped onto the scale to seat herself. Nicolas settled into the chair opposite, with Mr. and Mrs. McCandlish on either side.

Madame La Porte drew the curtains around her cabinet. Except for her hands, arms, and eyes she was obscured from view. The large dial of the scale behind and above her head was in plain sight. As she settled, the needle of the dial bounced, then registered at the 130-pound mark.

"Let's join hands, shall we?" Madame La Porte said. "Gaze into the light of the candle for some moments. I have a sense of ease this evening. We're among friends, and there's joy in the room at the return of a sympathetic visitor to the island."

"How kind," Nicolas said softly.

"Please . . . silence until a spirit makes itself known . . ."

Madame La Porte went still, her eyes blank. To Nicolas, it seemed like hours. His mind wandered, the happenings of the past days too intense, no matter how he stared at the candle. Perhaps the toddies didn't help.

Mrs. McCandlish began to snuffle, then quietly weep. The poor woman's misfortune was bringing Nicolas's mood low. He considered excusing himself from the circle. This folderol seemed unlikely to produce much.

Madame La Porte, her eyes dreamy and calm, broke the long silence. "My friends," she said, "I sense a gentle presence in the room. Let me tell you how we'd best reach out. It's called the alphabet method."

She explained that one member of the group would recite the alphabet, awaiting a "sign" at the correct letter, and thus, letter by letter, a message would be transmitted. This rather cumbersome method was effective for "first communications" with newly dead souls. "Please recite slowly," she said. "We must give our visitant time."

Madame La Porte then drew her cabinet tighter around herself, leaving only her arms extended. "I'm sensing the presence wishes to speak with you, Beatrice. Please state a simple question, then start the alphabet."

Mrs. McCandlish's voice faltered. "Are you . . . are you Jonathon? Is it my son?" She ran through the alphabet quickly, then stalled at the Y.

"Y? Y?"

"Go slowly, Beatrice," Madame La Porte said. "Spirits have all the time in the world."

Good heavens, Nicolas thought. *At this rate we'll take all night to get results.*

After several runs through the alphabet, a current of air passed through the room at Mrs. McCandlish's "Y." Nicolas gave a start and looked around to see if someone had lifted a window.

"Excellent, Beatrice," Madame La Porte said. "It appears you've established a connection."

At the next "E," the table trembled ever so slightly. Mrs. McCandlish gasped and squeezed Nicolas's hand.

"Take care not to break the circle, Beatrice," Madame La Porte warned. "Please continue."

A definite "Yes" was established by a powerful shake of the table at the "S." Mrs. McCandlish cried, "Jonathon! Are you all right?"

"Simple questions, Beatrice," Madame La Porte said.

"When did you die?"

Slowly, laboriously, the spirit spelt "Two weeks," which Mr. and Mrs. McCandlish enthusiastically confirmed as correct.

"Can you speak to us?"

At this, a rumble coursed through the parlour. The table legs rattled.

"I see something!" Mrs. McCandlish cried out. She began to rise from her chair; Nicolas and her husband pulled her back to prevent her breaking the circle.

All eyes went to the medium's cabinet, where the curtains parted slightly and Madame La Porte's face shone with serenity and peace. A faint, fluorescent blue cloud floated high over her head. The needle of the scale wavered and dipped downward a pound or two.

To the participants' astonishment, this blue vapour grew larger and brighter, and the face of a child materialized.

"Momma, I'm here," a child cried in a high-pitched voice that seemed to come through the ceiling. "I'm not lost."

Now the husband, Mr. McCandlish, leaned forward in his chair. "Come back to us, Son!" he cried, his bald pate shining in the blue glow. "Oh, good Lord, that damnable hospital . . . how I hated the place. I should've got ya there sooner, Son, but the cost . . . the cost. And now you're gone."

"Don't worry, Poppa," said the child. "It's fine here. It's warm and I like it. I wanted you to know . . . it's fine . . . it's fine."

The vapour dissipated and the boy's cries of "It's fine . . . It's fine" receded into the distance.

Madame La Porte peered out from her cabinet and glanced around the circle. She looked groggy, as if awakened from a deep sleep. Once calm was restored, she shut her curtains and joined hands with the others.

"There's more about this evening," she said. "I sense a more sinister presence, as if wrongs were done. Mr. Van Horne—begin, if you please."

"Who are you?" Nicolas asked. "Who's there?" He began reciting the alphabet, pronouncing each letter with care while holding tight to hands on both sides. No presence made itself known.

"Try a different tack," Madame La Porte said. "A direct question, but be forewarned. I'm sensing anger, or actual violence, in the room."

"Are you Adam?" Nicolas asked. "I'm sure you are, with your violent end."

A faint mist formed over the medium's cabinet, this time colorless, like a pale summer cloud . . . the cloud darkened until it was blood red. Mrs. McCandlish gasped. The red cloud dripped like a fresh, bleeding wound around Madame La Porte's curtained enclosure.

They heard mumbling in a foreign tongue, then a face took form in the cloud. Gradually, the face became more distinct—a man, young and robust—and straightaway the young man's face cleaved in two, gruesomely distorted, the two halves floating in air.

"I know him!" Nicolas cried, staring at the cleaved head of the murdered Canadian lumberjack, struck asunder by a vengeful woodsman's axe.

Mrs. McCandlish screamed and put her hands to her mouth, and the circle was broken. The appalling vision faded, its lips moving soundlessly.

"A sad case," Nicolas explained. "An evil man who was murdered for a heinous deed and . . . my daughter retrieved the body. I brought him here."

Madame La Porte pulled her curtains open. "He's on the island?"

"Yes."

"You seem to be trailed by a number of souls, Mr. Van Horne. How many have you brought?"

"Two dozen . . . more, counting Saint Louis."

"Oh, heavens. We may have a long night ahead." Madame La Porte withdrew into her cabinet. "Allow me to rest for a few moments."

81

A Second Revenant, This One Uninvited

Once Madame La Porte had recovered, she agreed to resume the circle and drew her cabinet shut. "I sense another presence," she said. "Quite distant at the moment. You may start, Mr. Van Horne. Let's hope for a better outcome."

"Are you Adam?" Nicolas asked. "Are you?" After repeated runs of the alphabet, a low, painful groan rumbled through the room at the letter "N."

"Then you're Ruth!"

A louder grumble at "N," then the alphabet went unanswered through several repetitions.

"You are Ruth. You must be. When did you die?"

The spirit spelt out "F-A-L-L."

"Then you are Ruth."

"N-O."

"Nonsense, spirit. It was in November that Ruth took her life."

"Simple questions, if you please," Madame La Porte said firmly.

"Tell me this, then," Nicolas said. "How many letters in your name?"

As Nicolas counted, a breeze passed through the room like a sigh at the number five and before Nicolas could say it, there was a whispered "*Six.*"

"Six? It must be four. Adam. Ruth. No matter which, it's four letters."

A vaporous apparition appeared over Madame La Porte's cabinet, but this visitant gave off a greenish tinge and the séance room filled with an abominable odor like that of rotted, maggot-infested flesh. A jolt of electricity shot from hand to hand around the table, but they all held firm.

"Dammit, we must see you," Nicolas said. "Who are you?"

A reply came in a deep, ear-splitting *"Thomas!"*—and the lone candle on the table flickered out.

"*I am Thomas Chubb*" echoed off the walls, which now shone an uncanny green from the aura the spirit threw out. A second massive electrical current pulsed round the table, Madame La Porte cried out behind her curtain, and the needle of her scale trembled and plummeted twenty pounds.

"Why you, Thomas?" Nicolas asked. "Why are you here?"

"*To tell the truth,*" Thomas Chubb replied. His booming bass shook the ceiling. "*To get the truth out—all of it. Tonight.*"

"I know the truth about you, Thomas."

"*No you don't, Nicolas.*" The undertaker's voice seemed filled with uncharacteristic remorse. "*You don't know. It's about the boys, Nicolas. Over the years, so many years, I've been a haunted man.*"

"I've discovered all about that—the orphans, the slave trade, how you took those who were murdered. Are you in hell now, Thomas?" Nicolas asked. "With all the evil you've seen, that's where you belong."

"I'm nowhere," Chubb replied. "They haven't told me what it's called. There's nothing here but emptiness. But they've given me this chance to tell the truth . . . and do a last good deed. You were my only friend, Nicolas. I must tell you about the boys."

"I know all about—"

"*Your sons, Nicolas. I'll tell you about your sons.*"

"My sons?"

"First, the young one."

"Ethan?"

"This boy, a sickly boy, would walk the lake trail. He knew me from town. I spoke with him often."

"Ethan."

"Such a bright boy, that boy of yours . . . and Ruth's. But he was so frail. I didn't mean harm. All I wanted was to show him my work, my calling . . . to be looked up to."

"You took Ethan to your house? Your funeral parlour?"

"He wanted to come. Like any curious boy, he wanted to see what a dead body looked like. But the cellar was damp and cold and he was frightened...perhaps it was the fumes. He turned blue. He couldn't get air. I covered him with blankets, kept him warm and talked to him. It was an attack, an attack of croup. I panicked. I knew I was in the wrong having him down there...then, it was too late."

"All my life . . . all my life," Nicolas said, choking on his words, "I thought he was lost in the woods."

"I buried him in the woods."

Nicolas jumped up, clutching the McCandlishes' hands so tightly they winced.

"*You cad! You . . . you son of a bitch!*"

"I went to Ruth and tried to tell her. We had been so close, once . . . I went to her, but Schuyler was a babe in her arms and I couldn't bear to tell her the truth. I swallowed it and she never knew. Never. In the end, she learned about me, my dealings in Buffalo . . . what an evil man I was. Those witches in Forestport told her. The Valdis crowd. Ruth knew she'd been touched by an evil man . . . in the end."

Nicolas dropped back into his chair and slumped, dejected.

"You took my firstborn son."

"There's more. I mean to tell all the truth tonight."

"What are you saying?"

"The boy I buried was your *only* son, Nicolas. *Ethan was your only son.*"

"But there's Schuyler."

"Schuyler is mine, Nicolas. He's my son. Ruth and I . . . we were together so little time. But it was enough."

"Schuyler?"

"I was foolish, Nicolas. Just out of the institute and chasing women, acting the gay blade. We were so young, so eager, Ruth and I, and you were away with your ice, you fool."

"*You cannot mean this! No!*" Nicolas pitched forward and ground his forehead on the table. "*No! No!*"

"Schuyler was such a talented boy. Finally, someone looked up to me. When we sat at the piano, I had the love of a son. My son."

"*Lies! Lies from the grave! Get your rotted soul back to—*" Nicolas jumped up, poker straight, and raised his hands, quivering, yet holding to the circle. "*Get back to hell!*"

"Nicolas, I came to do you a good deed."

"*You've shown me hell, isn't that enough?*"

"No, I brought you something you need . . . badly need . . . a gift . . . I brought you a memento of our business together, Nicolas, my friend. *I brought you this . . .*"

A rumbling like thunder came from overhead, the curtains parted, and Madame La Porte leaned forward, her hands like claws, her face twisted in agony. Directly over the table the ceiling shook and cracked wide open and out of the blackness tumbled a severed human hand.

With a *thump!* the hand fell onto the table in front of Nicolas. He stared, dumbfounded, recognizing at once the hand confiscated by the harbor inspector. The pinky was missing.

Beatrice McCandlish shrieked, raised her hands to her face in terror, and thus broke the circle. The ghastly green cloud spun down into the medium's cabinet. One by one, the shutters banged against the outside of the house and the windows threw themselves open. Cool night air poured in, clearing the stench from the room.

The visitant was gone, the séance ended.

Nicolas removed the tweed jacket he'd borrowed from Schuyler, gathered up the severed hand, wrapped the grisly appendage in the jacket, and stalked from the room. He did this without a word, leaving Beatrice McCandlish simpering in the arms of her husband and the medium slumped in her chair, unconscious.

In the hallway, Nicolas hesitated but didn't trouble himself to take Schuyler's hat from the hat tree. Instead, he tightened his clutch on the odious package under his arm and made for the door. From the second-floor landing, Basil Prangoulis called, "Good Lord! What is that smell?"

Nicolas glanced back into the séance room. Doing so, he noted that the scale on which Madame La Porte sat now registered 127 pounds, or three pounds less than at the start of their circle.

Three pounds, he reckoned, was the precise weight of a human hand with half the forearm attached.

82

In the Professor's Office

With long powerful strides Nicolas struck out to the medical college. He loped, then jog-trotted, and finally broke into a full-out run, his breath coming in a rapid staccato like a played-out steed on a steep mountain trail. Remnants of electricity pulsed down his limbs; Thomas Chubb's hideous revelations coursed round his brain.

Chubb had to be lying. The hideous rogue, it would be just like Thomas to take one last swipe at a lifelong associate.

A reasonable man shouldn't pay heed to lies told by a shade. Besides, the whole ridiculous circle was likely a trick of the mind played by Madame La Porte, nothing more than a ghastly green mist she'd somehow concocted from common chemicals. Life had more important worries. Better to attack what might be changed in the world than to dwell on the tricks of a medium or the lies of ghosts. It couldn't be true about Ethan. Ruth and Chubb? Schuyler not his? Still, the severed hand he carried had real weight, was real flesh. Strangely, it even felt warm, as if it had just been lifted from the sawmill floor.

Breathless, Nicolas pounded at the medical college's front door until a sleepy caretaker swung it open, and with the abhorrent package tucked under his arm, he bolted up the circular stairway.

Nicolas found Patrick, the student, working alone by the glow of the microscope's limelight in Keiller's laboratory. Bleary-eyed, pencil in hand, the youth looked up from his notebook and the sketch of the strange creature he'd been studying as Nicolas rushed by and burst into the office.

"Van Horne? At this hour?" the professor said. "What have you there?"

Wordlessly, Nicolas unwrapped Schuyler's ruined jacket from around his prize. The severed hand tumbled into the ring of light from the lamp on the desk. Keiller stared. "I'll not bother to ask how ye came onto this."

"I appreciate your discretion, Professor. The details are difficult to fathom even if one has seen them with one's own eyes."

"Hmm. Appears recently severed. Perfect. Tomorrow our new term begins, and this'll make a specimen for 'em, eh? If you'll excuse me, I'll take this to our storage facility and get it on some ice." Keiller delicately lifted the specimen by its wrist and hobbled toward the door. "Aye, there'll be hours of learning to be had with this one," he said, smiling.

Once Keiller left, Nicolas sank into the chair across from the professor's desk. He felt unnerved, yet strangely energized. Drained, yet exhilarated. His sprint to the college had released some deep-seated energy that left him confident, eager to act, even reckless.

The walls glowed an eerie red from the smoldering heap of coal in the fireplace. Nicolas stood, loosened his tie, and tossed off his jacket. He turned the lamp on Keiller's desk to its brightest. He probably should've accompanied Keiller. The old boy would be slow on those stairs.

The desk and the nearby table were heaped with academic works in progress, journals, and ponderous medical volumes. Nicolas opened a ledger filled with sketches and notes in Keiller's meticulous hand. Couldn't make much of that. He chose the thickest of the medical tomes, something entitled *Pathologic and Morbid Anatomy*, and began leafing through it. A faint buzz came from the mosquito cages piled on the far table; the lamp must've upset the deadly creatures.

Pathologic and Morbid Anatomy was filled with artists' three-color renditions and silvery photographic images of the most gruesome diseases of man. They appeared countless. Plague victims covered with weeping red sores. Syphilitic chancres. Page after page of mushrooming tumors, burst hearts, two-headed infants, and nameless monsters who'd strayed far from the mark in the dark womb of their making.

How cruel, this world, Nicolas thought. *So full of suffering.*

Ruth's illness replayed in his mind, its relentless downhill course, how the thing ate at her until she chose to end her own life. Dear Ruth. No one could blame her, with all she'd endured, with the awful knowledge she'd locked inside her. In his mind's eye Nicolas conjured the young, healthy Ruth, felt her body with a husband's knowledge and was saddened by the horror of her end, her anchor-rope tether, its rough hemp tight around her. *So much suffering . . . and so little time before some unspeakable contagion takes you.*

The lemony eyes of a fever victim stared back at him. Yellow Jack. Renée had said the fever killed more and more each summer, even the young and healthy. He shuddered, imagining the carts she'd described, laden with the dead rolling down the brick streets of Galveston at dawn.

Inexplicably, a choke lodged in Nicolas's throat. He tasted a trickle of tears and then, an uncontrollable stream . . . Surely it was Thomas Chubb's revelations doing this to him, yet even Thomas's betrayal seemed insignificant in view of the suffering on these pages.

He wiped an eye on his shirtsleeve. No man could stop the world's woes; no man dared even try. It was nature's way—most men believed that. The only ones thinking otherwise were Keiller and Renée. They dreamt of altering nature, worked at it every day. Nicolas was in the office of a rare man, indeed—one who believed in his own power to change the world. Keiller . . . his niece Renée . . . science . . . hope against the suffering of the world.

Nicolas closed the medical book and traced a slow circle around the room. The air in the office was warm as blood. *Damn that fireplace. Hot as Hades for Keiller's mosquitoes.* He paused by the fireplace. The cages nearby buzzed, their screening vibrating with invisible wings sensing warm blood nearby.

Nicolas thought of what Renée and Keiller had both told him about their science. They were desperate to perfect their anti-toxoid before next summer's epidemic, and all they needed was someone never exposed to the dread disease. An untouched, virginal subject to test their theories. A Northerner.

Nicolas admired the neat order of Keiller's insect cages in the cluttered office. He recalled how Keiller had shown off his laboratory when Nicolas first stepped onto the island, before he met Renée . . . before Nicolas's life had been irrevocably altered.

Now, he might be killed before he left this island. Or later. His life was tenuous, but then all of life was tenuous. Nicolas pictured the families shattered when summer drove the bloodthirsty mosquitoes from their swamps. He imagined those death carts . . . and how the Keillers, with a single experiment, might stop it all.

Nicolas took stock of the pile of mosquito cages, their frenzy of activity. He edged open the lid of a red cage, the noisiest, the most lethal, and slipped his right arm in. Yes, he would do it. He would be Keiller's guinea pig. It was the right thing to do with his own fragile life.

A sudden hush. A hundred faint pinpricks; a thousand. A wonderfully warm, burning sensation. The insects took their blood meal so easily, so quickly and, now, quietly. *Oh, messengers of death, carriers of Keiller's particle—so bloodthirsty, yet silent in your work.*

From behind him came a shout.

"What? What's this?" It was Keiller, returned. Nicolas gave a start but did not waver. "Van Horne! What've ya done? You're in my insectary! *What have you done?*"

"An experiment, Professor. An experiment of one, let's call it."

"What the . . . ? You're crazy!"

"You would do it, if you could."

"No, no, no. You don't understand. I'm a scientist, Nicolas."

"And now I'm your guinea pig."

Keiller blanched. "Damn you, Van Horne, you're too fine a gentleman for this." Keiller cautiously extracted Nicolas's arm from the cage and secured the lid. "Oh, my—you are badly bitten," he said. "Just yesterday Renée inoculated this cage with freshly prepared particles, our most virulent from last summer. You'll be infected, no doubt about it."

Keiller sat Nicolas down and called to the lab for Patrick. He instructed the youth to "find the quickest mount, ride at a gallop to the stables, and insist that Dr. Renée Keiller harvest as much anti-toxoid as possible."

"And tell her," the old man said, turned dead serious, "she must carry the anti-toxoid on ice to the laboratory and begin purifying *for the purpose of injection into a human being.*"

The youth's mouth dropped open.

"We'll begin immediately," Keiller said. "Go." He turned to Nicolas and reexamined his puffy, pink arm near the lamp.

"You see, Nicolas, the dose is unknown. A human will require a great deal of anti-toxoid, I'm afraid. We'll use our strongest."

When Keiller looked up, Patrick hadn't budged from the doorway, his face drained of blood. "An experiment?" the young man whined. "With him?"

"Get a horse, boy! Ride!"

Patrick stumbled out the door. Keiller limped behind his desk, pulled a bottle of Scotch from a drawer, and poured himself a stiff dollop. He downed it and poured another. "None of this for you, Van Horne. The anti-toxoid will be hard enough on your liver."

"What am I in for, Professor?"

"We'll inject anti-toxoid direct into your vein. Let's see—yellow fever incubates in three to six days . . . We'll give you three treatments, one a day over the next three days to beat the particle to the punch."

"We'll know in three days then?"

"That we will. The anti-toxoid will have side effects. Serious side effects. If you survive—"

"Survive?"

"I confess, Van Horne, the stuff's been killing our guinea pigs. About fifty percent mortality from the treatment alone. It's a mite hard on the internal organs."

"This infusion—where do you do it?"

"I'll arrange for a hospital bed on the General Men's Ward. I'm thinking two liters of purified anti-toxoid for a first dose. It should take only an hour to infuse, then you'll have to rest." Keiller's hand trembled as he reached for his whiskey and squinted through his spectacles, searching for a pen.

"I'll write the orders now. Renée and I will see to it."

83

First Treatment

Beds stretched in four long rows down the ward. Wrapped in a hospital gown, Nicolas lay between stiff white sheets. Electric lights blazed overhead. Florence Nightingales dashed to and fro in black frocks with white aprons and caps. A red rubber tube ran from the steel trocar in his forearm to a glass bottle of murky grey fluid. An empty bottle stood on the bedside table; the last of the anti-toxoid flowed; his veins pulsed with it.

It was late afternoon, nearly dusk. He must've passed out with the first treatment. All he could remember was a young physician stabbing him with that thick steel trocar and the room growing dim. The room was still fading in and out. His legs shook convulsively, his belly ached, and his arms seemed made of wood. A sea of strained faces washed by—nurses, students, doctors. Then Renée was at his side.

"Oh, Nick," she was saying under her breath. "Why in the world have you done this?"

"I . . . I . . ."

He must've dozed again because the next time he opened his eyes night was falling and his bed was surrounded by the solemn beards and white coats of physicians making their evening rounds. Keiller was lecturing, something about "adverse effects," "necrosis," and "organ damage."

"What's happened, Francis?"

"A wee reaction, quite bad, actually," Keiller said. "But you've taken it well enough."

The professor's face was drawn. Nicolas read doubt in the old man's eyes.

"Is it working, Professor?"

"As I've said, it'll be a few days before we have a verdict. Your veins are not much good, sir. It appears ye've punished 'em somethin' awful. Renée finally managed a passable vascular access for the second bottle."

"Can I go?"

"Oh, yes. Renée's preparing tomorrow's dose of anti-toxoid as we speak. Your job as the guinea pig . . . uh, the patient, Van Horne, is to get plenty of rest. And remember, no whiskey, sir. Be here on the ward promptly at noon tomorrow."

"Yes, Doctor."

"Must rush along now. Need to finish our rounds. You remember I've a special anatomy class to instruct this evening. We'll be dissectin' all through the night."

84

Abducted

He'd taken only the first step of the narrow, unlit stairwell to the flat when they struck. One step in the scant light from the street, and powerful arms encircled his neck and head from behind, a forearm the size of a fence post tightened against his throat. He sensed a second man, someone tall, his breath stinking of cigar and cognac wafting down as the strong one did his work.

He was so close to safety, surprised barely a dozen steps from Schuyler's snug front room and divan. Those bolts with piano wire strung between sprang to mind, the weapon that had nearly done him in at the rail of the *Jilted Lady*. The Russian assassin . . . the garroter he'd been dreading.

He saw metal flash . . . the steel bolts? No. Tinplate. A tin can. He struggled against unyielding arms. *Try to shout, shout out, but no air . . . no air . . .*

What is this? A wad of cotton clamped over his nose and mouth, the big man yanking his head back. He saw the tin can tipped overhead. The coolness of a volatile splashed onto his face. A familiar smell.

Ether.

He bucked against the fumes. Kicking, twisting, writhing, but *weaker . . . weaker.*

The next he knew he was on his side on a hardwood floor, his eyes trying to focus on . . . on his own feet, bound together so tight they ached. His wrists were bound together too, with coarse baling twine in front of him. A rag had been stuffed in his mouth. Weak light dodged around the room. Nausea rose in his craw—the familiar aftermath of ether narcosis—and he choked back vomit.

His cheek rested on a floor of polished red pine. The walls around him were carved . . . carved of fine cherry. *He was in Keiller's office* lying next to the professor's desk. A man's broad backside—it had to be a Russian, the same overstuffed suit of fine silk—kneeled in front of Keiller's safe. On the floor, Keiller's desk lamp was turned low. Nicolas heard the spin of the safe's dial, the click of its tumblers.

Behind him, through the door to the laboratory, came a harsh whisper: "All's ready. Hurry with that, then fix him and we—"

Lying as still as he could, Nicolas worked the rag in his mouth until it loosened and dropped free. The big Russian still stooped by the safe, concentrating. Nicolas chewed at the twine around his wrists. The twine tasted of engine oil but it loosened; he slipped one hand out and shook free.

The safe door creaked open. The Russian was scooping bills, gold eagles, and silver dollars into a canvas bag. He stuffed handful after handful into the pockets of his suit jacket.

Nicolas sat up and tugged at the bond on his ankles. As tight as a steel shackle. He'd have to go it with his ankles bound, mustering all his strength to have at the big man. Nicolas shuffled closer, got his bound legs under him. Surprise was his only hope. He waited, thinking back to football days. The perfect tackle.

When the big man straightened, the safe only half emptied, Nicolas lunged at the back of the man's knees, buckling them . . . but he didn't go down. Nicolas threw a roundhouse deep into soft belly flesh.

The Russian grunted and the money bag fell to the floor. Nicolas, still gripping his knees, thrust again and the big man toppled onto Keiller's insectary. Cages crashed to the floor and splintered. A buzzing cloud of mosquitoes rose toward the ceiling.

Nicolas lunged again but got nothing but air, as the Russian had gained his feet with surprising agility and sidestepped away.

Flat on the floor on his back, his legs still bound, Nicolas watched for the wire garrote from his assassin's pocket. Instead, the Russian stood with his hands on his hips, sneering . . . as a tall silhouette entered the doorway.

"Here, use this," the man in the shadows said, holding out a gallon jug of clear, colorless liquid. "No changing the plan. Not now."

The Russian inched over to the door, his eyes glued on Nicolas. He took the jug and sidled back to the safe, then bent down for the bag of money and tossed it on the floor next to Nicolas. He took a step forward and delivered a wicked kick to Nicolas's groin.

"The bag's for you, ice man."

A dull, crippling pain gripped Nicolas's belly. The Russian splashed the liquid in the jar onto Nicolas's pants and feet. A puddle formed on the floor. Nicolas recognized the fumes—alcohol, pure alcohol.

"You got lucky on boat," the Russian snarled. "But your luck run out now." He turned and reached for the lamp on the floor, smiling now. "See, this way we get two hares with one shot." The assassin lifted the lamp and turned its wick high. "Rabbits, you say."

"Get on with it," the man standing in the doorway growled. Light fell for a second on the lean, angular face, but pain so blinded Nicolas, he couldn't place that shadowy, twisted countenance, except that the man was ugly. Very ugly.

A flickering red-orange glow crept up the lab walls behind the tall man. "Light him," he said. "We need to get out." The man withdrew. The drone of the mosquitoes ratcheted to a higher pitch.

"Here you go, ice man. Try this." The Russian dashed Keiller's desk lamp to the floor at Nicolas's feet.

The lamp's kerosene flamed up with a roar, sending a dense, black cloud of smoke to the ceiling; the alcohol puddle caught with a low, blue flame. The ends of Nicolas's pant legs flared, the baggy, oversized pants he'd borrowed from Schuyler alight in blue flames. He batted madly with bare hands, then rolled furiously to the wall.

"Now I git," the Russian growled, running for the door straight through a cloud of enraged mosquitoes. He turned at the threshold, the tall man right behind him, both swatting at themselves. "Good-bye, ice man. Zhivakov tell me say good-bye, too."

With a wicked grin, the Russian slammed the door shut. The key turned with a clunk in the lock.

85

Good Samaritan

Smoke slowly filled the office. He'd snuffed the still-smoldering cuff of his pants. Righting himself, he shuffled across the floor and leaned his back against the locked door. It felt warm. He tried his bonds again; they were tight. *Scissors? A knife or letter opener?*

Nicolas edged around the burning lamp to the desk and pulled out a drawer, scattering its contents onto the floor. Nothing sharp. He was reaching for another drawer, choking now, when the door rattled and the key again turned in the lock. *They're back? For the money bag they left behind?*

The door flew open and a man ran in, a wild blur of a man with a wicked long knife drawn, a knife like Nicolas had seen used on the docks to open bales of cotton. But this man was much slighter than the killers who'd just bolted.

"You!"

With wild tresses streaming behind him, the Voodoo Doctor grasped Nicolas by the twine on his ankles and dragged him rudely out of the office and across the laboratory. Flames licked at the lab walls. The Keillers' laboratory was filled with smoke and heat.

On the landing the Voodoo Doctor, with a single well-aimed swipe of his knife, sliced the twine that had welded itself into the flesh of Nicolas's ankles. Nicolas wobbled onto rubbery legs. The door to the anatomy laboratory was closed, but flames flickered behind the door's glass.

The voodoo man slung Nicolas's arm over his shoulder and loped down the stairway at a clip with Nicolas stumbling alongside. An explosion rang out. With tendrils of smoke clinging to them, they burst out the main door of the medical college onto the portico.

Nicolas collapsed and was dragged to the sidewalk. Flames leapt from the topmost windows of the red stone building. A funnel of thick, black smoke and the reek of scorched human flesh rose from the skylights of the anatomy lab.

The Voodoo Doctor crouched beside Nicolas.

"Thank God for you," Nicolas gasped. "You followed me here?"

"My men were always with you. I suspected a plan for tonight, so I followed myself, went in after you, slipped into a doorway, and waited. I know who's behind this . . . well, at least I'm sure it's not you now, Van Horne."

"Who—"

The Voodoo Doctor glanced behind him. A fire wagon rolled to an abrupt stop, bells clanging, the team of horses wild eyed with excitement. In an instant, a hose snaked from the fire wagon around the building to the bay. Two men in shirtsleeves began working the wagon's pump; the hose pulsed; men in black rubber slickers dashed up the stairs past Nicolas and the Voodoo Doctor.

"I've got to get out of here," the Voodoo Doctor said.

"Tell me—who was the other man? The one with the Russian?"

"They'll stick this on me . . . I must go." He straightened and casually strode down the street.

Nicolas rubbed his bruised ankles. His hands were blistered, his trousers charred. He could hardly catch a young man like Sealy's mulatto son on foot. Not in his condition.

A second fire wagon was drawn up by two horses. The street filled with hospital staff, physicians, nurses, and patients in their scant gowns with blankets wrapped around them.

Nicolas gained his feet; he still stood near the bottom step to the medical college when a large landau thundered up. Long white coats tumbled out, and Renée rushed to him, her eyes wide with terror.

"Oh, God in heaven!" she cried. "What's happened?"

Nicolas stared blankly for a long moment. "Renée . . . it's horrible . . ."

"Tell me, Nick!" Renée grabbed his arm, steadied herself against the stone stairway. "Where's Uncle?"

"I—"

"Don't you realize? Uncle Francis was teaching anatomy lab tonight. He had some sort of special specimen."

86

Uncle

"No, you can't go." Nicolas took her by both arms to restrain the lady scientist. "Perhaps . . . perhaps he got out before . . . perhaps he escaped."

Men worked the second fire wagon's pump hard; two rubber hoses now wove their way up the central staircase. Brackish bay water tumbled down the stairs and out the front doors. Though the brave firefighters quickly staunched the flames, black puffs of smoke continued to burst sporadically from the broken windows of the top floor. Through the shattered glass Nicolas glimpsed the anatomy laboratory's whitewashed walls, thick with char. Patches of the star-filled sky showed through gaps in the roof where the skylights had been.

Renée began to sob. Then, two firefighters burst from the entranceway pulling behind them the limp body of Francis Keiller, his head lolling from side to side, his crooked back and game legs scuttling along lifelessly on the stone of the portico. Renée and Nicolas dashed up the stairs onto the portico.

"Uncle!"

Together they cradled Keiller in their arms. A sickening gurgle escaped from the old man's lungs; his face was coated with a thick layer of soot, his hair was singed, and his eyes were fixed in a demonic stare.

"My laboratory . . ." Keiller gasped. "I was assisting the dissection when I smelled smoke . . . the students ran but . . . but I was knocked down by a big man. Two men—one like a bear, one very tall. I . . . I . . . went into the lab, crawled into my office, the smoke, I saw . . . I saw—" Keiller sucked at another breath. "The solvents . . . alcohol, acetone . . . it all went up!"

"Oh, Francis," Nicolas whispered into the old man's ear, "as God is my witness, I shall get to the bottom of this."

Orderlies rushed onto the portico. Nicolas helped lift the professor to a stretcher and the orderlies dispatched him at a jog across the street and through the front doors of the Infirmary of the Ursuline Sisters of Charity.

While nurses prepared a bed and got the old man between clean white sheets, Nicolas waited with Renée in the hall outside the large, third-floor men's ward marked CONSUMPTIVES. But Renée was mute.

"He's in good hands now," Nicolas said. "They got him out in time."

A dark shadow crossed Renée's face. "I confess, Nick," she said, "I was thinking of you. Our retorts, columns, everything for purification from the horse serum was in the laboratory—it's all lost."

"How much anti-toxoid is left?"

"I must check, but I suspect . . . hardly any."

"Come. Let's see to your uncle."

The consumptives ward was long and narrow, its two rows of beds filled with patients. The bare, whitewashed walls echoed with groans and hacking coughs. Keiller, scrubbed and in a fresh hospital gown, was propped on pillows, his eyes dull, each breath a coarse whistle. Renée stood at the bedside smoothing back her uncle's scanty white hair.

Keiller's eyes brightened when he saw the ice merchant. "Nicolas . . . I'm sorry you're in this," he said, his voice a raspy whisper. "But you must find them, Nicolas. You must." The old man, fighting for breath, closed his eyes and went quiet.

"Let's give him a moment," Nicolas suggested. He stepped to a window and beckoned Renée from the bedside. "He'll recover, won't he?"

Renée shook her head. "There's no telling."

"But he wasn't badly burnt."

"It's his consumption, Nick. Over the years tuberculosis has taken its toll. His lungs are ravaged. His spine is full of it, and now, with the smoke . . ."

"Has he long?"

Renée turned away without answering, then whispered, "If he survives the night, it'll be a good sign. Now hush."

Keiller started awake. "Nicolas! You must . . . you must . . ."

Nicolas stepped to the professor's side. "Don't fear, Professor, I shall bring them to justice."

"No, no, you don't understand." Keiller struggled to raise his head. "The culprits must be found! They must be treated."

"Treated?" Nicolas turned to Renée. "What's he talking about?"

"The others! Those men!" Keiller croaked. "I saw my office . . . the cages overturned . . . ransacked and . . . the mosquitoes!" He fell back onto his pillow, gasping, his eyes wild.

"Nick?" Renée asked softly. "Did they loose the mosquitoes?"

"Yes. I saw clouds of them."

"Then the culprits were exposed, as Uncle said. A few bites, and with that potent particle from last summer, they're bound to be infected."

"The fools deserve worse."

"I agree, deep down, but as physicians we're obliged to treat them."

Panic, raw and undiluted, gripped Nicolas. "How much anti-toxoid did you say survived?"

"Only what we already have on the ward. Very little, I'm afraid. We can bleed the horses for more serum, but as I said, from here it looks like the fire destroyed everything in the lab. I'll need to jury-rig something."

"My task, then, is to find the two fiends so you can save their miserable hides." With a bewildered look, he turned to leave.

"Don't forget!" Renée called after him. "You're to be on the ward tomorrow for your second treatment. Best come at daybreak, without fail. I'll see to you personally with whatever anti-toxoid I can muster."

87

Businessmen

"Two hares with one shot." That's what the Russian had said—leave the ice man to roast in the fire, and close down the college with the same blow. *Two birds with one stone. Damn Russians.* His assassins wanted him dead, but, luckily, they'd failed. The two miserable curs succeeded in destroying the medical college, or at least they had burnt its heart out.

Who wanted the college gone?

Nicolas thought back to Keiller's office. The safe . . . the Russian. But who was the accomplice? Nicolas had the slightest glimpse of him, a sideways view lit by the glow of the early flames, before the big blowup. A tall, ugly man. Very tall, very slim . . . and Keiller had seen him, too . . .

Trey Sealy!

Nicolas recounted to himself how Trey Sealy, the son of the financier, and another man had accosted Renée at the Cotton Exchange. Perhaps it was Trey and his businessmen allies who had been vilifying the medical college all along. But how to prove that? How to get to Trey Sealy?

Hutchinson Sealy, father of the cotton trade and father of the biggest cotton trader—Trey Sealy—would know.

And where would old man Sealy be at this late hour? At least two or three hours had passed since the attack, which took place at the start of the supper hour. Like most businessmen, Nicolas realized, the chances were that Sealy would be dining on Restaurant Row, probably nearing brandy and cigars right now.

Nicolas hopped the first trolley to downtown and marched along Restaurant Row. The street was abuzz with news of the fire. Nicolas entered the first restaurant he came to and walked briskly through its dining rooms looking for Sealy. He passed table after table. Dressed as he was in Schuyler's oversized, disheveled, and smoky clothes, with the bottoms of his pant legs burnt and ragged, Nicolas wasn't surprised that eyes turned his way and diners grew unearthly quiet as he passed. Undaunted, Nicolas marched into every dining area, large and small, then moved down the street to the next restaurant.

It was in Trudeau's that Nicolas thought to ask a familiar-looking waiter about Mr. Sealy's dining habits. With a greenback slipped into the waiter's white jacket, Nicolas was led upstairs to a small, private dining room where Hutch Sealy sat at the head of the table with a handful of well-dressed business types. Their plates were empty, crumbs were scattered over the tablecloth, and the men leaned back in a blue cloud of cigar smoke.

Sealy met Nicolas's bloodshot eyes with his own for an instant, then settled his elbows heavily on the table and stared straight ahead, a half-smoked panatela motionless in his hand.

"You've got some nerve, Mr. Van Horne," he said, his side-whiskers quivering. "Barging in on our dinner after your misdeeds."

"You've heard what happened at the medical college, I take it," Nicolas asked.

"News travels fast on the island, Van Horne. Of course we've heard of your attack."

"*My attack?* Surely you joke."

"Hardly, sir. Everyone knows the destruction you caused."

Throats were cleared. For a long moment nothing was said, then the silence was broken by the elderly gentleman seated next to Sealy, a trim fellow with cleanly shaven cheeks, a neatly combed white goatee, and fervent blue eyes.

"I doubt any of us regrets terribly what you've done out there," the elderly gent said. "We all hate their unlawful dissecting and—"

"And their unholy experiments!" added another at the table.

"Good God!" Nicolas was aghast. "It appears you've been lied to, gentlemen. An outrageous lie, at that."

Sealy continued, more calmly. "Word is, they weren't meeting your price for your grisly supplies, Van Horne. Paid you nothing. And you in such dire straits, financially speaking. They're saying that the ice merchant's attack was foiled by his own blundering, and he's lucky he didn't burn himself to a crisp."

A gent with a heavy accent spoke up; Nicolas recognized the mustachioed Frenchman, Pierre Bonferri, preening his mustache at the far end of the table. "*Mon Dieu,* Van Horne! And how could you forget zee sack of money? Not like you at all, is it?"

"Gad, what lies you've been fed, Pierre . . . gentlemen," Nicolas countered. "Whoever's misled you is the one responsible for this fire. And he tried to kill me, too."

Bonferri raised an eyebrow. "Kill?"

"He tried to trap me in the building."

"*Mon ami*, your word of honor—it wasn't you who set zee fire?"

"My word. As I explained to Mr. Sealy here earlier, I've been pursuing a criminal element ever since my first visit to this island. Whoever set this fire wanted me dead and the medical college destroyed in one fell swoop. Fortunately for me, they were foiled on the one count."

When there was no response, Nicolas decided on a different tack.

"You must understand, gentlemen, one of Galveston's finest citizens was injured in tonight's heinous assault. Dr. Francis Keiller, the famous professor. And property, valuable property, was senselessly destroyed."

The table was stilled; trails of cigar smoke rose unwavering to the ceiling. Furtive glances were exchanged.

"Even if we believed you, Mr. Van Horne," Sealy said softly, "it's not us who burnt the damned college."

"Perhaps you know who did, Mr. Sealy—and I'd solicit your help in getting the culprit."

More silence.

"Ah, you're right," Bonferri admitted with a shake of his head. "It's gone too far. Damage to valuable property? Now that's unforgivable."

Sealy shifted uncomfortably in his seat. "Certainly there'll be an investigation," he said, looking off. "Our city constable will be on the case."

"You mean your cousin, Hutch?" the elderly gent with the goatee asked.

"I . . . I'm sure justice will be done. I'm sure."

The gentleman with the goatee frowned and turned to Nicolas. "You seem to know all about that place, sir. Would you kindly tell us about these experiments?"

"Yes, do," another diner added. "It's rumored they perform vivisection on imbeciles and such."

"I'll be glad to explain," Nicolas said, leaning wearily on the table. Bonferri pulled a chair from the next table and Nicolas fell into it, suddenly hit with a wave of fatigue like he'd never felt. Keiller's words *"organ damage . . . a wee reaction"* replayed through his mind.

Summoning all his energy, he straightened and told them in detail of Keiller's theories, the scientists' dedication and hard work, and their hope for a cure for yellow fever. At his mention of the dread disease, concern creased the men's faces one and all. Heads shook.

"It's true, *mon ami*," Bonferri said. "Not a family on the island escapes Mr. Jack."

"This Keiller fellow," Nicolas continued, "believes a certain particle causes the disease. The scientists have come to understand this particle through experiments . . . experiments on guinea pigs and horses kept at their barns."

Nicolas hesitated as he considered the impact of his next disclosure.

"And it so happens"—his gaze was steady—"I have joined them in an experiment, personally, of my own free will. I've exposed myself to this particle of the professor's."

"*Sacré bleu!*" Bonferri stared in astonishment. "You exposed yourself?"

"Yes, to test their cure."

"Yellow fever?" Sealy muttered. "Of your own free will?"

"If I prove that their antidote works, gentlemen—and I have confidence it will—come summer, the treatment will save your entire city. Merchant and stevedore, rich and poor alike. And Galveston will be famous as the place where the cure was discovered, all because of your medical college."

"You've a point there," Bonferri said with a nod. "For years, I tell you, I've heard these tales of body snatchers and vivisection. Who cares, anyway? The college is full of dedicated medical types, and they're fine gentlemen. I've always said that. We're lucky to have them in Galveston. Doctors searching for cures, students . . . and such lovely nurses." Bonferri contemplated the nurses for a moment. "Come to think of it"—he grinned—"I'm quite in favor of the college."

The elderly gent spoke up with a shake of his pure white beard. "I'm not so sure. Mother Nature has her laws."

"That's humbug," Bonferri scoffed. "It's a new age we're in. Man can change nature's laws, and why in hell shouldn't we?"

Nicolas jumped at Bonferri's lead. "I, for one, gentlemen, intend to back the medical college to the fullest, with all resources at my disposal, as you once did, Mr. Sealy."

Bonferri rose from his chair and looked around at his colleagues. "Van Horne's right," he said, giving the table a rap. "We need to be leaders in this, gentlemen, not followers."

Nicolas stood on unsteady legs. He pitched back, caught himself, and shut his eyes against the bright gaslight of the chandelier. His skull throbbed. *The anti-toxoid would have adverse effects, Keiller said. But will it work in time? Before the particle takes over?*

Bonferri offered a hand. "*Mon ami*, you're looking poorly."

"Perhaps it's the smoke I've inhaled. Nothing serious."

As he wobbled, exhausted and near fainting, Nicolas recalled one last bit of information he needed to impart. He'd contrived a clever ploy that just might unhinge one or another of these self-satisfied gentlemen.

"One other thing about their skullduggery," he said. "During the attack, the criminals broke the professor's insect cages and released his most dangerous mosquitoes. The deadly yellow fever particle is loosed on the town, gentlemen."

"Oh, come now, Van Horne," Sealy countered. "It's March. There's no yellow fever this time of year."

"That may change, gentlemen. Certainly for the criminals it will. The scientists are sure the attackers were bitten during their crime and will soon fall ill. As for the rest of the town, well, we can only hope."

Faces dropped. Chairs scraped.

"You're not at all well, Van Horne," Sealy said, looking particularly agitated as he stood and took Nicolas's arm. "My carriage is waiting. Let me have my man assist you to your lodgings."

At Trudeau's front doors, Hutch Sealy helped Nicolas slide onto the smooth leather seat of his personal brougham. "This business of the blasted college," he said, before sending his coach off. "You've made some good points, Van Horne. I suppose we mustn't have assassins running loose in our city. I'll ask around to see what I can learn. You get some rest."

Nicolas requested Sealy's coachman help him climb the stairs to the flat, where he found Schuyler pacing. An ashtray on the kitchen table overflowed with half-smoked cigarettes. His son Schuyler. His only living son. But was he really his son? The ghastly words of Thomas Chubb flooded back. Had Thomas's revelations from the other side of the grave made his son a stranger?

"What the hell happened?" Schuyler asked when he saw the sorry state of his father. "Look at you."

Nicolas stepped to the window. Schuyler joined him. It was near midnight; the streetlamps had been lit for hours. Clouds covered a full moon like mottled bruises.

"Damn, Father. Were you crazy enough to join the firefighters?"

Afraid of what he might see, Nicolas snuck a sideways look at his son. It was the youthful Ruth Stuyvesant's clear, intelligent eyes that struck him first, light hazel eyes full of humor and goodwill. But Schuyler's gentle eyes were set, Nicolas realized, in a broader, fuller countenance than his own, with something flamboyant, sensitive, and complicated about it—like Thomas Chubb.

"No, I was caught in the damned fire," Nicolas explained. "I've just been questioning the downtown businessmen about it."

No, he'd not allow Thomas Chubb's horrid secret to matter. Not in this lifetime. He'd simply take that secret to his own grave, untold.

"What did they tell you?" Schuyler asked.

"Nothing. At first, they blamed me." Nicolas paused, framing his words carefully. "But there's more I must tell you, Son. I've taken an experiment on myself, a very important experiment."

As Nicolas recounted how he'd come to this point, he watched concern grow on Schuyler's face until his son could no longer hold his tongue.

"You're so blasted headstrong, Father! Obstinate, that's what you are. Contrary. What about Abby and me, huh? What will we do without you if this crazy experiment of yours should fail?"

With his head pounding so, Nicolas could think of no reasonable reply.

88

Second Treatment

Foghorns sounded through the night. Nicolas never slept; he saw first light come creeping onto the island under a blanket of wintry fog. His mind was full of fog too, hazy, cottony, and his skull throbbed with each throaty bellow at sea. Was this pulsing of blood at his temples an effect of the treatment or Yellow Jack's first onslaught? Nicolas tried to shake the thought from his aching head.

In the tiny kitchen Schuyler spread crusts of bread with marmalade. There was cold coffee and no butter for the crusts. The plate sat before Nicolas untouched.

"You're making no sense," Schuyler said, pushing away his own meager breakfast. "I told you it was an insane idea. Come along. I'll accompany you to that damned infirmary. You'd never make it on your own."

Nicolas held tight to his son as they groped their way through the fog to the corner trolley stop. They heard the trolley's rancorous approach but saw nothing until the car broke through the bank of fog and screeched to a halt dead in front of them. Nicolas stretched out on one of the trolley's long, wooden benches. Out the window, a blank wall of whiteness crackled with electricity and resounded with the plosive clatter-clip of passing carriages.

The fog cleared for a moment at the hospital stop, revealing the Medical College of Galveston in the early dawn light. The building's once-stunning pink sandstone was coated with a black, tarry residue; the front doors were boarded shut; the shattered windows of the top floor gaped like the ragged mouth of a Halloween jack-o'-lantern . . . then, the sight was again lost in the fog.

Schuyler took Nicolas's arm and they inched their way across the street. The intricately decorated wrought iron fence of the Ursuline Sisters of Charity infirmary loomed out of the fog. At this early hour, the gates of the hospital's massive security fence were just being unlocked by a caretaker.

Schuyler threw the front doors open on an onslaught of human activity and brilliant electric light. Nurses in crisply starched aprons and caps raced to and fro; gurneys rattled by; orderlies swept down the hall behind wheelchairs of polished hardwood and cane.

Seeing all this, Schuyler backed toward the iron gate, mumbling to himself, "Oh, no. Definitely not my cup of tea. Good luck, Father."

Renée arrived on the ward with two bottles of anti-toxoid. "It's all that's left, I'm afraid. I'll entrust you to our able physicians to find a vein, while I cobble together a purification system."

A bed was readied, the red tubing unfurled and a bottle hung. The fluid was murkier than he remembered from his first treatment. Nicolas's arm burnt with the crude preparation. He closed his eyes when the first shiver hit and let the drip of the anti-toxoid waft him to a distant place.

During his conscious moments, Nicolas sensed that beds were made, nurses fussed, gurneys rolled by. The orderly checked his nearly empty bottle but left it hanging.

Now the orderly busied himself at the next bed. Where was the second bottle? What was he doing? Hanging Nicolas's second bottle of precious grey stuff at the next bed? A new patient?

Nicolas willed his eyes wide open, struggled to sit up and see who lay in the next bed. A stocky man in street clothes, his back to Nicolas, blocked the view. The orderly nodded and stepped away. The bottle was hung, running briskly. Then, the visitor turned and shot a fleeting glance at Nicolas.

"Mr. Sealy?"

The man ignored him, but those greying side beards were unmistakable. Hutchinson Sealy, Galveston's most prosperous financier, was visiting a patient so tall, his black socks stuck from under his bedsheet.

Nicolas tried to speak again, but the anti-toxoid had numbed his lips. He flopped back onto his pillow. Nicolas's mind, and his memory, worked well enough to recognize the tall, ugly son of Hutch Sealy and recall the man's nasty confrontation with Renée at the Cotton Exchange. Nicolas understood he shared the ward—and the precious anti-toxoid—with Galveston's link to the slave trade, Hutch Sealy's son Trey.

When Nicolas came to again, Trey Sealy slept soundly in the next bed. His father was gone. Renée was at Nicolas's bedside, unhooking the tubing and flushing it with clear fluid from another bottle at the bedside table. She set the bottle down and began rolling the tubing into neat loops. "Ah, good. You're conscious again," she said with a fleeting smile.

"In the next bed . . . that's Trey Sealy, isn't it, Renée?"

"Yes."

"Have you notified the constable?"

"I went to him, but he refused to look into it. Said he needed 'more evidence.' For now, the culprit needs treatment."

"The scoundrel. He tried to kill me. He should be in jail."

"His treatment went better than yours."

"Better?"

"You're having a bad time of it." She sighed, the exhaustion in her voice obvious. "Oh, Nick, everything's gone wrong." She threw the tubing down on the stainless steel table. "I'm doing all that's possible, but your veins are difficult, and you're prone to these adverse reactions . . ."

Nicolas saw tears at the corners of her eyes. "Will there be enough?" he asked. "Divided between us like this?"

She picked up the tubing and began rolling again, tighter and tighter. "I've made a makeshift lab in the hospital dispensary. God, I wish I could do more for you, Nick, but I took an oath to treat all men as equal—from the finest of gentlemen to the lowest of scoundrels." She set the roll of tubing on the bedside table, leaned over, and placed her hand over his. "Now I wish I'd never taken that damned oath."

With a grim look, Renée set off between the rows of beds. While the other physicians felt his forehead and prodded his belly, Nicolas tried to concentrate on the faint sweet smell of apple blossoms that hung in the air.

Once the doctors were satisfied Nicolas had weathered the treatment, he was told to dress. Trey Sealy slept soundly in the next bed, snoring, his mouth agape, his hawklike, pockmarked face in complete repose. The picture of innocence.

"There's nothing more to be done," the physicians told Nicolas, "until tomorrow's treatment—if there is one."

Nothing more to be done.

89

Jaundice and Delirium

Schuyler helped his father to a chair at the kitchen table. He lit cigarette after cigarette as he paced in circles around the flat's tiny kitchen, a thin trail of smoke rising to the ceiling behind him. "I can't believe this, Father. Look what you've done to yourself."

"It's the final stage of their cure, Son."

"They'll not cure a blasted thing. Quacks and charlatans, that's what everyone says."

Nicolas had no strength to argue. He bundled himself directly into bed. In the deep of the night a chill shook him. He was drenched in sweat. Suffocating. He threw off the blankets, staggered out of bed, and vomited thin, bilious strands into the chamber pot.

Schuyler came with a lamp and turned its wick full.

"My Lord, you're turning yellow!" he cried. "I must get you back to that wretched place."

Nicolas slumped to the floor, then everything faded. He had a dim memory of a hurried ride, again in Sealy's carriage, and of a high, vaulted ceiling viewed from a gurney clattering down a long hospital corridor. Then, moans. Bed after bed of woebegone men that came in every shade of yellow. Foul-smelling bedside slop buckets filled with dark fluids. As the gurney rolled down the aisle, the small metal plaques at the foot of each bed flashed past: LIVER WARD . . . LIVER WARD.

He was wheeled to a bed near the end of the row. Sheets were unfurled; nurses in white wrestled him into a hospital gown—white was everywhere, as if the room had suddenly filled with freshly ginned cotton.

Physicians leaned over him, mumbled Latin phrases, wrote in small notebooks, and nodded knowingly. Icy hands poked his belly. He was doused with alcohol; its vapours choked him and he retched into the bucket at his bedside until he was too weak to retch any more.

Then, a gentle hand was on his shoulder, and he heard Renée's voice in solemn discourse with her colleagues:

"I favor astringent. We've got to break the fever, no matter what caused it."

"One thing isn't clear, Dr. Keiller. Is it yellow fever or your treatment?"

His stupor deepened with evening. The moaning on the ward grew faint. When the weak light of morning was at the windows, the orderlies and nurses again shuffled across the hardwood floor, and the groans grew louder.

Nightfall followed dawn. Had it been days or weeks?

He had strange, intense dreams. In one, he was trackside at Saratoga; the horses were running and the summer air smelled of turf and well-lathered horses het up for the start. He was laying a bet on a pretty stallion when he spoke to a young woman in line. She was fetching, but she kept her distance, a lovely voice from the end of a long tunnel:

"Nick . . . oh, Nick. If only . . . if only I had . . ."

It was August and he smelled the meadows, saw the multicolored silks of the riders, their mounts' manes braided with bright red and yellow ribbons. The comely woman backed away and was swallowed by the trackside crowd.

"The fever . . . it's not breaking."

"I'm afraid the damage to the liver has advanced . . ."

A bitter, coppery taste blossomed at the back of his throat. His tongue was thick. His eyes were scorched, his lips split. He was going to die, he knew . . . but how simple a matter that would be, to follow all those who'd gone before to the grave, the icehouse, the anatomy lab. The way had been well marked.

Orderlies slammed shutters against a howling north wind. Nurses rushed to light gas heaters. It was morning again and those who had died in the night cooled on gurneys, awaiting transport to the morgue . . . but Nicolas wasn't loaded onto a gurney. Clean sheets were pulled under him. Cool hands laid on.

At his bedside, the familiar smell of horses.

"Don't, Nicolas. Don't try to talk. It's Renée. I've been at the horse barns, working on more anti-toxoid"—his eyes opened and he saw the ward clearly for the first time in . . . how long? days?—"but now I'm here."

"I swear I saw the culprit in the next bed, Renée. Trey Sealy. Did he . . . ?"

"He recovered and disappeared, left yesterday. Two doses of anti-toxoid did the trick. The other man—"

"Other—?"

Renée pointed to the gurneys covered by sheets near the window. "That's him. The large one."

"My assassin. The Russian."

"The fever set in quickly. I gave anti-toxoid, but his fever rose and his liver . . . his liver was ruined."

A second dream, a dream more vivid, more palpable than real life, came to him that night.

He was walking the shoreline trail near the outlet of Upper Spy Lake. It was early winter, peaceful, the smell of balsam in the woods. A thick, wet snow fell. He heard rustling on the trail behind him. A bear burst from the woods, an old, grey beast, snapping its jaws, rolling its shoulders. It was a big male crazed with hunger, laying on fat for the winter, eating everything in sight, its claws scraping along the lonely shoreline trail. Nicolas ran. His lungs were about to burst. The bear was closing in. He smelled its fetid breath. He turned toward the lake.

The ice was thin. He dared not venture out.

90

At Her Merchant's Bedside

She'd had her chance—foolish girl—but hadn't taken it. Now it was about to end. This fine gentleman, so kind, so clever, lost because of her foolishness. Tears ran; she tasted their salt; she traced their tortured course on her cheeks. *If only . . . if only . . .*

She'd felt close to him from the first moment of their meeting. It was like she'd always known the man. She should have said things, the right things at the right time. She knew the things to say; she'd had the chance but had not taken it. Foolish girl.

Saratoga . . . that's when she should have taken him for hers. If she had, they wouldn't have been at that roulette wheel. They would have been in each other's arms. But the proper thing, the right thing, was clear—when all the while her heart said yes.

She'd always done the right thing, and what had it brought her? Suffering. Grief. Her beloved husband had died. Her son had died. And now, a new love, a love like she'd never known, would die. For her, it seemed, what was love but a prelude to sorrow?

Nicolas Van Horne. Her Nick. What did right or wrong matter? Nothing mattered now. It was over . . . *if only she had . . . if only she had . . .*

He was stirring, inflamed with fever, jaundice deepening, bodily fluids leaking away until whatever it is that defines a life would leave; she'd seen it so many times, this feverish tossing while the liver died away bit by bit until finally, the whole body followed. The ghastly work of the killer Mr. Jack.

Even their strongest anti-toxoid hadn't saved Nick. Her best effort, so paltry, so off the mark. This science she practiced. This medicine. Out loud, she cursed the day those others—"Crude beasts!"—those real killers came to the infirmary door needing her precious anti-toxoid. She cursed the oath she'd taken. To do no harm, to treat men as equals . . . when there was one who had no equal, one she dreamt of with every living breath.

She'd had her chance and hadn't taken it. Foolish, foolish girl. Now her only task was to make a dying man comfortable. She would move him out of this horrid liver ward. She had already arranged the move to that vacant room on the upper floor. It was small, and unused because of the hurricane damage it took last September. The room needed paint, was under repair, and the balcony off the room was wobbly, but the breeze from the south at the back of the infirmary might prevent Nicolas's lungs from filling with pneumonia. That was her hope.

And the room would be private; there'd be no one to hear the things she had to tell him.

Nick would be as comfortable as a dying man could be. She would stay by him as a lover, not a physician, and visitors off the street wouldn't be traipsing up and down the aisles like in the liver ward. She'd allow only his son Schuyler in . . . and perhaps that business associate of Nick's who'd just arrived by train. A friend, someone who'd worked with Nick on the ice. A big fellow named Smith or Jones or one of those names that were so very common.

During one of Nick's lucid moments, a visit from a fellow trader might lift his spirits and certainly would do no harm. That was most important. To do no harm.

91

The Bear

Consciousness came in fits and starts. When he managed to open an eye, Nicolas saw a blurry shape looming at his bedside: feminine, the shape was tall and thin like Renée, and then she leaned over him and he saw her dark eyes, the green sparkle.

His mouth was parched, his lips pasted together with his first words. "How . . . long have I been out?"

"Two weeks, a little more since your first treatment." She moved away, became a shape again, a vague profile with weariness and worry in her voice. "I've had you moved to this new room. It was under repair but I've sent the workers off for now. You'll be alone and I've assigned the best nurses to you."

"Did the treatments work?"

"Oh, Nick, it's difficult to know, though we're doing everything we can. You've gotten four doses of anti-toxoid and I'm still not sure if you're like this because of yellow fever or the treatment. We've discussed your case on rounds and decided for one more dose of anti-toxoid."

To show him, she lifted a single bottle from the bedside table, which was cluttered with reels of the red tubing, steel trocars for injection, and a small surgical kit. "Your last dose."

"You don't sound convinced."

"Oh, Nick, you fade away for days. I . . . once I thought I lost you . . . I just don't know. You're looking a bit stronger today. Perhaps this last dose—"

"Why is this bottle so clear?"

"I've purified and filtered it for a week." Renée began unfurling the red tubing. "Let's get started." She opened the surgical kit, rummaged among the tools, and selected a pair of scissors to trim the tubing to the correct length.

Nicolas tried to focus his bleary eyes on her but it seemed like lead was weighing down his eyelids. No matter how he fought to watch her at her work, her shining dark hair, her precise movements, she faded . . .

He'd been out again—it must've been only a minute. Renée bent over his arm, about to insert a trocar. Red tubing ran to the bottle hung high above.

Then, he sensed a movement in the room, perhaps a gust from the balcony, and heard the door to the corridor click shut.

"Oh!" Renée glanced behind her, trocar in hand. "You must be…Mr.…."

Nicolas blinked. An ill-defined, shadowy shape loomed behind Renée. Nicolas shook his head to sharpen it. The shape wouldn't snap into focus. It was big shouldered . . . hulking. Too large for a man. *It's the bear from the dream! The bear by the lake!*

"I go by Wilson," the bear shape said. "But real name Russian, pretty lady. I am Zhivakov." The big Russian grabbed Renée's arm and jerked her toward him; she gasped. "How nice . . . I find the ice man with lady friend."

Grabbing the bed frame, Nicolas bolted upright and swung his rubbery legs over the edge of the bed.

"Get away from her—"

"Too bad she here, ice man. Too bad for her. See what I bring for you?" With his free hand Zhivakov reached into his jacket pocket and brought out the two steel bolts. He let one bolt slip, unwinding a length of piano wire, then swung his deadly garrote like a watch on a chain.

Nicolas felt the skin at the back of his neck tighten, a wild pounding in his chest. Where would he get the strength? He hadn't been on his feet in the last two weeks. The Russian had Renée's arm clamped like a vise.

"I ride train a long way to get you, ice man." Zhivakov smirked. "I heard how you ruin my business here. In Boston, too, they find my men and arrest them. Newspapers full of it. Now you going to join your pal the undertaker." He threw his head back and laughed maniacally. "You'll be deader than an undertaker. Ha!"

"Let her go. She's a doctor . . . has nothing to do with this."

"Lady doctor?" The big Russian frowned.

"Doesn't know anything about this. Nothing—"

"*Yeow!*" Zhivakov jumped like he was stung by a bee. "*Ow!* What in hell?"

Renée's trocar quivered in the back of his hand. As he pulled it out and threw it across the room, Renée dashed for the door. Zhivakov sprang after her with amazing speed for a big man and caught her in a few steps.

"*Suka! Dog!* Now you in real trouble." He growled, twisting Renée's right arm behind her back.

Zhivakov pushed Renée ahead toward the bed. "You regret that, pretty lady." As they passed the bedside table, Renée reached out, grabbed it, and pulled herself free of Zhivakov. She fell to the floor; the table toppled, scattering medical paraphernalia over her with a crash.

"Now you two come." Zhivakov grabbed Nicolas, then reached down for Renée and pushed them both out the balcony door. "Yes. Is perfect. A lover's leap."

Nicolas staggered beside him, a rag doll in the big man's grip.

Rubble from the stalled repairs sat in piles on the balcony. The bricks underfoot had cracked and loosened; the central railing of the stone balustrade leaned drunkenly outward. Zhivakov spun to kick the door shut, then threw Renée against the building. Dazed, she sank onto a pile of broken bricks and mortar dust.

He swung Nicolas around to face him. "Now you going to learn to fly. But before, I tell you what else—after you gone, I go get your pretty daughter, ice man. She's the one messed my business in Chicago. She join you soon. Ha! You, her, and undertaker, all one big family. Dead family."

Nicolas felt the boil of anger rise in his blood, hardening the muscles in his arms, steadying his legs. Calm settled over him.

Zhivakov shoved him toward the balustrade. Nicolas forced himself to glare into the big man's eyes—to keep his glance from straying to Renée, who was creeping up behind the Russian's broad back, her hand in the pocket of her white coat.

A six-inch-long surgical scalpel flashed in the sun—and came down on Zhivakov's right shoulder. "There! There!" Renée raised the steel blade again and again, stabbing to the bone.

Zhivakov spun. "*Suka ebonya!*" he shouted, swatting the scalpel away with his right hand. He balled his left and caught Renée's jaw with a crunching sound, laying her out on the deck.

The Russian's back was to him. Nicolas reached for a piece of broken brick. Cold, rough in his hand. He swung. A glancing blow, but blood seeped from the Russian's scalp. Zhivakov turned, his hand to his bloodied head, his eyes momentarily crossed. "You dead now."

Crouching, Nicolas backed toward the balustrade. "Come get me, you coward . . . you stinking Russian filthy bastard." Guessing the distance, Nicolas shifted to the left, using his old football moves.

The big Russian lunged and grabbed on to Nicolas's flimsy hospital gown. The gown tore. Nicolas ducked lower, let the big man's momentum carry him forward, toward the rail. He had the Russian's bloody jacket in his two hands, smelled his stinking breath as he gave a last desperate push. Zhivakov spun around, arms flailing, and went over backward, his eyes rolling up, his mouth a large, round O in the instant before he disappeared through the broken balustrade.

"Ahh!"

Nicolas lay on his stomach, panting. His arms and shoulders hung over the crumbling edge of the balcony. Bricks fell away. He reached back, clutching—no purchase. Rubble, mortar dust.

Then he felt a weight on him, counterbalancing. Renée, her arms wrapped around his knees, inched him back from the precipice.

Nicolas lay still and peered over the edge. Before he shut his eyes and let exhaustion take him into oblivion, he stared down at the bearlike body hung over the hospital's fence, impaled on wrought iron spikes. He thought he saw a twitch or two before the big bear's body went still.

92

Visitors

The next time he cracked an eye, the last of a bottleful of clear solution ran into his vein, and Schuyler was at the bedside. The grown man he called "son" wore a fresh shave, a crisply starched shirt and collar, and a lustrous purple chesterfield. His eyes looked bruised by worry, despite the snappy duds and the cigarette dangling from his lip.

"I'm hoping you'll be fine, Father, and soon. Dr. Renée tells me it was a close call. She refused to lay odds, but . . . she gave you two more treatments—that's your last running now. And the most amazing thing"—he guffawed—"Dr. Renée found a vein she never knew existed. Some sort of variant of anatomy. She's going to pen a report to present to a medical society in New York." He looked off to the busy hospital corridor. "This place isn't so bad, you know, if you're not sick."

Nicolas could only nod.

He slept fitfully during his last treatment and woke chilled to the bone. Another norther howled. Shutters rattled in their stone casings. Gusts blew through the room; an orderly arrived with blankets. Tiny beads of hail clattered against the brick building and skipped from the balcony and through the slats of the shutters and across the windowsills into sculpted piles, like beach sand scattered on the pine floor. Then, a cloth smelling of camphor dampened his face and was draped on his forehead.

"Rest, Nick. That's your only worry, now that—" Her voice broke. She went on in a whisper. "The look you had at your worst . . . I've seen it too many times. But now, it'll be all right."

Her cheek was badly bruised, her left eye blackened and swollen nearly shut. Through the camphor and disinfectant, Nicolas imagined he caught an apple blossom scent.

He opened his eyes to bright morning sunshine and the banging of shutters being thrown open. A gaunt, pallid Professor Francis Keiller leaned against the metal head of the bed.

"Aye, Van Horne, looks like you've come to. I know you can hear me. I'm pleased to tell you that yer experiment-of-one worked . . . sort of." Keiller beamed. "That blasted young Sealy, the scoundrel . . . he took one dose and recovered. Well, maybe they'll catch him. Anyway, we have a better idea about the doses, all thanks to you, good sir."

Nicolas managed a low whisper. "You can beat yellow fever?"

"Aye, we've the knowledge, I'm sayin', but we've not much of a medical college left." He laughed darkly. "We've been abandoned . . . the students . . . researchers . . . half the faculty gone."

Nicolas sat upright on the edge of the bed. He breathed deeply of the soap and antiseptic on his withered body. "Gone, Francis? All the scientists?"

"Practically all."

"Fernando, too?"

"Him? He was the first to flee. Like rats off a sinking ship, I tell you. We had six of those masqueraders. Scientists? Bah! Those traitors? I can't prove it, but I'm convinced they were sent by Toussaint, the sneak thief, not Pasteur."

"But why, Professor?"

"To steal my ideas, of course." Keiller shook his head in disgust. "Probably steal the particle itself. And, speaking of rats, I believe you've cleaned out a nest of 'em yourself."

"It was Renée, really."

"Aye, I'm sure. She's one lassie who'll take no guff from any man. And you can rest easy. The law will have all the facts on your little episode. What we're hearing from up north—that'll be taken into account, too, if I have anything to say about it."

Nicolas stepped through to the decrepit balcony, which had become their appointed meeting place. The doctors' rounds were ending soon; he felt his pulse quicken, waiting in the cool sunshine. When he saw her long white coat sweep into the room from the hospital corridor, her dark, satiny hair swaying, he felt the same catch in his throat he'd felt after they'd dashed the life out of Zhivakov and life flowed into him, knowing that the Russian's ghastly mark would never again be cut into the flesh of children.

"I see you continue to improve." Renée smiled and stepped into the sunshine. "You understand, your convalescence will be long."

"Yes, Doctor," Nicolas said with a giddy smirk. "I'm glad you're healing nicely, too, Doctor."

"A bit of powder goes a long way. Now remember, travel by rail is forbidden, at least for a few weeks."

"Perhaps longer." He slid his hands around her waist, pulled her to him, and pushed the balcony door shut behind her. The morning light falling over his shoulder lit her coat, but the shadow of a turret atop the hospital roof shaded her face and he couldn't read what was there. "Let's get serious and discuss business, then, shall we?"

"And what business would that be, Mr. Van Horne?" she asked. "Something about ice?"

"No, not ice. I mean the business of us, Renée. You and me."

What is he saying? she thought as she broke free and took a step closer to the broken balustrade.

He keeps talking so seriously of the future. Our future. What could the man be thinking? He's daffy from the fever. In two or three months he'll be on a northbound train if his convalescence goes well, and if it doesn't . . . Well, she didn't want to consider that hideous possibility.

No, she had to ignore this emotional tie growing between them. She would allow herself only the faintest hope it might someday re-form, like a chemical bond, an attraction of elements that could not be kept apart. Unseen forces acting between two bodies. Thermodynamics. That would be a test, wouldn't it? A test of their chemistry, their thermodynamics.

It was all a daydream, this kind of thinking. A foolish girl's daydream. She was a grown woman; she had her science, her life's work. Years from now, in their separate lives, they'd look back at this brief interlude as a wonderful mistake . . . and nothing more.

"Oh, you dreamer," she said. "You, sir, are a born Northerner. You'll be back at your lake soon enough."

"You just said I'm to stay for weeks. Doctor's orders."

"Well, yes, follow my prescriptions and rest. Remember, Nick, the fever damaged your liver. I'm afraid there'll be no whiskey for you, sir."

"I can live without whiskey, but I can't live without you, Renée."

She took him firmly by the shoulders and looked into his eyes.

"Nick—you're my favorite patient."

The morning Madame La Porte came to visit, after offering the customary pleasantries and well wishes, she stepped into the slats of light near the shuttered window and drew the collar of her blouse aside. "Look here," she said. "See what he did."

A reddish discoloration ran like a healing gash down the right side of her neck.

"It's the exit site, you see, of your visitant's preternatural ectoplasm. You summoned a powerful thing, Mr. Van Horne," she said. "His was a soul heavy with misdeeds."

"I'm sure he's paying the price, madame."

Nicolas watched springtime unfold from his broken balcony high above the housetops: the redbud trees' glorious foliage pulsed like blood, the scent of honeysuckle filled the early morning stillness, and the evenings were redolent with night-blooming jasmine.

Basil Prangoulis, the jolly gent, visited at midday. He carried a jug of a sturdy soup, a "Prangoulis specialty" of shrimp and crab, with a color as bright vermilion as the redbud blossoms.

"I've learned much from my Russian friends," he said as he set the jug of soup and a spoon on a tray. "Such horrid dealings, these children on the docks."

"Thank heavens it's coming to an end."

"Naturally, I've dwelled on this from a religious viewpoint. Our commandments—yours and mine both—forbid taking a life, but to enslave is to take a life also, is it not?"

"Wisely stated, Basil."

"And to enslave children, even worse, eh? . . . Now eat your soup."

One tepid spring evening, quite late after supper, Renée tapped unexpectedly at the door.

"May I?"

"But it's late."

"I've spoken to the nurse. She'll not be around tonight."

There was a congenial visit, then a gentle kiss in the balmy evening, and another; promises for the next evening. A long embrace. She stayed. Smooth arms entwined, a touch, and Nicolas's heart swelled with returning strength, and love for this woman.

"At last I have you."

"And I have you."

93

Appointment at Myer's Shop

Once he was fully on his feet, Nicolas ventured downtown to the offices of Hutchinson Sealy & Son. Galveston's financial district seemed far too frenetic for a convalescing man, and the smells of Restaurant Row were not enticing. Nicolas's weight had suffered with his illness; one saw it in his sallow, fleshless cheeks and how his trousers hung like drapes on his hips. He availed himself of the Cotton Exchange's new electric lift to reach the upper floor and was quickly ushered into Sealy's inner office.

"You've heard that Trey remains . . . vanished," Sealy said.

"Yes."

"No sign whatsoever. I had no idea about his involvement, you know. Oh, I warned him years ago that cheap, unskilled labor never pays. Still, I never surmised . . . those mere boys . . . until the night of the fire."

"But surely he fell in with that crowd some time ago."

"I believe it began when he acquired holdings in the Sugar Land plantation, just across the bay. A massive operation, and highly profitable; I recall the unusually young crews he imported to cut cane and boil molasses. But when his associates tried to bring them onto the docks—"

"They ran into your other son."

"And to think, all these years I fought to keep him a secret."

"You have one good son, Hutch, and the wharves firmly in Sealy hands. What more could you ask for, eh?"

"I realize that, Nicolas. I truly do . . . Be sure to keep me posted on progress at the college, now. Remember, my purse is open to them."

Nicolas took the long marble stairs of the Cotton Exchange slowly. For a bit of light exercise he ambled nearly the length of the Strand to the shop of Mr. Myer, supplier of fine men's clothing, where Renée had promised to assist with the purchase of attire more fitting for the tropical climate. She was quick with her selections.

"I think this summer wool's perfect on you," she said, smoothing the jacket over his gaunt shoulders.

Mr. Myer, doting over his new customers, agreed. "At Myer's," he said, "we employ the finest tailors from Europe. A proper and comfortable fit is assured."

"That's good," Renée said, turning to Nicolas. "Because we must fatten you up, my dear. With luck, you'll be needing alterations in a few weeks' time."

"I believe the walk has piqued my appetite."

"Well, then, let's get you to Trudeau's."

"Will there be champagne?"

"Perhaps a glass, no more."

"We'll make it a French one, then."

94

A Daughter's Letter

21 June 1890

Galveston, Texas

Dearest Abigail,

I am quickly becoming the happiest man in the world, sweet daughter, & to think that just a few months ago I stood at the doorstep of Death. I'm sure you've been reading the newspapers as they trumpet "Child Slaves Exposed," "Russki Ring Broken," etc. etc. The latest news in the Boston Globe *was most welcome & I'm grateful they've kept us out of it, so far at least.*

Presently I busy myself with matters at the college; Schuyler departs for NYC in the coming week to pursue his youthful schemes & I've come to realize I've delayed for too long the urgent request I now put to you, dearest Abby —I wish to pass you the reins of the Van Horne business, including the ice harvest & all related matters. Foremost among these matters, as we've discussed, is the salvation of whatever orphaned youths you can put to honest labor on the ice of Upper Spy. The alliances you've forged with the ladies in Chicago should serve you well there.

I have the utmost confidence you will succeed in this, Abby. Your fortitude & determination, even in a man's world, are beyond question. I shall provide guidance, but from afar, for

I intend to remain in Galveston with my new love. Imagine! Your father, a tropical gentleman! (I'll be needing an entire new wardrobe.)

Do not think this a foolhardy decision, dear daughter. I am assured of its wisdom whenever I set eyes upon my sweet Renée. She works tirelessly to defeat the growing epidemic & with her uncle's failing health, I know that I am doing the right thing by supporting her noble endeavor. I cannot wait for you to meet my dear Renée. You are two accomplished women who enjoy many lovely attributes in common.

I confess my hope that Renée & I will someday marry. For now, her researches consume her & she prevaricates, yet my persistence in this matter of the heart shall not waver. My fondest dream is that you & Schuyler will someday see us wed, and what a glorious event it will be. Saratoga in August would be perfect.

As you see, our plans are not yet firm & my time is largely taken up by the new program to gather cadavers. (The professors tell me this is surely the better word.) Now my task is to travel to Austin, their capital city, to change the laws to allow for legal donation of one's body for scientific purpose. It is a battle I shall win & all my energy will be spent in the name of it.

All the best to you, sweet daughter, & to your dear friend Hilda I extend my warmest wishes for health & happiness. God willing, we will all be together at a future wedding.

Yrs affectionately,

Father

95

Pier 28

Nicolas thought it best to hand-carry his meticulously sealed letter to the main postal office in the railway station, thus ensuring its expeditious departure from the island on the earliest U.S. Mail Express.

"I'll accompany," Renée said, hanging her black rubber apron on its hook.

"You deserve a change of scenery," Nicolas said.

It was late afternoon and no carriages were to be found near the medical college, so the couple hiked posthaste down the harborside. As Pier 28 came into view, Nicolas's soul swelled with pride at the sight of the icehouse so expertly executed by Schuyler. The VAN HORNE & SON in three-foot-high red letters on its side remained crisp and bright after these many months in the sea air—indeed the building still appeared new.

Then, a disconcerting thought struck the merchant of ice, and he halted on the spot. "No, this just won't do," he muttered to himself.

"What is it?"

"I must speak to Schuyler about a good painter."

The incongruity between the lettering on the icehouse and the letter in his jacket pocket was too great. It wouldn't be right to remove "& Son"—not after Schuyler's superb effort, even though the boy would soon be pounding the ivories in some New York gin mill. And how could he give Abigail her due? He'd never seen an enterprise labeled "& daughter."

After a few moments' thought, Nicolas decided on "Van Horne Family's Famous Northern Ice." That would do nicely. Surely Abby would approve. Schuyler, too.

With a prideful grin back on his face, he whisked Renée down the street, doffing his new homburg to passersby and acquaintances as he went: the corner grocer; a dry-goods man he'd dealt with; a milliner whose fashionable work Renée admired. And who was this just ahead? They were about to overtake the Galveston postmaster himself! Now here was a stroke of good fortune.

"Say, sir!" Nicolas rushed to catch up. "A good evening to you." A brief exchange ensued and the postmaster, who was on his way to man the late shift at the main postal office, tucked Nicolas's letter into his pocket—along with the pennies for postage.

"It's a very important communication," Nicolas explained, "and somewhat complicated."

"Well, then, trust it to me," replied the postmaster. "Good evening, sir . . . miss."

They turned back to the college, but, on a whim, Nicolas persuaded Renée to divert onto Pier 28 for a few moments. He strode onto the dock, pulling his key ring from his pants pocket to search for the icehouse key; his key ring had gathered so many recent additions. Once they'd stepped into the icehouse, Nicolas was forced to light a lamp, so tight were the siding and roof of Schuyler's construction. He slid the door shut on its rails and, taking Renée's hand, wove down the familiar canyons of ice to the heart of the mammoth icehouse, where blocks of ice reached nearly to the ceiling. The only sound in the bone–chilling hush was the tap of their boots on the hardwood, and even that was muffled by sawdust.

"Magnificent," he muttered.

"I've always said it's gorgeous ice, Nick . . . but I'm cold."

"Just a moment more."

As he locked the icehouse door behind them, Nicolas was hit with the briny heat of a June day on the docks. It was near dusk and commerce was winding down. Ships were made fast at their berths; only a few longshoremen lingered, leaning on ships' ropes, smoking, passing a bottle.

Nicolas and Renée strolled to the end of the pier where the berth left empty by a paddle wheeler steaming off gave a full view of Galveston Bay. Nicolas settled onto a wooden tea crate; Renée stood behind, her hands on his shoulders. Together, they watched two brown pelicans glide by, their great wings beating soundlessly as they skimmed within inches of the salty, opalescent water.

"How elegant," she said.

The birds were headed north, toward the mainland, hunting up supper. They were big, heavy Texas birds; Nicolas thought pelicans such clumsy, lumbering buffoons on land, yet so full of grace and power once launched into an evening sky that, too, seemed bigger in Texas.

The tangy salt air, the sultry gusts off the water, and the red blaze gathering on the horizon hit Nicolas with a pang of wonder, and doubt. Would he never again smell the cool balsam scent of summer or set foot on the frozen expanse of Upper Spy Lake in the stillness of a winter morning?

Cutting ice was Nicolas's life; he already pined for Upper Spy, even as he strove to put his Yankee ways to use on this tropical island. Galveston boasted newly bricked thoroughfares, modern trolleys, an electricity plant—Nicolas had even heard talk of crossing the bay with a roadway for carriages and a public water line—but it wasn't her streets or architecture that drew Nicolas Van Horne, ice merchant, to this thriving city. It was the strength and goodwill of her citizens . . . and a very special woman.

The pelicans doubled back, cutting a straight line to their nest in the island's wetlands . . . big birds, winging their way south under a big Texas sky.

"We must get back, Nick."

Nicolas glanced over his shoulder. Renée's wry smile told him that the love of his life was already in her laboratory, wrapping herself in black rubber.

"We'll go soon enough, my dear."

Nicolas allowed himself a last, long look at Galveston Bay. Its salty surface, rippled to a pinkish, fluorescent sheen, gleamed like the sides of a North Country trout as it leapt into the last of the day's sunlight. Galveston Bay. Lovely water, really. Still . . . it was lovely water that would never, ever, turn to ice.

"Let's go," he said, offering his arm. "There's much to be done."

CPSIA information can be obtained
at www.ICGtesting.com
Printed in the USA
FFOW02n2351290916
28077FF